إلى الأب المحترم
أبونا انطونيوس
مع محبة

جمال فهمي

THE
HAZE

The Haze

by

Burnaby Hawkes

ATHENA
BOOK TAVERN

Any action, thought, trait, or dialogue in this book—whether pertaining to imagined or real-life characters, dead or alive, standing up or sitting down—is completely fictitious. The island of Pulau is not Singapore nor any other tropical haven the author is aware of. (You Alaskans wish.) Similarly, the American Institute of Middle Eastern Studies in Cairo is not a real university in the Middle East or North America. This is a novel.

Published in 2020 by Athena Book Tavern
www.athenabooktavern.com

ISBN-13: 978-1-7772024-5-3

In memory of my father

[It] is an abominable mystery.

CHARLES DARWIN, 1879

A good tree cannot bring forth evil fruit,
neither can a corrupt tree bring forth good
fruit. Every tree that bringeth not forth good
fruit is hewn down, and cast into the fire.
Wherefore by their fruits ye shall know them.

MATTHEW 7:19

PRELUDE

Pulau, Southeast Asia
Friday, May 17, 2013

I t was smoggy and stinky as hell, but Pinocchio hankered for a cigarette: this blue, comforting poison. He was standing on a deserted part of the Disraeli river's shoreline, with Peel Quay's vigorous lights barely visible a hundred feet off, through the haze.

His handlers had said they couldn't risk picking him up there, at the Quay, because of CCTV. And how on earth could he even argue with that?

Hugging himself as though in a blizzard, he paced the haunted shore, coughing. And suddenly, he stopped and listened. The boat was drawing near. He knew that by the droning sound it made. It came from the opposite side of Peel Quay, from the South China Sea. Soon, it glided into view and swayed to a stop on the haze-covered water.

It was a small patrol cruiser carrying the unique flag of the nation of Pulau, the mermaid goddess. Pinocchio vaguely recognized the two men on the boat. Both were Chinese and wearing the pervasive N-95 mask.

"Sir, come, fast!" cried the tubbier of the two, gesticulating wildly with his arms.

"Is he on board?" Pinocchio shouted.

"You're in big danger!"

You don't say, Pinocchio thought querulously.

"You Borat friend, right?" asked the other sailor.

Nearly twenty meters stood between the shore and the boat. Pinocchio took off his shoes and socks and silently waded into the river, gnashing his left foot only three steps in. It was painful, but he kept going. The coast was steeper than he was expecting. He had to swim half the distance to get to the starboard, the Chinese having tossed down their Jacobs ladder for him.

They helped him aboard, and he jerked himself free from their grips. "You don't happen to carry cigarettes around here, do you?" he asked.

"Not healthy."

Pinocchio shook his head and proceeded to the taffrail, dropping there to examine his injured sole. The wound was deep and it looked hideous. "Is he gone already?" he said.

No reply.

He raised his eyes and saw the tubby sailor holding a gun, his hands trembling. "Sorry," the sailor said, "this is my first time."

He shot him in the stomach. Pinocchio yelped and tried to pull himself up using the taffrail. The sailor jerked the slide and reshot him, six times in the chest and back, until Pinocchio dropped and stopped moving.

"See?" the other sailor said. "This is why *they* should do it. Their spies are like cats."

They dumped his body on their way back to the South China Sea.

PART ONE

4 . *The Haze*

1

RENDEZVOUS

TWO DAYS AGO

O
n his second day in Pulau, Hector Kane—the youngest professor at the American Institute of Middle Eastern Studies in Cairo—retired to his apartment early. Shortly after lunch, he feigned jet lag and excused himself politely from his students and wife. He would pop some melatonin, he said, and call it a day. Have a great evening, everyone.

And before he got bogged down by any questions, he hastened through the gate of the National University of Pulau's residence, nodded to the concierge who was patrolling the garden, then leaped up the stairs to his apartment on the third floor of the boys' dormitory. He would hunker down there until, at least, eight-thirty p.m. His rendezvous with the Company was at eight-fifty.

They were seven travelers in all. Besides Hector and his wife, Yubi, five graduate students—a small summer class—had come along. Those students didn't pose a threat to Hector's scheme.

They'd bye-byed casually to him and said, "Take it easy, Dr Kane. See you tomorrow, okay?" before going their separate ways.

All five of them had plans for the evening.

Baxter and Fifi, to begin with, had been clear: They would get wasted on gin slings and tequila in local bars, hopefully through midnight.

As for Ahmed and Zainab, the devout Muslim newlyweds, they must be by now celebrating the finale of their honeymoon at Peel Quay—the yacht-gorged harbor on the Disraeli river—before the "very exciting Night Safari ride, doctor," which Zainab had yapped about during breakfast.

Even Kero—his problematic student, who'd been slow to make a decision—got out of Hector's way eventually: He would tour Orchard Road's upscale galleries with a very beautiful woman.

Hector was the successful author of all this, the reason for everybody's excitement about Pulau. From the outset, he'd sown in his students' heads a stellar fantasy that still thrived despite the post-landing shock. A tropical island like Pulau, he'd said to titillate them, came to free singles and bonding couples once in a lifetime. Pulau was Southeast Asia's Las Vegas, a cyberpunk Camelot, the surfaced Atlantis. It was the city, after all, of Our Lady the Mermaid.

So he was sure none of his students would bother him tonight.

His equally excited wife, though, was the problem. He needed to elude her, too.

Despite the CIA's questionably liberal view that Hector's Asian wife might be "helpful" in Asia, Hector had done his best to dissuade her from coming. Yet Yubi was friends with his students, and his fiction about Pulau seemed to hit a romantic chord with her in particular. "We never had a honeymoon," she said, "and I think we need one."

Even though they hadn't been intimate since their son's death last year, Yubi had stayed, battling to rebuild their marriage. Hector could only admire her tenacity.

She would drop by his office at the Institute without notice, plan dates that never took off or did then crashed in the same ditch: He was "giving up" on them, "not putting in the effort," or—more recently—*lying* to her.

"Are you back in that Spy Losers Club?"

"I wish." He laughed.

"I talked to Elena"—his teaching assistant—"and she said you canceled your class today. Where'd you go? Your phone was turned off."

"My battery died. I was with Jeff."

"The biggest loser of them all, eh? But I've got news for you. I called him and he hasn't seen you in weeks."

"You don't have his number."

"I called his office."

Pause. "You called the United States ambassador to Cairo, asking about your husband during his lunch break?"

"It wasn't a lunch break."

"I'll tell you what, I'm guilty. Sweet dreams, honey."

Late at night, she usually came to wake him up, kneeling beside his couch. She couldn't stop thinking. She wanted to share something with him.

Something like what, Yubi?

There was her Chinese father, and the fentanyl overdose that had killed him. He'd been having a difficult life in Canada, her father.

And Yubi's mom who, despite having loved her husband and done everything to make him happy, still thought she was responsible for his death.

There was the mob of mean girls who'd tortured Yubi in middle school.

And the generic, curly-haired boy who'd broken Yubi's heart at A. Y. Jackson Secondary in North York, Ontario.

She would open up to him, then demand the same from him. "Tell me something I don't know about you."

"But I told you everything when we first met. Besides, I'm a new man now."

"New how?"

He yawned.

"Hector, are you seriously bored here? Do you hate Cairo? We can move to Toron'o, if you want. You can work at U of T or York U or anywhere. They wouldn't dream of having you there."

"Right, right. Can we talk about this later? I need to be up at seven sharp. And you, too."

At which point, she relented and stood up.

In the syrupy night light, he saw the sheen of her violet nightie and, behind her, the sheets of her empty queen bed piled on the floor. "Want me to come inside?" he said.

"*Um.* Maybe tomorrow? I'm too messed up now. Or in Pulau. We're leaving in two days, anyway."

Yes, Yubi. Maybe in Pulau.

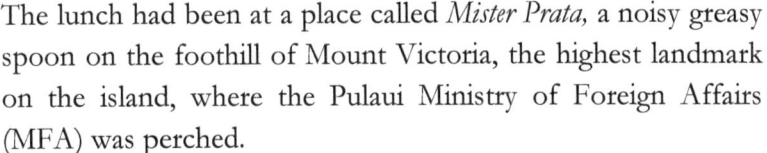

But he'd blown his chances today.

Sitting now in his lonely Pulaui apartment, Hector felt a mix of pride and guilt about the success of his ugly scheme.

At breakfast, he'd joined Ahmed and Zainab at their table, knowing full well how Yubi loathed Ahmed.

Then at the Ministry of Environment, he'd scandalized Yubi in public by flirting with a French blonde the Pulauis had contracted to advise them on their carbon emissions.

Later at the Music Box Museum—where they experienced the joys of the *pipa*, *erhu*, and *suona* and came upon rare photos of The Beatles, Pink Floyd, and Tina Turner in historic concerts—Hector dodged Yubi whenever she balked, crossed her arms, and looked ready to start a fight with him.

And by lunch… she'd given up on him.

It was heartbreaking, but he did what he had to do to protect her. It was during this lunch that Yubi had convinced Kero to escort her on a shopping spree in Orchard Road's famous stores—and Hector had received the instructions for his long-awaited rendezvous with the Company.

The lunch had been at a place called *Mister Prata,* a noisy greasy spoon on the foothill of Mount Victoria, the highest landmark on the island, where the Pulaui Ministry of Foreign Affairs (MFA) was perched.

By all means, it was not a splendid lunch. Most of Hector's students found the food strange and were quite upset because

Ambassador Lee, the celebrity who'd undersigned their travel invitations, had stood them up at the MFA.

Tommy Lee was an international lawyer who'd served two stints as Pulau's permanent representative to the UN. He'd taught international law at Harvard and Sciences Po and had written over fifty books. In a recent TV interview, Lee had said that he penned five to six books a year but published only three. "This way"—the old fox had winked at the BBC brunette— "there'll always be some juice in me when I kick the bucket."

Hector had groaned watching this. He believed Tommy Lee was no more than a scam, a beautifully publicized one, at that. Still, he preached about him to his students as if he were preaching about some sort of god.

Otherwise, how on earth could one spy convince five intelligent adults to join him on a trip to the equator in mid-May? *Pilgrimage, pilgrimage, pilgrimage!* There was not a mightier magnet in the universe.

The MFA comprised eighteen directorates, and they all reported to Lee. Eleven directorates dealt with administrative or economic issues. Only seven were diplomatic, broken up by different world regions. Hector and his group were guests of the Middle East Directorate (MED). The strange thing about the MED was that for most of its history, it had been dormant, its personnel serving in other directorates. Never once in recorded history had an Arab diplomat received a Happy New Year card from a Pulaui counterpart. Until the Arab Spring had happened. Suddenly, the Middle East became sexy in everyone's eyes.

Hector was slugging through his hot curry rice and chicken when the MED director, Fred Zhang, touched his elbow and grimaced, Fred's unhealed acne a topography of gorges in his saucepan face.

"How do you like the restaurant?" Fred said. "It's pretty cozy, and the food is amazing."

Hector looked out the clerestory windows at a sky heavy with smog. Even with the thick aromas of food, he smelled the stench awaiting them outside. He said the place was good, yes.

Fred balled his fist and coughed into it. Then he flung his neatly clipped fingers toward a picture of Lord Ganesha on the wall tapestry. "Fine people, these Indians. The gods watch over their foods and monies and sex. They don't go anywhere without them. They wear them in necklaces and tattoos, write poetry and make great movies about them. They are, in analogy, the Catholics of Asia."

"But isn't that the case with Buddhists also?" Hector asked. "Director, as you may know, my wife is Buddhist, and she has her saints, too."

Fred murmured a perfunctory concurrence, restraining his eyes from moving toward Yubi, who sat at his one o'clock between Kero and Fifi. "It is funny, Mr Kane, that we have accidentally stumbled into the touchy subject of religion. I have a question for you, you being a Western man. What do you call a high priest in Rome? A man who isn't a pope and dresses in a red robe? Is he a bishop? A pope deputy, perhaps?" And the director let out a quiet, breezy laugh.

Hector was irked by this "Mister," an honorific he'd acquired since landing and hadn't managed to shake. If he were free to make assumptions, he would have thought the MED wanted to dismiss his academic qualifications whenever they were out of earshot. Was this the Pulaui way of endearment? Of patronizing? Or of despising!

"Your last name is Kane. That's Irish, no?"

"Indeed, Irish-Canadian. And American on top of that."

"Oh, a multinational." Fred stabbed his last samosa with his fork. "A man with many passports and a strong sense of himself." He chomped. "A Westerner, throughout."

"Your insight is astonishing, director." Hector downed the insult with a glassful of lukewarm water.

"Do you practice religion, Mr Kane?"

"I'm afraid not. My father was Methodist, my mother a Catholic. But I don't really go to church, no."

The director arched his eyebrows and argued, "But you still know your Western religion. We have a fellow…" He turned his head toward the right end of the table, where his men were gathered. Then he redirected himself. "I met a man, a very holy man. What do you call—Oh, Mr Kane, you haven't answered my question!"

"A Cardinal," Hector provided quietly.

And Fred blessed this answer with a nod of his forefinger and forehead. "That's what he is, then. A Cardinal. I wonder why I forget so often. It's early dementia, for all I know. So, Mr Kane, I met this Cardinal yesterday. He's almost seventy, but sharp and spry like a wolf in his prime. Very holy, a very holy man. He lives close to where you're staying with your students. Middle Road and Prinsep Street. Number eight, unit fifty. We should go visit him sometime. Maybe tonight if you can manage to free yourself up."

That was before the conversation had veered, miraculously, into discussing the weather.

2

VINTAGE

I
n the ten weeks since his reactivation, Hector had gone to the CIA's Cairo station over a dozen times. They weren't crazy about seeing him there, since he was undercover. But he imposed all the same.

He needed to know where he stood.

He understood he'd been laid off then taken back on, but he wasn't sure of the terms of his *reemployment,* so to speak.

Hector had lost all trust in the Company ever since they'd dropped him without proper notice thirty-one months earlier. His measly biweekly deposits had actually stopped on the same August 2010 day he'd walked out of the Cairo station on an ostensible "assignment" at the American Institute of Middle Eastern Studies in Cairo (AIMES). He'd been a professor at AIMES now for about three years. But his life, to this day, had been *hazy*.

Haze is doubt, uncertainty, open-endedness.

The haze is eternity. It's where life "intussuscepts," as the doctor who'd declared his son dead had said. It's the middle ground between good and bad. It's where you lose your insight and become a zombie. It's where lies taste like candy.

It's where Hector had been, in early March 2013, when a woman called his office.

"Dr Kane's office. How can I help you?" said Elena, his teaching assistant, a delicious Italian girl who dated a professor next door.

It was Katherine Schmidt from the Goethe-Institut. (Or some such nonsense.)

"Oh, I shall transfer you to the professor right now. Dr Kane, a lady is calling from the German center."

Hector welcomed the call gullibly.

And, as it turned out, it was no Frau Schmidt. It was Lisa McConkey from Murphy & Associates, the cover firm for the CIA's Cairo station.

O Lisa. Your fake optimism, red hair, and feline eyes.

Your cocoa hand cream, warm body, and dry kisses.

Long time no see, Lisa.

"What is it now?" He was thrilled in spite of himself. "You want me to shoot your ex?"

"He can't shoot himself, can he?"

They rendezvoused on a felucca on the same afternoon. The Nile was quiet and shiny and just mythical. Lisa brushed his hand more often than she should, then quietly said, "I need you for a new operation."

But I'm junk, Lisa. A discounted reject. An axed CIA agent turned bad teacher to lead callow hopefuls on. Oh, you should come and see them, Lisa. The Farm churns them out by the dozen, and I burnish and oil them, drill more mumbo-jumbo into their cracked heads. A chump giving other chumps the ins and outs of the post-9/11 apocalypse.

"Syria? Libya? An Egyptian power gamble? Screw all that.

I'm retired," he said.

"No, you're not." She was kind enough to correct him. "You were fired. But we'll take you back. After this mission, you're golden. Fabio is retiring and I need a replacement. And as much as I hate you, Hickey, you're the best candidate out there."

She used her pet name for him, making him soften up. "When can I leave my teaching job?"

"Not yet. Actually, your mission *is* your teaching job."

"I don't understand."

"You will. Soon."

"I just have to be in on everything. What happened before the Revolution won't fly with me anymore."

"It's a one-man job, and that man is *you*." She knew how to play to a man's ego. "After that, you're stuck with me for good."

And after he agreed, she threaded her fingers through her hair—blazing red in the sunshine—and broached the lingering subject. "So… I heard you got married again."

And for eight weeks, Lisa had fed him only candy. Lies. He was given chores, Asian diplomats to visit and buddy up to, a summer class at AIMES to assemble, but never the full truth about his "one-man job."

Driven mad by curiosity, Hector employed a trick that had done him well in the past. It was the same tactic, in fact, that had landed him his AIMES job—even though it would slowly, and cruelly, transpire that AIMES had been his severance package at the time.

Before the end of April, Hector barged into Lisa's office with his typical three-page torture-to-read resignation. And he vomited his spiel. I'm not respected, here, Lisa. Find yourself another pushover. I told you this would happen… Et cetera.

Then he spun and held the doorknob. And he waited.

Lisa looked up from her desk and sighed. "Don't be silly, Hector. Please."

"Is that what you're keeping me in the dark for? I'm a grown man. I'm not 'silly,' Lisa."

"We've been through this before, haven't we?"

"When?"

No reply. She wouldn't play his game.

"This time is for real, then," he said.

She stood up and approached him. "You're not ready yet. I'm not keeping you out because I want to."

"That's not persuasive enough."

She shook her chestnut tresses. "Hickey—"

"That ain't gonna work either."

"Okay, fair. Would you be interested in reading our intel on the Nomans?"

A chill lapped over him. "The Nomans? What's their part in this?"

"They *are* this."

The Nomans were the most influential family in the Middle East in this post–Arab Spring reality. Their influence reached far and wide, but it centered in Cairo and belonged to one man: Ibrahim Noman, the godfather of the Egyptian Revolution.

He and Hector had a dark history.

"What have you gotten me into, exactly?" he asked.

"Nothing you can't handle."

"Then I demand to see your curious 'intel.' Maybe that's something I can handle, after all."

"Wait here, okay? I need to get the okay on this first."

She lurched out, and Hector puffed and paced her office.

——————— · ———————

Lisa's office was a train wreck. Her chipped veneered desk was cluttered, on that day, with every species of needless stationery—a jammed blue stapler, a shriveled eraser, a flip calendar dating two years back, two empty fountain pens stuck to a peeling blotter pad, dog-eared Post-it notes, rubber bands—and behind the desk was a window overlooking the Nile Corniche behind dusty, crooked venetian blinds.

The floor was never mopped. The north wall of the room carried posters of the world map, Francis Fukuyama, Henry Kissinger, and *New Kids on the Block* (mid-eighties vintage, when both Wahlbergs were still with them). Hector looked at that last poster and smiled. Oh, Lisa, Lisa, Lisa.

He turned and paced toward the opposite wall. This one was occupied, floor to ceiling, by the station's short-term memory, a platoon of wine-red high-tech cabinets. From one of these cabinets Hector's teaching job had emerged thirty-two months earlier. They were always locked, those cabinets of secrets, unless Lisa needed to review or store a file. Each cabinet—twenty-four in total—opened to a unique set of digits, punched to a threshold of three failed attempts before the contents perished in a ruthless system of automatic shredding.

Something caught his attention. A glitch. An anomaly.

The gliding wooden ladder—the same sort used in libraries—was parked on the far right. And up there was a bulge. The topmost drawer was open. Obviously, Lisa had been in the process of storing or retrieving a piece of intel when his intrusion had interrupted her.

Hector started with the desk. He inspected the papers on the blotter pad and found nothing significant. Only a dry update on a natural gas find in the Mediterranean—which was old news by now—besides the regular business report on Egypt's economy, which didn't augur well.

He then moved to the door and peered out at the open-plan hall. He saw Lisa speaking on the phone, while Fabio Torres—her soon-retiring deputy—mimed and gesticulated to her. The three other "risk analysts"—CIA agents, all of them—seemed moonstruck by their computer screens. Lisa was a rare bird in the intelligence community. She held no faith in computers. Her cabinets were her RAM memory, her cranky brain her hard drive.

Opportunity knocking, his curiosity eating away his inhibitions, Hector mounted the right-flushed ladder and peeked into the open cabinet.

There were two files inside. The first had a shopping list of required supplies to the Syrians in their struggle against the tyrant Bashar al-Assad, each given a monetary estimate. The last line read:

P B H thru Gen

Which Hector translated without any difficulty whatsoever. *Prince bin Hakam through Geneva.*

Hector, in fact, had anticipated this. Prince Mohamed bin Hakam was a Saudi royal whose affair with Washington went back a ways. What had started out as a bypass to feed a training school for spooks in Cairo had grown into the aorta of Syrian resistance. Prince bin Hakam supplied the rebels with everything, from rice to condoms to RPGs.

And in the second file Hector found honorable examples of

those *rebels*. He pulled one photo out and looked hard at it. The kid—he couldn't be over twenty—had a sharp face underlined by a mothy beard, stretched in a rabbity smile, central incisors jutting and yellowed by tobacco and tea stains. Behind him was a rolling cropland broken by a parked jeep. Hector turned the photo over and read:

K GRANT GUY M H

Which was… impossible to translate.

"What're you doing?"

Lisa was frozen at the door. She quickly looked back, then closed the door quietly.

Hector tried to keep his cool. "Keeping you safe."

He slammed the cabinet shut, and it beeped to declare the activation of the locking mechanism. He climbed down.

"You shouldn't have done that."

"I know. I'm sorry, Liz."

Behind her round glasses, Lisa's green eyes wobbled. Her cheeks and forehead reddened. "Hector, don't call me Liz."

"I know. I'm so—"

"And don't *ever* lie to me again. Understood?"

Hector was silent.

She slapped a single paper in his palm, dashing past him to her desk.

Hector looked at the paper, which read:

April 28, 2013

Which was this coming Sunday. Today was Friday.

"That's it?"

"He wants to see you," she said.

"Who?"

"Who do you think? Your mentor. Your confidante. The reason for your existence and all your troubles." She popped two gum cuboids into her mouth. "The Cardinal."

3

BULLDOG ROCKET

T he helicopter had deposited the three CIA agents on a hilly tongue of land extending between the Mediterranean and the brackish smash of lakes gathered in its lagoon. The location was a few miles west of Port Said, the city grown out of the Suez Canal laborers' huts. There was a trailer there, which Lisa, Fabio, and Hector waited in until the Cardinal arrived.

And an hour later, the Cardinal alighted, escorted by a coterie of Muslim Brotherhood scouts.

But only Hector got to take a walk with him.

The spy and the master wandered away in silence. Then they came upon a promontory that overlooked the frothy waves of the Mediterranean. The Cardinal climbed a rock with his left foot and took in gulps of the warm sea air. He looked like *The Wanderer above the Sea of Fog*—Caspar David Friedrich's famous painting—with his dark green suit and rumpled white hair. The promontory wasn't lofty. It stood barely twenty feet above sea level. Yet the horizon looked like the smooth edge of a flat earth. It was only by the mercy of a drilling platform on the sea-cusp, and two ships threading their way back, that the two men were spared the vertiginous shock of their minuteness before nature.

George Moore, the CIA director, was known in the dark corridors of espionage as "the Cardinal," a sobriquet he didn't so much like as begrudgingly accept. When he'd taken office last December, he'd said in a *Washington Post* interview that returning to Langley had been his "true calling." It had made the spooks' joke of the year.

The reason for this being that Moore had spent a year as a Jesuit monk novice before Langley had come into his life. Strangely, Moore would later divorce from religion and its three sisters: literature, art, and philosophy. He hated sophisticated memos, avoided unnecessary performances, and shut his spies up before they rationalized their mishaps and failures. He came off more as a fierce army general than a seasoned spook, and his dour demeanor emphasized this impression. He was so proud of being called a "jingo."

Moore was the most esteemed CIA director since 9/11. He was a Company man. As if it were a magical vine, he'd climbed Langley's ladder in less than three rushed decades—from the swamp of the Directorate of Operations analysts during the Cold War, to an operative then station chief of Riyadh, to head of the Near East and South Asia Division (shortly before the Second Gulf War), to director of Operations (which was later termed "The National Clandestine Service") shortly after 9/11, then to director of the whole Company.

Moore was a good family man, too, father of four, grandfather of seven. Not a sloppy womanizer like his predecessor, or a Snepp-sympathizer like a certain director of Analysis who'd almost beat him to office (before the DA's college diary, somehow, resurfaced on the Seventh Floor). He was a technocrat *distingué*, having served as special adviser to the president on terrorism for four years before retracing his steps back to Langley.

The only crime the Cardinal was guilty of, perhaps, was the "orange terror alert" he'd undersigned, among other hotheads, in the lead-up to the Iraq War. The media had used that against him when the Senate discussed his nomination for the directorship. He was called "The Mastermind of the Iraqi WMD Scandal," and a "War Criminal." Still, his nomination had passed with the necessary majority vote.

And here he was, five months later, steering the global ship without so much as moving a finger.

———※———

Hector was sweltering under the Egyptian sun. He'd left his jacket in the trailer and felt grateful for it. Now he put on his *Predators*. Those were the dark Ray-Ban sunglasses CIA men started wearing in the late '90s as a spoof of the *Men in Black* franchise. Behind his *Predators,* Hector now shut his eyes and waited for the Cardinal's revelation.

At length, the Cardinal landed his brown oxford on the sand and walked alongside the precipice.

Hector followed humbly.

"Look at the sea and take the measure of the stakes, Hector. Thirty trillion cubic feet of high-quality gas. I've seen it with my own eyes, but can't for the life of me believe in it. The president is skeptic as well, and well he should be."

Hector squinted at the sea. It was the bluest he'd ever seen. The sky was awfully clear, the sun hanging low like a glowing sauna stone. Who would think this natural beauty harbored the biggest abscess in the Mediterranean? The stuff for a new Opium War. Operation OIL Phase II.

The Cardinal stopped and pinned his eyes on the sea-cusp. "And the strangest thing is that this is only one third of their deal."

Hector had to voice two enquiries into the nature of the other two thirds.

Of the first, the Cardinal said it was a naval base, a place near Alexandria. The ousted Mubarak regime had been adamant not to allow any foreign military bases on Egyptian soil. Obviously, this was about to change with the Muslim Brotherhood now in power.

"And the last piece of the puzzle, sir?"

The Cardinal was silent.

"Sir?"

"Syria," the director said heavily. "They will clean up our mess in Syria."

Hector jerked his head and scanned the two helicopters parked at either side of the trailer. In truth, this was a frightening scene. A squad of Egyptian soldiers carried Kalashnikovs and guarded the helicopters. And spattered close on the sand, emaciated bearded men bore M16s and smoked cheap *Cleopatra* cigarettes, glowering at the two Americans conspiring at the precipice.

Unlike the Salafi-Wahhabi ideal, Muslim-Brotherhood scouts grew their mustaches, trimmed their beards, accepted the pants and the T-shirt, shook hands with women and infidels, and wore a fixed grin on their mugs at all times. They told you they wanted to take over the world, kill unbelievers, enslave women, abolish the arts, all with kindly smiles and pats on the back.

No one had foreseen that those utopian crazies would one

day rule the Kingdom of the Nile—no one except the toppled President Mubarak, a veteran of a three-decade reign of tyranny. It took a tyrant to spot another that far away.

The Brotherhood borrowed their brand from Turkey. If Turkey's Islamists were *Justice & Development,* the Brotherhood were *Freedom & Justice.* This copycat rhyme had a name in poetry. *Epanalepsis:* when one clause ended with the first word of another. *The king is dead, long live the king!*

Politicians are lucky people, Hector mused. They kill using mere words. Pretty, rhyming words.

"Sir, we can't," he hissed. "We've danced with so many devils already, we can't afford Satan himself. And if you want my honest opinion, sir, I won't touch a Muslim-Brotherhood deal with a ten-foot pole. These folks don't honor anything!"

"Calm down, son," the Cardinal said.

But Hector was more ireful than the sauna stone above. "Things are moving quickly in Syria, sir. The rebels are making progress. Soon Assad and his buddies will be out of the way. The Qatari pipeline should reach Bulgaria in under a year, and cheap gas will flood Europe. The Russians will bite the dust! No more Cold War nostalgia or multipolar bickering. World peace, sir. World peace! If Langley is making a U-turn, please don't let me stand here and watch it, sir."

"Things are moving quickly in Syria," the Cardinal echoed his takeaway from the rant. "Hector, I'll be honest with you. I made a big mistake when I recruited you."

Hector was silent.

The Cardinal turned and walked closer to the edge. His toecaps towered over the crashing waves twenty feet below. He sucked his upper left molars. "You had a lot of gusto. Tragedy, too. Both make for a perfect spy. But in your case, your emotions took a life of their own. Did you ever wonder why we laid you off just before the Arab Spring?"

"Is it because of my *thing* with the Nomans?"

"It's because you were a fool once, and we couldn't afford fools anymore." The Cardinal looked at his feet, the frothy waves below, and he breathed deeply. "So you'll practice self-control this time around, Hector. No runaway emotions. And whatever comes your way, let your brain deal with it first. Am I making myself clear?"

The Cardinal was clarity incarnate.

"Now let's get back to the trailer," the Cardinal said. "We've seen enough of the heartrending outdoors."

In the trailer, the Cardinal pointed him to the one empty booth, where Hector's abandoned jacket hung from the sill of a small window. Lisa and Fabio had taken liberties with the generous Egyptian stocks to create the atmosphere of a cozy living room. There was Arabic pop music, biscuits and coffee, and macaroni béchamel in the oven.

Once Hector was seated, Lisa handed her mitt to her deputy and came to sit across from Hector. The Cardinal sat beside her. Something about Lisa's demeanor, at this exact moment, reminded Hector of Judge Judy—if Ms Judy had a bubblegum problem, and if she had a seedy, despondent view of the opposite sex, as Lisa did. Before Cairo, Hector had met her only once. Back in 2005, Lisa had come to guest-lecture Farm cadets on the new security challenges of the Arab world in the post-9/11 era. She had been an operative in Baghdad then, and her lecture had been incoherent at best. But make no mistake. Even with all

Hector knew about her, Lisa wouldn't have made it to station chief of Cairo without some sort of talent, something which Hector had yet to see.

She took a red paper file from her Banana Republic bag and opened it on the enameled table. The file hosted multiple satellite shots of warships that Hector recognized as belonging to the Russian Navy. Comment bubbles denoted each ship's class and description.

"The Russians are doing a navy workout in the Mediterranean," Lisa said, blowing a blue gum bubble. "The biggest since the end of the Cold War. Their ships are patrolling the Syrian coast as of right now. Tartus is back in business, baby, and it's not looking good."

"So the Russians are keeping their property in shape," Hector said. "So what? Tartus is a junkyard, pretty much. Four piers tops. I don't see the Russians being that stupid. They won't afford another war on top of the Ukraine and North Caucasus. This"—he moved his forefinger over the first photo—"this is a waste of time."

Fabio came with the béchamel and laid a heavy, steaming lump in Hector's plate. "We love to keep our agents healthy," he said with an unhealthy grin.

Fabio had always reminded Hector of Mikhail Bulgakov's cat, the one in *The Master and Margarita*. Behemoth. If Behemoth had an actual mustache and if he were, perhaps, a tad slicker.

The Cardinal spoke softly. "We know for a fact the Russians are coming, Hector. In a few months, they'll be sending *Admiral Kuznetsov* back. That's their only aircraft carrier, so they're taking this utterly seriously."

Hector decided not to ask however the Cardinal had access to this information. The Cardinal turned to his Cairo chief and gave her a nod.

While Fabio pushed Hector in and Hector crawled till his jacket brushed his left ear, Lisa rooted out a photo a few layers down in her file. "Waste of your Highness's time, huh? Take a good look at this."

Hector examined this new photo and a few more Lisa dealt to him one by one. This series of photos was different. Some were a bit grainy, some shiny, but they were all taken in the same location. A warehouse of sorts. Photo One showed a pale finger—or what Hector mistook for a finger—up the left corner. Photos Two and Three zoomed in on this finger.

Hector did not need a bubble to comment on this finger, nor tell him what it meant for the war in Syria.

Eight years ago, in 2005, while still a junior operations officer fresh off the Farm, Hector had listened to Ozgur Alexopolous— his supervisor and, later on, his friend—poke fun at this exact same finger.

It was the first operation Hector had taken part in, a Russian secrets deal taking place in Paris. Two weeks earlier, a man had walked into the US Embassy in Paris claiming to be a *starshy leytenant* in the Russian Ground Forces with invaluable secrets to sell. It was a dubious affair from the getgo, and later on would turn out to be no more than a booby trap, but the Cardinal— then-director of Operations—had deemed it a valid opportunity to train one of his best recruits: Hector Kane.

So for two weeks, Ozgur showed up at Hector's 18th Arrondissement hotel at six p.m. sharp, to guide him through their nightly surveillance of this "defector." And on this particular day, Ozgur had come carrying a paper bag with a heap of clothes in it—a floral tunic, a beaded necklace, a pair of dusky harems, rainbow sunglasses, and sandals—and asked Hector to put them on.

"You're kidding me. Right?"

"Nope."

Ozgur was in his stellar Armani suit as usual, bleeding Tom Ford's *Neroli Portofino* unto the air, no disguise heeded: It simply didn't work with Ozgur's persona. Ozgur had the looks, slyness, and ostentation of a fox. In comparison, Hector paled big time.

But now this hippie outfit promised to make him glow. Which wasn't necessarily a good thing.

Besides the clothes, Ozgur had also brought a teaching material: the latest issue of *National Defense*.

"Here, look at this smoking gadget." Ozgur had opened the glossy pages to a featured story, reclining on Hector's bed. "*Yakhont*. Like in *ruby*. You see a pattern there? Same thing with the 'secrets' our *leytenant* is feeding us. Take a good look, buddy. What'd you see? A bulldog!" He boomed. "*Huh huh huh*. I might wanna patent that. *The Bulldog Rocket*. Hey, you should get the Russkies better than I do. You're Canadian. When you live in minus twenty all your dreary life, good taste becomes like fine wine. You hear about it, you lie about it, but you don't really get it. And when you get it, you don't like it. And you don't want others to like it, either. So what'd you do? You make the ugliest rocket in the history of warfare, and you make it so good that even your enemies will line up at your doorstep to get a piece. That, mon ami, is the Russian secret, how they win. They make things so ugly you can't even resist."

How about the tunic and harems, Ozzie? What's their secret?

"Oh, those. Just to demonstrate. Found 'em in a flea market at Clignancourt. Nice Jewish gal. She said they were ugly enough, and I took her word for it. And, oh boy, who can resist you right now!"

Vain, snarky, and suicidal: Ozgur, may you rest in peace, wherever you are.

———— ❧ ————

"But, sir..." Hector's larynx jammed.

"The Stooge is on board, Hector," said the Cardinal. "The Tsar has fed the Lion."

The Yakhont was a thirty-foot monster with a dipped ramjet engine that looked—verily—like a bulldog's nose. And this was the pale finger Hector had seen in the first photo.

Earlier this year, there had been reports of a Russian "sample" sent to the Syrian Army as part of a marketing campaign. Most CIA analysts believed this was a bluff. The Russians wanted the West to take them seriously and, maybe, they promoted their stocks of ugly missiles, too.

Photos Two and Three had already corroborated this conclusion. A Yakhont missile—the "Bulldog Rocket"—had been sent to al-Assad's camp. But Photos Four, Five, and Six backed a different theory, confirming the director's ominous metaphor.

The Americans were sordidly naïve, Hector realized, drunk on their fine homegrown wine. Not only were there more missiles than you could count in the photos, but these missiles were loaded onto TELAR vehicles, the Syrian flag in red, white, and black—doubly, greenly starred—stamped on the vehicles. This meant that the Russians had handed the Syrian *Lion*—the literal meaning of Assad's name in Arabic—their comprehensive

K-300-P Bastion-P (which NATO reclassified as SS-C-5 *Stooge*), one of the mightiest anti-ship missile systems in the world.

And this… changed everything.

Eyes glued to the bulldog rockets, Hector said, "I need more info."

"That's not gonna happen," said Lisa. "We're only showing you this to make you see what's at stake."

"Then what do you want me to do?"

"It's more a matter of *where* we want you to go," Fabio said.

"Are you familiar with the nation of Pulau?" Lisa asked.

"Southeast Asia? What's that to do with the Arab Spring or Syria or anything?"

"You'll know everything once you get there," the Cardinal said. "But first, let's talk family. Does your wife know you're a CIA agent?"

"She thinks I'm retired."

"Good. Let's keep it at that," the Cardinal said. "Ignorance, in her case, is bliss."

"She's Asian," said Fabio. "Is she not?"

"Yes, Fabio. My wife *is* Asian. Is that going to be a problem?"

The Cairo deputy shrugged innocently. "Never crossed my mind, man. I was just thinking. You're going to Asia, and she might be helpful there."

4

GYPSY DOLL IN VIENNA

ector put on a pair of blue jeans with an untucked gray short-sleeve on top and light black Vans to match, and at eight thirty-five he tiptoed out of his apartment and climbed down the stairs.

The Pulauis had given him and Yubi Unit 301, right beside the stairs. The boys' dormitory was well-conditioned. So when Hector existed to the garden, the poisonous air jolted him, made him pull his mask up over his nose. *The haze* had gotten much worse over the evening.

The haze was a perennial curse to Southeast Asian communities. Every summer, huge clouds of smoke traveled the Malay Archipelago, conquered the happy cities. People suffocated on the souls of dead trees, Gaia's retribution in full swing.

Conspiracy theories and blame-dodging abounded in Asia, but the bottom line was there was no smoke without fire and that the fire was in Indonesia. There were people there whose livelihoods depended on the slashing and burning. They cleared their land of vegetation, then sold it—for peanuts, really—to corporations expanding their pulpwood and palm oil plantations in Southeast Asia.

More trees to burn for more money to print. What a bargain!

Yet even those made rich by this bargain (there was no denying it, the Pulauis were members of this club) were not happy.

"The scourge of every summer" was how Fred Zhang had described the haze at the airport, yesterday.

And another diplomat—who gave his full name as the ludicrous "Sylvester Fan"—pouted. "We're as unlucky as you are, professor. We didn't expect any of this before June." Sylvester raised his arm to the dusty clouds concealing the skies outside the terminal's glass dome. "It's like hell has descended on earth. Atrocious, really. Worse than all the previous years. Even with Sumatra on hold."

Yubi inquired, "Why Sumatra—"

But a squat, bespectacled man called Paul jumped in. "Anyway, you're all set. The bus will take you to the National University's residence in Prinsep Street. The driver is at your beck and call throughout your week in Pulau."

"But unfortunately, you'll have to buy your own masks," Fred added, folding his wrists on the flat derriere of his buff suit. "The malls in Orchard Road are excellent. Also, check Ion Orchard and the Mandarin Gallery. Both are close to the res."

Paul touched a hand to his right cheek in embarrassment. "It was really short notice for us."

"We'll see you at lunch tomorrow," a smiling John chimed in. "Ambassador Lee is looking forward to seeing you all. And, please, professor, do not give up on Mermaid City yet. She has a lot to offer."

Fred, Sylvester, Paul, and John. The four horsemen of the Middle East Directorate. White teeth, broad smiles, Chinese, polite, and inscrutable. Their ministry was up the mountain.

They called Pulau *Mermaid City* for two reasons.

Actually, it was a reason built upon another reason.

In ancient Sumatra, there was this folktale wherein the island of Pulau had sprung into existence from the body of a mermaid. That story was hardly known outside the Malay Archipelago. In fact, most Pulauis hadn't heard about it before the late eighties, when their affluence called for a national history to be written.

By which time, however, the Malays—the historical inhabitants of Pulau—had shrunk into a minority in their own land, outnumbered first by Chinese settlers, then by the passels of Indian migrant workers coming during the *New Deal* economic boom of the 1970s and '80s. Cosmopolitanism was never considered an option by Pulau's leadership, so the Pulauis settled for a formal merger. Myths were jumbled to create a revised version of the island's creation myth. The Malayan/Sumatran meat of the tale was kept. But it was married to Chinese folklore, not without a Hindu blessing.

The Mermaid was now the goddess of Pulau, its protectress and emblem. They painted her on their flag and erected a gargantuan temple for her: a famous lighthouse on the south coast. Travel guides promised fertility and eternal youth for those who kissed at the goddess's feet.

You can imagine how romantic the idea had seemed, then, spending a week on this tropical, magical island of love and fertility. And everybody on the trip had braced themselves for a good deal of surprises.

But not *this*. Not the haze. The haze was no surprise: It was a catastrophe.

⸺ ❧ ⸻

As Hector threaded his way in the haze-suffused garden, he recalled his first step on the airstair. How horrific. All those memories of teargas, the blood and skirmishes in Tahrir Square, had come back to him.

And he'd been able to hear and feel his students' frustration.

"What was I drinking when I signed up before Googling the weather!" said Baxter.

"They didn't buy us masks on purpose," said Fifi. "They're mean as hell, I can smell it. *Arrrgh.*"

"Congratulations, guys," said Kero. "We survived a revolution to die on a remote island in the middle of nowhere."

"It makes for a perfect absurdist story," said Ahmed slyly.

"Maybe a nightmare, not a story," corrected Zainab.

"Hey, Yubi, quick question," Fifi said. "Did your husband bring us here to die?"

After the MED men had left them, they had to rely on their luck to locate the bus. The airport parking was drowned in the smog, the lines of cars looking like infinite V's. And there seemed to be no boundary between parking and street. So many times, they wandered off onto a sidewalk teeming with masked strollers.

They'd lost all hope, when they finally came upon it. It was a white Toyota minibus, parked under a pedestrian bridge with a placard tucked under its wipers, reading in all-caps:

PROFESSOR K. FROM AMERICAN UNIVERSITY IN AFRICA

They found the driver dozing inside. Hector pounded on the glass door, and the figure inside started then jerked the door open.

He was a sixtyish Chinese man wearing Coke-bottle glasses behind which a pair of pinpoint eyes cut them down to size. He was uniformed in black slacks topped by a white tunic that had the bus company's logo stitched to its left breast in Chinese letters. The man banged his fist over this very logo and spurted something about letting the bus company know.

"Let the company know about what, sir?" Hector asked.

"Always tell the company!" The driver threatened with his forefinger. "I think you went back to Africa, so I sleep. The haze make people go back. You America people do not respect."

The students slipped into verbal combat with him, but the driver was too fast, too sour, too old to be gained upon. To resolve the situation, Hector asked his male students to help:

"Mr...?"

"Li," the driver allowed.

"Please, guys, help Mr Li with the bags. If you need a hand, let me know."

Fifi seated herself beside him on the bus. Hector looked at the rearview mirror to follow the outcome of his diplomacy. He saw the driver arguing with the boys over the size and heft of every single bag they wished to jam into the narrow trunk. Yubi and Zainab were giggling in the backseat.

"This is weird, doc," Fifi said.

"*Uh-huh?*"

"This trip, it's weird."

Fifi—Fatima Noman—was the dean's niece. Like all the Nomans, she was a celebrity. Fifi's father was the world-famous Ibrahim Noman, the man whose name had become synonymous with the Egyptian Revolution. When Fifi had signed up for this trip, *the Big No*—as Mr Noman was known throughout the Middle East—had objected to her going, fearing for her safety. But Fifi had insisted, hooked on Hector's intricate myths about Pulau and Asia. So the Big No had relented: He'd called Hector in person and asked him to bring Fatima home safe. And Hector had promised him he would.

Now, despite being the dean's niece, Fifi effaced herself. She barely spoke at all in class: only moved her gazelle's eyes among her classmates and nodded at whatever they said. Hector believed she was struggling to make friends. No wonder there. Fifi's second passport—Austrian —bestowed upon her the benefits of a European citizen, a gift millions of her fellow Egyptians would kill for. But that made Fifi also a stranger among them.

She wasn't pretty. Her skull was too big and her skin hirsute and rough. Her cheeks were stamped by butterfly freckles that made her smiley always, even when she cried (which happened a lot and resolved without explanation). Her brown hair was wavy and dry and very, very lush. Her father had married a Gypsy woman toward the end of his stint in Vienna as secretary-general of the Organization of the Petroleum Exporting Countries (OPEC). Exile had been rather elective than compulsory for the international lawyer, and he thought he'd finally found love, a benevolent recompense for a life half-wasted trying to fix corrupt Arab regimes, half-gone arguing with stiff-necked European academics bored to death by the lack of a new great war to historicize.

His *Roma* had given him what he'd failed to achieve all his life: an extension out of himself, a baby girl whom he named *Fatima*, after the Prophet's daughter.

But like a good joke, the punchline hit him hard. His *Roma* died three years later. Pancreatic cancer. No family history, no alcoholism, and despite being seventeen years his junior, an athlete with a silver medal in synchronized swimming.

Hector had held this medal in his own hand, weighed the heft of its naked presence on the Big No's Dickensian oak desk in Vienna, five years ago.

In the mid-to-late 2000s, Hector had been stationed in Europe. It was a unique arrangement with the National Clandestine Service, by which he worked part-time and got to roam the think tanks of the Old Continent as a political researcher. Hector still regarded that period as the peak of his life.

Until one day in December 2008, when his life's curve began to come down.

The CIA had gotten word that the former secretary-general had grown a beard, started working on a memoir in Arabic, had reconnected with fringe activists in the Arab world. Had the ex-secretary-general, then, been radicalized? The Cardinal was on fire.

He showed up at Hector's Stockholm apartment and ordered him to fly to Vienna pronto. "Someone needs to suss this guy out," the then-director of the NCS said. "Ozgur is waiting for you there."

And for six days and six nights, Hector and Ozgur lived in a white Ford Transit parked across from the Nomans' Leopoldstadt address. The former secretary-general and his teenage daughter lived on the second floor of a building risen from the ashes of a synagogue zapped during the

Reichskristallnacht. They seldom went out, seldom conversed, never received visitors.

"What are they doing here?" Hector marveled. "I would go back to Egypt if I were them."

"Why don't you?" Ozgur said.

"That's exactly the point. I'm not."

Viennese winter is solemn and lonely. But Ozgur, impeccably dressed up and perfumed as always, kept Hector entertained. They'd grown close over the years. Since their first meeting in New York in 2003, and later their joint surveillance of the *starshy leytenant* in Paris, they had forged a bond that served them well in various risky operations in Europe. Naturally, they had a lot to reminisce about while the Nomans were refusing to budge from the flat. That Algerian fellow who recruited imbeciles for al-Qaeda in Marseilles, remember the gay porn on his PC? *Hah hah ha.* And that chips factory near Prague, Ozzie, you threatened to throw a Pakistani ISI tracker inside one of those slicers. The guy bawled like a baby, "I'm not important, I'm not important, ask my wife!" And you said to him, "Well, if you're not important, no one will miss you, uh?" And don't forget the pharmacy explosion of Venice. Oh, my goodness. And the adventure with the Moroccan brothers who cooked tabun in a hot-dog cart in Brussels...

And they laughed and guzzled gallons of strong Viennese coffee, ate dangerous amounts of apple strudel and *sachertorte,* took turns showering in a single bedroom the Agency had suffered them at a nearby two-star hotel, and waited and waited for the impossible to happen, for the Nomans to be away from the flat at the same time.

Which didn't happen until December 13, when the former secretary-general allowed his daughter to see him off at the airport, where he was scheduled to fly to Oran, Algeria, to attend the 151st OPEC Conference.

"I thought I'd die before they moved their butts," Hector said.

"You go up," said Ozgur. "I'll call the boss and catch up."

That had been the last time he'd seen Ozgur.

———— ❧ ————

Weird, Fifi? Let me tell you what's *weird.*

I found your hidden condoms, opened up your laptop and saw the nude pictures you sent to a boy called Jonas. I read your sexts. I photocopied your *Gypsy Doll in Vienna* diary. Your daddy's memoir, Fifi? It was useless to us. Listen to this:

Last night I dreamed of it. The rising East. The gestating Revolution in the hearts of millions. I am a prophet and to my prophecy I am wedlocked.

Or this masterpiece:

If humanity is ever to eradicate inequality, the Plebeians must rise and demolish their Idol... an Idol that the Patrician has sculpted especially for them... an Idol called Democracy!

Crazy guy, huh?

Uh-unh. There is a better way of nailing him:

A lazy bastard... an old fart who's lost his male drive... a spewed-up cog of the system. Even in his country they don't

respect him so very much. What the hell am I doing here
with him? He is totally insane!
I HATE him!!!!

Sounds familiar? Your father, the man you despised in your diary, turned out to be the highest achiever of the century.

But you didn't see that coming, Fatima. Did you? And neither did *I*.

I read your diary… and I believed you.

I advocated for you. Your shallow teenage epiphanies were my gospel. I copied whole passages of your "analysis" of your father into my memo. I dismissed the old man's open declarations as manifestations of dementia. And because of you, I rammed my CIA career into a wall.

Fast-forward three years, and here we are, sitting right next to each other in this hell of a country.

That, Fifi… that is *weird*.

"I know what you're thinking," Hector said to her on the bus. "But you're overthinking it like everybody else. They said they didn't expect this haze till June, and I believe them. Pulauis are very good people, and I'd like everyone to give them a chance."

"No, doctor, I mean something different."

Recently, Fifi had fallen into this Egyptian habit of calling all her professors "doctor," with a distinct Arabic drawl that made it sound more like "doc-tour." But Hector took this as a good sign she was adapting well to her home country.

"Different like what?" he asked.

"Doctor, remember our class on realism? You said the currency of the international system was power, right?"

"Mearsheimer. Structural realism. Right."

"But what is power, doc?"

"Well, that's an interesting question, Fifi. Basically, what we mean by power in realist theory is military and economic might. The governing structure of the international system is—"

"Anarchy," she said.

"I knew you were paying attention in class."

He hoped the sarcasm in his words wasn't audible. For many months now, Fifi had been skipping classes and asking for extraordinary extensions for her assignments. The reason for that being her daddy's new political venture: *Tamarod*, which stood for "mutiny" in Arabic. Tamarod sought to depose the Muslim-Brotherhood president of Egypt and redo the last election. It had come as a shock to most CIA analysts who'd thought the Big No's first memoir—blasphemous anti-democratic babble—had been a satire. Fifi's activism had negatively affected her school performance, and she probably wouldn't pass at all if she wasn't, A, famous, and B, the dean's niece.

Now she laughed and covered her big lips. "Sorry, doctor. Of course I wasn't. How can you say that? You know how crazy things are right now."

"Then I'm glad you've found the time to come with us on this trip," Hector said.

She fidgeted in her seat. "I just needed a vacation. Cairo is like a warzone. I don't know when things will settle down if they ever will. Everyone is like everyone's enemy for no good reason."

"That's what we call democracy, Fifi."

She rolled her eyes. "That's what Hitler and Lenin had said, before they came to power. Dad thinks the Muslim Brotherhood are even worse. They'll kill us all if they think we stand between them and the Caliphate."

Hector shook his head, then decided to change the subject. "How's Ernest, by the way? You guys in touch?"

Ernest was a former student and friend of Hector's. Yet ever since he'd left Cairo, he'd neither called nor emailed Hector. Hector had tried to reach him on an old email account he had, but there had been no reply.

"Oh, yeah. He mentioned this same subject the other week, said anarchy was the rule in today's world. And he mentioned you, too, doctor."

"Really? What'd he say?"

"Not much. Just that he misses everyone. He misses Cairo and the shisha and the Revolution and everything. He says life in DC sucks. He just sits there at his desk and does nothing."

Ernest had a privileged but unusual background. He was the illegitimate son of Prince Mohamed bin Hakam, a fact which Ernest himself hadn't been privy to until three years ago. Following his son's smooth graduation from AIMES in October, Prince bin Hakam had called in his chits with Washington to secure a stable job for his American son. Now Prince Mohamed was so popular in Washington that his son wouldn't need to do any work to get paid. To say that some people had it too easy was an understatement.

"That's post-graduation blues for you," Hector said. "Tell him to stick to his job in the Treasury. Most fresh grads wouldn't dream of being in his shoes right now, especially in this economy."

"But he *hates* it. It sucks his soul." She shook her vast forest of brown curls. "What a waste of talent. Ernest was the best of us."

Hector saw fit now to return to the original subject. "Anway, Fifi, to answer your question, realists believe that our world compels states to seek power. Call it leverage, security, or peace if you will. *Si vis pacem para bellum.*"

"Oh, I know what that means. *If you want peace, prepare for war.*"

The phrase was from Hector's first lecture this summer. He deemed his students worthy of a passing grade if they retained this single line from Vegetius: It summed up the entire discipline of political science.

"Good job," he said. "So states constantly amass weapons, compete over resources, seek out investments. And that, Fifi, that is power."

Fifi turned this over in her mind before posing a subquestion. "And people?"

"What about them?"

"Do countries compete with one other over the number of their human resources, too?"

Now *that* was a tricky question, and Hector knew exactly where it'd originated. Kero, of course. Being a persecuted Coptic Christian in Islamic Egypt, Kero was perhaps too fond of alt-right propaganda.

"Well, Fifi, I'm not saying demography is completely out of the question. The common wisdom has always been that demography is the mother of all politics. But still… Africa is very populous, and it's not powerful in any sense of the word."

Fifi was silent awhile, gazing out her window. "Doctor, they're funding this trip. Right?"

"They're good and generous people."

"Why?"

"I beg your pardon?"

"What's in it for them?"

Hector tried to hide his face. He looked back at the rearview mirror and saw the luggage warfare still in full swing. "Don't worry about them, Fifi. Pulau has a first-world economy. They can afford to be curious about us."

"I know exactly what they're doing," she said. "They're trying to be friends with my dad. But it's pointless. Dad doesn't care. He doesn't even care about me."

"Don't say that. I'm sure your father loves you very much."

"You don't know him. He's doesn't know how to relate to people."

To say that about the man who mobilized the biggest revolution in human history was rather uncanny. Hector remembered her stupid diary and cursed himself for not seeing this teenage know-it-all-ness in advance. "The more you grow, the more you lose touch with your parents," said the man who lost his only son, the man who was only eleven at his parents' funeral. "That's a fact of life you need to get used to."

"Thanks for the heads-up, anyway," she said flatly.

After the bags were somehow crammed in the trunk, Hector's male students began filing onto the bus. Baxter squeezed his way past Hector and Fifi, smiling like a prized boxer. Kero followed and plopped in the seat behind them, ballooning and deflating his thin cheeks. Ahmed lurched through to his wife in the back, his prayer mark like a painful bruise on his forehead. Both Ahmed and Zainab were members of the Muslim Brotherhood. Zainab was born into the creed, and her husband had married his way in only last month. Still, it was Ahmed who was more outspoken and, thereby, hated. Yubi rose the instant she spotted him coming her way.

Pointing her middle finger at Ahmed, Fifi said, audible enough, "Why is he even with us on this trip? He's a terrorist."

"*Shshsh,* shshsh," Hector hissed. "That's not a nice thing to say about a classmate, Fifi."

Finally, Mr Li climbed on the bus. He kicked the door shut and turned to glower at them all with his pinpoint eyes. "Next time you put masks inside bus!" he roared. "We take no disease from Africa."

Then he clambered to his right-sided seat, and started the engine.

5

C.O.R.O.N.A

The Presbyterian church beside the residence was swimming in darkness as Hector passed it on his way to Prinsep Street's intersection with Middle Road. He walked by a Subway, a sushi bar, and a couple of pubs, before the intersection loomed. There was roadwork there, the workers helmeted and vested in phosphorescent orange. They were eight workers in all: A Malay, two Indians, and five Chinese. Pulau's demography in a nutshell. *The mother of all politics.*

Across the road, Hector recognized a cavansite-blue Mercedes beckoning to him with its four-way flashers. He approached the car and opened the right back door.

The car instantly set out on its journey.

———

A fragrance tickled Hector's nose. Soap with orange and bergamot notes. Only one son of a dandy he knew worshiped *Neroli Portofino* to such a degree the perfume seemed to percolate through his skin. But it couldn't be. Could it? Hector twisted his neck and glared at the ghost seated beside him.

The ghost was in his early fifties now, his head buzzed, his ears big and flappy, and the veins in his forehead gorged like serpents. He was decked out in an off-white, double-breasted Soho suit, which did justice to his shredded Grecian physique. His eyes were still narrow and blue, lupine, but they looked more muted than Hector recalled.

Ozgur was a former wasp from the CIA's Special Activities Division. His job title was forever vague, but it was assumed he cleaned the Cardinal's table. Assassinations, rescues, interrogations, groceries, you name it, he was the man for it all. When the Cardinal had transferred to the White House in January 2009, Ozgur had shortly disappeared. Then word came he'd been torn to pieces in an explosion in the Turkish province of Kilis in April 2010. At his funeral, Hector had shared memories of Ozzie's "holy coffee grail," his outlandish birthday presents (think of a Beretta Cheetah handgun shipped via FedEx), his blonde-a-year dating ritual, his stale breath. All was improvised on the spot because nobody—not even Ozgur himself, apparently—had taken his death seriously.

Still, it was eerie seeing him after all this time.

"Well, well, well," Hector said. "Look who's got a new coat. Oh, is it you, Mr Turncoat?"

"Too much perfume," justified the deserter of Vienna of 2008, pointing at his midsection for some reason.

"What are you two talking about?" asked the driver.

"Nothing," said Ozgur.

"And what're *you* doing here?" Hector inquired of the driver. "Thought this was a solo job."

"You know, Hickey, sometimes I amaze even myself," Fabio

said, wrestling with the wheel from his ectopic right-sided driver's seat.

"Well, don't get too amazed there, Han Solo," Ozgur said. "They put people behind bars for breaking the speed limit here."

"It's like *Alice Through the Looking Glass*." Fabio made too wide a right turn at the next intersection. "Dimensions are all gone, man. Goddamn."

"The Brits have their fingerprints all over this place," Ozgur said disdainfully.

The car climbed onto an overpass. And with the nightmarish overview of a city drowning in the haze, Hector grew strangely relaxed. He'd not been in a real operation in nearly four years. This one, with its first passel of surprises, augured well.

The car shot through the nightlife of Pulau. Despite the tyranny of the haze, the city lived up to its reputation. Dazzling lights enlivening its streets and adorning its billion trees. People as plentiful as fish. Gooseneck lampposts bowing in alternating arabesques on the sides of the winding roads. Casinos and eateries battling to steal your attention. Skyscrapers reclining like sumptuous women in a Turkish bath. And a sky that was leaden, ominous, exquisite.

Slowly the roads closed in, and the car descended into a tunnel. What came on the other end was the necessary part of every city. The fleshpots were three miles south of the US naval base at the island's northern tip, which Hector suspected was their final destination. Hundreds of wooden shacks nursed a smattering of cloth-covered souqs, where Squids in their khaki uniforms laughed and brawled, prostitutes slouched in dusty doorways, and street vendors shouted their stir-fried noodles and dumplings.

The car whizzed past. After a while, Hector realized they weren't headed for the naval base.

"Where are we going?" he asked.

"You're getting angsty, Hickey." Fabio swerved onto a highway that wound a steep path around Mount Victoria. And a few minutes later, he landed the car along the island's west coast.

There were silent fences there. A few were factory warehouses, but most belonged to the National Army barracks. The water looked like over-brewed coffee, muddy brown and vapory. Across the other side, a lively civilization was visible, about three miles away. Hector made out the outlines of skyscrapers, minarets, and a star-topped tower. A few military launches cruised the water, and Hector followed their trajectories. And it wasn't long before he visualized it. What his academic life was all about. The invisible wall. The international border.

The city across the water must be Kuantan, Hector judged, the capital of the Malaysian state of Pahang which gave this water passage its name: *the Strait of Pahang*. Here the first East India Company ship had landed, nearly three centuries ago. Yet because of Pulau's rocky nature and harsh weather, it was dismissed as a geographical glitch, a funny joke from God.

It wasn't until Sir Robert Fullerton, governor of the Straits Settlements at the time, had had a series of dreams featuring a circus—in another version, a mermaid—here, on this piece of rock, that Pulau's modern history began. Sir Fullerton established the port on the east coast, naming it after his king. He built schools, hospitals, opera houses, churches, mosques, transforming Pulau into the Switzerland of the Malay

Archipelago. He breathed life into it. And insofar as Hector was aware, the Pulauis were still grateful.

Hector rolled down his window. The haze was light and, indeed, breathable. So it's true, he thought.

Malaysia exported natural gas and drinkable water to Pulau. Yet this arrangement was hit-or-miss on the best of days. Only last October, the Malaysian president had publicly ridiculed Pulau as this "red spit of dust" that, without their help, would "parch to death." And the Pulauis had been outraged.

But then came the death of Pulau's long-term leader and independence hero, Fei Guo, in December. The Malaysian president attended the funeral himself and gave a historical eulogy for Fei Guo. Fei Guo had been his "rival and conscience," he said. "Looking back, I see one man riding the stallion of our modern history. Not me. No. Allah may continue to bless me with humility. But Fei Guo. Yes. Without Fei's foresight, his good heart, his tenacity for the peace and progress of Southeast Asia, we would have continued to bicker ad infinitum, as the West pointed its fore-talon at us and guffawed." There had been plenty of weeping and hugs. We're neighbors and kinsmen, after all. And the Malaysian flags were lowered for three days, because Fei Guo was himself, by birth, a Malaysian.

Yet soon, another tribute came from Indonesia, this leviathan of the Archipelago, that drove a wedge into this whole reconciliation soap opera.

Hector recalled what he'd read about the subject with guilty delight. Even though the Indonesian islands of Borneo and Sulawesi were the main sources of the haze, Sumatra—the Titanic-shaped island across from the Malaysian state of Malacca—was a furnace in its own right also. This year, however, the incineration of the forest was put on hold there. A year of silence to honor Fei Guo's cremation, the Indonesians said. *Let his ashes swirl highly and fill the atmosphere,* tweeted one Indonesian poet, *hover, unadulterated, over Malaysia, the country of his birth that rejected him, stranded him on a "spit of dust," which before him wasn't worth a shilling.*

⁂

Hector fixed his eyes on a launch that kept pace with the car. Ozgur leaned over his shoulder and saluted two Pulaui officers in olive-green uniforms. The officers looked straight at them, but did not requite the salute.

"Pawns." Ozgur crinkled his nose.

"Can't tell a friend when they see one," added Fabio.

"Where're we going?" Hector demanded.

"Right over there." Fabio indicated a gated edifice drawing near.

Hector recognized the place right away. Yubi had shown him its picture in her *Lonely Planet* book and said it'd been one of the fewest relics that'd survived the Japanese invasion of '42 and the purge that'd followed Pulau's independence.

Hector whistled. "It's not open to visitors. Is it?"

"You'd make a perfect spy, Hickey," Fabio said. "It is not."

The double, harp-shaped gate opened for the car, then closed automatically when it passed. The Mercedes threaded its way on a stamped concrete driveway through a thick garden of plum, mango, and palm trees.

Finally, the car stopped next to a seahorse fountain made of black stone. And standing before the fountain was the historic monument. It was a three-story Georgian edifice of limestone and wood, complete with side gables, pilasters, and freshly painted quoins. Rifled security guards in deep blue uniforms stood before its double wooden doors, which had fancy iron grilles and transom windows.

"Gentlemen," Fabio exulted, "welcome to the US Embassy. Formerly, the Fullerton Palace."

———— ⁂ ————

Fabio closed the door and took four quick paces to sit at the head of the table. It was an aged teak table situated, mercilessly, under a candelabrum hanging too low over their heads. The lighting was wane, and it gave the room a macabre feel. Over the mantelpiece, Sir Fullerton—gold-buttoned, neckclothed, disdainful—glared down at the three Americans.

And the Cardinal looked the bygone master back in the eye. "Victorians were funny people," he said. "They had all those portraits and mirrors to keep looking at themselves."

Hector felt like informing the Cardinal that Sir Fullerton was not "Victorian," but thought the better of it and remained silent.

The Cardinal was dressed in a blue twill shirt with the sleeves rolled up. He picked his teeth with a pencil and turned to Hector. "What do you make of this place? Two billion bucks for this hen house."

"It isn't a hen house if it's two billion."

The Cardinal nodded and raised his hoary eyebrows in approval.

By which time, Fabio had opened a leather Gucci briefcase: It contained a few paper files and a MacBook. The Cairo deputy kept the MacBook, then sent the briefcase skating to his director.

The Cardinal picked a slim maroon file from inside the briefcase and passed it to Hector with a relaxed grip. "Simple logic. You're a smart guy, and it won't take you five minutes to get the gist of it. Are you sure you don't want a drink?"

Hector shook his head. He still couldn't shake his confusion. He had correctly decoded a message about a meeting with the Cardinal. But up until ten minutes ago, he'd assumed he would meet with a dispatcher from the NCS or a local operative from the Far East Division. Not the CIA director himself, again. This was unnecessary, if not outright illogical. Even Fabio's presence, which had surprised him in the car, seemed now overblown, ominous. As for the resurrected Ozgur, why he'd desisted from taking part in this meeting was a mystery unto itself.

Hector began reading the maroon file. It was the slimmest operation dossier he'd ever seen, three pages in all, all grainy photocopies of US EYES ONLY documents. The first page was a feasibility forecast, putting the success rate of "Operation C.O.R.O.N.A" at eighty-six percent. The second and third pages detailed this weird-sounding operation, and they boiled down to this:

To safeguard against the reversal of democracy in volatile, post-Revolution Egypt, Mr Ibrahim Noman's daughter had to be "comforted." Comforted how? That was Hector's job, his babysitting duty. So "Agent Starry Night 03"—Hector—would work on Fatima's millennial agnosticism to reprogram her, show her the underbelly of this benevolent dictatorship called Pulau, impress upon her pliant head the Kantian tenet that democracy was a categorical imperative, a rule both universal and good, never to be broken.

In other words, in order to prevent one man from turning against democracy, his daughter needed to hate a rich dictatorship? That didn't make any sense! And a fiasco like this could only have come from a brain with generic, template ideas, a bureaucrat's, such as Fabio's.

Hector was now livid. All his hopes for an Armageddon to restore his name had been squashed. How could he be so gullible? Langley didn't accept penitents. She fed on your guilt, dismissed your exploits like a toxic lover. *Never celebrate successes, never explain failures*, thus went her ignoble motto. And she lived up to it, Langley. One fat mistake, and you're out, Hector. No purgatory. And you're lucky enough if offered a spot in a theoretical limbo called AIMES. If anything, it kept you complacent, within the fold but not part of the clergy.

Never part of the clergy.

Which meant that their promise of a Cairo deputyship was just a dirty lie, a ruse to drag him here and make him partake of whatever plan they didn't deem him worthy of knowing.

He was just a *pawn* to them.

"You think you can do that?" the Cardinal said, studying his face. "It's not much, and she and her family trust you. I'll give you that, you're a trustworthy guy. That's why we need you, Hector. Any questions?"

"Sir, I have to tell you," Hector said, rising, his lips quivering, "you're full of shit."

And he walked out.

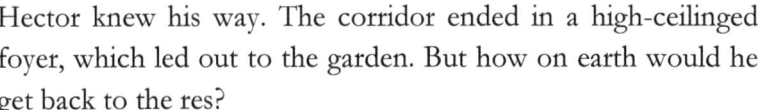

Hector knew his way. The corridor ended in a high-ceilinged foyer, which led out to the garden. But how on earth would he get back to the res?

He was thinking about this as he shot past Ozgur, who was seated on a padded chair between two big vases across from the door. Ozgur called out to him, and when he caught up with him, in the vaulted corridor, he took hold of Hector's elbow and whispered into his right ear, "We'll take a walk."

In the foyer, a group of people was gathered at the bottom of a sweeping red-carpeted staircase leading to the palace's upper two floors. Hector didn't establish eye contact with any of them, fixing his eyes on the curlicued grilles of the front door. Yet a vague impulse—maybe it was the decrescendo of the mirth as they passed by, or a particular laugh, sharp and guttural—made him turn his head.

And he was obliged to make a stop.

They were five people. One was a British diplomat who excused himself politely the moment Hector and Ozgur approached. The others were two girls and two lusty-looking men. One of the girls was the same French blonde—the environmentalist—Hector had flirted with this morning. She wore a revealing red halter dress and held a half-empty glass of white wine in her left hand. He'd forgotten her name, yet—both to his dismay and delight—she remembered his.

"Hector, howdy?" She high-fived him with a slender, diaphoretic palm.

The other girl was a petite black girl in a white cashmere blouse and pale denim tights. She introduced herself quickly, in Louisiana Creole, as a public affairs student at the National University, fiddling with a goldenrod pendant over her bosom and fixing Hector with a smile that made him uneasy. The two men were white Americans. One of them looked to be in his early thirties, with trained pectorals and prominent facial bones and, overall, looked vaguely familiar: Something about his beaming face, as he stated his designation—"I'm the Embassy's agricultural attaché"—suggested a spook or, more specifically, the *idea* of a spook. The other man was in his forties or early fifties, haggard (or inebriated), and authoritative in tone. He introduced himself as "the visa clerk," adding slyly, "keeping the Chinese at bay," with a wink.

The French environmentalist wobbled on her wedged heels and talked at length about her job. Hector found her, at length, tedious. But Ozgur seemed to enjoy her hoity-toity ramble.

"The Pulauis are so stupid," she said. "All those sycamores, locust trees, and oaks, they release VOCs—"

"VO-*what?*" Ozgur said, a grin swallowing half of his face.

"Volatile organic compounds. The moment a VOC meets nitrogen oxide, what d'you get?"

"Babies!" Ozgur boomed.

The girl giggled. "Ozone, stupid."

"That sounds like my name," Ozgur said.

"The haze is of their own making," the French girl went on. "Trees aren't always benign as you may think. This jungle they built, it's crazy, it's killing them."

"But I thought…" Hector chimed in, then changed his mind.

"His wife is very pretty." The girl took a long sip of her wine. "She came up to me and she was like, 'Why're you flirting with my husband?' And I was like, 'I'm not flirting with *anybody*.' So she was like, 'You're so pretty.' And I was like, 'No, *you*'re so pretty.' So pretty. We're friends on Facebook now."

The conversation meandered for another twenty minutes. It went through subjects as banal as cheap hotels in Kuala Lumpur and as serious as the People's Liberation Army's naval capabilities. Eventually, it slowed down and it became convenient for Hector and Ozgur to excuse themselves.

Hector realized only then that, despite having chatted with these people for nearly half an hour, none of them had offered his or her name.

———— ❧ ————

The Fraternity Bridge was not far from the Embassy. It crossed the narrowest section of the Pahang Strait—2.7 miles—and rose some thirty feet above sea level. It looked like the mummy of a steel-and-concrete insect. The piers gleamed, sent colored ripples through the water when cars juddered on. Two pylons, cast in the image of the Mermaid, propped two cable fans. And once in a calculated while—as if on a timer—a border patrol launch would skid under the bridge then veer fifteen or twenty feet away from the two spooks lurking in the great shadow. Hector and Ozgur would wave their hands to the officers, but the officers would not wave back.

Ozgur picked a pebble and skipped it. It was hard to see if it bounced, but he cheered anyway. "A woman like that, giving you the eye, and you're like, I'm married, here is my wife? What's wrong with you?"

"Two marriages can do wonders to a man," Hector said. "She took a shine to you, by the way. Go knock yourself out."

Ozgur dropped his pebble and swiveled to face him. "What's eating you, huh?"

Hector paused awhile. "Ozgur, what exactly is Operation Corona?"

"What's anything? It's all rhetoric."

"Lisa was vague with me. 'A one-man job,' she said. 'Operation Corona. It's like a Mexican beer on a sizzling day.'" Hector looked listlessly back at the palace. The thin haze swirling around its gables. The serenity with which it had acquiesced to the new landlords. "She said it would all make sense here."

"And it does. COunter-Revolution with uppercase C, O, and

R; uppercase ON; Arrest. CORONA. Get it?"

Hector looked at the colored piers, hypnotized. "We had a fling once, Lisa and me. It should've worked, but I was in a rough place, a loser with a PhD. I drank. It helped for a while. I worked very hard. But the Company booted me out anyway."

"I didn't realize we did that," Ozgur lied.

"Thirty-one months. It was the longest period of my life. I got married, had a kid, then lost him. You lose your mind if you live like other people. We're not cut out for it, the normal life. I couldn't stand it, the slow afternoons and the demons screaming in my head. I needed to get out." Hector picked up a stone and lobbed it. It missed the launch only by a yard, and the officers did not look happy about it. "So when Lisa called, finally, you can imagine how it felt. It wasn't like going back, but being born again." They walked away from the bridge, and Hector sat down on a warm rock.

Ozgur remained standing. "And then what?" Ozgur asked.

"We met on a felucca. Thinking about it now, part of me wanted it to be a date. Her lipstick was red like blood, and her bubblegum smelled of peach. She smiled and toyed with her hair and she was rude at first, but I knew she was happy to see me. And she told me a funny story."

"Story? What story?"

"There was an agent before me in Cairo. His name was Courtney. Courtney as in a guy called Courtney. In Sweet Home Alabama they bullied him, so he moved to Cairo thinking he would find peace there. And he was right, but wrong. Anyway, this Courtney, he got lost in Cairo. When Lisa recruited him, he was a teacher at a language school in Maadi, some elite thing for local consumption. Lisa wanted him because some of his filthy-rich students were being recruited by a *jamaa Islamiya* seeking out filthy-rich Muslim kids. At first, Courtney seemed like a godsend.

He was passionate, fast, and he helped Cairo preempt a bomb at the British Council, sometime in twenty-O-five. But he 'smelled like poop,' as Lisa put it. Something wasn't right about him. Her suspicion doubled when he refused to sip at the toast to the victory. 'I don't drink anymore,' he said. So Lisa upped her game. She dropped by his Mohandeseen apartment and said she wanted to discuss a 'secret project' with him. He let her in, and she bugged the bathroom and the hall. 'I brought you some milk,' she said. 'Water buffalo. *Uh-unh*. You got your last toast. This time, you have to work for it.' And she stripped for him. But the bastard wouldn't do it. He was in a long-distance relationship, *blah-blah-blah*. So Cairo monitored his apartment. No boys. And no prostitutes. No-thing. Not even porn. Something stood out, though. And guess what? Courtney was whispering in his dreams. They rewound and rewound the tapes, slowed them down, and it was everybody's worst nightmare. Courtney was reciting al-Quran. Next, they got a visual into his apartment from the opposite rooftop. Courtney read Sayed Qutb and Anwar and al-Awlaki. He prayed five times a day. When Lisa interrogated him, he said he was indebted to Langley. Had they not recruited him, he wouldn't have seen 'the light.' And therefore, he was loyal to America, as long as America let him practice his religion freely."

"What a strange story," Ozgur said. "What's your take on it?"

"Lisa said it was the air. Cairo's air. 'Seven thousand years of civilization, Hickey. The rot, the decay of two hundred generations. We're breathing dead Pharaohs, Ptolemaic merchants, Roman soldiers, prophets, gods, Jews, Arabs. It's a big tomb and we're buried in it, breathing its curse.' Her Maine Coon cat had gone feral after she'd moved to Cairo, she said, and it was then that she'd known. She thought she was going nuts, too."

"So she went *carpe diem* on you." Ozgur walked the orbit of his confessing friend.

"It didn't work. The mood was off, for both of us. Lisa was annoyed about what was going on in Egypt. Two years after this big revolution, and people were protesting day in, day out. Nothing was getting done. Unemployment high. Power outages everywhere. And the country was going bankrupt. The Islamists had come to power by democracy, yeah, but the people weren't happy about that. They hated the *Ikhwan* so much, they would've replaced the old tyrant on the throne if they could."

Ozgur stood behind him and leaned over. "Bring it on, my friend. Keep going. It's easier when you look your devil straight in the eye."

A sudden movement by the pier stole Hector's attention. For a second, he thought he'd seen a silhouette, a flicker under the bridge. But then the launch returned and with its strong headlamp, it dissolved the shadow. "I was recovering from Wayne's death. My boy."

Ozgur resumed his orbit.

"His anniversary was getting close. Two weeks after my rendezvous with Lisa, he would've been twenty months. Poor kid. Yubi hasn't been the same."

"Do you still love her?"

"I don't know anything anymore. She's been very strange lately."

"In what way?"

"Stop right there and look at me!" Hector shouted. "What the hell is Corona? I must know!"

Only then did Ozgur stop. He considered his friend with a morose face, then said, "You have a lot of problems. You sure you wanna add to that?"

"What are you, my therapist?"

Sniffing the stench of the air, Ozgur raised his gray eyes to the leaden sky. "Knowledge is like medicine. It can cure, but it can also kill you."

"Then I prefer to die."

Ozgur nodded slowly. "Welcome back, Agent Kane."

On their way back to the Embassy, Hector picked up a pebble and skipped it. It hit the side of the spying launch. One officer—the tubbier of the two—raised his fist in what the spooks took for a salute. So they saluted him back cheerfully.

With the extras in the foyer dismissed and half of a Hennessy bottle consumed by the Cardinal and Fabio—Sir Fullerton looked gloomier, his cheeks saggier, and a definite frown was visible on his brow—Hector received a presentiment of what was to come.

"You need a drink," insisted a soused Cardinal, and Fabio poured half a mugful of the liquor.

Hector took his drink and seated himself on the nearest chair.

Fabio walked back to the far end of the table and returned with his MacBook. "Take your time." He patted Hector's shoulder.

It was a PDF file. Hector read...

February 6/2013

MEMORANDUM FOR: George Moore, Director of
Central Intelligence
FROM: Thomas Bolgers, Director of the
National Clandestine Service
SUBJECT: Project C.O.R.O.N.A

1. The purpose of Project C.O.R.O.N.A
is to abort the Egyptian anti-democratic
movement known as Tamarod. Since December
2012, Tamarod has gathered the signatures
of over 25 million Egyptians, most of whom
supporters of the deposed Mubarak regime.
Tamarod seeks to annul the June 2012
presidential election, which has brought
the Muslim Brotherhood to power by a
narrow 51.7%. It also seeks to repeal the
Constitution passed in December of the
same year. Tamarod stands for Mutiny in
the Arabic language. The campaign poses a
serious threat to democracy in the Middle
East. If democracy falls in the biggest
country in the region, fledgling
democracies in smaller Arab Spring states
such as Libya and Tunisia will likely
collapse as well.

2. Tamarod's initiator, Mr. Ibrahim
Noman, 72, is a former OPEC Secretary-
General (1999-2007). He follows the Sufi
method of Islam and is a vehement anti-

vaxxer and anti-modern medicine. Our psychologists suggest that both his late religiosity and his reaction to science are results of his late wife's death of pancreatic cancer in 1992. Mr. Noman's NGO Haram was the main platform for political activism during the 2011 Egyptian Revolution. Egyptian revolutionaries have given Mr. Noman the title of "The Godfather of the Revolution," but colloquially he is better known as "The Big No."

3. Former Agent Starry Night 03 is serving a stint as a professor of political science at the American Institute of Middle Eastern Studies in Cairo (AIMES) where Mr. Noman's daughter (Fatima), 24, is a student. Agent S. N. 03 is to be reinstated into his last-held position at the Cairo Station. Agent S. N. 03 will arrange for Ms. Noman to enroll in a summer class and coordinate with the Pulaui Embassy in Cairo for a study trip.

4. Agent S. N. 03's duties are to Triple-Eye Ms. Noman: Isolate, Immunize, then Import her back to Cairo. Following the success of his mission, Agent S. N. 03 will be promoted to Deputy Chief of the Cairo Station. Our Pulaui partners will

cover the travel costs and offer generous per diems. They will also arrange for Ms. Noman to be injected with KV-19, a coronavirus similar to SARS which the Pulauis have borrowed from the Chinese PLA laboratories at our behest. KV-19 causes severe respiratory symptoms after an incubation period of one to two weeks, by which time Ms. Noman should be back in Cairo.

5. Once the symptoms occur, Mr. Noman will be contacted by our Cairo office and be offered medical help in exchange for his unswerving loyalty: as manifested, for the time being, in aborting his anti-democratic movement, Tamarod. Our agents in Asia and Cairo will endeavor to accomplish their missions without compromising the CIA's core values of Service, Integrity, and Excellence.

On the drive back from the Embassy, Hector couldn't stop thinking about what he'd pledged to do. He didn't for a second doubt that democracy was a good force. He wouldn't go so far as to believe that democracies didn't fight, or that they made people rich. Democracy, in his opinion, wasn't designed for that. What democracy offered people in principle was *maturity:* It made people the masters of their own destiny.

Which brought him back to his current dilemma. Which held more weight: one person's life or the growth of millions?

He listened to Ozgur and Fabio's testing jest, too profoundly confused to play along.

"Say, what's a cold bite?"

"A frostbite."

"Nah, a frost hickey. *Hah hah.*"

"Who killed the electric car?"

"Mercedes."

"*Uh-unh*. OPEL with a C."

"*Huh*. Good one. Take this—"

"No, take this. Guy gets the hook."

"He's depressed."

"No, he's married. *Hah hah hah hah.*"

Hector plummeted deeper and deeper into himself. He'd been there before: the day his parents had died, for example, and the day his baby Wayne had passed away. He did not like what he saw there, so the trip back to the surface had to be quick.

The Mercedes dropped him three intersections away from the residence, way back west on Dickens Road. He walked a few steps, then realized the car was making the walk with him.

"Wanna get sick or what?" Ozgur was holding his forgotten mask through the window, the tattoo on his wrist spelling *retired* in two spaced syllables: RE TIRED, and above the tattoo was the sword-and-shield emblem of the Special Activities Division.

Hector took the mask.

"Take it easy, Hickey," Fabio said from the driver's seat. "You have my number if you need me."

Hector watched the Mercedes go to the end of the street, then vanish into the haze.

He wondered if the past two hours had been a dream.

If this *island* was a dream.

6

CITY OF DOGS

I n July 2009, Mr Ibrahim Noman resigned from his adjunct teaching position at the University of Natural Resources and Life Sciences (BOKU) in Vienna, subleased the Leopoldstadt flat, and booked two one-way tickets for himself and his daughter to Cairo.

Once in Cairo, having run a sweeper to his parents' rundown house in Old Cairo, the former OPEC secretary-general called in his chits with the dean of Cairo University to enroll Fifi there. His sister's institute was a no-go zone at the time, because of a family dispute that would settle later.

After that, the Big No started up an NGO, which he named *Haram*, after the Arabic word for *sin* or generally *wrong*.

Haram called for electoral reform, stricter laws against corruption, and accountability for police brutality. Soon the Nomans' Old Cairo house—Haram's HQ—became a Mecca for all political desperadoes of Egypt. Haram grew so quickly like a tumor, despite its founder's early pessimism:

"Egyptians cannot tell a ballot box from a fruit box," the Big No had said in a notorious TV interview that had cost him a thick swathe of his popularity a few months after his return.

No one had seen it coming. People from all streams of life converted to the new creed. Callow idealists. Stiffened skeptics. Lefties. Islamists. Technocrats. Nubians. Copts. Couch Party sloths.

Yet even then, the Egyptian government kept its cool. We've seen it all before, they said. Can grassroots do anything? They just toke and shout at one another. Let them play, let them play.

Before the year rounded, though, the government had blown a fuse or two. Haram activists had mustered their courage to go out on a few protests. Noman had also refused every honorary position he'd been offered. The West was supporting him, evidently, since he was visited by a miscellany of envoys from around the globe. Something was not right about him, for unlike the human-rights and democracy mongers of Cairo, he refused all aids and donations. The Egyptian Intelligence monitored his finances closely. They monitored *him*. They paid people to join his movement.

So when the Revolution finally erupted, it took everyone by storm. Even the Big No was surprised.

History has taught me never to take Him for granted

He wrote in his bestselling second memoir.

———— ༓ ————

In Europe, Hector had been feeling the heat, but his spying prowess had not taken him far.

By this time, the Cardinal had left the CIA for the White

House gig and Hector was bossed by the DO's new director, Thomas Bolgers, the lanky albino from Palo Alto who seemed so sociable and easygoing but was in fact a psycho whose sport was feeding his agents hogwash.

Hector tasted this hogwash himself when he handed Bolgers a 72-page memo on the reviving defense industries of Europe and what that meant for the future of NATO, only for Bolgers to stare at him behind his squarish, gold-rimmed glasses, and say, "Now I'll be damned. I was joking with you, brother. Jesus." Bolgers held the heavy, double-spaced, black-wired memo, then added, "I'll put it to good use, though. Someone in the DIA may find this handy. Meanwhile, you may want to take a breather... especially after Ozgur, you know. You guys were close. And emotions can dampen a spy's judgment. You can't work with me if you'll lose your acumen, Hector. Now get out."

Ozgur's death had flung Hector into a maelstrom. But in truth, he'd grown weary of Europe long before. He could definitely use a breather to recover, cogitate, and regain at least a smidgen of his earlier excitement about the trade. But at this point in his career—as happens to the best of spies—he didn't want to go any farther. And the idea of resignation seemed too defeating. He didn't want to do or undo anything. He just drifted on, hoping for the worst to pass without his interference.

Thus April 2010 had passed. Peacefuly. Hector buried himself in his day job and was rewarded with a good raise. Since 2005, he'd bounced all over the Continent from one think tank to another, procreating his legend, as instructed. He met diplomats, professors, and scientists from every community on earth. He'd objected to this arrangement at first, desiring a full-time commitment like Ozgur's, but slowly he came to appreciate his cover: It wasn't love, but respect, or simply gratitude.

Political analysts are a downtrodden bunch: They hardly get

paid at all, and if they do, not for long, and not much. Not Hector. The Company had given him a lucrative job at one of the pinnacles of political research: the Stockholm International Peace Research Institute (SIPRI). It was a dream job even for someone who took it merely as a cover.

This job had come his way as a direct placement, which was unusual for a Langley boy. Previously, the Company had desisted from influencing his cover, fearing smudges on his legend. But in February 2008, six pounds of enriched Uranium were intercepted in Helsinki. The source was the dismantled Soviet strategic arsenal in the near abroad, the lab confirmed. One lead led to another, and the CIA ended up tilting at windmills in Latvia. The chase had been a farce, but it had proved Hector's theory about a nuclear smuggling network across the Baltic—a theory that hadn't come out of his spying work, but through the drudgery of his cover job.

The Company had wanted him in Scandinavia, fast, so they risked making a few phone calls.

And in Stockholm, he'd soon floundered into a new relationship.

This one was called Lyra, like *The Golden Compass* character— though born long before the book had been conceived—but she pronounced the Y as an A. Everyone called her "Lara." She was the least beautiful of all his girlfriends: too skinny, too sweaty, her eyes protruded a bit, and her chin was sharp like a witch's. Yet she was the sweetest gal a man could meet. A physiotherapist, she tickled her patients' stiff knees and hips and chanted ABBA songs to them and made them dance with her smiles. Everyone loved her. Life loved Lyra, and Lyra loved life, and Hector. Why? His looks, for the most part, plus the spleeny moods he dropped into after sex. Often Lyra realized he didn't like her very much. But he'd stuck with her for over a year and had shown no signs of fleeing, which reassured her to some extent.

Before Lyra, Hector had had only two girlfriends in Europe. Hayley was a professional chef based in Notting Hill whom he'd met while working for Chatham House. In a quirky way, she took Hector up as a reprieve from a controlled life. She took him to cheap Irish pubs, seamy underground clubs, and crack sessions. They didn't bond, and after five months they broke up amicably.

With Maureen, his coworker at the French Institute of International Relations, Hector had finally contemplated settling down, or in the least, extending his stint in Paris. Maureen was a smashing five-foot-four blonde, with a PhD in non-proliferation and disarmament. She spoke four languages and had a brown belt in judo. Barely beyond the dreaded thirty, she pushed him hard toward the cage of spousehood. But Hector was adamant he couldn't, because his "career" was "rocky." After a passionate—verging on violent—one-year romance, the relationship ended with her cheating on him, in a stuffy 10th Arrondissement basement, with Guillaume, their goateed, soccer-crazed, favorite bartender. Hector was devastated. He saw her only once after that. It was at a conference in Amsterdam. She looked older and wise in a cruel way. She gave him a warm hug and pecked his cheeks. Then she said she would love to visit him in Stockholm sometime.

Thank God, she never had.

What was new about Stockholm—and Lyra, by association—was the quietness. The Swedes were lovely people: too polite, too smiley, too handsome. They struck Hector as a refined version of his early countrymen, the Canadians. Something about the snowy North appealed to him in general. The frozenness of his fingers near Christmas. The short days.

The heaters. The tuques. The close alleys of Gamla Stan when they pulsed with electricity and music. Stockholm was a place where he could retire. And Lyra would make the perfect wife.

———— ✿ ————

One day, a week or so after the raise, Hector went home to find the lights turned off. He lived in a spare, two-bedroom rooftop apartment overlooking Stureplan Square. You could see the Spy Bar's steeple on your left, and the Sturegallerian shopping center across, with its flags and façade assailed by headlights. An unexpected guest was standing on his balcony.

Hector closed the front door and fumbled his way past the dark furniture. "What would have happened if she opened the door?" he asked.

"She won't be back before midnight," the Cardinal said, leaning over the mildewed railing. "We made sure of that. Good view, by the way."

Hector joined him in the balcony. "What are you doing here, sir? Not enough action in Washington?"

"It never stops."

"Then what? Bolgers didn't say anything."

"About what?"

"Whatever job you're here for."

"You don't like your current job?" the Cardinal said with a turn of his face.

"I never said that."

"*Hmm.* You don't like *her* then."

Hector didn't respond. He grabbed the railing with both hands and leaned over. Down on the street, in front of a

Starbucks, seven adolescents lounged on their bikes, sipping frappuccinos and moaning in unison about a bad movie they'd watched. Stureplan was busy but never quite noisy. If a cat mewed a hundred feet off, Hector would hear it.

"I came to say congrats," the Cardinal said, "for the promotion."

"It's only a raise, sir. Bolgers got it all mixed up." Hector puffed.

"He said you needed fine-tuning for your ears, and I can see why," said the Cardinal.

"Why're you really here? A new operation?"

Despite the optimism Hector had brought with him to Scandinavia, a nuclear dealership network across the Baltic had never been found. Hector had spent the past thirteen months doing what he'd been doing in Western Europe: Islamic terrorism stuff. And he was tired of it all.

"It's time you moved on," the Cardinal said.

"Where to?"

"Cairo. A full-time job. That's the promotion I came to congratulate you on."

Incidentally, a car honked on the street, and Hector felt queasy, as if he were going to plummet there. He'd accepted a floater position in Europe principally to avoid Cairo. He would use his political science background, he had convinced the Cardinal many years ago, along with his three languages— English, French, and Arabic—to serve at any station in Europe. At one point even, he'd considered applying for a desk job at the Directorate of Analysis to avoid a vacancy in Baghdad for which he'd been rumored to be "a strong candidate."

Hector and the Cardinal left the balcony, and Hector went to the kitchen to boil water for two cups of Earl Grey tea. He was distraught. It took him a long while to calm down and prepare the drinks, during which he revisited his entire childhood.

Cairo? How could he go back there after all he'd been through? And why now? There must be a strong reason. He wasn't the sole Arabic-speaking agent in Langley's registry. Not by a long shot. Far more capable agents would kill to prove their mettle before America's new nemesis, Islam. So why him?

The boiler whistled, for the second time, and Hector poured the water and took the tea out to his guest. The Cardinal was bracing one foot on the coffee table. Hector placed the mug inches from the Cardinal's polished boot.

"You haven't asked why," said the Cardinal.

"I don't need to." Hector seated himself in a brocaded seat across from him and sipped his tea. "Orders are orders."

"You're a good lad."

Hector took a deep breath. "I think I do want to move, sir. I've been in Europe far too long. There is this book I read, it says a man must specialize in his thirties. Europe is pretty, but a man can't specialize here."

"How old are you now?"

"Thirty-eight."

"Still a puppy."

"I don't like pets."

"Well, you'll have to adapt." The Cardinal reached for his mug. "Cairo is teeming with dogs."

Hector hadn't mulled over why the Cardinal, a former spook at the time, had bothered to deliver the promotion himself. But he should have. It took him a year after the transfer to rethink that visit and marvel at his stupidity.

In Langley's dogma, the sins of the recruits were always visited upon the recruiters.

The Cardinal had come to admire the view from his Stockholm balcony not to deliver a promotion, but a punishment.

Cairo was Hector's sentence.

7

CREDIT

I n Cairo, Hector had been installed as a political risk analyst at a firm called "Murphy & Associates," a façade for the CIA's Cairo station. The firm overlooked the Nile from two high-ceilinged flats in the Corniche. You could see the feluccas swarming with tourists, the roasted beans and lupin vendors with their carts and catcalls and brawls, the juvenile lovers venturing forbidden kisses.

Lisa McConkey, the station chief, called it "the Crazy Horse of the CIA family," an analogy that only she was able to decipher. Aside from the two flats in the Nile Corniche, the Crazy Horse had a safe house in Sayeda Zainab—the poor neighborhood of the Hussein Mausoleum and Mosque—and three rooms in the US Embassy, which was a stone's throw away from the firm.

"Forget who you are," Lisa instructed him on day one. "Kiss and make love to Cairo. And remember always, Murphy and Ass is a real company. We do business here. People get fired." Then she touched her steel ruler to his left and right shoulders, conferring her accolade on him. "Got it, Hickey?"

Fabio, her deputy, whistled then tilted his back in a whiplash on his creaking chair, snickering.

Lisa had a black velvet mask that she used when she slept. And she shrieked like a zebra during sex. But every morning, she cried her eyes out.

One night, she slobbered and clung to his hairy chest like a terrified goatling.

What's bothering you, Lisa?

Her husband. He was a CNN guy. Rishmawi was his name. A Christian, of Palestinian extraction, raised in Jordan, who now carried an American passport. A man so lost among identities that when he finally found himself, it was in the tangles of the Somali Civil War, from which he never returned.

Does he ever contact you?

Last Christmas, that deserter had sent her a video, apologizing for not being able to carry on with his husbandly duties and asking for her forgiveness. After the divorce, you know, she struggled to convince people—herself before others—that she'd come out of the trial stronger. She married herself to her job. She grew upbeat and bubbly, as if to show them—people—that she could laugh in the face of misery. She gave money to charity. She even thought of getting another cat.

"Let's go on a trip," Hector proposed. "Petra, or Athens. I've got a lot of Air Miles and not much going on anyway."

He kissed her sweaty scalp, her hands on his chest. Her green eyes were open, the sleep mask discarded at her legs. And as her breaths grew shallower and steadier, her eyes remained open.

In June, a rumor went around that President Mubarak's latest surgery in Germany had been, in fact, palliative.

"The old lion is dying," a Haram activist celebrated in a groundbreaking YouTube video. "We're coming for you, Gamal!"

But most Egyptians whispered cautiously. Although heartened by the gossip, they couldn't picture another tyrant on Mubarak's throne. After all, he'd ruled the country for three decades. He'd done bad things, but good things also—like the Metro, the libraries, and the many irrigation projects in the Western Desert—not to forget that he was rich. They'd *made him rich*. A young starved president would take forever to be "full."

So a new Pharaoh? Impossible!

People could only laugh at the notion that Mubarak's eldest son, Gamal, could succeed him. That sort of succession happened in Jordan and Syria, and was the tradition in the Arab Gulf states. Yet "this forty-six-year-old child?" as one army general put it to Hector, at an Embassy luncheon. "We would take *Iblis*"—Satan—"over him."

Washington was ambivalent as well. For years, Gamal had insinuated his cronies into the domestic politics of Egypt, which caused them to have monopolies over whole sectors of the economy: such as steel, cotton, and poultry. Those actions were frowned upon by the opposition and were used to call for democratic reform. Which was good. Yet a feedback loop had slowly ensued, whereby corruption fed opposition like a patron.

"Without them being so careless," a journalist said to Hector and Fabio over shisha, "we won't have anything to say, will we?"

Five months later, in November 2010, Gamal would take his transgressions to a whole new level. Taking advantage of his father's dwindling health, he directed the parliamentary elections, giving most of the seats to his National Democratic Party and only one seat to the Muslim Brotherhood. The MB would lose nearly ninety percent of their seats from the previous elections, when they had swept the two houses of Parliament.

And this last move would make the gods of democracy in DC very angry with Gamal.

July 2010 was the month of Lisa's chewed-up, flighty pronouncements, thrown hastily among them as she zipped through their pods flinging her red arms about.

And of Hector's burgeoning friendship with Jeff Trevor, the chronically constipated US ambassador to Cairo.

What had bonded them, on their first meeting, was Jeff's professed hatred for Cairo, which struck a kindred chord with Hector.

Jeff said he'd wanted a job in Estonia or Bulgaria or any post-Soviet hungover state but had been hurled to Cairo regardless. "Islam and the political mess of the Middle East? Allah and his suicidal saints? Fossilized Arab dictatorships? No, man, I'd rather flip burgers in DC. But my moment will come. Cheers!"

Their high-spirited camaraderie soared.

The Embassy's wall was vandalized with graffiti in mid-July. An informer called Sherif emailed Hector a video of a radical imam wailing about "the Crusaders' castle in the Land of the *Kenanah!*"

"*Kenanah?* What the devil does this mean?" Jeff rested his

fleshy palm on the pool table's rail. He overextended his thumb to cuddle the stick—Jeff's thumb could bend over backward to touch itself—and aimed. His right eye winked and when it opened, the blue in it remained below its size in the left eye. His beer gut was tight under a merlot-red shirt. His armpits were wet despite the chilling AC on the prince's yacht.

"A quiver, Your Excellency," Prince Mohamed bin Hakam answered, coming through the back door of the cabin.

A beefy cigar was in his teeth. The prince was wearing a sheeny black tux without a tie around his thick neck. As for His Highness's head, it was a controversy. The hair on either side of his bald crown was white like cotton, and he ponytailed it with a red scrunchy studded with emeralds. His Highness's well-trimmed beard matched his hair. His skin was ruddy, glowing like melted sand. So perfect, well-scrubbed, and creamed was the prince's skin, except for a crescent three-inch scar on the left cheekbone that reached to the eyebrow under a black leather patch.

The prince scripted the following verse from Surat Hood, in deep orange citrine, over his eye patch:

إن الحسنات يذهبن السيئات

(Good deeds do away with misdeeds)

Mohamed bin Hakam had mentioned to Hector, once, that he'd lost this eye in a children's scimitar play with his cousin, the Saudi crown prince. "Our family is cursed," the prince had lamented, "with weak hearts. We forgive. We forgive way too easily."

Hector always wondered why the prince hadn't concealed the scar as he had the eye. (Or better, correct both.) Definitely, he didn't lack the money. Yet from what he'd seen from storytellers—and there were wardfuls of these in espionage—he knew the answer wouldn't add up. The prince only shared cathartic mutations of the truth. Any serious inquiry into his soppy tale would topple the whole story-verse.

"Oh, hullo, Mohamed," Jeff lackadaisically greeted their host. He banged the striped 13 ball. The ball bounced at an obtuse angle and hit Solid 6, which dropped into the corner pocket.

"Scratch," Hector said, squeezing his way to the distant end of the table. "Step aside, Your Highness, give us some space, uh."

The prince relocated to a golden tray beside the fridge and poured a double shot of Tanqueray No. Ten. He rocked his drink and looked into the tumbler for a while. Then he said, "The Prophet was taken by Egypt when he conquered it. It wasn't, you know, always like this. He blessed it and called it *Kenanatu Allah*. God's own quiver." The prince tasted the gin and his one eye constricted in an approving grimace. "The Western image of an Arab is a savage head-chopper. But you are way, way misguided, my friends. Arabs were great romantics. We still are. Even in war we write great poems. Our grandfathers were brave men, not barbarians, not primitive savages. They were knights. Archers. Spearmen. And—yes, of course—swordsmen. No shame about it, no shame at all. Were the Romans peaceful in their conquests? Were the Spartans that you worship in films? Come on, my friends, I know you are listening. Agent Kane?"

He had walked to the table and stood behind Hector as Hector leaned to take his shot.

"It's Mr Kane, if you don't mind." Hector straightened and simpered at the prince and the elk head mounted on the wall behind his funny head. "Or you can just call me Hector."

Hector bowed and aimed again. Solid 2 went into the side pocket. Hector moved to take aim at 4.

"Kane—Hector, sorry—has a PhD. So feel free to call him a doctor." Jeff winked to Hector, his arms folded, his legs shaking to dispel the colic in his dilated gut.

"I didn't know that. You never mentioned it. You think you know a man." The prince swigged his gin. "And what sort of doctor are you, my dear Doctor Hector?"

"Not one who can treat you, I'm afraid," Hector murmured, before striking the ball.

Hector and the prince had met over a dozen times before, first in the Crazy Horse then at random events in Cairo, and Hector's PhD had come up at least twice. Mohamed bin Hakam was a generous host, a patron of strangers, and a quick and easy friend, but his memory didn't measure up to his gregarious appetite. The Americans used his two yachts moored in the Nile, his Maadi villa, his three limos for work and to party. They made fun of him on his own property, and the prince forgot about it all in a blink. That was why they loved him.

The prince walked back to his minibar and poured a triple shot of the same liquor. "Yes, yes. Lisa. How stupid I am. I was going to visit her today, but I forgot. Stupid Prince Mohamed," he repeated. "Stupid Prince Mohamed."

"Are you okay, Your Highness?" Jeff voiced. "Maybe you should put the drink down and call it a day."

The prince glanced into his tumbler for a moment, then plonked it on the golden tray. He took a step back toward Hector. "Of course. Now it makes sense. She put your name forward as one of her most capable guys. A PhD. Good. So tell me, Hector, is it true?"

"Is *what* 'true'?"

"This treasure up north."

Prince Mohamed was not the biggest shark in the water, perhaps, but he was a heavyweight investor. His business empire—HakamCo—was ranked highly on Lisa's clientele list, especially for her new project, the Zohr gas field.

Hector had thought it a hoax at first. Yet geology didn't lie. Not to money. And according to the leaked seismic reports from the Italian gas company Eni, the biggest gas field in the Mediterranean had just been found, niched a few kilometers within the Egyptian maritime border with Cyprus. Zohr boasted double the size of Israel's Leviathan. Thirty trillion cubic feet of fortune lay in wait of bold drillers. And normally, a find like this would make Murphy & Ass the biggest consulting firm in the Middle East.

But Langley didn't like that prospect.

Only two days earlier, orders had come: The project was to be closed, and suitors dismissed.

Hector paced by the prince to the bar. He held up a Black Pearl Louis XIII and poured himself a shot. "Nothing for sure, prince. If you want my honest opinion, it's all hot air."

He heard three *schnick*s of the prince's lighter as the prince remembered his cigar. "Will your boss be happy with you telling me this? She promised me the moon."

"The moon is not for sale, Your Highness."

The prince smoke avidly, as if with a grudge against himself. Jeff said he needed some fresh air, and the two Americans stepped out of the cabin, through an automatic sliding door. They climbed two steps, which lit and pinged as they stepped on them, and finally they walked onto the open deck.

The moon was a full circle, the sky a dirty mat. Far north, on the opposite shore, the Egyptian National Radio and Television center—Maspero—blazed like a colossal birthday cake. In its shadow the cuboid HQ of the Ministry of Foreign Affairs glowed wanly, blending surreptitiously into the dirty night.

Jeff said, "Sing your song."

"Don't let me down!"

"Come on, man."

"I'm in love for the first time!"

Jeff followed Hector to the taffrail, scratching his stubble. They looked down at the two lower decks and the dark river cupping the yacht's aft. On the deck beneath them, two hands—blond, downy—massaged their bones and tendons. Beside these, a pair of flail brown forearms were crossed at the wrists. Once in a long while blond and brown touched.

The main deck was full of life. A dozen or so inebriated men circled a belly dancer glimmering in gold. Hector was aroused. He took a chestful of the river's fecundity. Catfish and baltics. Dead hyacinth. Daily garbage. He closed his eyes.

"I have work at eight a.m." Jeff looked at his gleaming blue-dial Omega and began rolling down his sleeves.

"Oh, you work?"

"You're a funny guy. Anyway, what have you got for me?"

"Like I said. A crazy guy in Imbaba."

"Fantastic. I'll let you deal with him, then."

Hector was still taken by the belly dancer. But right then the prince came on deck. He dispersed the dance circle, then gripped the girl's left arm. She smiled widely at him. Healthy teeth, smeared by melting rouge. Slowly, without resistance, the prince towed his prize out of sight. The music didn't stop.

"Sounds like a plan," Hector said.

As a State Security captain worth his salt, Mourad *Bey* was plainly clothed and groomed. Though it was still July, he wore a biker's black leather jacket, black jeans, and a pressed blue shirt. His thick mustache was oiled. So was his thin scalp. And a pack of red Dunhill cigarettes stood before him on the desk.

Hector measured him up. A man for all seasons, laidback, ruthless, bargainable.

"Do you drink *khamra*, Mr Hector?" The *bey*'s chipped desk was empty. The room was religiously bare, cubical, with pale indigo paint covering three quarters of its height. Behind the *bey* was a high window blocked by four rusty bars. A ceiling fan whirred softly.

"I don't drink, *maaly el-bey*," Hector lied, stretching his hand over his chest and leaning slightly forward: a gesture of humble decline.

"Good, 'cause we don't carry wine or *beera* or whiskey for you. An alert man, then. We like that. How can we help you? We have work to do."

Hector laid his hands obsequiously upon his knees. "The incidents at the Embassy, *maaly el-bey*, we can't control them. But maybe you can? The United States would be very appreciative of your help in this regard. After all, we are fighting the same enemy."

Mourad *Bey* took a cigarette and lit it with a match. He threw the match away and shrugged. "If you say so."

"We're only asking for peace and security. Your name, *maaly el-bey*, stands out. General Salmawy pointed you out. I've come here with his card." Hector stood up and, with a bow, presented the general's card to the captain.

The captain gave the card a cursory look, then slipped it into his jacket's inside pocket. He swung back and raised his black boots to his desktop. "Begin, speak."

"There's this very hateful imam in Imbaba. His name, I believe, is Sayed Dosouky. He said very bad things about us, the Americans in Cairo, and we fear we are in grave danger. Our ambassador is very concerned."

Hector thought he'd seen the ghost of a smirk.

"And you, Mr Hector, who are you?"

"I am a concerned American, *maaly el-bey*. But I'm friends with many notable decision-makers in Cairo. I'm here to represent the American Embassy in this delicate matter, as per the Embassy's request."

"And your Arabic, when and how did you learn it?"

"Oh, that's a long story, *maaly el-bey*. I grew up here with my parents, in the seventies, a long time ago."

Mourad *Bey* had, by this time, got bored with his cigarette and flicked it away. Coughing, he reached into his pocket and removed Hector's passport: Hector had obediently handed it in at the Interior Ministry's gate as proof of his identity.

Hector retrieved his passport, and the captain planted his feet and stood up. With his index and middle fingers, Mourad *Bey* motioned for Hector to follow him.

Men in black uniforms ebbed away as the *bey* and his guest walked the windowless yet—as if by stored sunshine—bright corridors of the Ministry of Interior. The two men passed by a canteen where a soccer match was playing. (Expletives mingled with hearty laughter.) Finally, Mourad *Bey* pushed open a door to a set of exit stairs and they went four floors down.

They entered a cell with an open steel door. The compound stench of sweat, urine, and feces welcomed them, and Hector sucked his belly in and bit his lips. He peeled his eyes till he accommodated to the dimness.

There were four men inside the cell. Three were plainly clothed but without the rugged trademark of a high-ranking officer. The fourth was definitely an outsider: He was strapped from wrist to wrist to a wooden bench, naked, sore, his legs splayed.

Hector had not recognized the man at first. But slowly, his identity became indisputable.

"What's your mama's name?" imposed an acromegalic man in a tight black T-shirt and sea-green chinos, his voice ringing between the concrete walls.

"I don't know," cried Sayed Dosouky.

"Repeat after me: My mama's name is *Sharmota.*"

"Your mother is—*Aaaah!*"

Two bamboo sticks—wielded by the two other men—had landed on the imam's naked back and buttocks.

"Okay, Hamada, forget about your mama. What's your papa's name?"

"*Leave me alone! This is haram!*"

"Papa's name is 'Uncle.' Repeat after me…"

"*You infidels! You sons of dogs!*"

The lynching continued.

"Let this be a lesson to you," Mourad *Bey* whispered into Hector's ear. "We don't wait for anybody to come and tell us how to deal with our people. Tell your bosses to sleep tight."

———⁂———

The belly dancer on the boat was Ukrainian. Her stage name was Marina. Every Thursday they went to see her at *Cabaret Lyaly.* She was famous for her *raqsat shaitaniya*—Satanic moves—with her limbs slicker than eels, her breasts the size of watermelons, and her giggles that set fire to the loins of many men.

Fabio couldn't control himself. He clambered up to the stage and danced with her. They waltzed the *balady* together, locked a cane between their navels, and rocked their hips in sync. A sheik came and sprinkled them both with a thick wad of America's hot currency.

The cabaret rocked with laughter.

"Yoooou're expensive," Jeff said, sipping his Sakara beer with two straws, red-faced, and squinty, after Fabio had climbed down.

Jeff and Hector had arrived an hour earlier. Fabio had been waiting outside, smoking. He'd walked all the way from the Corniche office to the Abdeen cabaret, "*moto-regl,*" as he'd put it, on foot-engine. For weeks, Fabio had been working overtime. Hector had been sent home early today, like every day.

"So what's new, Fab?" Hector asked.

Fabio dipped a crouton into his baba ghanoush salad. He was still panting from the dance. He silently shrugged.

"Come on. What're you working on so late?"

"Yearly audit. Something you don't have to worry about."

"I'm becoming more like Jeff here, man."

"What's that supposed to mean?" Jeff protested.

"Can I help with the 'audit'?" Hector asked.

"Why would you?" Fabio asked with a full mouth.

"I'm all humbled down now. Please, Fab, I'm begging. I can't stand this. Do you wanna step outside to talk?"

"Maybe *I* should leave!" Jeff said.

"It's like credit, Hickey," Fabio said. "The more you take, the more you owe. Take it easy on yourself, man. You're lucky."

8

FREE AGENT

ork had been vague since early July. Hector wrote dozens of reports, shot the breeze with randoms: tradesmen, students, old-fangled pan-Arabists, penitent communists, university professors, penniless authors. Then he set up meetings for Lisa and Fabio: with a YouTube celebrity, with a couple who ran a human rights NGO, with a pop band, with soccer ultras, with two Muslim Brotherhood leaders (who came to Murphy & Ass dressed as women in tarry niqabs), and with the Big No himself—the only invitee who hung up on him, so Lisa had to go visit him herself.

And then there was the mysterious Serbia trip.

It was around the second week of August, when Hector was given the *List of Eleven* to organize a trip for. No explanation or context. He met with them individually and endeavored to deduce their common denominator. All eleven were high-society kids fed up with the mosque and the church and the pyramid, devoted to modernizing Egypt.

Besides that, they were all Haram activists.

Hector broke them into six groups: five couples and a single, each bound for a different European city. Cyprus or Tuscany or Barcelona or Paris or Vienna or Berlin. Hotels were booked for a solid month. For the first two nights, Hector instructed them to wander outside, enjoy the city. "Take lots of pictures and kiss, if you can. Post on Facebook."

On the third night, they would slink out of the hotel, bagless, and rendezvous with a contact who would hand them their new passports and tickets to Timisoara, Romania.

Once in Timisoara, a team of CIA operatives would receive them then drive them to a camp just out of Belgrade.

"A camp, like a boot camp?" an Australia-born brunette asked.

"It's a summer youth camp. Something along the lines of Solidarity International."

"What's it called?"

Hector didn't know the exact name of the camp, but he'd traced two of his online partners to a foundation in Midtown Manhattan, one belonging to a Hungarian billionaire who was the focus of many of the world's conspiracy theories.

"That I'm not free to disclose. But are you comfortable with traveling still?"

"I guess."

Hector dropped his three-page, torture-to-read resignation on her desk, and vomited his spiel. He wasn't respected here. He was a CIA agent not a clerk. He'd rather go back to Europe... Et cetera.

Lisa looked up at him. She pushed her glasses up her hooked

nose and said, "It might get crazy soon. We'll give you something to do, if that's what you're looking for."

"It's not that, Liz." Her nickname tasted like acid on his tongue. "I deserve better, I deserve real work. And you don't give me real work here. No work, I go. Simple."

She removed her glasses and let them hang from the chain around her neck. She'd grown plumper and had been kind of morose lately. She wrapped her arms over her breasts and rocked in her chair. "You had a day job in Europe."

"I had covers."

"Intelligence is a tough sport. Tougher for a part-timer going full-time all at once."

"It's easier to file one tax return, so I'll pass."

He'd already turned the doorknob, when she said, "Don't be silly. Close the door."

She then rose and stepped to the file cabinets occupying her southern wall. "I'd like you to take on a side gig."

"Like a side project?"

She shook her head, punching the dial pad on one cabinet to the left. "It's a liaison. With the Pentagon. Are you interested?"

The Pentagon and the CIA. What do they have in common? Nothing and everything.

"That's a waste of my time." He opened the door. "Adieu, Lisa."

"What do you know about AIMES?"

He stopped at the doorstep, then returned and closed the door. "The Institute?"

"*Uh-huh.*"

"They have a new campus in New Cairo. A hundred feddans or so. My father used to teach there. Not in the new campus, but the old one."

"Perfect," she exulted. "Perfect match."

"'Match' for what?"

She dropped a heavy dossier on his extended forearms. It was a rough-grained khaki file with the acronym *AIMES* scribbled on it in whiteout. A hundred and fifty sheets or so. Hole-punched. Tied together with a pink ribbon.

Classic, higgledy-piggledy McConkey!

"Your PhD still good?" she asked.

"I'll check the expiry date."

"*Huh*. Funny. You'll need that sense of humor with the students."

"But I don't know anything about teaching, Liz."

"Ridiculous." She swished her arm dismissively, returning to her desk. "Give 'em good grades and make 'em laugh."

"Can I keep my desk here?"

After some thought, she said, "You may, if you want. But I want you to settle there first. Okey-dokey?"

Hector looked at the heavy file, then nodded.

"Ah—and Hector, don't call us. When we need you, we'll call you. It's a great job. Good luck."

It took Hector more than three hours to finish reading the dossier. And it boiled down to this:

AIMES was an independent postsecondary institute accredited by the Southern Association of Colleges and Schools Commission on Colleges in the state of Louisiana. It was founded by Presbyterian missionaries in the 1930s. And as of 2010, it hovered in the middle tier of *The Times Higher Education World University Rankings*.

AIMES boasted many notable alumni: a Nobel prize winner in economics, a Saudi royal, a Middle East adviser to the US president, and many actors and journalists.

What was missing from the official record, though, was that AIMES was more than just a school.

In the mid-sixties, the Pentagon had seen in this overseas oasis a safe board from which military personnel could jump into Arabic waters without arousing much suspicion. So the Pentagon courted the Institute. And the Institute didn't know how to say no.

For decades, AIMES's affair with the Pentagon had been smooth. Soldiers and spooks went there disguised as students, and their tuitions were paid by Uncle Sam. Issues began when the Institute's academic reputation rose over the years. A certain cadre of Arab aristocracy sent their kids there, bragging about the heavy tuitions they paid. AIMES was becoming more financially secure and was getting attention from other parties. And our generals in Arlington were not happy about that. So they wired more money to keep the Institute loyal.

After a few heavy transactions—which the Egyptians got wind of right away—rescue came in the form of an alumnus of the Institute, a Saudi royal, *a friend of the American people*—as the dossier described him—named Mohamed bin Hakam.

The prince would be the donkey to carry the Pentagon's gifts.

A female voice greeted him after the third beep. Hector stated his name and title and requested an appointment with the dean.

Luckily, a time slot was readily available this afternoon: A staff meeting had just been canceled. Would he like to take it?

"Three-thirty to four-thirty. Fine, I'll take it."

He printed off his résumé, dropped the dossier into the shredder, picked up his jacket and briefcase, then gave his pod a final look.

Thirty-one months would pass before he would see this place again.

———

Down on Corniche Street, Hector flagged a taxi. It was closing on two p.m. and the sun was vicious.

The taxi driver was a leathery man of about fifty, a cigarette dangling from the corner of his mouth. "You go to where, mister? Hotel? I know a good hotel it's very good."

"*La, la,*" Hector corrected in Arabic. He wanted to go to the American Institute of Middle Eastern Studies, please.

"You Egyptian?"

Hector made the grave mistake of denying.

"The Arabic is good," the driver reverted to English, waiting for his customer to close the door before he pulled away. "You tourist or work in university, mister?"

"Drive fast, please. I'll give you a big *baksheesh.*"

On their way, Hector had to reroute the driver to AIMES's new campus in New Cairo, since the driver was heading toward the old campus in Zamalek.

"Long way," the driver complained. "I take two hundred dollar."

"Two hundred *what?* Hey, listen, I'll give you two hundred Egyptian or no deal. And for a round trip."

"Cheap," the driver muttered in Egyptian. But he drove on.

New Cairo was roughly thirty kilometers east of Cairo. Hector noticed the clean air and modern villas. No trash. No stray cats. No beggars. No dearth of restaurants, shisha bars, or shopping centers in this new incarnation of the capital. But still, most of those walking under the sun were maids or contractors. Grunt workers coming from the old capital.

No city can escape its past, Hector thought. And no *one.*

AIMES's high limestone walls, its thick iron gates, and the thoroughness of its security personnel left a good impression on Hector. The guards called the dean's office to confirm his appointment, since he wasn't on their visitors' list. Then a paunchy guard, decked out in dazzling white, handed the driver a yellow parking permit and Hector his passport back. "We are sorry for the waiting," he said.

"It's all right. Would you mind giving directions to the driver?"

"Cars don't enter. There is gate inside. You walk not long after the inside gate."

As Hector strolled AIMES's cobbled streets... beheld its angular masonry, the buildings planted in rolling grass... as his skin was tickled by the balmy breeze... and the more and more and more AIMES's timeless decor sucked him in (be it Pharaonic, Ptolemaic, Roman, or Arabian)... the one thing Hector had longed for titillated his heart.

It wasn't peace, but reconciliation. In this Institute reincarnate, he would relive his past.

The dean's secretary was a pretty veiled girl called Zainab. She rose and gave his hand a coy brush of a handshake. Her kohl-lined eyes were apricots. She was strong-built and stood at five feet five. Hector was happy just to look at her.

"Hello, doctor. We spoke on the telephone. Dr Amira is

excited about meeting you. Please sit down and I will go and tell her."

Hector sank into a posh white sofa and listened to Zainab's *click-clock*s disappear into the dean's office. Then, to his astonishment, the dean came out in less than a minute.

"Welcome, welcome," the lovely dean said, clad in a honey silk blouse and a black dirndl skirt. "It's a great pleasure. Come on in, please."

Hector followed her inside and seated himself on a wooden chair in front of her modest desk. It was a vast room. A divided-lite window walked the eastern wall and overlooked a flagstoned, palmy court. There were dozens of bookshelves on the southern and western walls and two couches and a coffee table in the center.

"My apologies for the short notice," Hector said.

"We're glad to receive distinguished guests such as yourself anytime."

Everything about her—her enticing voice, her gentle smile, her serene eyes—encouraged him.

"I would like to apply for a teaching position at AIMES. I have a PhD in political science from Columbia. And I've held many positions, at SIPRI, double-I-S-S, Chatham House, and others."

And he handed her his résumé.

The dean took a pair of glasses from a black case and put them on. She skimmed through the first two pages—Hector's résumé was nine pages long—then she swiveled her iMac screen to give him a good view of it. "When Zainab mentioned your name, I did a little bit of research," she said. "Well, it looks research is your forté, not mine." And she laughed a perfect laugh, low-pitched and far-reaching. "Your track record is very impressive. You coauthored two articles for Foreign Policy, and your name comes up in Brookings, the Boston Review, and the British Journal of Political Science." She swiveled her screen back, and her face grew earnest. "But why us? Why Cairo in the first place?"

Hector hesitated for a second, then decided to take the plunge. "My father, Roger Kane—"

"I knew it!" The dean banged her fist on her glass desktop.

"—used to teach here. He desired that I follow in his footsteps."

"Don't fathers always." There was a sarcasm in the dean's voice. She leaned forward and interlaced her bejeweled digits. "But tell me, Dr Kane. First, can I call you 'doctor'?"

"Of course," he said without batting an eye.

"Dr Kane, are you personally interested in AIMES, or is this a tribute to your dead old man? Excuse my bluntness. We all labor under invisible influences, family first and foremost. Freedom comes from agency, not duty. So be honest with me. This is not necessarily going to affect your application. Are you a loyal son, or a free agent?"

Agent? Hector thought to himself. Had Lisa, by any chance, called the dean to *assign* him here? If that was the case, whatever he said wouldn't make the slightest difference.

"It is my own desire," Hector said, not knowing whether he was speaking truth or falsity. "I've always wanted to come back to where I grew up. You may be interested to know, ma'am, that my PhD dissertation was about Nasser's Pan-Arabism. So the Middle East isn't just in my heart, but in my brain. I'm absolutely interested in this job, beyond measure."

The dean pouted and shook her head. "A tragedy. Dr Kane—your father—was a rare academic. We read and reread him tirelessly. Such a treasure from the past."

Hector didn't like the tone of her words, but he smiled evenly.

"Do you have kids?" she asked.

"I'm afraid not."

The dean rose and walked to a small table beside the divided-lite window. There stood a tulips vase and a framed photo. She brought the photo to Hector. The photo showed a girl in polka-dot shorts and a yellow T-shirt knotted above her bellybutton: She raised her slim arms before a nightly view of the Arc de Triomphe, and her pose implied blocking the traffic through the great Arc. She was beaming. A millennial in control of the world.

"Is she your daughter?" Hector asked.

"She's my niece, Fatima. Fifi, as we call her. I don't have kids, no, but this one is like a daughter to me."

"Nice." Hector grinned.

The dean replaced the frame on the table. Then she came back and dropped behind her desk. Her face had changed. "Did you find a place to stay yet?"

"I'm renting a place in Doqqi. But my lease ends August."

"No worries. We have a few apartments in our hostel in Zamalek. You'll like the neighborhood." She looked at the divided-lite window for a long time. "I'll make a few phone calls," she had concluded. "If all is well, we can sign the contract today."

9

TRAMA

ector walked down Dickens Road. Dickens was a neighborhood of modern houses, street-numbered by steel lozenges pinned to rose-redolent trees. These trees were huge, some reaching fifteen or twenty feet high. Yet the strangest thing about them was the blood-oozing gashes in their bark.

Hector had learned that morning that these gashes were intentional. Sylvester, the MED guide for the day, had told them that the trees were called "angsanas," and they were among the first green imports to Mermaid City a good five decades ago. The angsanas were also the first "F" in the founding fathers' green gradebook. Nobody had expected this bleeding behavior. Most of the Dickens residents at the time, Malay Muslims, deemed the land unclean because of them. So the few Europeans on the island had gotten themselves a good bargain. The Europeans bought Dickens off, erected a great cathedral, and regularly injured the bark to keep the Muslims away. Yet a decade or so later, the ire of postcolonialism pushed the Europeans away. Affluent Chinese families moved in. These new landlords didn't care about religion, but they let the *Weeping Maries*—as the angsanas were now called—stay, a bleeding relic from the bygone masters.

As Hector reminisced on that story, a figure came upon him, snapped him out of his introspection.

The girl was wearing a sleeveless chambray top. The *knock-knock*s of her golden sandals echoed endlessly across the road. Hector's heart leaped. She had a big mask on, a brand different from his and his group's. But that didn't seem to matter. Neither did the Bermuda shorts, which matched her top—but not the person in his head.

She had the right eyes, a close-enough stature (five-two-ish), and she had caught him off guard.

He was about to call out to her, when he saw *him*. The other man.

From around the corner of a cash exchange shop, a Chinese man, stocky and round-bellied, strutted up to her. The girl was obviously tipsy and had scampered ahead, driven by a giggly fantasy. She tottered to a stop when she realized so and awaited her man, who came and cuddled her on his buffed breast.

And together they walked by a flustered Hector.

Hector had mistaken a total stranger for his own wife.

The residence was nearly invisible across the boom gate. Only two lights were on in the garden. Even the concierge's kiosk was dark.

Hector didn't bother with the door beside the kiosk. He knew it would be locked. "This facility closes at ten o'clock," their difficult concierge had stipulated upon their checking in. "No late-comes allowed. And I will not open any door. You call me, I say, 'No, I'm a-sleeping, my friend. I will not come this night or any hour before five in morning time. You must wait all the night outside.'"

Hector bowed under the boom, then walked on the asphalt driveway.

And he wasn't ten feet in when a voice called from his right: "Hello, doc."

The voice's owner was standing before the only lightbulb in the vicinity. The voice was shaky, and it took Hector a while to identify the silhouette.

"Oh, hi, Keroloss," Hector said finally.

Kero was a short guy, barely five feet three. His body was emaciated, an effect he usually amplified with a rastacap mounted on his dreadlocks, which made his head look like a giant wasp's bottom. Not today, though. Today, Kero wore his dreadlocks *au naturel*.

"Where did you go, doctor?" Kero asked.

"I took a short stroll." Hector checked his wristwatch, and it was eleven-twenty. He was counting on them being away until at least midnight. "You guys came back already?"

Kero lurched closer and Hector saw the Beats headphones slung around Kero's scraggy neck. Kero had purchased these during the layover in Dubai, thanks to the generous Pulaui per diem. There was an audible tone coming from them, a faint eulogy. Hector asked him what it was.

"It's a French song. *J'ai demanda à la luna*. I can't say it right."

Kero wasn't wearing his mask and was also holding a cigarette. His big nose looked like a furnace in the haze. He was wearing a black T-shirt with the jaundiced face of Bart Simpson as a motif. Below this was a pair of blue jeans, shredded to show

Kero's lumpy knees. His black Converse fidgeted on the gravel.

Kero stubbed his cigarette in a Ming aralia pot resting at his feet. Ming aralias had thick, erect leaflets resembling supplicating hands, and there were eleven of these pots dotting the perimeter of the reception *Bungalow*—which was actually a reception laundry complex.

"Kero, have you lost your mask?" Hector asked. "You know it's very dangerous to walk around without a mask in this weather."

"Oh, I don't know. I think I lost it. Hey, doc, can I ask you a favor?"

"Be my guest."

"Call me 'Careless.' My new name is 'Careless.'"

"What happened to Keroloss?"

"It's the name of a great saint. I'm not a saint, doctor. Do you think I'm a saint?" And the kid staggered close and bowed his heavy head. "Do you see my horns? I'm the devil."

"Aren't we all," Hector muttered.

"But your name, doctor, it's Hector of Troy. Is that right? He was a great fighter, a hero. My name comes from Cyril of Alexandria, who was a miracles man. I don't even believe in God. I'm half-Protestant, half-atheist. Any Copt would be ashamed of me. I'm a disgrace! I can't even think of a subject for my thesis. How can I be a miracles man!"

Kero was shouting. He was obviously under the influence.

Hector looked at his watch again. "So Yubi is up there, huh?"

Kero suddenly froze. "I don't know."

"What do you mean you 'don't know'? You guys went out together."

Kero took a step back and turned toward the Bungalow to hide his face. "I don't know," he repeated. "I don't know."

Hector was furious. "Kero, let's step inside," he said. "I need to have a word with you."

The Bungalow's wooden door was so well-lubed, so light to the touch, it felt as if made of solidified air. And it was cold inside, the AC fans *vroom*ing. And it was noisy: There was a gurgling washer in the laundry compartment. Hector hit the light switch, and a soothing neon light flooded the place. The reception area took up three quarters of the Bungalow. There was a burgundy leatherette couch, two matching seats, a coffee table, a foosball setup missing two players, two vending machines for Chinese soft drinks, and a cumbersome dusty TV that functioned as an accessory rack for books or magazines. Eight bookshelves stood beside it, and Kero lingered there and flipped through the volumes.

"Looking for inspiration, Kero?"

The kid shook his head. "I already finished my novel, doctor."

"Your novel... Is this your first?"

"No. I wrote one before, before the play, but it didn't succeed."

Three years ago, Kero had written a very successful play. As far as Hector knew, it was regularly staged in Cairo.

"That's wonderful," Hector said. "I'll be looking forward to reading it."

"Seriously, doc? I can give it to you. It's in English. You will find it very... different."

Hector was trapped. He'd seen the production of Kero's play and had not disliked it. Yet the play was fraught with memories he'd rather let go of.

"Sure, sure," Hector said quickly.

Kero was excited. "I'll give it to you, then. Promise me, doctor. You'll read it quickly and give it back to me. It's not long and won't take you more than a day to read. I must have it back before we leave this island."

"Can you just email it to me, then?"

"I didn't type it on a computer, unfortunately. It's in a red notebook. This is my best work and I wanted to feel like old writers like Balzac and Chekhov. Did you know he was a doctor, doctor? Chekhov. He was fast and expressive and very good."

"You'll be even better, Kero."

"Thank you, doctor. Sorry for the way I shouted outside. I have a headache."

Hector screened the titles on the shelves. Fei Guo's books topped the list. The deceased founder was thumped through and through. *The Pulau Story: Island, City, and Nation. ASEAN vs The World. Remapping a Multipolar Asia…* All the way to his final, and only, chapbook.

On the shelf below were books about China written by Western authors. Hector saw Henry Kissinger's *On China* and Martin Jacques's *When China Rules the World* among many others.

The rest of the shelves were crammed with financial self-help books and translations of Harry Potter and Twilight and the like, all in Chinese.

"So you will read it and tell me your honest opinion, doctor?"

"Yeah, sure," Hector said. "Let's sit down."

Hector ushered him to the burgundy seat and seated himself on the couch. Hector assumed an open posture, something he'd learned on the Farm and applied to good results later: parallel legs, relaxed arms, leaning slightly forward, and holding intermittent eye contact with his target.

Kero's eyes glanced away, his knees shook, his neck jerked. He looked at the laundry section over Hector's right shoulder, then to the parquet floor, then to his hands, then to his dry meatless thighs. He started humming. His dreadlocks seemed to be weighing on him.

"Turn this thing off," Hector requested.

"*Hah?*"

"The music. Turn it off. Please, Kero."

Kero produced his iPhone from his jeans pocket and blinked at the screen for a bit. Hector gently repeated his request.

"I have to go soon, doctor."

"Are you drunk?"

Kero stammered before he confessed. "It's trama. Sorry, I felt so bad and tired I thought a trama pill would make me happy."

"Are you drunk, too?"

The dreadlocks shook in denial. "No. Trama is bad with alcohol."

"Kero, do you know the penalty for carrying drugs into this country? They don't care if you have a medical degree. It's a life sentence. Do you want to go to prison?"

The dreadlocks trembled. "Not me, not me, it's him!"

"It's *who?*"

"Baxter."

That made sense. Quite a lot actually. Baxter had a badge of honor for serving his country in its endless wars. A leg injury. So he was rewarded with a collection of painkillers. Despite their lack of a spark, Kero and Baxter were put together in Unit 302, next to Hector and Yubi. And is there a better way to buddy up to a roommate—or to keep him out of your way—than to get him high? Especially for someone like Kero, no keef surpassed tramadol, this highly addictive China-made opioid that had drugged millions of Egyptians during the Revolution, rendering them insensitive to blood and bullets.

"Does Yubi know about this?" Hector asked.

"I don't know, doctor. She... I... I haven't seen her in a while."

"In a while," Hector echoed.

"We were shopping in this mall. Beautiful mall, doctor. Armani and Boss and other brands I don't know. And I was feeling sick, so I came back. She's okay. She's very brave."

"Very brave." Hector interlaced his digits and bowed and felt his rage build up again.

It wasn't that Hector feared for Yubi's safety—she knew how to defend herself—or that he thought she wouldn't find her way back. It wasn't even a surprise. (Kero had abandoned Elena, Hector's TA, at a violent protest in downtown Cairo five months ago.)

Hector just... felt pity for this kid.

10

WATER-VENDOR'S STATUE

T wo months ago, shortly after Hector's reinstatement into the CIA, Hector and Yubi had joined the Graduate Students Association at AIMES on a trip to Paris. They thought the trip would rekindle their romance.

But for a whole week, all they got was Kero's embarrassing, loud, and *unwanted* company.

Who would believe this skin-and-bones malingerer was a celebrated author, a surgeon, and a Revolutionary hero!

Before Paris, Kero—a single male in his late twenties, a Copt in Islamic Egypt who dreamed about breaking out of *dhimmi*tude ever since his eyes opened to the world—had been turned down by every Western flag in Cairo. *No strong ties to home country,* read all his visa rejection letters. The US Embassy had gone so far as to block him, having been, let's say, too slow to budge after his last visa interview.

Kero had been the only AIMES student denied entry to the Embassy's Halloween party last October. Not even Hector's friendship with the ambassador could get him in.

Hector soon made it up to Kero, though.

"*C'est un pauvre type, Votre Excellence,*" Hector intimated to Philippe Lachance, the French consul, over the phone, "*mais on lui donne le salaire d'un roi.*" Hector outlined Kero's privileges at AIMES: a four-thousand-pound monthly stipend, plus free lodging at AIMES's hostel in Zamalek, plus a books allowance, plus free transportation. "It's a good bargain for all sides," Hector said. "The donor is a most generous man. He keeps the Institute solvent and the poor bright kids happy. Prince bin Hakam. You remember him from our weekend in Dahab? Yes, yes, Your Excellency. Right on. Big fellow, ponytailed, and he wore a striped swimsuit on the *plage* like Elvis in a reggae *Jailhouse Rock* of sorts. *Ha ha ha.* With a big difference, though. No, not that. The prince loves his women as much as he loves his yachts. But he doesn't have to dance to get them. They dance for him."

Without this call, and a formal letter Hector had the dean cosign—pledging responsibility if Kero scooted to his twenty cousins in Amsterdam or thirty uncles in Milan and, as with most Copts, filed for asylum—Kero would neither have seen nor fallen prey to the City of Light.

Think of a wretched monk after Lent—to repast finally on the ambrosia of God!

Of a virgin bride on her wedding night.

Of Bastille Day.

So he couldn't handle it, the poor kid. He binge-drank, wasted all his euros in a single day (cadged through the rest), and bled his past in pathetic, masochistic spurts.

———— ⁂ ————

In the few weeks leading up to the Egyptian Revolution, Kero had been given Haram's social media accounts to administer. A computer geek by hobby—a reprieve from medical practice, which he wasn't so keen on—he did a pretty good job.

So good, in fact, that the State Security Police whisked him away for a second interrogation.

The first interrogation had been seven months earlier, in June 2010. During that time, Kero had been so despondent about leaving Egypt. A Coward by nature, he committed himself to a rather silly suicide plan. He sought to provoke the despotic government. Kero created a Facebook group called *Egyptians Against Injustice*. Nothing original. Better and more active groups had been around for months. But by dint of copying others alone, he was dragged from work to stand before a solemn State Security officer. The officer saw a penniless physician, a mumbling dwarf, and a Copt—someone with born antipathy to the government's biggest nemesis, the Muslim Brotherhood— so he settled for a gentle reprimand. "Your country gave you a degree in medicine," the officer said. "Use it. Don't hang out with those glue-sniffers, those lefties. They're no doctors or engineers or anyone useful. Look after your mother and sisters, who'll be raped and cannibalized if the *Ikhwan* reaches power."

Kero had been tagged as "low-risk" and let go.

Come December 2010, Kero's play *Pharaohstan* was staged in Cairo, to huge success. And thanks to that, Kero got to meet the demigods of society. Actors. Musicians. Writers. Vloggers. Politicians. And finally the new angry prophet of the opposition's Torah: Ibrahim Noman, a man with a thousand faces (lawyer, Sufi, secularist, aristocrat) who anointed Kero as the wizard who would mobilize the masses with his digital wand.

"Do you see these marks?" Kero would bare up his torso and hunch over the table, in Paris, physically misshapen like a doll that had fallen into a bonfire. On his scoliotic back and his flanks and buttocks, the lynching scars stretched.

So the State Security goons had hauled him off for a second interrogation, this time from his bed, at three a.m. They tried to pry a confession out of him. They tortured his soul. Waterboarding. Cockroaches. Lynching. Sleep deprivation. False promises. Sex. A pretty *interrogatorice* (Kero yowled the world) stripped down for him, excited his organ then danced a lighter underneath, made him evacuate his lust on the floor then slapped him and finally opened the door for a big man—who was tall with a bony face like Lurch in *The Addams Family*—to come and rape him. "But I bite," Kero reassured the startled ladies. "Not even *Iblis* could get a piece of me. *Ha ha ha.*"

A week into this horror, the SSP invited his family over. Kero had two pretty sisters—Janette and Lydia, twenty-one and -two—both pharmacy students because Kero had forced them to avoid medicine. His mother—Madiha—was a widow with osteoarthritic knees who worked as a cleaning lady and had been waiting on Kero to open up his own clinic so she could retire.

Kero saw them all through a one-way mirror. The SSP officers were bored with his childish pigheadedness, they told him. They really wished he hadn't pushed them so. "But we gave up on you. What do you expect? We have families, too. But what kind of doctor would leave his family in such poverty? *Tut-tut.* Bad Cuckoo. Bad Cuckoo."

They knew how to break him. The reticent hero vomited hysterical babble: Haram's codenames and phone numbers and social media accounts, their secret operations room, the blueprints for the planned riots, everything.

Then one sixtyish general genuflected beside him and crooned into his ear. "Listen, Cuckoo, listen." A banshee screech echoed in the dark, horrific yet distinctly wordy. "See? We don't need you anymore. You're not just an infidel and a traitor, but stupid too." The general's voice was almost sensual. Kero lost his sense of reality. The general waggled his middle finger toward Kero's family behind the one-way mirror. "You'll never see your family *ever* again. Decent citizens like these do not deserve a piece of feces like you. Godspeed, my boy."

They blindfolded him, choked him with a rotten eggplant, wrapped him up in a flour bag, and jammed him with many other bodies in a garbage truck.

When Kero came to, he saw a framed icon on a bright lemon-green wall.

Where am I?

You're in Garbage City, brother. We saw the tattooed cross on your wrist so we knew you're one of us. You're in good Christian hands. Drink this holy water. Slowly. It's a miracle you're alive at all. Blessed be Saint Saman the Shoemaker!

"Garbage City, then." Kero hiccupped in Paris. The place of his resurrection was a dunghill whose creation myth was biblical: a piecemeal relocation by a saintly shoemaker contracted by the pope to convert the Sultan. "Is it a wonder that I don't believe in anything anymore? Cheers!"

On their third day in Paris, they had winded up in a Lost Generation shrine—*Café de Flore* or *Les Deux Magots*—Hector couldn't recall which. What he recalled, though, was the picture of Picasso and Dora Maar on the wall: Picasso in a white tank top and Maar in a floral pleated dress she slyly hitched over her knees. Hector was so fed up with Kero's emotional extortion, he sipped his white wine and did his best to space out.

Yet Yubi, all glistening eyes, her delectable chin cuddled in a half-rolled fist, her smooth elbow precariously propped on the table's damask beside her Rully rouge glass, was wholly engaged. "You didn't find them, Kero? Oh, I'm so sorry to bring it all back to you."

"Dad did everything he could," Fifi said, her dad the god of everything Revolution. "There simply is no record."

"Everything was eaten by the flames," Kero said.

"Of course," Fifi said, "to hide their crimes."

"No. I mean *us*," Kero said. "*We* burned everything up." Clap. Clap. "*Khalas. Finito.* No records."

———— ❧ ————

On Friday, January 28, 2011, clashes between the Egyptian protesters and the police had descended into chaos. Rocks flying. Gunfire amok. Teargas replacing air. And massive arrests, killings, and rapes (which were termed "virginity checks" by state-sponsored media).

The state media also accused the Muslim Brotherhood of this Armageddon. As for the "glue-sniffers," those Haram deplorables, they were lost souls, zombies employed by *Iblis* and foreign powers, and the Muslim Brotherhood took them for an easy lay.

"Death to all traitors!" one zealous radio host proclaimed. "They will all be arrested and executed. Long live the Arab Republic of Egypt!"

"Oh, I remember that day," Yubi said in Paris, tingly with the red wine, making a circle with a manicured finger on the damask. "Do you remember, baby?"

A nod from the disgruntled husband. How could he ever forget!

———— ❧ ————

She has been insisting on seeing the protests for days, and he has reluctantly agreed.

Yubi is so excited, clapping her hands. She's beginning to appreciate being married to a spy, she tells him, and she prints a kiss on his lips. She can't wait to see the world through his eyes. She looks into his eyes and kisses him again. Isn't that what he always wanted? For her to love him the way he is?

His strategy for her disguise is simple: Any woman will blend in easily in the Muslim world if, and only if, she succumbs to the hijab. So, contracting the wardrobe of her girlfriend Alyaa, Hector will offer his wife, for one day, to Allah.

Yubi checks herself in the mirror and snickers. She scampers around the bedroom like a schoolgirl in a new pinafore. Her veil is nothing garish, a blue chiffon, and Alyaa has coupled that with a full-sleeve, floor-length, carrot-speckled blue dress.

Enter the concerned father-to-be, and he tells the wife, "Wear these, honey."

Ew... The despicable *Coach* sunglasses she thought she threw away a lifetime ago? The ones with the spotty violet? No, thank you.

"Your body is covered? Check. Your Asian eyes?" Hector shakes his head, hand outstretched with the sunglasses. *"Uh-unh."*

Her jaw drops, eyes popping. "You're racist. Do you know that?"

"I'm a Nazi if you don't wear 'em. I'll keep you safe or there is no going out."

She snaps the accursed sunglasses. "Fine!"

Hector has got himself a pair of double-pleated black slacks, a checkered cotton shirt, and a bomber jacket, all for a song from Attaba, the low-buck market in central Cairo. Button by button, sock by sock, Yubi dresses him up. He's aroused and wants to throw her in bed, but he looks at the wall clock and thinks of the dangerous streets outside.

They walk out of the Zamalek hostel hand in hand, destination Tahrir Square, a good three kilometers away. They blend smoothly into the zillion couples seeking the Revolution's hub. Hector is glad they haven't been found out. Not that it matters much. Blood has been shed already, and bleakness has been married to sobriety. No one would bother about two disguised foreigners wandering the angry streets wanting to get themselves killed.

Tahrir is so crowded Yubi nestles under his arm, and he squeezes her tight. Shouts. Placards. Bandaged faces. Bloodied beards. Is this the glorious Revolution?

The convivialities of previous days have dissipated, giving way to a choleric miasma. Yubi says, "It's like a migraine aura."

"You're having one of those?" Her migraines have gotten worse during the pregnancy, since she's stopped taking her pills. "Let's get you back home."

She tenses under his arm. "It's not *me* you're worried about. Are you?"

"Right," he whispers into her veiled ear. "It's my *heir*. Think how many socks I have to pass on."

"Now I remember why I didn't like you." She disconnects herself. "You think you're funny."

They crawl on silently. They breathe the sulfur and soot in the air. Their eyes burn.

Once in a while, Hector comes across a face that makes him freeze.

This short fellow, with the mole on his left eyebrow, isn't he the single from the Serbia trip?

And that chick over there, who's climbed the lamppost and is waving the flag and squealing. She's married to a human rights activist of a high status…

And that bandaged brunette. Isn't she…?

God, I know these people. They're my *List of Eleven!*

"What're you looking at?" Yubi stiffens beside him.

He shakes his head and devotes his attention to the potbellied functionary, the jobless university grad, and the Nile Delta *fellah*.

He shows her his spying prowess. He lures Egyptians into dialog. No one suspects him, thanks to his native fluency. Hector has black hair, fair skin, and green eyes. Many Egyptians are mixed-race anyway. Lots have a streak of Turkish or European blood, especially among the aristocracy. They see the beauty of his face and assume he is rich—despite his shoddy clothes.

"And you, *hajja*," Hector says to a widow who sells sugared *simit*, "what are you protesting?"

She? She's mad about the stolen subsidies. Every time she goes to the Supply Bureau to receive her monthly rations of sugar and oil and flour, there isn't much of any. "Where does it go, mister? Tell me, for the Prophet's sake!"

Hector snickers. "Maybe the supply and demand don't go hand in hand."

But she shakes her scarfed head and swears to him it's the Bureau's infidels: They cook the books and sell the staples for double and triple the prices in the black market.

"And how about you, young man? Why are you so vexed?"

"You look like a decent man, so I'll let in on a secret. You see those police officers in pressed uniforms who're slaying us? I wanted to be one of them. I'm not ashamed of it, because my family is way under and we need social prestige to rise and see the world. But they rejected me at the Police Academy just because of that. Because I have no connections, you see. Now I'm going to bring it down on their heads and the heads of their families."

By noon, the *muezzin*s' calls for the Zohr prayer interlace in a polyphony. The godfather of the revolt himself is seeking council with Allah in the nearby Omar Makram Mosque. All mosques are chock full and most people pray out in the open: They face themselves toward Mecca, follow the imam's lead and recite *al-Fatiha*, bow and erect, then prostrate themselves, and soon rise again. The few Copts are holding hands, a picket fence around their Muslim brethren.

Once the prayer concludes, the Big No emerges from the mosque and comes to mount a high platform set in front of the vandalized KFC. He blares into his mic: "I have faith in our people's will. We will triumph, and we will triumph, and we will triumph!"

Chants quake the square:

> *People want*
> *To bring down the Regime!*

> *Leave!*
> *Leave!*

> *Down, down with Hosni Mubarak!*

And the occasional:

> *Allah Akbar!*

A thud echoes. Everyone is flustered: *What's going on?*

Screams. Bullets whiz past.

Yubi stumbles and falls on the ground. "Hector!" she cries.

Hector pulls her up, and they run in the stampede.

———— ✼ ————

"We call it *Friday of Rage,*" Fifi said in Paris. She set down her Heineken bottle gently on the table and added, "I wish they really did that, you know. Like the radio guy said, arrest and kill them. Not Daddy or us, of course. I mean those Muslim Brotherhood animals."

And threading her digits through her pressed hair—it was a passing phase of hers, and she had looked stunning!—the daughter of the most influential man of the century looked around her in fear.

The Muslim Brotherhood had eyes and ears everywhere. Even in Paris. *Especially* in Paris. For example, their classmate Zainab, the dean's secretary who would be married to Mr Tough Guy, Ahmed al-Shatby, in less than a month.

Ahmed al-Shatby, this new and mysterious student at AIMES. This uppity who hung out with Westerners only. Who refused to sit with them in a café serving alcohol.

"Isn't he like a gold merchant or something?" Fifi said. "What's a gold-merchant doing studying anything? Oh, I know now. He's not a gold-merchant. *Uh-unh.* He's a *gold-digger!*"

"But they did arrest some Brotherhood leaders," Hector deflected. "Didn't they?"

Fifi took a moment to think, then said, "It was a bargain from the start. They couldn't make a deal with Dad, so they made a deal with *them.* It was just a play. So cheap and ugly."

Kero, legitimately hammered now, lost his grip on his fourth

Stella bottle. The bottle smashed with a bang on the floor. Unfazed, or maybe encouraged by the attention, Kero shouted, "What's the difference? The Muslims won anyway!"

Hector was livid. Yubi reached a hand to press his under the table.

A blonde waitress in a tux and a white apron came to dust off the mess on the floor. Kero asked for "*un Stella encore, ma belle amie.*" But Hector shook his head to the waitress.

"Where'd you learn your French?" Hector asked Kero.

"I learn very fast, doctor. My brain is like a nuclear engine."

"Is that so?"

"Yes. It's my only asset." Cockily, Kero winked at Fifi, then at Yubi, and when his eyes met Hector's, he dropped his face and looked about to cry.

So he fell back on his soppy tragedy.

Once violence had been confirmed as the new reality of Egypt, he said, protesters chose to burn their country down. From the ashes Egypt will rise! The Egyptian Museum, police stations, the National Democratic Party, the Ministry of Interior, all were vandalized and torched.

Kero had been—he claimed—one of the daredevils who attacked the Interior Ministry's HQ in Lazoghly Square.

"Do you know what—who—Lazoghly was, doctor? It's a statue there. It was sculpted by a French artist called Jacquemart. The story is very literary. I have always wanted to write a story about it. So this man, Lazoghly, was a prime minister of Mohamed Ali Pasha. He was a very good person, maybe, because after so many years the Khedive Ismail remembered him and wanted to make a statue of him. The Khedive wanted to make Cairo like Paris, you know, very beautiful. But because of this ambition Egypt was drowned in debt and the British came. So anyway, Jacquemart the artist came and asked the Khedive, 'Okay, where is this man I must make a statue for?' And the Khedive was like, 'No, monsieur, *désolé*. Mr Lazoghly died many years ago.' So what can the artist do? He asked around and the people told him Lazoghly looked like this guy over there. 'Who is this guy?' He was… a water vendor, a *saqqa*. *Ha ha ha*. So funny, doctor, this statue we walk beside every day is a statue of a water vendor… Why are you not laughing, doctor?"

Yubi is bleeding. A bullet has brushed her right earlobe, missing her skull by a narrow half-inch. She will cover this ear forever, she sobs.

She tears off her veil and dumps it and stomps on it and she shrieks in Allah's face.

She soon collapses into Hector's arms.

The Beards stare at her, and at him. But the fray presently claims the Beards' attention.

There is a life-or-death battle with the police forces afoot. So Hector carries his wife and takes shelter at the feet of an idol in the center of a nearby square.

One hand of this idol is clutching the hilt of a scimitar. The other is steeped, condemningly, toward the rioting masses. The idol's bronze brow and oversized turban bolster the contempt in its eyes.

From the idol's pedestal and over to the besieged ministries of Justice and Interior, water-cannons battle the suicidal protesters.

Shrieks echo from the deeps of hell.

Teargas hovers over the corpses like the mist over the Styx.

The sky is red. God is angry. And Yubi is crying.

———◦———

So much for romance in Paris. Thank you, Kero!

11

NIGHT VISITOR

he problem with well-lubed doors is that they move at the timidest touch.

The Bungalow's door opened without a sound. Fifi was frozen there, like a hare bracing for a bolt.

"Hi, Fatima." Hector addressed her formally. "Come on in."

"*Err…* Hey." She was dressed in a pair of baggy sweatpants and a tank top. Like Kero, she wasn't wearing her mask. Her hair was messy and her eyes a bit puffy. She looked like she'd just gotten up from a very tumultuous sleep.

"Come on in," Hector repeated. "You all right?"

"Yeah, yeah." She sidled toward the vending machines. Then she stopped there with a curse. "I forgot my money, man!"

"I have some coins," Kero offered, pulling out his wallet.

But the girl rejected him with a rigid, erected palm. "Thanks," she breathed, barely audible. She turned to the right vending machine and kicked it with her slipper. "Doc, you're a good guy and won't hand me in, will you?"

"What makes you say that?"

"'Cause you are." She knelt by the machine and hugged it

with her right arm. "A good guy."

Fifi slithered her left hand through the takeout port up to the goodies. When she straightened up, she was holding a Clamato can with a Chinese label. She popped the can open and gulped.

"*Yum, yum, yum.*" She licked her big lips. "Can you read Chinese, doc?"

"I don't read Chinese, Fatima."

"*Fatima?*" A chortle rippled through her chest. "What's up with that?"

Kero, standing between him and her, now flopped into his seat with a frown.

"Don't call me 'doctor' again." Hector pointed his forefinger at her. "It's 'professor' from now on."

"But I like 'doctor' better," she moaned.

Hector turned to Kero. "Goodnight, guys."

"Come on. Doctor," Fifi called.

But Hector ignored her and walked to the door.

"Prof, wait," Kero called.

Hector stopped. "Yes, Kero."

"Tell Yubi I'm okay. Okay? My mobile was uncharged but now it's well-charged."

Hector looked at him for a moment. "See you at seven sharp tomorrow."

Hector wasn't ten paces away when Fifi rushed past him toward the girls' dormitory, dropping her Clamato can on the way.

"Fifi, what's going on?" Hector called.

Her sobs were audible until she disappeared through the dorm's door.

Yubi came after midnight. Quarter to one precisely. She was carrying two bags of pricey merchandise, Gap and Ashley Isham. She showed off to him. A pair of snakeskin, wedge-heeled red shoes. A wide-neck, kind of blotchy tie-dyed T-shirt that looked awful to him but he said it was lovely. A natural silk jet-black bolero.

"How much is all that?" he asked.

"Not much."

"No, seriously. How much?"

"Baby, you said buy whatever you want. You forgot? Oh, poor baby. It's been a long day for you. You look so tired."

Yubi was wearing a duplicate of the sleeveless chambray top that had deceived her husband a couple of hours earlier (on another woman's body) and below that a pair of white linen slacks. She took off her hair clip, and her heavy black hair dropped with grace over her shoulders, highlighting the smoothness and narrowness of her neck. Her eyes were quiet and clear and—yes—Asian. Yubi was a great beauty even if she didn't pay it much attention. And the most gripping thing about her was not even her beauty per se. But her voice. It wasn't singsongy or smooth: It was nasal, low-pitched, and rather shrewish. You couldn't make out what she said without looking into her eyes and reading her full lips. Thus, the halo of her femininity, the anger in her obsidian irises, made her scream with life. She was so much *there*.

And it was this *there*ness about her that triggered Hector's reaction.

"Where have you been?" he inquired.

"Where have *I* been?" She rolled her eyes. "Where have *you*?

Kero saw you coming from a 'stroll.' Where did your legs take you?"

He ignored her question. "I called you like ten times. Why didn't you answer?"

Yubi folded her bolero and dropped it in the bag. "Did you have dinner yet?"

"Answer me!"

She hitched her two shopping bags with a muted groan. She marched into the bedroom and slammed the door shut with her ankle.

Day two on Romantic Island, Hector. And tonight, you'll be sleeping on the couch as usual.

For a long time after the fight with Yubi, Hector couldn't muster any appetite for sleep. Muttering a litany of curses, he reached for the TV remote control on the coffee table. He muted the sound and worked his way through the settings till he hit the subtitles toggle.

The residence cable had only a handful of channels available for students and guests. All were in Mandarin or Cantonese, except two: a Hollywood-Bollywood streaming service overwhelmed by ads, and the regional brand of the BBC, self-proclaimed as "BBC Asian." The latter was Hector's only window to the world. So he stuck with it and hoped the stories would distract him.

The first story on BBC Asian was, strangely, not Asian. It was an update on the situation in a torn country known as Syria. The rebels had overtaken the town of Qaysa and were engaging in bloody skirmishes with Assad's army in Damascus. Over a hundred people had been killed. The report added that the UN's fresh estimate on the death toll had reached beyond 80,000 souls. In effect, the General Assembly had passed a resolution "demanding that all sides end hostilities," which Russia and China had both nayed. An end to this debilitating war was not forthcoming.

Many people, Hector included, had assumed that after the death of Mosa al-Damashqy—the symbol of Syrian resistance—the rebels would go suicidal *en masse* to avenge him, simply win. Mosa al-Damashqy—Moses of Damascus, notoriously nicknamed "Mosa al-Damawy," or Bloody Moses—was Syria's Jeanne d'Arc. But he didn't wait for the enemies to come and capture him. He went for them. Deplorably, Mosa's death had little if any impact on the war. And only now Hector saw things from the Cardinal's perspective. America didn't understand the Middle East. Only a regional power, such as the Muslim Brotherhood, could untangle this mess.

Which did little to assure Hector that he was doing the right thing by pledging to carry on with his part in Operation C.O.R.O.N.A.

The next stories on BBC Asian *were* Asian.

One was about a widow in India who used her late husband's hundred and eleven pairs of shoes to cremate him. "He was a lovely man," said the widow. "He loved to wear good footwear and he spent a lot of money on them. My daughter and I decided to send his collection after him on the trip of *samsara*. In his new life, my dear Prateek should be happy to relive his life as a pair of winklepickers."

The story after that was about a diplomatic crisis between Pulau and the Netherlands. A Dutchwoman had been caught handing out 5 chewing gum to three callous Pulaui girls on a transit bus. Chewing gum was a serious crime in Pulau, something to do with a gum epidemic in the late '60s that had driven Fei Guo insane. The Dutchwoman had been sentenced to six years in prison. The Netherlands had withdrawn its ambassador, but there was no Pulaui response as yet.

On another sphere, the fuss over China's avian flu epidemic had finally been addressed by the government. A spokesperson for the Chinese Ministry of Health had confirmed that most deaths reported were due to "natural causes." One was a ruptured brain aneurysm, another myocardial infarction, a third spontaneous combustion. Only one death was a legitimate flu case, but this was regular seasonal influenza. Not subtype H7N9, the cause of so much ado about nothing among the Chinese people.

In Japan, the thirtieth anniversary of the silver-screen phenomenon *Oshin* had been hosted by the empress consort herself. Thousands of photos were shared on social media featuring the hale, septuagenarian first lady posing with fans from all around the world. Especially Pulaui fans: They dominated the festival. One Pei Fen Chong—a Chinese-Pulaui infant swaddled in a golden layette—won the empress's heart and millions of likes on her mom's Instagram account.

Hector leaned forward and squinted at the screen. The infant was crying throughout. Yet every adult in the photos looked one step away from the Pearly Gates.

Hector remembered his dead child and closed his eyes.

He stood up and went to the bathroom. When he came back, the Japanese story was still on. Pei Fen Chong, the Chinese-Pulaui, was the princess of the Japanese festival.

Hector marveled at how the Chinese and the Japanese had made it up so well. Of all Asian communities, these two were, if not mortal enemies, then hateful neighbors.

Once upon a time Japan, like most Asian polities, was part of China's ancient *Tribute System*. Japanese rulers were vassals of the Chinese emperor. They adopted Chinese calligraphy and customs out of deference. But collapse had finally come to this master-follower hierarchy in the nineteenth century—thanks to the British.

The British had come with their barges and their breeches and their lust for opium, and inflicted severe damage upon China's legacy. It had been a "century of national humiliation," as Chinese pundits still described it. China was wrist-locked into unfair treaties, and large swathes of its landmass were wrung out of its control. Soon the Japanese, those former followers, declared themselves superior to Chinese men. They invaded China and sought to dominate their former masters.

It wasn't until China had reformed its economy—divorced both ideology and nostalgia, both with their crippling sensitives—that its dignity was restored.

Now, not only was a reconciliation with Japan possible, but also the celebration of Japanese drama by so many Chinese people.

But that didn't explain how Chinese-*Pulauis*, of all people, flooded to attend the Japanese festival.

Who could forget the bloody Japanese occupation of Pulau during the Second World War! It was the single most national disaster in Pulaui history.

Hector was confused now. And the new story on BBC Asian made him more so. It made him even question his grasp on his discipline, on political science.

The story was about Pulau's Golden Jubilee celebrations of last Friday, which marked half a century of independence from Britain in '63. Hector watched the carnivalesque processions of

Disney characters, of Chinese mythical creatures, of Buddhas, of Jesuses and Marys, and of big-eyed Hindu gods. There mingled in the crowds millions of Chinese, Indians, Malays, besides the table-salt modicum of whites, Arabs, and other newcomers. All were hoisting the island's spectacular flag: Our Lady the Mermaid, sketched in blue, crowned in gold, crouched in a sea of milk.

Newcomers who celebrated a date most of them hadn't even seen.

And they broadcast it on Britain's own mouthpiece—the BBC that called itself "Asian."

They were masked in a haze of their own making.

Nothing made sense at all. Not his operation, not Asia, not even the world at large.

Hector shut down the TV and paced his hall. There was no liquor in the fridge—damned Pulauis!—and the only book around, Davies's *The Rebel Angels,* reminded him of his silly early twenties at the University of Toronto.

His brain seemed to have exhausted its data plan to download any good memories. His head ached.

He went twice to check on Yubi, propelled by a drudgerous libido. Each time, her pose made it harder for him to relax. Yubi slept on her left side, her left arm curled—like a saint's halo—over her head, her right thigh flexed at the hip.

He did a few pushups on the frieze carpet to weary himself up, but his ears caught something interesting. He stopped. There was a soft creak at the next door.

This was followed by hasty footsteps rushing past his door, then down the stairs.

Hector straightened and cocked his ears. The world was now silent. He referred to his watch. Two-seventeen a.m. Not high time for a nightly stroll or a morning jog.

He walked into his flipflops and opened the front door. Instantly the smell of clean soap and bergamot flooded him—a souvenir from the incredible rendezvous only five hours earlier.

The sealed windows of the hallway commanded a hazy view of the illuminated pond and the wooden bridge arching over it, and of the girls' dormitory across: five stories of pastel beige, a replica of the one he was looking from. Hector fixed his eyes on the bridge and waited three minutes. No one showed there. This was the main route out of his side. A flagged trail walked you alongside the girls' dormitory to the marigold and dahlia pots ring after that, then finally onto the asphalt driveway.

Theoretically, however, there were two alternate routes.

The boys' dormitory had two exits. One of them lay three floors under Hector's feet, close to the bridge over the pond. Another exit, more to the northwest, gave onto a grassed mini-backyard that bordered the ring trail. It was fairly possible to skip the bridge altogether and climb a mere four-foot hedge to the ring trail.

Or, more savagely, you could crowd through the cashew, neem, and breadfruit trees neighboring the mini-backyard and from there extract yourself some twenty feet after onto the asphalt driveway.

Either way was not conventional. But Hector knew his night visitor: He wasn't one for convention.

Hector waited another minute to see if the night visitor would pop up on the ring trail. He did not. So Hector walked to the end of the hallway. And there, by Unit 312, his suspicion was confirmed: The lush branches of cashew, neem, and breadfruit were stirring, in a definite course toward the driveway.

It wasn't possible to follow it all the way through, though. The burly, lush arms of a mango tree covered Ozgur's egress from the residence.

———— ❧ ————

Baxter opened the door but held it close to shut down any thoughts of a possible invitation. His grin was his trademark and when Baxter grinned, his violet lips parted and his pearly teeth rear-marched. He stood there shirtless, barefoot in pewter cotton boxers. His six-packs and his obliques wiggled as he rebalanced his weight, from his right to his left leg, where the shrapnel scars were visible.

Baxter, a former 101st Airborne Division sergeant, had been injured four years ago in Kabul. His unit had been the famed *Band of Brothers* 4th Brigade Combat Team, a detail he never tired of repeating. He didn't look it, but Baxter was close to his professor's age—early forties—and, according to rumor, "dishonorably discharged." Yet you couldn't be sure of anything with Baxter.

"Yessir."

Hector would have responded with his comradely "Sergeant" had the visit been at a more convenient hour. "Hey, Baxter, is Kero there?"

"Nope. Haven't seen him in like forever."

"You know where he went?"

Baxter shook his shaved ebony head, the door moving infinitesimally in his grasp.

Hector got the message and was about to turn away, when he remembered, "How was the bar scene by the way? Any good places around?"

"Yeah, some of them are good. Spiffy Dapper or something was a pretty good one. And Exclusive near Chinatown. There's also this place called Djang or Djing where you get a cantaloupe tequila for six bucks. Good times, boss."

Baxter always called him "boss," a welcome variation from the incorrigible "doctor."

"Did you have a few drinks, then?"

Baxter looked utterly, if not disappointedly, sober, but he nodded. "Yeah, I had a few."

"And Fifi... did she hold up okay?"

Baxter's grin buckled. "Man, this girl never had a drink in her life or somethin'? She couldn't hold it. I paid for her Uber ride home. Won't let her throw up on my shirt, no thank you." He shook his head. "Never again."

Hector still didn't leave. "Baxter... Yubi is having one of her bad headaches. Can I borrow some of your pills?"

The embattled sergeant considered his professor with an amused look. "Sure, boss." He released the door. "Tylenol. Advil—"

"Actually, I was thinking tramadol."

Hector sniffed the air. It was unmistakable: Ozgur's perfume was all over the apartment.

Baxter scratched his smooth chin. "Okay. I don't have that. But I've got other stuff. You into hardcore: Chalk and Oxy and all that?"

"You're kidding me. Do you *have* that?"

"No way, man." Baxter chortled. "I'm just kinda measuring you up. You know what... Forget it. Anyway, you want this trama junk? I don't like it, but I know someone who does."

Hector waited patiently while Baxter disappeared into the one bedroom. The apartment was a mirror-image copy of Hector and Yubi's: a bedroom, a tiny washroom, and a modest hall with a kitchenette, a teal-upholstered sofa, a glass table, and a big Samsung plasma TV. Pulauis were open-handed, yes, but by no means ostentatious.

Baxter came back. He opened his left fist to show six yellow caps. "It's Kero's. I don't think he'll mind, though. You have a paper on you?"

Hector said no.

Baxter limped back inside, then returned with a printout of their itinerary. As Baxter tore out a paper and rolled it into a cone, Hector read *City Hall* and *National Museum*, which were the first two visits for the day.

Baxter saw him off at the door. "Hey, boss, what did Ernest say that campaign was called? The one about farming in China?"

Hector recalled Ernest's defense last September, which everybody had attended. Hector had been Ernest's supervisor, and he had passed him on the first go. It was well-deserved, for the prince's wunderkind of a son had written one of the most original theses in AIMES's history.

Ernest's thesis was a comparative analysis of Sadat's *Infitah* versus Deng Xiaoping's Opening-Up. Both economic reforms had happened around the same period and boasted similar agendas. But only China had thrived. Egypt had flopped big time. Ernest defended the hypothesis that the Egyptian president at the time—Anwar al-Sadat—had implemented a mock reform, a ploy to trick his new ally, the United States, into believing he'd divorced socialism forever. Thus *Infitah*—literally "opening-up"—was no match for Mr Deng's extensive Four Modernizations and his sincere will to move China past Mao's earlier ideological disasters.

"You mean Mao's economic whims? Forcing the Chinese society to jump from agricultural to communist to socialist? It was called the Great Leap Forward, Baxter, and you should always remember that it was an atrocity."

"Yeah yeah yeah," Baxter said. "The Leap Forward. So this thing I gave you, boss, is gonna give you a good leap forward—if you can read me."

"I don't read you, sergeant."

"I mean take it easy on the dame. We're tired and we wanna have a couple hours of sleep before the sun come up. See you soon, boss."

And with a wink, Baxter shut his door.

12

UNKNOWN

T he commingling of sunshine and mist on the yawning verdure compensated Hector for his rocky night. Life was suffused with magic. The roses, the lipstick flowers in the pots outside the Bungalow, the mango trees across with their ruby-red low-hanging fruit, all awakened his desire to partake of the world—be an active *agent* in promoting beauty and justice.

He found Kero inside the Bungalow. The kid's megalith of a head was resting on the couch, his legs straight on the floor.

"Kero… Kero." Hector pressed his shoulders.

Kero started, then stared at his professor with congested eyes. "Yeah."

Hector sniffed the air. "Have you been smoking here?"

"It's like Auschwitz outside." Kero decided to rise. "We should get a coffee pot or something. I'm having a bad headache now."

"Don't ever smoke here again. You hear me?"

The boy nodded.

"You had a fight with Baxter or what?"

"No."

"Then what's keeping you away from your room?"

Kero shrugged. "The AC here is cool."

Hector gave him a long look. Kero was wearing the same Bart Simpson T-shirt and the shredded jeans he hadn't changed out of, nor probably washed, since Cairo. His face was greasy, his eyes gunky, and his dreadlocks looked more hoboish.

"Tell you what." Hector pushed him to the door. "Go and do yourself a favor. It's a long day and we won't be back till eight or nine. Besides, Ambassador Lee is meeting us at the ministry today, for certain. We still have about ten minutes till the bus comes. Take a shower and wear something neat. Business casual. Jeans are okay, but nice jeans. Not *these*. Put a nice shirt on. Borrow one from Baxter if you have to… Hey, and don't forget your mask!"

Hector was neatly dressed himself. He had on a navy-blue Zegna suit with a micro-houndstooth pattern, which he hadn't used since he'd left Stockholm. He'd hoped the suit would reveal to him that Europe was behind him—bolster a sense of presentness, if anything—but instead it made him feel stuck in time. Despite the ruthless fitness regimen Hector had espoused since his dismissal from the Agency in August 2010—weightlifting, swimming, jogging, rock-climbing—his body had remained more or less the same. He'd not been aware of this fact until a half-hour ago, when he'd slipped into his old suit.

He paced the Bungalow and thought about last night. Ozgur's secret visit to his neighbor didn't so much surprise as worry him. From the outset he didn't trust Baxter. Every vet who came to AIMES was intelligence until proven otherwise. But this meant that Langley was cooking something up behind Hector's back. What was it?

Hector was still pacing around when the door swung open.

"You need manners," the concierge said.

He was a Subcontinental middle-aged man wearing blue cargo pants with a white short-sleeve bearing the university's acronym—NUP—on the left breast and epaulets. He was masked and mean as usual.

"Good morning to you too," Hector said.

The concierge held something up in his hand, as if to shame Hector forever. It was an empty Clamato can.

Hector said, "And?"

"You dirty people. Clean after yourselfes. This facility is cleaner than palace of Arabia."

Hector took the Clamato can and tossed it into the garbage box beside the vending machines. "Are we good now?" he said.

"You're a violent person." The concierge took a step back. "Please don't do that."

"You violent people. You all are criminals," the concierge said.

Hector asked him to be so kind as to elaborate.

"I show you," said the concierge.

Hector followed him out to his kiosk by the boom gate. On the sliding window facing the street, the toothed showcase lock was smashed deep, sending rivulets of cracks into the glass.

Yet that wasn't the interesting part.

Printed on the smashed glass was one word in blood-red lipstick:

HICKEY

"Some," the concierge said, hands behind his back, his proud paunch tipping up, "of your ladies like attention. Yes?"

Hector looked hard at him. "Are you bored, sir?"

The man's eyes popped out.

Hector hovered his index and middle fingers over the letters on the smashed glass, which seemed to have caused more damage to this man's karma than anything he'd ever seen on this serene island. "'Cause here is how I see it. A man like you sits here all day just annoying people. You must be really bored to smash your own window."

"Enough! Enough!" the concierge shouted, raising both hands and rotating right and left, as if to seek a witness. "Who are you? You can't be a good professor from America. You're criminal! Yes, gang mobster. I call police right now. My job is to clean the residence of you and people like you!"

Panting behind his mask, the concierge lumbered around into his kiosk, and shut the door.

Hector looked at the broken window one last time. What's this about, now, Ozgur? he wondered.

———— ❧ ————

By seven-twenty everyone was seated on the bus, except for Fifi. She hadn't responded to the dozens of texts her classmates had sent her. Hector asked if anyone would mind going up and checking on her. And when no one replied, he suggested: "Zainab?"

But Zainab malingered, retreating into her husband's arms. "I don't even know where her room is."

Ahmed al-Shatby, the accomplished post-honeymoon hubby, nodded conspiratorially to Hector. Whether Ahmed had a fleet of sunflower-yellow shirts, or brought only one shirt with him, Hector wasn't sure.

"I'll go." Yubi finally volunteered.

"Thank you, honey," Hector said.

She squeezed past his legs without a word.

By the time Yubi crouched under the boom—the concierge wouldn't open it for the bus, nor unlock the side door anymore—Hector turned to Kero, who'd been gazing silently out his window. "You okay, Kero?"

"*Uh...* Yeah, yeah."

Kero had taken Hector's advice to borrow from his roommate's wardrobe to heart. Baxter's XL white shirt made him look like a schoolchild acting a snowman onstage. His pigeon chest and spindly arms moved invisibly inside. The starched collar hid his ears. As for Kero's mask—cigarette-stained and crumpled—it hung over his larynx like goiter. He had switched his jeans for a worse pair, frayed not only at the knees but on the hips and along the seams as well. He tucked his shirt there and cinched it with a peeling black belt fitted with a wrestler's buckle shaped like a skull. On his feet were the same black Converse. He definitely didn't shower—his face was still oily and grubby—and his rastacap was back on.

Hector averted his eyes in pain. "Baxter, where is your mask?"

Baxter, in the backseat, inched forward and took his squashed mask from his back pocket. He was wearing a blood-red Lacoste polo shirt with deep blue gabardine pants. He looked clean-cut and good.

Hector revisited Ahmed & wife. They were seated in the two seats in front of Baxter. "You guys had fun last night?"

"We ate lamb meat," Zainab bragged, "and caviar. We went to see the wild animals in the Safari. And we took a boat in the ocean around the island. It's very romantic, I want to go back."

"Then go!" Kero muttered.

Zainab either didn't notice or deliberately ignored him. "You should go, doctor," she said. "You and Yubi. I'll tell her all the good romantic places when she comes."

Hector thanked her and said Yubi would be very pleased. "And you, Ahmed, how did you find the island?"

Ahmed pouted his lower lip and shrugged. Then he smiled. And at length, he talked. "My mistake, I thought they all geeks here. But these Asian people are very good. I mean..." He frowned, fishing for the word. "They enjoy good life. They are very rich here. But they don't support Israel, doctor, do they?"

Hector hadn't expected this angle of the conversation. So he tried to override it with a brisk remark. "Great, great, let's keep our spirits up today, guys. We have more wonderful places to see."

Yet Kero here barked, "And what *if?* What *if* they support Israel?"

"I see the Israeli Embassy here yesterday," the MB scout said quietly. "Doctor, they have embassy for the Zionist entity. Then they support the occupation?"

"It's different here!" Kero continued. "There's no religious discrimination or tyranny!"

"They have Jewish people on the island maybe?" Ahmed said sarcastically. "Where? I see no one."

"Ask your mother!"

"Kero!" Hector roared. "Apologize. Now!"

"He started it," Kero said.

"The Muslims they persecute all the time," Ahmed said. "I never see a one Muslim who is anyone important here. The Chinese took the island from the Malay Muslims and they make them slaves. Right, Mr Paul?" He addressed their guide, who'd been hitherto silent in the first passenger seat, on the left of the driver.

Paul was a pudgy man, clad in a brown suit and a caramel shirt without the trammel of a tie. Unlike the demure man he'd been at the airport, today he was perhaps *too* outspoken. He'd stated his age *and his religion* to everyone once they'd stepped onto the bus. "Hello, my name is Paul Wong. I am forty-six years old, a Christian, and I am honored to represent the Ministry of Foreign Affairs to guide you through Mermaid City today."

"Our country is multicultural," Paul said. "We love and honor every ingredient of our unique experience. We do have a Jewish minority, yes. And no, sir, we do not persecute the Malays, nor any other ethnic group for that matter. Pulau is famous for peace, and to peace we have bound our destiny."

Bravo, Hector thought.

"You have Palestinian Embassy too, then?" Ahmed returned.

"What kind of stupid question is that?" Kero muttered.

"We've done better than that," Paul said.

"What 'better'?" Ahmed said.

"Our government, sir, has given sixty-five million dollars in assistance to different Palestinian organizations during the last Gaza War. We also provide Palestinian technicians and medics with free training in our institutions. Our bilateral trade volume with the Palestinians is measured in billions, and we have a representative for the Palestinian National Authority—"

"State!" Ahmed rejoined. "It's State of Palestine since UN Resolution of last year!"

Paul did not lose his cool. "Please do no raise your voice, sir. We can discuss semantics later. But suffice it to say, we do and have always helped those people—whatever you choose to call them."

Ahmed's eyeballs rocked in their cavelets. His wife had

detached her fuchsia-scarfed head from his rising and falling chest and was now beseeching him with her eyes.

"You do not respect," the driver said. "I worked with Africa people before, and they are good people. You, you do not respect. Driver time is precious."

"Sorry, Mr Li," Hector said, happy with the diversion. "Well—there they are."

Yubi and then Fifi climbed inside. Without a word, Fifi sat beside Kero. She was wearing a short black dress showing her smooth rounded knees. Around her neck was a golden necklace with the Arabic calligraphy for "Allah" pending there. She was cheerful.

"It's a beautiful day," she said. "The haze looks much less than yesterday, doctor, don't you think?"

"Yes, I believe you're right," Hector lied.

"The Weather app says it's gonna ease up tonight," Yubi said.

"Today is another day." Fifi took a deep breath.

"Tomorrow," Kero said, looking out his window. *"Tomorrow* is another day."

"Whatever," she said.

McDonald's was busy. Yubi and the students stood in the queue, while Hector and Paul reserved two tables.

"Will we see Mr Lee today?" Hector asked.

"I cannot confirm."

"My students were very disappointed yesterday. You see, he's got quite a reputation."

Yubi approached them with a look of discomfort on her face. She hadn't wasted any time taking advantage of her spoils from yesterday: The tie-dyed T-shirt screamed against her black silk bolero and slacks. Her long neck, the grace of her skin over her clavicles, opened up the men's appetites.

"Everything is too expensive here," she said.

"*He's* paying." Hector pointed at Paul with a smile. "What's on the menu?"

"They have the regular, plus some specials if you wanna try some."

"Get the McSpicy if you can handle it," Paul said with a smile to Yubi—which Yubi didn't reciprocate.

Hector said he would take that too.

After she left, Paul said, "She's a fascinating woman."

"Because she's Asian?" Hector said.

"Because she's your wife. Not many women can handle your *trade*, Mr Kane."

Hector looked around. They were seated in the center of the eatery. The booths were mostly behind Paul's back, the cash-registers and the food-handlers behind his. Most of the clientele were teenagers. They were probably safe.

Do you think you're ready for this?" Paul said. "This whole operation is a crime against God."

Hector closed and opened his eyes. Across the table, Paul was still there. "Are you for real?" he said.

"As real as I can *ever* be."

Hector fell into careful silence. "Tell me more about you. What's your code?"

Paul looked at his hands, then looked back up ruefully. "Ever heard of Typhoon Nina?"

Hector said there were two Ninas he knew of.

"I'm talking about the first. Nineteen seventy-five."

"Yes. What about it?"

"What about it?" Paul shook his head. "What about it? I *lived* it. I was eight at the time."

"That doesn't explain anything."

Paul sighed. "Then listen, Mr Kane. It's a strange story, but it will make you understand how we operate. Here is the story of my late conversion, how I became Pulau's first Christian spy."

And Paul's story was one of the strangest Hector had ever heard.

———— ❧ ————

"I was born in China," Paul said, "in Henan. And it wasn't until Nina came along that I moved here to Pulau. My parents were Chinese Christians, followers of the Three-Self Church, and my village didn't like us very much. They thought we followed 'the British God.' So when the Banqiao Dam broke down, our hut was gone in a jiffy, but no one cared to save my parents. Everyone was gone but me. A neighboring family picked me up. Their daughter had drowned in the Ru, so I was taken as her replacement.

"Seven weeks later, we sailed to Pulau. We were refugees. We took on new identities and forgot about our Chinese past. This may come as a surprise to you, but Pulau is very good at making you forget. Here the world itself is foreign. Your past seems like a closed book. Progress was our only deity for so long. Fei Guo's work! But, alas, Fei Guo passed away in December. And so, after decades of kneeling to progress, I found myself looking back— and I wasn't alone. Fei Guo's death made us all look back. We are his orphans, so to speak.

"Weeks after Fei Guo's funeral, I heard about an American pastor coming to Pulau. I was reluctant, but my legs carried me there. I remembered my biological parents and hoped to make a reconciliation with my past. The pastor was of Chinese descent, and his words touched my heart. He spoke of God's strange ways and said that everything in the universe served a holistic purpose. He was funny too, despite a physical deformity that made looking at him rather painful. He said it was a 'thorn in the flesh,' which he appreciated. I cried so much. And I swear to you, Mr Kane, I saw Fei Guo himself hovering over the pulpit, in a cloud of light. It was a sign! I walked to the pulpit and declared my faith on the spot. The MFA was at first shocked by this transformation. But they have allowed me to keep my job. Most of my colleagues also have found new creeds, new loyalties. It was Ambassador Tommy Lee, in fact, who suggested that believing in a celestial god was perhaps better than falling for 'the cult of the political,' as he called it. He said he would use me as a prop, a device to measure the cunning of the MFA. And he coupled me with another spy. We call him 'the middle-middle man.' I'm one end of the measuring stick, he's the other. And together, we balance the MFA—after it's gone mad after Fei Guo's death."

———— ❦ ————

City Hall lay in the center of town, in a neighborhood known collectively as *The City*. The City comprised four neighborhoods: the Central Business District, Chinatown, Little India, and Arab Street. Most of Pulau's touristic attractions were located there, and that made the narrow streets always crowded with tourists. This had also prompted Pulau's City Council to impose a car-free zone over a half-mile radius. Luckily, though, both City Hall and the National Museum were equidistant from the parking lot, so their first two visits shouldn't take more than a couple of hours—Paul assured them.

The streets were cobblestoned and teeming with all sorts of people. Yet Europeans by far dominated the scene. Boonies— it's strange how everybody falls in love with them abroad—cargo shorts, sandals, backpacks, and Nikon cameras were everywhere.

"Ladies and gentlemen." Paul was backstepping and clapping his hands. "A brief history here. As you can see, City Hall is built like a Greek temple. And not just *any* Greek temple. This design comes from the *Temple of Diana*, also known as *Artemis*. It used to be one of the seven wonders of the ancient world."

They rose their eyes to the reborn miracle.

Nested in the hazy clouds, clothed in vines, a temple rose to a hundred feet of white marble. It boasted elegant, fluted columns. "Ionic order," as Paul said, distinct from the older "Doric" order by its feminine spirit: The Ionic columns were slimmer and more ornate and they capitalized into a spiral wig-like sculpture called the "volute," which comes from the Greek word *voluta,* meaning a scroll.

"Where is this temple?" Ahmed asked, holding his wife's hand, a step ahead of everybody.

"Excuse me?" Paul said.

"I get you." Fifi looked at Ahmed then at Paul, and shook her head. "He means the original temple. His Highness thinks it's still kicking around somewhere."

Here Zainab snapped, "I don't like your attitude. Your words are not decent."

"English, please," Hector required.

"We're sorry, doctor," Ahmed said. "But I ask a question to the guide, not to anybody who doesn't like us."

Paul defused the situation by simply answering the question. "Well, the original temple doesn't exist anymore. It was destroyed by a man called Herostratus, around three-fifty BC. It's funny that you ask, Mr al-Shatby. Legend has it he was seeking to make his name last forever. The same night he set fire to the temple, was the birth night of Alexander the Great. Excellent question. Any more before we go in?"

Hector felt a vibration on his forearm. It was hot and he was carrying his jacket and tie.

Yubi looked at him.

"I'll catch up in a sec," he said, digging his phone out.

He looked at the screen.

UNKNOWN CALLER

Hector dodged a wave of German tourists and paced slowly to the ceramic patio of the temple. There were balloons and other decorations from the Golden Jubilee celebration of last Friday. Some were taped to a red fire hydrant and some to the food carts hemming the patio in a semicircle: selling roasted beans, pork cabbage, and ice cream sandwiches. At the center of the patio was a fountain, inside which stood a white marble statue of Diana the Mermaid—Pulau's rendering of the Greek goddess— arching an arrow at her naughty visitors.

Hector didn't need a guide to speak of the sacrilege he was witnessing. Diana was the goddess of the hunt in Ephesus. People believed she bestowed protection and wealth on their city. Thus when Paul, the Apostle, started proselytizing the Ephesians, he found himself at loggerheads with the artisans whose livelihoods depended on making Diana's statuettes.

Needless to say, Paul and his followers had won, big time.

She was the first feminist in history, this Diana, a virgin for Zeus who devoted herself to fighting the devious tactics of the Romeos.

And as Hector stood there, debating whether to answer this mysterious call, he concluded that the Romeos had won, too.

Three teenage girls were teetering with laughter as three boys vied for fondling the Greek goddess. Selfies galore.

Hector decided to answer. "Yes?"

A pause. A deep, rasping cough. "Hector. Are you alone?"

Neither the time nor the place. "Yes, Your Highness. Yes, yes, I'm alone. How are you?"

"I need to speak with you," Prince Mohamed bin Hakam said in a diminished tone, gliding over the syllables as would one in a surgical bed. "Something bad has happened. Are you aware or not?"

Hector felt his heart thump against his chest. He walked around the fountain. "I'm not sure I know—yet. What's happened?"

The prince hemmed and hawed then blew out a heave. He was evidently smoking. "My son. He is taken."

"Your son." Hector was briefly stunned. "Ernest?"

"The Chinese have him. Hector, are you aware—"

"Are you sure?" Hector dropped his jacket on the ceramic floor. "Tell me, how'd it happen?"

"I received their messenger today. They knew how to find me."

"Yeah, yeah, and what'd they want?"

"I cannot discuss this with you. I'm not calling you for this reason."

"Then what are you calling me for?"

"They will kill him if I inform the Agency. They have... certain conditions for him to be released. These conditions won't make you happy."

"Right. Conditions and demands you can't disclose. So why're you calling me, for God's sake? To cry and weep on my shoulder? And how did you get this number anyway?"

"Your dean gave it to me." The prince paused and Hector heard the sizzle of the burning cigar. "I am in Venice. I'm newly married. I was not expecting this."

"Congratulations! What'd you expect? Of course they got to him. You treated him like a pet. They figured *you* out, so they figured *him* out."

"No, it wasn't like that." A quick, nervous drag. "They lured him to where you are."

Hector felt himself turn into a marble statue. He was one with the goddess. His eyes fidgeted in his head. Yet he could not move.

The German group were discussing the statue's significance and taking photos of City Hall. A Chinese boy was drinking off the goddess's nipples.

Hector picked up his jacket in slow motion.

"Hector, are you with me?"

"Prince, are you smoking regular tobacco or hashish? 'Cause what you're saying doesn't make any sense."

"He went to Pulau to run away with your wife," the prince said.

Hector stopped. "Pardon me?"

"You heard me!" The prince's tone crescendoed. "Your wife seduced him. He left his job in DC and bragged to his mother that he would run away with the professor's hot wife. Are you still with me, you stupid cuck—"

"Hey, prince… Listen… Listen… They're messing with your head. This can't—"

"No. *You* listen to me. I know he's with them. I've seen the videos. They blindfolded him and they're keeping him with them till I submit to their demands. He used my credit card to book your wife's bedroom at the Sands Hotel. Wake up, my friend, wake up!" The prince took a deeper drag of his cigar and coughed, thousands of miles away. At length, the prince becalmed himself. "How could they take advantage of you? This is dangerous, Hector. Everything will collapse if I submit to them. The Russians want Syria and everything. We live in very dangerous times."

"The Russians? I thought they were Chinese."

"I'm not here to teach you your trade."

Hector was silent.

"Hector."

"They told you not to call the Company. What made you call me?"

"I called to let you know of this. The ball is in your court now. You want to tell your buddies, go ahead. But make sure you tell them about your Chinese spy wife, too."

"Prince… my wife… she isn't a spy. I'm pretty sure there is—"

"Do you have children, Hector?" the prince cut him short.

"You know I don't, anymore."

"Well, I have nineteen. And these are the ones I know of."

"I don't get you."

A sigh. "I mean I didn't raise this kid. I met him three years ago, same year you did. He doesn't carry my name, and I won't lose a tooth if I lose him."

"Are you serious?"

"May Allah have mercy upon him," the prince said. "Goodbye, Hector."

"What? Wait!"

But the prince had disconnected.

PART TWO

13

SEWAGE YEARS

S ome people find love at the bar, others in church, and
some in the drudgery of career.

But Hector didn't have to do any of that.

Love had come *running* to him.

AIMES had an extensive network of green courts
and jogging trails. The longest of these trails toured the
whole campus: It skirted the six main buildings and
passed by the four gates: It traversed the O'Donnell Park then
walked between the two fields where agriculture students worked
day and night on their projects: It glimpsed a view of the most
distant point on campus, the Wishing Pond, where singles
pitched coins and lovers kissed.

It was Hector's favorite trail.

Running was a way to get more acquainted with AIMES and
to battle depression. Ever since he'd walked out of Murphy &
Associates last month, he'd not been able to get in touch with
any of his Company contacts. Two sturdy Egyptian guards *lived*
outside Lisa's firm with clear instructions to keep him away. The
Sayeda Zainab safe house had magically metamorphosed into a
physiotherapist's clinic (with a two-year history *ex nihilo*). Calls

went straight to voicemail or were answered by the wrong voice. Soon the truth was inescapable: He'd been kicked out of the Company. He had to resign himself to this fact and move on.

It was on a rarely mild morning in September 2010 that Hector was jogging back from the Wishing Pond when a fellow jogger joined him from a side trail.

"Hey," Hector wheezed. "Do I know you?"

Earphones in place, she reservedly smiled. She had on a blue-on-white Nike top and black tights. She was very athletic and looked much younger than he was. But perhaps not *too* young?

"So, Amanda?"

Her ponytail waggled. No.

"Tiffany, then."

Silent giggles. Nope.

"Lucy Liu?"

"Hey, not funny." She ran away.

His side stitches were killing him. He gave up. Bending over and gasping, he promised himself: Next time, I'll get it right.

And there was a next time. Only two days later. This time it was at the Edgar Hoover Library, in the elevator. She was wearing horn-rimmed glasses, and scrubs, but he recognized her right away.

"Goodness," he said. "And I thought I went to elite schools."

"Lobby?" she asked sharply, hovering violet-manicured digits near the touch pad.

"Is that where you're going?"

"Hey, look—"

"I'm sorry, I must've acted like a jerk."

He introduced himself and shook her reticent hand. He was dressed in his dusky herringbone Harry Rosen suit, and held a brown leather briefcase, which he hoped would enhance his professional air. His cheeks radiated a heavy musk aftershave he'd brought from Stockholm. He smiled to show his good teeth.

Gradually, she opened up. She told him she was the registered nurse at the campus clinic and that she had been working there for approximately four years.

They walked out to the plaza, Hector pulling his *Predators* from his pocket and donning them. She looked at him, squinting.

He asked, "Where'd you move from?"

"Toronto."

"No way."

"Why? You think I'm from Shanghai or something?"

"Where in Toron'o?" He let the hint of his Canadian-ness sink in, as he pointed her toward the shady arcade of Prince Mohamed bin Hakam Building. The building hosted the departments of Public Policy and Political Science on the second and third floors respectively.

"You know Toron'o?" she asked. "I'm from North York."

"Chinese immigrants and Seneca College. The Peanut Plaza."

"Oh my. You're a Canuck, aren't you?"

"Yes ma'am. The Blue Jays jersey is under my shirt. Do you want me to show you?"

Too late now. She rolled her eyes and excused herself. "Nice to meet you. I gotta go now."

And she walked away.

In his turbulent teens, Hector had suffered from a severe upper respiratory infection that had left a perennial legacy in his sinuses.

"Bite torch here," enjoined the doctor. "Nurse, turn off light. Good employer save money to university."

Yubi hit the lights and the examination room floated in darkness broken only by Hector's incandescent cheeks and skull bones. Hector moaned his objection to this backward procedure. He could hear Yubi's muted giggles.

The physician was a six-foot, rich-bellied man whose copper name tag—sweeping precariously close to Hector's wide eyes as the great clinician set about pressing and percussing Hector's head—read *Dr Afanasy Zharkov.*

"Take photo of sinus," Dr Zharkov instructed Yubi, who traipsed, giggly, inside the room with a Sony camera. The physician jammed the lit torch against Hector's palate and Hector groaned.

Yubi took a few photos.

"You have left maxillary sinusitis, my friend," Afanasy Zharkov concluded, removing his torch at long last.

"I know!" Hector said. "I told you so!"

Yubi had a hard time controlling her laughter as she withdrew to her desk, switching on the lights on her way.

"You doctor?" Afanasy frowned.

"You know what? Peace." Hector slid down the examination table and slipped his feet into his loafers. "What do you think, doctor? Do I need antibiotics this time around?"

The physician returned to his massive mahogany desk and plopped onto a posh executive chair. "I write good prescription for you. You say you professor here?"

"Uh-huh."

"When you started?"

"Technically this month."

Dr Zharkov nodded multiple times, bent over his prescriptions notebook. "Insurance cover basic things. Not high medicine. Not specialist things. We need special fee for this." But then he raised his grizzly head and smirked. "For you, my friend, for you... today is free doctoring."

"Right, right," Hector said. "Doctor, I'll wait outside."

Yubi beamed at him, and he wasted no time. "How do you survive here?" He pointed his index and middle fingers to his right temple and closed his thumb, like a gun.

Afanasy came out of the office and placed his prescription on Yubi's tanker desk. Yubi covered her lips and broke out in laughter.

———— ❧ ————

The following Friday he picked her up from her home. She lived on an upscale block in Mohandeseen. The building's *bawab* devoured her bare shoulders and thighs with his thick spectacles and spat brown phlegm on the floor as he said, "Take key. We no open door to stranger men in middle of nights. We fear God."

In the car, and later at *Bellini,* she warmed up to him.

She told him about her Palestinian roommate Ali, an AIMES sophomore with a congenital heart disease that required an open-heart surgery every five years, but Ali still smoked shisha and drank araq every night with his British girlfriend whose name was, funny, Brittany.

About her year of depression in Toronto following the breakup with her boyfriend Harry, a retail visual merchandiser and aspiring actor who had a decent role in *The Boys in the Photograph* for two performances, no more, and he sang and played the piano, didn't smoke or drink, and he adored his dog

Casper more than her, and finally said he had wasn't ready for a relationship.

About why Cairo of all cities for soul-searching:

"I was desperate for a sign and there it was one night on the floor. I was given a cute girl I still remember very well. Shyanne. She had pneumonia and her grandma was there and she was reading her a book with an awful title: *Death Comes as the End*. I can't allow her to read that, I thought. So I took the book and kept it with me. It turned out to be a really nice novel, an Agatha Christie mystery set in Ancient Egypt. I'd never heard of it, so I Googled Egypt." She sipped her tequila. "And here I am."

Hector ordered another Bloody Mary. He felt confident enough to cuddle her. She did not resist. He spoke softly, told her life was so beautiful in Cairo.

"Do you really think so?"

"*Uh-hmm.*"

"You don't look happy. I don't know. Something about the way you talk, I guess."

He chuckled silently.

"It's kinda gritty here," she added, "and rough."

"My past was way, way grittier, believe me."

"Why, what did you do?"

"You're not gonna believe this."

"Try me."

"I was a CIA agent."

She was silent a moment. "Dude, come on."

"I can prove it." He touched her chin with his fingertips. "I kiss like James Bond."

It wasn't until they'd been dating for two months that she opened up about her distaste for that "spy business."

From now on, she wanted him to be her cute boyfriend, the youngest—and most desired—professor on campus. She liked his knowledge of wine and music and museums in Vienna and Paris. But blood and politics? No, please, no!

Good luck saying that to the man who sailed a gondola under Il Ponte dei Sospiri with two corpses tarped at his feet, throwing kisses in the air like a bona-fide Venetian.

Who bought nuclear blueprints from the Big Khan himself, in the Dancing House of Prague.

Who defused a chemical bomb in the EU's very capital.

"And you want me to forget about *all that!*"

"Hector, I know enough about you. Keep your ugly memories to yourself, please."

But despite her objection, she listened.

She always listened.

———— ·· ————

She memorized by heart, for example, the story of his New York's "Sewage Years."

For two years after his graduation from Columbia University, Hector had jettisoned every opportunity at having a life.

Probably because the day he'd passed his PhD viva was 9/11.

He got drunk and burned his dissertation right at the Morningside campus gate. (He was barred from Columbia for life.)

The Congressman for whom he interned for three months after, Hector called "stinky" in a press conference.

He wasted a whole year writing a novel that would never see the light of day, a *roman à clef* about his childhood in the Middle East and his ultimate adult failure. The final scene was at a Bushwick bar, in Brooklyn. It started with Hector hitting on many random women, to be killed mercifully by an angry boyfriend at the end.

He subleased his Queens apartment to a bunch of Senegalese immigrants and couch-surfed at the homes of former friends who didn't want to know him anymore.

Desperate enough, he'd seriously considered flushing his PhD down the toilet and starting anew in a trade. Preferably plumbing. He'd always envied plumbers for their brawny arms and their humor.

Thus his wisdom to Nicole: "Life is like a plumbing. You run the wrong pipe and end up drifting in a sewer like me. Next time, meet the right plumber, Nicole."

Nicole? Who's Nicole? Yubi asks.

Nicole, who were you really?

He'd met her at Columbia. Unlike him, though, she had the right connections, artistic talent, *and* the guts to drop out. He proposed to her in October '99, on the sixteenth anniversary of his parents' death.

Six months later, though, they both realized the graveness of their mistake. Hector moved out, but Nicole agreed not to file for divorce before he got his citizenship.

Nicole was a true talent. It didn't take her long to establish herself as one of New York's bestselling pastichists. And Hector—he played his role with gusto. He was her tagalong husband, her spellbound aficionado, her dervish.

He ogled her *Lipstick Mona Lisa* with lust, dropped before her *Guernica in Eyeshadows* with a swoon, possessed by the sad angels of color.

He worshiped her most celebrated work to date, a rendition of van Gogh's *A Starry Night* made entirely out of toothpaste: He wept and muttered in tongues.

And it was at one of Nicole's exhibitions that the Company men came for him at last.

The sheikh had come on a rainy day in March 2003. In his company was a well-cologned man in a striped suit and polka-dot tie. Together, these two weirdos toured Nicole's exhibition guided by Tabitha Diamond, Hauser & Wirth's director of exhibitions, who quickly introduced them to the artist and her husband.

"Sheikh Hamid and… well, dear… his assistant?" Tabitha smiled to cover her awkwardness.

"How can we help you?" Hector eyed the man in the *thawb*, *keffieyh*, and *aqal* with apparent disgust.

The sheikh bowed and pecked Nicole's hand. "Hamid bin Suleiman al-Hashem. I have come from Riyadh to steal your *Starry Night*, my princess. Will you allow me the honor?"

Nicole was walking on clouds.

But Hector intervened and said no.

"You have a strange husband, my princess. *Ha ha ha ha.* Oh, we like him. We like him very good. How much is he worth?" The sheikh turned to his dandy assistant and said in the phoniest Arabic Hector had ever heard, "Two million riyals for the husband and a half for the painting. Fetch my checkbook from the car."

"Get lost. You and your clown. Or I'll call the police,"

Hector said.

"We'll go out, yes. But please show us the way, Mr Kane," the sheikh entreated—now in stellar Arabic.

At *Club 7*, West 16th Street, the pact was forged.

The sheikh raised his watermelon martini, knocked it into Hector's Glenfiddich, and cheered, "To democracy!"

"To the Hashemites," Hector returned.

Two Chinese lanterns hung too low over the bar, signaling a calculated oddity against the sweeping Beverly Hills decor. There were potted palms and bushy murals, striped monochrome couches, red strobe lights, and seamy music. At the heart of the dance floor was a girl with a black python slung around her glimmering shoulders, go-go dancing. Across from her stood a shirtless indigenous-looking man, who ate and spat fire to the rhythm. And about them dozens of bodies discoed, all dead drunk, grinning with waxed faces, safe in the security of their fame and money.

Hector spotted an Emmy-award-winning actress, a retired comedian, a Calvin Klein model, and the very *New York Times* arts editor who'd hailed Nicole's exhibition last week. *Club 7* was Chelsea's new fad, an upscale exclusive club for whose membership someone with Hector's bank account did not qualify. Still, this mysterious sheikh and his companion had walked him right in, without a whisper from the bouncers at the door.

No side glances intruded on their privacy at the bar, either. Everyone was so courteous to the sheikh. This was post-9/11 America: Having zipped through *denial, anger, bargaining,* and *depression,* it was now in the *acceptance* stage.

The sheikh took advantage of his elephant-in-the-room status by winking to whoever walked by their stools. He didn't touch his martini. He beamed at Hector, then said, "Hector, *habibi*, you've got yourself a good wife."

"Obliged." Hector lapped his tongue into his scotch.

"But are you a good husband too?"

"Excuse me?"

"My English is bad. Excuse me. But I tip my *aqal* to you." And he did. "You do know how to choose a wife."

Hector put his glass down on the bar. "Who *are* you?"

"Who are *you?*"

Hector was in a good mood. The liquor. The lights. The uplifting atmosphere. He said, "I don't know, sheikh. Sometimes you lose track of yourself. You learn a language, visit a new city, and you learn something new and travel to a new city, and it goes round and round. You end up questioning yourself. Does this ever happen to you?"

"Every day. But I have something over you."

"Which is?"

"A home country. An anchor."

"My life is my home." Hector drained his scotch.

"Think of home in the *broader* sense."

"Like the human race?"

"You have a PhD in international relations. Is humanity home to anyone?"

"The globalists say it is."

The sheikh flicked his hands and swung back with a scowl. "You're avoiding the truth. Are we even going to argue this? Globalism is pretty much dead after 9/11."

"Says the sheikh in New York."

"We both know I'm not a real sheikh."

"Which brings us to the real question. *Who are you?*"

"Before I answer that," said the sheikh, "you might want to think of other questions."

Hector ordered another Glenfiddich. Meanwhile, the sheikh glanced at his assistant, who stood by the murals, nearly obscured by the disco lights. The clown flickered, and Hector saw he was cross-fisted and looking at them.

Hector rotated his new tumbler. "There is, of course, the necessary question of why the bad script. The Hashemites were the historical rulers of Hejaz, today's Saudi Arabia. But they're not there anymore. The lucky ones fled to Jordan." Hector took a sip. "Hamid bin Suleiman al-Hashem, sir, could not *possibly* have come from Saudi Arabia."

The impossible Saudi signaled to his dandy assistant, smiling triumphantly. The dandy came, as the DJ switched to Beyoncé's *Crazy in Love*—eliciting wide clamor from the crowd. The dandy dragged a stool and planted it beside Hector. He sat and his kneecaps pressed Hector's left quad.

"This is going to sound strange, my man," the dandy said. "But we used to know your father."

"My father… who died twenty years ago?"

This was preposterous. Up to this moment, Hector was half-expecting his companions to declare themselves Immigration and Customs Enforcement (ICE) officers. Hector had become an American citizen only three months ago. His marriage to Nicole had thankfully cut his physical-presence requirement to three years, and he'd filed for naturalization in October. And the approval had been quick—quicker than any case Hector had known or heard of—just two months! But for the past four weeks, he and Nicole had been harassed by a mysterious ICE officer with a snowman's skin, who'd basically asked them to confess to immigration fraud. Nicole complained that she was stuck with this marriage forever, it seemed. And many of their common friends were questioned about the nature of this strange union: How could they explain the separate addresses and the separate bank accounts—not to mention the boyfriend Nicole kept in her Upper West Side apartment?

"The cardinal," the dandy crooned into Hector's ear. "Remember the cardinal, Hector."

Hector gazed at the sheikh's face, who frowned like a priest who anticipated the worst from this confessor.

In the shifting light, the layers of the sheikh's face melted. Hector saw a new face. An old face. Younger with eyes the color of a raging storm.

"Beirut, eighty-three, April eighteen," the dandy began. "Your father's been invited to lecture at the American University of Beirut. But it's Monday, and the lecture is on Wednesday. You've just landed from Casablanca, where you enjoyed the fancy-dancy hospitality of the king himself. Your father is a famous man. But his fame is reserved for the right kind of people. He's a *helper*, as they call him. He helps people get along. Arabs and Europeans. Israelis and Palestinians. East and West. Who's the ghostwriter of Sadat's speech to the Knesset? Rocky Kane. The mastermind of the Camp David Accords? Rocky Kane. Who's the real negotiator of the eighty-two evacuation of Lebanon?"

"My father," Hector intoned, a sudden hotness welling in his eyes.

"Good recall, buddy. Your father. And you were only eleven at the time."

"Magda," Hector said. "Magda's house."

"Your parents left you at your mum's auntie's, Magda. They were invited to a get-together at the American Embassy, where a hullabaloo of people were waiting to see them. Lebanese Civil War adversaries. American diplomats. Israelis." He paused before adding, "Even CIA agents."

The sheikh kept eye contact with Hector, as his man dredged up the gruesome history.

"You didn't see it happen, Hector. Lord's mercy. But you were told about it by a man who popped up at Magda's house in East Beirut. A Maronite cardinal who crouched beside Magda's white-lily pots and told you your parents had gone to heaven after an explosion at the Embassy."

Hector was looking at the messenger of death. The Cardinal, who'd taken him to the airport on the same evening his parents had been killed in war-torn Beirut in 1983.

"In the car you kept asking about your father's lucky charm, an evil-eye amulet that he used as a key fob, did it not save his life? About your mommy's Catholic devotion, how could she die if she believed in Saint Andrew Avellino, the patron of sudden death? About your grandfather in Cayuga, Ontario, and how you hated his guts. And about the killers you wanted to kill and the lie that your parents were dead after all. Then you wept silently and stared out the window. The veiled women and the miniskirts. The Kalashnikoved vigilantes and the carefree hippies. You had an epiphany that you *shared* with the Cardinal. Do you remember, Hector?"

The Cardinal finally lifted his martini and began sipping, his eyes locked on to Hector's.

"The chaos," Hector said.

"The chaos."

"The science of chaos."

"The science of anarchy."

"Political science." Hector was startled.

"Bin-go," approved the dandy. "You said you wanted to be the man who brought order to this chaos when you grew up. You said you would do *anything* to avenge your parents' death."

Hector ordered another Glenfiddich. Presently, a barmaid dressed in a white Navy outfit replaced his tumbler. Hector downed the shot and attempted to clear his head.

The song playing was Sean Paul's *Get Busy,* too crammed with lyrics.

"Who are you?" He looked at both men.

"I'm the Cardinal," said the sheikh.

"And who is the 'Cardinal'?"

"An old friend and your new boss."

"I don't need a boss."

"You need a job."

"I haven't applied for one."

"Nobody applies for this kind of job."

Hector asked for another scotch, but the dandy raised a flat hand to the barmaid.

Hector turned to the dandy. "And you, who are you?"

"Call me 'Ozgur.'"

"A Turk? Welcome to my life. My mother was half-Armenian."

"A Cypriot," corrected the Turk.

"What kind of job?" Again he asked both men.

Only the Cardinal answered. "The Company."

"And what's the Company to do with someone like me? I'm a bum." The drinks, the surprises, the music, lights—all this made him sick.

"You're a rare bird, Hector," the Cardinal said. "You simply do not belong. Irish-Lebanese-Armenian by blood. A child in the Middle East. A teenager in Canada. An adult in America. I'm offering you a final way out."

"Of what?" Hector pressed his temples.

"Of homelessness, of despair, of loss."

"God, I'm so lost!"

"No, you're not, Hector." The Cardinal had smiled, his face breaking into a thousand little lines. "We've got you."

14

ALASKAN PRINCE

ector hadn't seen Ernest since Halloween. Ernest
had hung around a few weeks after defending his
thesis, and repeatedly expressed his sorriness for
ever leaving Cairo.

His professor had seen this many times before.
Cairo had a way of keeping you in her thralls.

Ernest was actually lucky to have come to
Egypt before the Arab Spring, when plans wouldn't be suddenly
canceled because of an explosion or a massacre, when
Westerners were safe—or at the worst, cash cows for street
crooks—and when the ingredients of the Egyptian Revolution
were cooking.

What a treasure to political science those days had been!

Ernest was a CASA fellow for a year before starting at
AIMES. The Center for Arabic Study Abroad—CASA—was a
Harvard scholarship that sponsored the cream of the crop of
American students wishing to study Arabic abroad. Every year,
a swarm of hopefuls, wanderers, and misfits would fly to the
Middle East to live, eat, and breathe Arabic among *natives*.

An imperial mindset for sure. (Think of the millions of Arab-

Americans who would be more than glad to take whatever jobs CASA fellows were eligible for.) But CASA had gained traction after 9/11, and it had allowed Ernest Perkins, of Homer, Alaska (a town often ridiculed as "the end of the road") to move to Cairo, Egypt, the cultural beacon of the Middle East—where his parents had first, and last, met.

There he was finally, in the ignoble bedroom of his conception.

Make no mistake, Ernest was sick of Cairo at first. The pollution. The harassment. The scams. The loss of personal space. The lump in his throat when he saw two men clobbering each other on the street (before they, inexplicably, made up). It was all so bizarre, frightening.

But eventually Cairo won him over. He got inured to its spontaneity and roughness.

And before he knew it, the Alaskan fell with every bit of his bones in love with Cairo.

Last Halloween—it was the day prior to Ernest's departure—Hector had run into him on the way out of the Zamalek hostel. Ernest had been pacing the hostel's little garden smoking a cigarette, curved on his midsection courtesy of a recent gym craze devoted—as all overnight bodybuilders were—to his pecs and abs.

Ernest was a good-looking kid: six feet, wiry, his face symmetrical, and his skin clean and olivey. At twenty-five, his hair had thinned gracefully, pushing back the bays on either side of his forehead, leaving only a thin peninsula of trimmed, oiled black hair. His eyes were sea-blue and always looked surprised. His nose was strong and wide, like an Arabian steed's.

His friendship with Hector dated two years back. Shortly after Hector's move to the Crazy Horse, the Company had thrown a party at the Greek Club, where Fabio, Hector, and two other agents had done everything in the book to buddy up to Prince bin Hakam's newfound son.

But only Hector and Ernest had struck up a bond. And this bond continued to grow through Ernest's studies at AIMES— in spite, if not in defiance, of AIMES's academic-integrity guidelines.

Ernest suggested that they go for shisha, and Hector, despite his appointment with the dean, accepted.

They strolled the streets of Zamalek like teenagers after school, shouting recklessly and arguing about politics, books, movies, and girls. Zamalek was a neighborhood of embassies and diplomatic cars. Its streets were quiet and balmy. It was full of spectacular villas, Italian restaurants, gorgeous girls, bikers, and shisha cafés.

Their café soon presented itself. They stumbled into a vacant table on the pavement and sat there. Egyptian cafés always did that. The police would come and fine the cafés for this illegal appropriation of the pavement, but one they were gone, the tables came back up on the pavement.

They ordered a big shisha for two, and Hector took the first drag of the cool, minted smoke. The shisha stem was bandaged with ice bags, and ice cubes danced in the water like harbor buoys. Hector bragged about his knowledge of Cairo's cafés. In some swanky places, he told Ernest, they used gutted apples as bowls.

Ernest listened silently. Then he stretched and said, "The air is heavy with stories, Hec. I can feel and smell it. I really wish there was a way I can stay."

Hector was aware that Ernest's departure wasn't by choice. Prince bin Hakam's legitimate family had gotten wind of this sudden potential inheritor, so they forced the prince to send the Alaskan back where he came from.

"You're a romantic," Hector said. "You think the East is important because of the poverty and the noise. A white boy like you comes here, gets awed by the five-hundred-year house and the six-thousand-year pyramid. You see people who make less than fifty bucks a year. Throw in the corruption, the fights, the Revolution. And what d'you get? You get high on your fantasies, kid. The flags and the songs and the Sufis! You think you're in some *Arabian Nights* tale."

"That's so Orientalist," Ernest objected.

"We're all Orientalists. Let me ask you a question. Would you still like Egypt if it didn't revolt?"

"But that's exactly the point. Egypt has shown us she can kick and scream."

"'She'?" Hector smiled. "Listen to yourself. Do Egyptians speak the same way about America?"

"What's that to do with anything?"

"You personify their country as a *she*. Who gave you that authority?"

"They call Egypt a woman all the time."

"Did it ever occur to you that's their bloody country?"

Ernest took the hose, replaced the plastic mouth tip, and dragged off the smoke. "You're misunderstanding, Hec. I mean no disrespect to anybody. I just love this country as if it were mine."

"But Egypt isn't *yours*, Ernest. You're an *ajnabi*. An imperialist Westerner. My advice to you is to go back home and never look back."

While Ernest smoked, Hector raised his eyes to the sky. There was never much sky in Cairo. Wherever you looked, something had to block you. A balcony. A wire. A sign to promote so or so in the People's Assembly or the Consultative Council elections. Or it was Cairo's glow itself that overlaid the sky, a commercial screen mixed with dust and smoke. Above Hector now there was a rope bowed between two balconies: It bore late Ramadan decorations, your typical Christmas tapestry married to the pervasive China-made lantern. The residents must be too lazy or too pious to remove the decorations, Hector thought. Two months had passed since Eid al-Fitr.

"So you agree it's more romantic here?" Ernest said.

"What? I never said anything like that."

"But I think you did."

"I said *you* were romantic. As for romance itself, it's a fantasy. And in your case—your fantasy of a mystical East."

"Don't you feel it, Hec?" Ernest said with passion. "The vibes! Something *is* going to happen here. I'm sure of it."

"More than it already has?" Hector said snarkily.

Ernest then put the hose on his thighs and flipped into a sulk. Hector was about to broach the subject of Ernest's exciting first job—in the Treasury—when Ernest said, "Did you see that monkey the other day? Oh, man, what a tragedy! What a tragedy, Hec!"

Calling the Egyptian president a "monkey" wasn't uncommon then. The presidency itself had lost its sanctity with the Revolution, when millions of angry protesters had faced the soles of their shoes to a consternated President Mubarak—a war hero and an imposing tyrant—during his three nervous speeches.

Imagine how they treated his replacement.

The Muslim-Brotherhood president had none of Mubarak's charisma. He was a short, pudgy man with lewd eyes and a strange proclivity for suggestive humor that cracked his listeners up. He was not the nation's first choice, nor his group's. The MB had proposed him as an alternative to a strong leader who'd been ruled out on the pretext of a smudge on his criminal record. The Egyptians, a joke-loving people, toyed with this for months, calling their would-be president a "spare-tire" candidate. Hector knew a young woman who literally referred to her car tires by the president's name, front so-and-so, rear so-and-so. The Muslim Brotherhood had been the lesser evil for the electorate, though. The only other option was an army general and former prime minister for Mubarak, who'd been against the Revolution from the first.

Yet the Brotherhood didn't seem to comprehend this fact. After their narrow win, they thought that Egyptians had bought into their Caliphate drivel. In effect, they neglected Egypt for their dreams of global domination.

Strangely, the Brotherhood paid excessive, almost unhealthy, interest in national ceremonies, though.

In his first hundred days as president, their "spare tire" president gave over fifty speeches, ludicrous hours-long ramblings that tickled his audience to death.

The last of these disasters had been three weeks earlier, on the thirty-ninth anniversary of Egypt's victory over Israel in the Yum Kippur War. Mr President had toured Cairo National Stadium in an open jeep, raising his fists and bouncing before a howling crowd of Islamist supporters.

The rest of the country, watching this on television, called this "a crowd of monkeys."

And he was a "monkey president" ever since.

———— ❧ ————

"Well, Mubarak was a tyrant," Hector said to Ernest at the café. "People deposed him and elected your 'monkey.' What's your problem? You're not even Egyptian, Ernest. So funny we preach democracy to others, and when it doesn't get us someone we like we grumble and philosophize."

"America wants the monkey and his tribe in power, Hec. Don't fool yourself," Ernest snapped.

"And why is that?"

"Because they're easy to make a deal with. They're too obsessed with their global goals to see reality. And we love that."

"We?"

Ernest gave him the hose and said, "Maybe not ordinaries like you and me, but our watchmen at Langley."

———— ❧ ————

Funnily, Ernest himself had flirted with the idea of intelligence as a possible career after graduation.

Why wouldn't he? They were all Edward Saids, better Arabists than Bernard Lewis. All were Paul Bowles, new Durrells, Graham Greenes, Maughams, modern Conrads, and Hemingways. An expat is a bloated daydream in essence.

Yet all the expats of Cairo had at least one privilege over the prince's son. They were *nobodies*. And Ernest couldn't be a nobody even if his daddy were to spend billions of dollars to obscure his identity.

Ernest wasn't a nobody when his mother had wasted half of her life whitewashing him in the Great White North. He knew he wasn't a local boyfriend's son before his mother—a hairdresser who spent way more than she earned, bought him a brand new Audi A6 for his eighteenth birthday, promised to send him through Ivy League, no worries about the money, hon—spilled it out, thanks to his emotional bullying. (Do Chugachs grow beards at fourteen, Ernest? Get hair loss at sixteen?) Yes, you aren't any of theirs, she confessed. Your father was an Eastern guy I met on a trip. No, Ernest, I don't know! Don't even remember guy's name. Now you know what your mom really is. Why does it grate on you so much? Finding him won't solve any problems. Careful what you wish for.

Ernest had related to Hector—being his friend and "a true intellectual who needs to know how bureaucracy has destroyed America"—the story of his second big disappointment in life (the first, of course, being finding his father).

With all the zeal of youth, Ernest had flown to Benghazi in July 2012 to meet the US ambassador his father had cajoled into meeting him (the same ambassador who would be slain, along with two CIAs and an IT guy, in the militant attack on Benghazi in September). The American ambassador took him to a sunny boardroom overlooking the compound's bustling yard: armed vehicles, Libyan militiamen with their red berets and sweaty faces, jumpy visitors, hungry journalists. Then a heavy man with rimless glasses came and introduced himself as "Jonathan Beach." (Hector knew there was no such agent.)

So, Ernest, what kinda degree do you have? Are you trained

in martial arts? What's your IQ? Myers-Briggs Personality type? First and other languages?... So, Ernest, why do you wish to apply to Central Intelligence? Oh, is it Perkins I see here? Have you changed your name? I see. I see. And Arabic is your second language, nonetheless. Thank you, Ernest. No, don't contact us. If you're a successful candidate, we'll be contacting you.

· · ·

"Even the army won't take me, Hec," Ernest said at the café. "Is this the end of me?"

"You'll do just fine staying away from the army."

"It's like Fukuyama said. *The end of history.*"

"He was a romantic."

"But still, he thought history would end after the Cold War. No war, no conflict, happy people, no art—"

"Or romance."

Ernest looked at his shoes, the din of the street enveloping them—guffaws and raspy coughs, spoon clanks, bicycle bells, order shouts, the usual symphony of car horns.

"I don't know why you keep saying that," he said. "I forgot about romance a long time ago."

"In DC you'll find a girl. Tell her your dad is rich, and she'll make you forget all about Cairo, politics, and me for that matter. Live the good life, kid. Never go back to school."

Ernest blushed. He took short, jerky drags of the smoke, and leaned forward with a frown.

Hector yawned and looked at his watch. Five-twenty p.m. His meeting with the dean was at six. "What time is your flight?" he asked.

Ten a.m.

"We'll have a drink tonight, then."

"Tonight?... Oh, Halloween. God, I forgot."

"No, don't. Your classmates will be there. Yubi, too. They'll love to say goodbye."

"Okay," Ernest said.

Hector rose. "I'll take you out today. My treat."

He called the waiter and handed him fifty pounds and told him to keep the change. The waiter looked like he'd won the lottery: He scurried back to the kitchen. Hector walked to the end of the street and flagged a taxi. He gave the driver the dean's address in Doqqi and bargained a fare: Fifteen pounds was his limit. He slipped into the car and waved to Ernest.

But Ernest looked straight at him with a strange face. He was simpering and smiling at the same time.

And then there was the Halloween party.

Right at the Embassy's Lazoghly gate, Kero had been screened out. Fifi, the European citizen, assailed the guards with words then with rocks and called them "American mules"— before leaving with him.

The air smelled of smoldering cars and teargas. But it smelled of stability, too. Compared to how other Arab Spring states were faring, Egypt was the Switzerland of North Africa. The Muslim Brotherhood were terrorists, sure, but they were *bad* terrorists. Where was the restored Caliphate? The halal economy? The morality squads scouring the streets hunting down decadent daters? We didn't see the Christians enter the religion of Allah in multitudes, the atheists' heads embellish the squares, nor the

American Crusaders booted out of the Land of the *Kenanah*. In fact, America and the Brotherhood got along like a country on fire. No more attacks on Embassy, no cut-downs on military personnel, and no frozen aids.

This explained why, in Cairo, Westerners were partying all year round. Cairo was the new Bohemia, Paul Bowles's Morocco, Allan Watts's Japan, Hemingway's Paris. Everyone came here to be enlightened, get high, and get laid. A moveable feast at least has a destination. Cairo was a carousel.

Hector was dressed as a Pharaoh, Yubi as a pixie, her eyelashes glittering in green. And she smelled good, a Michael Kors fragrance with blackcurrant and bergamot Hector had bought for her from the *City Stars* mall.

She and Hector lingered at the bar. Hector got tipsy fast.

"Do you wanna dance?" he asked, pawing her bare back.

"I'm tired," she said, pushing his hand away.

"Hey, boss. Another one?" Baxter asked. He was one of the two bartenders dressed in Greek tunics.

Hector ordered another Samuel Adams.

"That's like what, your fifth?" Yubi said.

"I can hold up to ten," Hector said.

And then *he* walked in, His Highness the Alaskan Prince, decked out in a white Bond tuxedo. His thin hair was oiled, his gait uninhibited. He bumped into so many people as he threaded his way to them at the bar. He was indubitably high.

"Sorry for being late, guys," he breathed. "Where is everyone?"

"With your Caruso," Hector said, before turning to Baxter to take his Samuel Adams.

And when he turned back, he saw that Yubi was holding Ernest's wrist. "Come, Ernest," she said. "You're leaving tomorrow, right? I'll give you a goodbye dance."

"Are you okay with that, Hec?" Ernest asked.

"Just don't crush her toes," Hector had said, tipping his beer over his lips.

15

TIME MACHINE

W hat's wrong?" Yubi asked him when he rejoined the group.

Hector shook his head. Nothing.

They were walking toward the National Museum, threading their way through the masses in a conga line, Yubi the dancer he was tagging.

Finally they came upon a glass-and-steel truss dome, within which resided a marmoreal growth from the same era the founding fathers of Pulau were so besotted with.

Now if City Hall was the Temple of Artemis, what could the National Museum be, but a dwelling place for all the gods—in a word, a Pantheon?

Paul ambled to the box office, while Yubi turned to Hector. "Who was it?"

"Who was who?"

"You caller. Did something happen, in Cairo?"

"It was the Egyptian ambassador." Hector raised his eyebrows and shook his head. "This woman doesn't know when to stop."

On their first day in Pulau, the Egyptian ambassador had

treated them to dinner at her house: a double-terraced villa niched on the slope of Mount Victoria in a savanna of olive trees and wild grass. The place was close to the Ministry of Foreign Affairs on the hilltop and to *Mister Prata* down at the foothill. But they would make stops at both locations on the next day without calling on her, and they would ignore her phone calls ever since.

"Wash up your dishes when you're done!" she had shouted to her guests. "Fatima, pick up that salami piece you dropped. Now! Be clean or get out. The Embassy cannot afford a cleaning lady to clean all of your mess. It's been rather tight since your daddy made a Revolution. It's like a march a day keeps the doctor away these days. Interesting times. Very interesting times. Is that what your daddy taught you, Fatima: to drop garbage in other people's homes? How did he raise you all by himself, I wonder? Did he invite any ladies over? People talk. *Tut-tut.* Why does he want to destroy the country a second time? Answer me! Hey, don't cry on my carpet!"

Later, she had apologized and wept and put it all down on *Iblis,* an evil spirit that had penetrated her house. "Did you bring pork-eaters to my house, Dr Kane? Don't be offended. It's been scientifically proven. Oh, I feel so bad now. We'll hang out later and patch it up. Hug Fatima for me and tell her I'm sorry. I'll hug her myself tomorrow when she's calmer. Do you need a drive home? My car is yours anytime. Please take the rest of the pizza with you. Flies hang around here all day."

———※———

Paul returned with the tickets and they followed him into the museum. And soon the dome cut them off from the horrors of the outside crematorium. Tchaikovsky's fifth symphony was playing in the background, a piece of music so perfect, so victorious, it was its own universe.

And the air was cool and redolent of blueberries and jasmine. They breathed, and they were cured of all worry.

They were in a courtyard peppered by souvenir stalls and flanked by double-storied colonnades. Entrances to side exhibitions were on the ground floors of the colonnades. As for the court, it was a work of art: Lit by the glare penetrating the glass dome, a ceramic chessboard rolled endlessly.

Baxter whistled. "Looks like the White House is over there," he said, referring to an edifice crouching on the horizon.

Paul corrected him. "That is the Pantheon, Mr Simmons. It looks like your White House, absolutely, but the copyright belongs elsewhere," he said with a smile.

Hector clapped his hands. "It's a big place," he said, "so we'll break into groups." He set himself, Paul, Baxter, and Kero in one group to tour the exhibitions in the Pantheon. The others, he said, could explore the side galleries in the colonnades.

Yubi averted her face, but he could afford that.

The four men raced to the Pantheon, driven by Hector's outspoken zeal for the old monument. Once they reached the white stone steps, Hector came up with a fresh tactic to isolate his guide. Unlike the original Pantheon in Rome, this one was multi-storied. Hector had anticipated this by measuring it up from afar. It looked—it had to be—bigger. The columned portico alone rose over two hundred feet and, behind it, the rotunda to almost twice that height. The bold architects of this island had copied but not wholly succumbed to the Classics.

"We'll split again," Hector said. "There's too much to cover. You guys take pictures of everything 'cause we need to put that up on the Institute's website. Any questions?"

"I don't care." Kero shrugged.

Baxter extracted his Samsung Galaxy from his back pocket and flashed Hector a smile. "Anything you say, boss."

Hector wasted no more time. He skipped the exhibitions and took his guide up the staircase to the fourth floor. The staircase ceased and a sign greeted them:

WELCOME TO THE TIME MACHINE

"Something is up," Hector began. "I must—"

Paul muted him with an erect forefinger, his eyes rolling twice to indicate the ceiling cameras. He quickly made for a bald, elderly Chinese man standing behind a table carrying audio appliances set in numerical order. Paul picked a couple of headphones and returned to Hector. "Follow me," he said.

Hector followed him through a pair of heavy bronze-clad doors and found himself under the Pantheon's trademark: the perforated dome.

During his stint in Europe, Hector had visited the real Pantheon with his then-girlfriend, Maureen, and he recalled every word his Italian guide had told them at the time. The perforated dome was a wonder in itself, a solid proof that our ancestors were not behind us in brainpower. One of the major structural problems with building a dome, Hector recollected, was preventing it from falling under its own weight. So the Romans came up with a little trick: They gouged the dome. Besides the thirty-foot hole known as the "oculus," the dome boasted five levels of indentations called "coffers." These helped strip the dome of all unnecessary weight, making it lighter, helping it stand tall against time.

The museum's Time Machine was nothing like the circular

chamber of Rome's Pantheon, however. It was circular all right, but the vaulted cornices, the holy shrines, the columns, even the veneered walls were absent here. A silver shaft of light descended from the oculus onto a clock engraved on the stone floor. The light hit the "X" mark, and visitors' shadows shuffled around this sundial.

Tourists are too quick to be tingled by awe, and Hector was not an exception. And the moment he shrugged off his awe, he found that he'd lost his guide.

Then a metallic creak made him wince. A display started up. The smooth, cylindrical wall came alive with all varieties of color. The Time Machine had taken off.

A female British voice crooned into his ears:

'Pulau: A Day in the Life *is a geopolitical utopia in praise of the Pulaui miracle. It is a gift from the British people to the Pulaui people, a token of our enduring friendship. Copyright two thousand eight…"*

Images burst on the wall, circling around in tiles. There were no benches so everybody's heads had to endure the dazzling lights. Paul was at the opposite end, Hector spotted him: filmed over by reeling frames of schoolchildren. He gestured to Hector to stay put. Patience.

Landscapes of barren rocks. Mountains lush with verdure. Huts. Skyscrapers. Barefoot children at the port. Snazzy businessmen. And throughout, a hypnotizing mantra interlaced with a Wagneresque soundtrack:

Trrn trrn trrn ta, Pulau. Trrn ta, Pulau. Trrn ta, trrn ta, Pulau.

So the mantra went, repetitive, hypnotic.

Date stamps or captions helped the time-travelers connect

the dots, accompany Mermaid City from its cradle to the vigor of its current youth. And the pictures were often savage. Japanese soldiers shooting poor Pulauis in front of their own homes. Potbellied starved babies. Mutilated fishermen. Et cetera.

The Brits highlighted the kinks in the road, the bad stuff. Not much emphasis was put on the glamorous Sumatran past, for example. Even the island's creation myth, which Yubi had related to him on the airplane, was not here.

"Asia is a funny place," his wife had said in the air. "Everything starts and ends with a woman. I kinda like that. At least we have an appreciation for the feminine. So there is this sea goddess, Matsu, who is a mermaid. She has a fight with her husband, so she leaves him and goes up to the surface to stay alone for a while. She sprays some dust to make the water solid to stay and that's the earth, how it becomes. But guess what? Her husband sends his ugly pet dragon after her, trying to get her back. And she isn't going back now, no way. So what's she do? She takes her knife and stabs it in the dragon's back. The beast tosses and screams, but he wont' die. So... Where was I? Oh, yeah, so she stabs the beast. But... *Uh-unh.* Just listen. Do you wanna hear the story or not?

"So a few days later, her husband comes up and he's like crying and saying he's changed and all that. She believes him, silly woman, and they have a very romantic night... Huh? What did you say? Yeah. Sorry. So they make love and have lots of kids. And these are the humans who fill the planet and multiply. And the mother-goddess goes back down with her husband, thinking he's really changed.

"But that's not how it ends. Did I really say that? Strange. Sometimes I get too far ahead of myself. Anyway, things go on as usual with her husband. He's not taking care of her, and she's not happy. And after a few centuries, a hottie Sumatran king called Sang Nila Utama crashes his ship into the sleepy dragon. You got it. Of course, you're right. You're always right. No, I'm not being sarcastic. Anyway, I'm kinda sleepy now...

"Oh, the dragon. His name is really funny. Gong-Bong or Gong-Gong or something. I'll check the *Lonely Planet*. The knife is sticking out of his back, and he rages and tears the king's crew to pieces. And he's about to finish off with the king himself, this Nila Utama guy, 'cept then the mermaid comes up angry from the sea. And she grabs her knife from the dragon's back and she pushes it deep and hard into his heart. And she kills the beast for ever.

"Peace now, right? No dragon, the earth is happy. But not really. Things don't end up good for her at all. The mermaid-goddess, this miserable wife, she kinda... takes a liking to the hot king. He's been super nice to her, and she's been having a difficult time with her husband. Her husband won't spend time with her or take her places or anything. And she's so lonely...

"So after many years, her husband finally remembers her existence. He comes up, and he sees them together. So he loses his head. He takes out his sword, and he stabs his own wife and throws her body into the sea. So cruel. And her lover, he runs away. That's what they always do, they run away.

"And this is how Pulau is born, from the body of the mermaid-goddess. She was so full of life, this island, but now she's just a piece of rock. So empty. So dead. So lonely in the cold China Sea..."

———— ❧ ————

Between one bleak picture and the next was a balmy snapshot. Mount Victoria, for example, first bald and creepy then exploding with verdure. THE FORBIDDEN HILL, read the caption in all caps. It was something to do with having been a sacred burial site for the ancient Malays. Not anymore, not in this Chinese Las Vegas, this secular Olympus. (Besides, cremation was a faster way to heaven.)

The Japanese occupation, interestingly, got the lion's share of the show. Why this was in a British documentary was a question political scientists would spar over. Postcolonial guilt? Globalist apologia? Stressing the obvious so it lost its poignancy?

Everyone knew how hideous this episode of Pulau's history was. In late 1942, Imperial Japan had attacked one peripheral British colony called Pulau. Although local Loyalists had raised the Union Jack and refused to bow to the emperor, the British did not respond to Pulau's repeated calls for help. And by 1945, Pulau's population had shrunken to a third of its prewar size.

This was something the Malays would never forget, for it'd cost them what counted for everything in Asia: their demographic majority.

Thus Hector's sly theory for the film: The R-rated Japanese content was but a wink from one colonist to another. We made you into a demographic majority of this geopolitical utopia, the Brits were saying to the Chinese.

Suddenly the music stopped in his ears. Hector started. He jerked his head. None of the other time-travelers looked troubled. Wide-hulled boats and luxury yachts, hot girls in bikinis, Victorian brick mansions fading into wiggly skyscrapers, winding overpasses. They watched with uninterrupted absorption.

"I'm here," said a new voice in his head.

Saint Paul the Invisible. Hector couldn't see him anywhere.

"Stop searching for me," Saint Paul said. "You'll just attract attention. How can I help you?"

"Paul, I need to see someone."

"Who?"

"Your boss, Tommy Lee. I must see him in private. ASAP."

"I don't think I can do that, Mr Kane. Ambassador Lee is fully booked."

"Tell him it's about my wife, then."

Silence.

Steamers edged along the coast, followed by a bird's eye view of one of the city's large parks. THE JUNGLE FLAME, the caption read. Red-orange bushes made up a massive Twitter logo.

"I can only arrange a meeting with our middle-middle man," said Saint Paul, the Invisible. "You're asking for too much. I don't understand. This is not standard policy."

"Screw the policy," Hector said. "I'll take my chances, man."

A picture of the Royal Botanic Gardens' SUPERTREE GROVE flashed on the wall. Giant escalators of genetically engineered oaks stood in a circle, brilliant in all sorts of colors against a somber sky. Up between the supertrees stretched a skyway of fortified glass: Passers were hilariously terrified.

"May I ask what the problem is?" Paul said. "I might be able to help you."

"By doing what? Praying for me? Hook me up with someone dirty, Paul. You're too clean for my taste. And for the love of your God get me outta here!"

"A category to file your request under, sir?"

"Emergency!" Hector nearly bellowed, sickened to his stomach by the sappy pictures of Pulau's Royal Flying Club, equally stocked with bi-planes and street-children.

"The show is almost over," Paul said. "Please be patient."

"Now! Now, Paul!" Hector stormed about in the room, bumping into shoulders and jaws. "Get me outta here, now!"

Hey, mister!

Aw!

What's wrong with you!

"You're panicking." Paul's voice rolled over a picture of Deng Xiaoping's hand shaking Fei Guo's at the airport. "Sir... Sir...?"

Hector opened his eyes to the network of steel trusses keeping the dome from coming down on the thousands milling about.

He was lying on his back. His legs were flexed. Something hard was pressed against the back of his head.

And then someone gently slapped his cheeks. "You all right?" A tanned Chinese face. Bald. Gray tufts on the sides. Wrinkles. Must be over eighty.

The Time Machine operator. Hector recognized him after a few blinks.

Hector slowly sat up then sniffled and looked around him. He was in some kind of busy balcony. The stone balustrade's lower ridge was his hard pillow. Hector could see the chessboard court below. He turned to his rescuer and thanked him.

"You have medication?" the operator said.

Hector shook his head.

A new voice said something in patois. "*Ah-chek*"—which Hector knew meant "Uncle"—followed by a string of guttural compliments. Paul, then, replaced the operator, knelt at Hector's right side. "We'll get you back to the residence."

"No, I'm okay."

"I'm not a physician but this guy is." Paul referred to the elderly operator. "He's a retired cardiologist volunteering here. He thinks you had a breakdown."

"Vasovagal attack," corrected the retired doctor.

Using the balustrade, Hector rose to his feet. He avoided looking down at the low ground. It wasn't so bad: His legs were solid. He pawed around his chest and neck but didn't feel his jacket. He asked for it, and a moment of shuffling feet went by. Then a young boy wearing a baseball hat came and handed him his jacket.

In a gush of tears, Hector kissed the kid's hand.

16

OLYMPIANS

fter stressing to Paul not to breathe a word about his syncope to anyone, Hector made for the washroom. Inside, he popped one of Baxter's—or Kero's—tramadol caplets. "Five in the vault," he muttered, patting his breast pocket. Then he washed and dried his face and headed to the bus.

The drug kicked in fifteen minutes later. He hugged Yubi's back and printed an affectionate kiss on her sweaty forehead. She was put out but didn't mind.

Hector, then, engaged his students in a quick academic diversion.

"Tracks of diplomacy, Ahmed."

Ahmed was brought up short. "Shuttle?"

"That's not a track, that's a style. Okay, give me a name there."

"Me! Me!" Fifi raised her hand.

"Ahmed?"

"I don't know."

Hector had never seen someone so proud of his ignorance.

"How about you, Zainab?"

"Kissinger." She pronounced the name with a hard G.

"Me! Me!" Fifi again, bobbing in her seat like a bouncing ball.

Yubi laughed, twirling Hector's shirt buttons.

"Okay, Fifi. Go."

"Track one, official. Meetings between presidents and whatnot. Two—"

"Unofficial," Kero cut her off, a cocky smile on his face.

"—which is like between imams and priests," Fifi picked up without giving him a glance. "Three, people-to-people. Grassroots and so on."

Hector got slightly annoyed by her gusto. The haze outside his window made him queasy again. Paul was eying him closely in the rearview. "You missed one," Hector said.

"Four?" Fifi said.

"One and a half," the unlikely Ahmed answered.

"Thanks, Ahmed," Hector said. "Track one-point-five is official and nonofficial endeavors. That usually happens when the stakes are high. Like on the verge of wars. So there's a dire need to establish rapport before things spiral out of control." He glanced at the rearview mirror. Saint Paul's eyes were still watching him. "The Great Leap Forward, Baxter. Can you give your classmates a summary on that?"

Yubi purred over her husband's chest. His legs were warming up.

And Baxter produced the necessary contribution to the show.

But then Baxter went on, on his own. "But that's history. Now they're just like us, believe in some prosperity gospel."

And Kero—daftly—disagreed. "Big difference between the Western civilization and Asia, man. Asians are rich, but they have crazy beliefs. Ever heard of something called the Cultural

Revolution? They killed millions of people in the name of fighting capitalism."

A painful silence hovered on the bus. The drone of the engine was heard for a whole minute.

Then Paul said, "I'll correct you as politely as I can, Mr Mikhail. The Cultural Revolution was a political purge in China that happened nearly six decades ago. Are you, with all my respect, lost, or do you think that Asians are clones with the same culture and memory?"

Paul, then, pointed his finger at Yubi. "Is she Asian?" he quizzed the whole bus.

And when nobody replied, he quizzed Yubi in person, "Do you think you're Chinese, ma'am?"

But Yubi did not reply either.

———— ⚜ ————

The Ministry of Education was a simple, inviting cottage, circled by a circus of trees.

Trees with pink flowers dead on the ground like confetti.

Trees with slim branches yielding red horned fruit.

Trees with leaves looking like tassels.

And trees with mottled bark and balding crowns, the sight of which made you alarmed since they looked like leopards.

The place was near the bell-shaped bottom of the Pahang Strait. It was a malevolently meshy part of the island, too overpowered by greenery, very unlike the threadbare north of the Strait where the US Embassy sentineled the Fraternity Bridge.

An Indian lady in a miniskirt and sleeveless blouse came from inside the cottage and welcomed them. "Mrs Chu has been looking forward to meeting you. Sorry about the weather. Usually it's good in May."

"Yeah, yeah," scoffed Kero.

The classroom was equipped with tableted chairs and a projector. Mrs Chu—the Pulaui minister of education—was a lady who used a wheelchair and had a crown of glorious white hair. She was polite, but reserved.

As soon as they were seated, she began her lecture.

So excited was she to meet "the Arab visitors" finally. "It's time you saw how special you are to our national progress."

"Oh, my God, she's so nice." Fifi almost wept with emotion.

"Fei Guo was born in Malacca City." Chu danced a laser dot on the founder's face. Snow hairlets flanked the liver-spotted crown. A depressed Mongolian nose. Prominent cheek arches. Rawboned. Yet he had it, the dead devil, the gleam of genius, to the very end of his life. "His parents were real estate agents," Chu continued, "and he was very patriotic to his home country, Malaysia. In fact, we're not ashamed to say, his biggest dream was to become the leader of this great mosaic makeup of Malaysia." Chu ripped with her pointer the handsome face of another man, also in his dotage, but ebullient, fuller, bestowed with a cap of silvery hair. "But, alas, the powers of darkness caught up with Fei Guo. The current president of Malaysia was a political comrade of his. They fought over everything. Religion. Nationalism. Relations with the West. And in the end, they went their separate ways. One would become a great leader and a global example, the other a radical old man."

There, Ahmed raised a stiffened hand. "Miss. Miss. Please."

Hector heard Fifi hiss to Yubi, "This is going to be embarrassing."

"Yes?" the minister said.

"Why the anti-Islamic propaganda here, please? This man you don't like is great Islamic leader. He made Malaysia a great Asian Tiger and he is a good Muslim man we love and cherish with all our hearts. My wife are—is—and I, too, are Muslims. This is not respectful."

Yubi turned to give her husband an amused look, but Hector's seat was empty.

———— ❧ ————

In the foyer, Hector leaned on the French window and gazed at the geraniums and yellow orchids swimming in the light haze. His mind was racing.

He looked at his phone and checked the world clock. It was a quarter after noon in Pulau, which meant six-fifteen in Cairo. Today was a Thursday, though: AIMES's busiest day. Everyone struggled to finish the week's work before Friday, the Islamic weekend. And the dean was no exception. She had a regular staff meeting at nine. Yet even before that, she needed to be at her office to undersign a litany of papers: paychecks, budgets, claimed bills, content for the website, scripts for the weekly podcast... et cetera. She should be awake by now.

He tried Skype. Then her cell phone. When both went unanswered, he tried her home number.

A sleepy voice answered him. It was the husband. He said his wife had already left for work. Any messages, Hector?

Hector thanked him and apologized for waking him up, then disconnected quickly before the man inquired after his wife's niece.

Hector was about to give up on his plan and go back to the fray afoot in the classroom when he thought of a special person to make the recipient of his urgent call.

This one hardly ever slept, not out of busyness, but thanks to drudgery. Despite the tectonic instability of Egyptian politics, the American ambassador to Cairo was as hapless a bore as ever.

Jeff answered after the third Skype beep. "Hector," he cheered. "Howdy, buddy? So good to hear from you. What're you up to?"

"Jeff, listen. I need to ask you something."

"What?"

"A man I want you to run for me."

"A man? What man? Hey, Hickey, I don't do this type of work. Have you asked Lisa or Fab—"

"They can't know about this. I'm asking you for something private, off the books." Hector paused. "You don't have to do this if you don't want to."

Their booze binges. Their shisha and pool hangouts. The Ukrainian belly dancer and *Cabaret Lyaly* with its seamy buzz. His Excellency would say yes.

And His Excellency did.

"Thanks, bud," Hector said. "I owe you one."

"You owe me more than that. But anyway. Lay it all out. Who's the lucky guy?"

"He's the doctor on the AIMES campus. This guy is Russian. Afanasy Zharkov, that's his name." Hector spelled the first and last names of his suspect. "So here's how to go about this. What's her name, your cultural affairs specialist?"

"*Umm.* Nada."

"Yes, Nada. She'll make the call. Invite him to a conference or an exchange program. Someone just canceled, and the flight is next week. You need his passport right now to issue the visa. He'll fall for it. He's vain and will do anything to get noticed."

"So is this Zharkov dude a spy or what?"

"Nothing for sure, yet."

"He works for AIMES. That's dangerous, man. I have like five of my people taking courses there."

"That's why no one should know, till we know what we're dealing with, okay?"

"Another mortal to check off."

"Jeff, are you drinking?"

"This fella's name is funny. Afanasy Zharkov. The Mortal Cold-Weather Man. I know some Russian, you know, have always wanted to go to Eastern Europe. It's like a toy factory over there, Hickey. Even the sky is pink."

"I like how your imagination works. Do a good job, then. If this is what I think it is, you'll have a chip to bargain with the secretary of state."

"Any more orders?"

"That's enough for one day. Call me if you hit bone. Skype. No emails."

"All-righty." Jeff didn't sound very excited. "Where are you, anyway? I haven't seen you since Halloween. Your wife called me once. It was strange."

"Yes, Jeff." Hector sighed. "It is really strange."

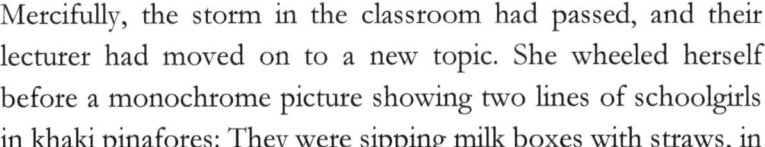

Mercifully, the storm in the classroom had passed, and their lecturer had moved on to a new topic. She wheeled herself before a monochrome picture showing two lines of schoolgirls in khaki pinafores: They were sipping milk boxes with straws, in the picture, and smiling.

"I'll make your road shorter," she said. "If you take a good look at the screen, you'll see a shy girl in the periphery. She's so scared of the flash her eyes are popping out. That girl is me. And this picture dates back to sixty-six, when our nation was just three years old. Phase one of our educational system was tagged *National Duty*. Getting an education then was extremely competitive. We didn't have many schools—where are the teachers, for one thing?—so we made a draw, a national lottery, and took the few luckies who won. Our country was starving, but we fed the children, their minds and their bellies. They were Pulau's only hope. Mind you, my generation was educated to serve, not to be happy, or to follow silly individualistic dreams. If our nation needed doctors, we became doctors. Engineers, so be it. Accountants, why not? Even if we hated it. We grew up to serve our nation, not to satisfy our desires. Up until..." She stopped, fingertips touching, head bowed in deep thought. "Up until you, Arabs, destroyed us."

"What the heck?" Fifi blurted out.

The lecturer responded by leveling the fingers of accusation—all ten—at Noman's helpless daughter. Then she moved her hands to include Ahmed and his wife, and finally the ashen-faced Kero: the Copt who rejected any Arabic association to his name.

"Your Yum Kippur War with Israel in seventy-three," Chu said, her face dark with incrimination.

"Nonsense!" Fifi cried. "What's that to do with your little island here?"

"The world is connected in ways only your professor can explain." The lecturer looked at Hector. "But I'll tell you our side of the tale, our humble side story. What started as a new conflict in the Middle East ended up in a global oil crisis. Arab Gulf states imposed an embargo on all flags they perceived to be supporting the Jewish state. We didn't care either way—we still don't, to be brutally honest—but we found ourselves in a very unfortunate situation. Oil prices had risen fourfold and our economy was not that strong. Officially we followed no world camp. We concocted our own political recipe: We borrowed from the Soviets their social programs and from the West their business model. But we weren't as rich as either camp. Other Asian Tigers were moving fast, but we were satisfied with our slow, steady progress. Come the global oil crisis, we were drowning in debt. Local businesses went bankrupt, many social programs were canceled, and many of us were falling into starvation again. So, unfortunately, Fei Guo had to make a choice. He picked the side we were accused of supporting. He chose to open our country to the United States."

Everybody was silent for a long moment. Paul, saintly, flaccidly, sat with one ankle overextended under his chair, barely breathing. Ahmed and wife were cross-hugging, as though this were some show at a movie theater. Kero looked detached, perhaps even bored. Fifi was frowning. Baxter coughed into his fist.

Only Yubi was watching with her full attention, the pulses in her neck visible. She looked slumped and somewhat distorted, as if melting down to the heat of the argument.

"That was the end of our silly dream of self-made glory," the Pulaui minister of education concluded. "Our educational system was remapped. Thus phase two, ladies and gentlemen, phase two! *Global Ambition.* We no longer seek to fulfill our families' needs, but the world's. And what does the world need from Pulau? A happy retreat. A new Cayman Island. A science-fiction city with kinky skyscrapers and robots for your selfies. A green utopia—yes—to make up for your environmental sins. Does it ever surprise you how good our English is? I dare you to hate us. You love Pulau not because it's in your own image, but in the image of your dreams."

————— ❧ —————

The Ministry of Foreign Affairs stood on top of Mount Victoria. The road up there was crowded by trees, narrow, and snakelike. But the apex was bald. Trees were either weeded out or never took root there.

There was no wall to the MFA, no need for one, and in fact it would have interfered with the location's benefit: The diplomats/spies overlooked the entire island from their Olympian HQ, CCTV cameras galore.

And other than Hector's group, there were no visitors. This was perhaps the only xenophobic foreign ministry on the planet.

The building itself was a patchwork of lumber and red brick. It had a cross-gabled structure, a high steep roof, and a distinct arch over a light rosewood door. It screamed *rustic* into the air, and it reminded Hector of the cottage of their doleful last visit.

"Tudor Revival," Paul said, sucking on his teeth. "Was a baron's house but we did a few renovations. We still have mice in the attic."

The security guards were not friendly. They combed them for contraband. And Baxter shined twice on their metal detectors: once for his leg plates, another for a Swiss knife he kept in his back pocket.

"I ain't killed no one." Baxter tried to have a laugh about it, but the guards were not amused.

"Weapons not permitted on premises," one guard said. "You can go to prison for this."

The guards insisted on an incident report, which Baxter and

his professor jointly undersigned. A guard bagged the knife and gave Hector a receipt for it, smiling oddly. "If he committed a crime, it's your crime now. Welcome to the Foreign Ministry."

They waited inside a conference room on the second floor. Through a couple of divided-lite windows they had a panoramic view of the dirty, dilapidated north coast of the island.

And after about half an hour, a man came through the door and announced, "His Excellency, Ambassador Tommy Lee, is unavailable."

Hector blew out a breath.

"Well then, that's that." Paul was about to rise from his chair, but Hector's hand was faster.

"Did you tell him it's Professor Kane and his students?" Hector asked the harbinger of insult.

The man—over seventy, South Indian, decked out in a vested charcoal suit—allowed a nod. He had informed His Excellency so, yes.

Hector stood up. "I must see Mr Lee. It is paramount. I can't leave without having this honor."

The man opened his lips, but Paul silenced him with a gesture of his hand. "Thanks, Siva. I'll walk Professor Kane to His Excellency's office myself. You go. Professor, please follow me."

Relief washed over Hector. He relaxed his fists in his pockets. His eyes widened. His heart broke into a steady rhythm.

The clouds enshrouding the Central Business District and, beyond it, the rest of The City were dirty and turbid, as seen through the divided-lite windows on his left. Overhead, wooden arches formed the underbelly of the hallway's ceiling. And to his right, between each white door and the next, a portrait of a former minister or ambassador smirked at him. All were men, Chinese, and mellowly aged. Pulau, after all, was a healthy work environment. The schism between agencies did not exist here, nor did the pyramidal hierarchy of labor common in the West. Departments overlapped brotherly. A chemist in the Environment Ministry, for instance, had written a proposal for a new defense strategy, as Director Zhang had bombastically related to Hector the other day. "It wasn't approved. Still, our man received a warm call from Fei Guo himself! Tell me, Mr Kane, how many calls have you received from your president? And your Canadian prime minister? What a shame. You should look into applying for a Pulaui residence, then. *Ha ha ha ha*. After all, you have fallen, like many men before you, for an Asian beauty."

How could he have been so stupid? The clues had been staring him in the face all along. And he, so insidiously blindfolded by his marital crisis, had fallen prey to his own wife!

Whoever you are, Yubi, I promise you, I *will* find out.

He followed Saint Paul through a double white door at the end of the hall.

17

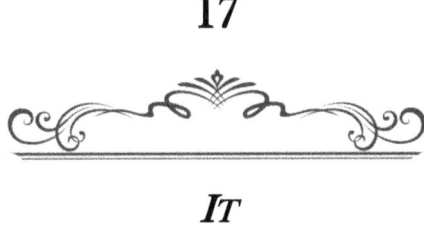

*I*T

Here's what I don't get," Ernest had said, bending his left leg under his thigh on the couch. "You've been dating for…?"

"Four months, more or less."

"And she's already moved in?"

"*Uh-huh.*"

"I call that 'lightspeed dating.' Certainly women are taking over. I'm happy for you, Hec. You're getting old and who knows."

"Oh, shut up."

"So, how was the trip?"

Hector summarized their recent trip to Upper Egypt. Yubi had taken maybe a thousand pictures posing before Abu Simbel, licking a ram's horn in Karnak, or ogling Ramses II's frown while hugging his giant stone legs. As for Hector, he didn't like Luxor very much. The barefoot children hounding him and his girlfriend with their "Give me a camera!" and "Give me money!" demands. The garbage piled up in close proximity to the great temples. The shameless men who devoured Yubi's bare arms and legs with their eyes. The tour guide's bad English. The waiters and boatmen demanding their *baksheesh* with the audacity of pirates. And Yubi's indifference to all of it.

Following their return, she buried herself in Egyptian music and drama. And she worked as an English tutor at St Mark's Cathedral in Abbassiya on Fridays. She often invited some of her students over, and she let them teach her all the juicy Egyptian expressions and recipes. She was happy. She told Hector "I love you" five times a day.

"Does she smoke or drink?"

"Doesn't even let me bring beer in."

"She's perfect, Hec."

"Yeah, isn't she?"

They shared a small joint. Afghani hash, the real deal. Fortunately, Ernest's apartment was close to the Zamalek hostel. He lived on the eleventh floor of a tower known as *Metro Tower,* named after a *Metro* supermarket on its ground floor. Hector would come here and toke whenever his schedule—and Yubi—allowed.

Hector passed the joint to Ernest, then relaxed and crossed his ankles on the table.

"What's the problem?" Ernest said, flipping through the channels.

"Who said there was one?"

"You look kinda obtuse."

"I'm just bored," Hector said.

"You can take your woman on another trip."

"Can't afford it."

"You're a professor and professors travel for free, Hec. Don't give me that."

"I'm still a novice at AIMES. They won't let me go anywhere. No conferences, no nothing. I'm stuck here with you."

"Grow some balls and go talk to your boss."

Hector changed the subject. "What's up with you? You don't look all right."

"You've rubbed it off on me."

"Let's go out." It was a warm and sunny day in January, something a Canadian would never fail to appreciate. "Let's go visit the Pyramids."

"*Hah*. Last time they accused me of idolatry. Not sure what they'll come up with this time."

Hector had totally forgotten. In the early stages of their friendship, the CIA had tasked Hector with taking bin Hakam's son to explore Cairo. So Hector contracted a local guide, who took them to the Giza Pyramids. And there, Ernest had lost his senses: He jumped over the barricade, pawed the Sphinx, and dropped on his knees and yelled to the Almighty God thanking Him for human creativity. They were promptly arrested by the Egyptian Tourism Police. And if it hadn't been for a timely call to Prince bin Hakam—who phoned the interior minister directly—they could have ended up in jail, or worse.

"So now what?" Hector puffed.

"You tell me." Ernest was still flipping through channels.

"She wants me to go see this silly play. I need an excuse. You're no good."

"Go see her play and don't be a jerk." Ernest toked, peering at the TV screen with a frown. "Strange, strange, very strange!"

"What's so strange?"

"Nothing on Bouazizi."

"Who?" Hector knew exactly who Bouazizi was, but he feigned ignorance.

"This guy who set himself on fire in Tunisia."

"Why's that bug you? Some people just get bored with misery."

Ernest looked at him with raised eyebrows.

"I know," Hector said guiltily.

"You grew up here. Why're you so mean? You remind me of this one prince I know. *Uh-unh*. Let me finish. Except that they aren't 'bored with misery.' They're smart, strong, and hopeful."

"Hopeful about what? The sun? They take it for granted. And they *hate* it. Even the Nile is drying up with those dams in Ethiopia. Romance is a disease. Hey, let's go swimming, how about that?"

"Where?"

"The Marriott."

"Hec, you're not taking this seriously."

"So, no swimming?"

"This is real." Ernest, wide-eyed, passed the joint back. "History is happening here in the Middle East. Tunisians are protesting, chanting, and it's super beautiful. I've seen it on CNN."

Hector finished off the joint then crashed the stub in the ashtray.

"But when you see nothing about that on Egyptian news," Ernest continued, "you know something is up."

Hector coughed.

"Some kids are planning protests in Egypt," Ernest said.

"*Huh,* good luck with that."

"Do you wanna bet?"

"On what?"

"Revolution, Hec."

The French campaign to Egypt was a bad idea. It lasted only

three years—1798-1801— and Napoleon's army soon retreated to fill what, for almost a century, would remain a post-revolutionary vacuum.

Some pundits, following the success of the Egyptian Revolution, would posit that it had been "the spirit of the French Revolution" that inspired the Egyptians. True. But it was this spirit also that bred the march-a-day-keeps-the-dictator-away ideal.

The Egyptian Revolutionaries, so much like their French role models, would prove very hard to please.

Hector would reflect on all this later, when the Egyptian Revolution would be a fact. But on the warm January 2010 day he'd left Ernest's apartment, mildly stoned, to meet his girlfriend, his association of the French and the Egyptians came from a totally different angle.

It just occurred to him, as he made for *Costa,* that in both cultures the café was a theater. Only in Paris, only in Cairo, a café was a cultural saloon, a hot date spot, a preacher's corner, a business conference room, and a political debate forum.

Costa was crowded. Pretty girls, as dainty as the macarons this café was famous for, giggled and chirped and smoked. A burst of strong sunshine came through the windows, and this made the girls squint, their fair skins blush. They must be talking about other men, Hector thought blithely. Some of them glanced at him, recognizing him from AIMES or the neighborhood. A few smiled.

One student of his waved a spaghetti arm. Elena. She would graduate this semester but hadn't found a job yet. He knew that from the man sitting across from her: a Subcontinental fellow who turned around and nodded conspiratorially at Hector. Professor Banerjee, from Law.

Hector ordered and cashed out, then waited at the counter

and chatted up his favorite barista, Hassan.

Hassan was a bald man with the gloomy air of someone mulling over the design of his own casket. Hector asked him how life was, Hassan, and Hassan said, in half-English, half-Egyptian, "My situation is good, *alhamdulillah*. How are you, *Ostaz* Hector?"

"I'm good, Hassan. Haven't seen you in a while. You told me you had two sons? How are they?"

"Good," Hassan said tersely. He finished Hector's mocha and came balancing a huge china on a saucer. Hector saw the barista's ingenious trademark: Hector's first name drizzled on the foam in *riqaa* Arabic. He rewarded the skilled artist with a twenty-pound note.

Hassan took the note and kissed it, then slipped it into his breast pocket.

Hector took his mug and turned to go. But then Hassan said, in slangy Egyptian, "Your honorable wife was here, by the way."

She was?

The sardonic barista winked a saggy left eye. They both knew Yubi was no wife, but *sahbah*—girlfriend—didn't strike the right tone.

"She was with another man," Hassan said. "And oh, what man, my *ostaz!* A two-ton dolphin, for all I care."

Hassan shook his head grievously, as if the dishonor were his own. He turned around to meet his next customer with a bright smile.

Hector thought about this piece of intel for a long time after he sat down. So Yubi had been here earlier. With another man.

What man? From Hassan's description, the man could be Afanasy Zharkov, that quack! But what did she meet him for? Today was Friday, the Egyptian weekend, so no work. And Afanasy lived very far.

He texted her. She did not reply. It was gaining on two p.m. and he'd been waiting for half an hour now. What took her so long?

Finally, she entered the café. She was smartly dressed in a tight lemony bodice with a square neckline. She had on a knee-length black skirt for contrast. Her petite feet were in her glittery golden flat shoes, which she'd purchased in Luxor, and she held a small black purse with both hands.

She was glowing, but she was not smiling.

"Hey." She lowered herself on the chair. "The play is starting soon. Are you ready?"

Hector had left home fully dressed, just in case Ernest turned him down, which Ernest had. Hector was wearing a light brown checkered suit with a cream shirt. He'd availed himself of Ernest's Cigar perfume and some mints to mask the stench of the weed.

He looked at her pale smooth neck and questioned if she wouldn't be cold later on in the evening.

"I'll use your jacket," she said simply. She'd fallen into this flirtatious practice ever since she'd moved in. Her facial expressions betrayed no flirtation whatsoever, though.

"What's the play about?" he asked.

"It's about this medieval castle and the king dies and nobody wants to accept it. His body rots and they keep him there and turn things around so they don't have to get his signature on anything. So strange. But it's a good play, got many good reviews. One of the guys I taught English to at the cathedral actually wrote it. He gave me free tickets."

"How do you know it's a good play? You hardly know any Arabic."

She rolled her eyes—there was a case of her overusing the kohl—and said, "Why are you arguing? It's gonna be okay."

"If you say so."

"Have you paid yet?" She turned and smiled to the same barista who'd backstabbed her less than an hour ago.

"Let's go." Hector rose.

They caught a taxi in a minute. Yubi was silent, leaning on her window with open eyes.

Hector looked at the dirty overcrowded streets. "So what did you do?"

"…Huh?"

"What did you do this morning?"

"Not much. TV and such."

The traffic thickened. The car stopped. Out his window Hector saw a little girl covered head-to-toe in a brown *khumar*. The girl knocked on his glass and pantomimed to sell her jasmine necklaces. Hector rolled down his window and handed the girl a ten-pound note for two.

He offered the jasmine to Yubi, but Yubi shook her head.

"I'll take them," the driver said. He slung them over the rearview mirror from which he regularly checked on Yubi.

"We'll talk later, okay?" Yubi said. "I just wanna enjoy myself today. Can we? Can we do that?"

And she broke out in tears.

———

Cairo National Theater was located in Attaba, a neighborhood of cheap retail stores and booksellers. Despite the cultural significance, Hector had deemed the neighborhood unsafe and shouted at the driver to take a different, less crowded route.

Yet the play was more popular than Hector had anticipated. Their taxi, inevitably, got stuck in the lineup before the gate. Hector paid then held Yubi's hand and they got out from his side.

They walked quickly. And they weren't two steps into the theater's yard when a voice called, unsteady with laughter, "Oh, my God-ness, is this Mr Hector? Wait, wait, I swear to God we missed you!"

Hector turned and, to his alarm, it was the State Security officer whom he had approached during the Embassy incident a few months earlier. He gripped Yubi's hand and doubled his speed.

"Who's that?" Yubi asked. "Slow down, you're running!"

"Know the devil? This chap is his silly cousin." He undid the second button on his shirt.

"'Chap'?"

"Where are your friends?"

In the taxi she'd told him she was rendezvousing with a couple of friends.

Now they were introduced on the mezzanine of the theater. Georgette and her husband, Ihab. Georgette was a bubbly, big-eyed woman in a shimmery black dress, and Ihab a shy bespectacled man in a full gray suit. Both were six feet tall and considerably meaty. Ihab shook Hector's hand with a slight bow, a gold watch glinting on his right wrist. "Good to meet you," he said in English.

A beautiful girl ushered them to their seats. They had perfect spots: front center. Ihab took the rightmost seat and his wife sat on the other side, beside Yubi. Their decorum, it appeared, did not allow for separating the *ajanib* couple.

Ihab flicked his big digits and said, "We know the writer. He is my colleague."

"And what do you do exactly, *Ostaz* Ihab?"

Hector's fluency seemed to take the man by surprise. He jerked his head and stared at him. "I've never met a single *ajnabi* who speaks Arabic without an accent."

"I grew up here. Long story. But anyhow, you told me you were…?"

"I'm an obstetrician." There was softness to Ihab's mien, a melting of the early shyness. He looked over at his wife. "So far, I guess. We are leaving for Canada soon. I'm not sure what I'm going to do there. Seventy-five thousand dollars we've put down so far. Fifteen each. We have three kids, and they all want to get out of here. Sooner or later this country is going down, Hector. The Islamists are sooner or later coming."

A wave of applause cut their conversation off. On the stage a small man walked slowly into the spotlight. He wore a full tuxedo and introduced himself as the playwright and a part-time surgeon. People laughed. He talked briefly about the play and where it'd come from. It was a loose adaptation of a dream he'd had, he said, and he had pitched it to the director while excising the latter's ingrowing toenail. People roared with laughter. Someone shouted he must have drugged the poor man, and the playwright-surgeon replied a doctor had to make a living, hadn't he? They laughed again, the surgeon himself snorting. Applause. Then he carried on. He heaped praise on the director, who was the real star of the show. He hoped people would like his play and bowed out.

As the lights faded, the obstetrician nudged Hector's forearm and whispered, "Ah, forgot to tell you, *bel-monasba.*

Congratulations. May he be raised in your fortune."

———— ⋅⋅ ————

And later that night—standing on a lake of broken china, engulfed by her howls of false rejection—he popped the question.

Next Sunday, they were husband and wife.

———— ⋅⋅ ————

Above Wayne's cradle they hung mobile toys of cowboys and Indians. "Wayne" after—well—Gretzky. So much for a father who blamed his own father for his namesake: Toe (Hector) Blake.

Wayne had his mother's obsidian and, yes, Asian eyes. Plus Yubi's fair skin. On the dad side he got Hector's V-shaped hairline, his dimples, and Rocky's bumpy nose and large ears.

Ernest rocks the cradle. "My future drinking buddy! What's the Indians and cowboys for, Yubi?"

"John Wayne," she says definitely.

"She doesn't like the name," Hector says, reading the local newspaper on the couch. "She thinks it's too *hokey.*"

"It's a creepy name for a kid, to be honest." Ernest takes Yubi's side.

Hector contains them both with a dubious glance. "We were all once kids, kid."

He resumes reading his newspaper but senses movement. He turns back to see Yubi breastfeeding the infant with only a half-rotation toward the hall, while the prince's son—a foot at least over her—smiles at them both.

———— ❧ ————

Yubi, a devout nurse, insisted on breastfeeding. Breastfeeding as you know baby immunizes the baby 'gainst so and so, boosts his brainpower, and it's all scientific, you know.

Yeah, yeah, yeah, yeah. Hector would marvel at her exactness. Isn't that a ritual of becoming-human or whatever you call it, that religion of yours?

It's human-becoming! And it's not a religion. Some guy who hated her professor at Loyalist College said it was a religion, but it is not true.

"So what is it, then, sweetie pie?"

She's not a child. Don't sweetie-pie her. And you know exactly what's what, Hector baby. You act dumb and forgetful, but you fake it and very badly at that. You're a very bad liar.

Yeah, yeah. (In their first month of shacking-up, they'd gone to war over this "human-becoming" philosophy of care. He knew she wouldn't let it drop.)

"So tell me," he says. "You think it's human?"

"Oh my God. *It*?"

"Pronouns don't mean nothing."

"No, you're dangerous. Pronouns are everything!"

"Okay, okay, cool down."

"I am. Cooled down."

"Right." With a murmur, he downs his sherry.

"And *he* is, yes. *He* is human. I get what you're driving at."

"I'm not fit to drive anywhere in this condition."

She rolls her eyes and bares her left breast, the one without the nipple fissure. She's on antibiotics and Tylenol though she skips the Tylenol when she can because she doesn't want anything to go through to her baby in the milk. Her migraines are also getting more frequent and worse. "He's more human than you," she says.

"Did you ask *his* opinion about your holy milk, then?"

"I'm doing what's best for him. I want him to have a better life than both of us."

Hector pauses. "What's wrong with *your* life, Yubi?"

She considers that with a philosophical frown. Then she turns away, the baby suckling on her gorged bosom. "I'm just a mother now," she says in ultimate wisdom.

———— ⁂ ————

Human-becoming or becoming-human, it's the same loony fustian, thinks Hector. But withal, it takes the father a long time to admit that his son *is* a fellow human being—not an *it*.

Throughout Yubi's pregnancy, and months after, a funny devil takes possession of Hector. He becomes convinced that his baby is but the embodiment of the Egyptian Revolution.

It starts with Yubi's injury on the horrible *Friday of Rage*. And ever since, Hector is quick to tie any pregnancy or growth milestone to the riots, the killings, the precarious politics of the region his son would be born in.

Morning sickness! Hector exults. *It* is sickened by us, by America's president. His "closely monitoring the situation," his "deep concern." *Huh huh he-he-he*. Do you think anybody is buying that? They think we're the devil. Who buys from the devil, honey? Unless your soul is worth something!

Fetal heartbeats—*ddup-ddup-ddup*—are Mubarak's three

speeches. The first *ddup* is forcible, imposing. Mubarak, that lousy aged lion, declaims his authority, warns of "a fine line... between freedom and chaos," sucks you into his presence instantly.

Second *ddup*... softer, like a harp's note. Mubarak says he ain't running for president no more. *Blah blah blah blah.* People are softening: They love the old rascal. He's a good egg, after all, a war hero, one foot in the grave. So, let him be.

Third *ddup*... Dr Ihab swipes the sonar piece, the beat loses its volume but is sharper. And this, baby, is Mubarak's final speech. Broken. Almost scared. With an aggressive patina to it. Definitely insecure. He is haughty as hell and refuses to leave. Goodbye dear old President Mubarak. Say hi to Uncle Ben Ali in Saudi when you get there. Oh, you're staying? Cool. It's prison then. Don't worry. Best room service in the republic!

Now the baby is kicking fast, Hector. Why is he torturing me so? Hector hymns, Lord, Lord, are you truly in this womb? Yubi says, "What?" And he genuflects at her feet, kissing and licking them, rises to stick his auricle to her navel. Yes. Verily I hear the miracle. Lord, now lettest thou thy servant depart in peace. "What're you saying?" Yubi is pale, glaring at him. But Hector laughs and stands up, and she is slightly relieved. "What is the matter?" she asks. "Don't you know it?" he says. "Know what?" "Sweetie"—he laughs again—"you should know better, being the Mother. Today, Bin Laden is dead."

Hector. Hector. My water just broke. "*It* is paying you back," he admonishes her in the elevator, where it is happening. "You shouldn't have insisted on going out," he adds. Has he lost his mind? she shouts at him, pushing herself to the elevator's wall for some reason. He must get her to the hospital right now. So they go back down, Hector making calls on his cell phone, Yubi sobbing and freaking out. The hostel is gloomy, lights are off, the streets of Zamalek devoid of humans. Everyone is in Tahrir Square, revolting. *Friday of Revolution First,* they have dubbed it— way too many Fridays—and Hector and Yubi have actually just returned. Tahrir was congested, Islamists everywhere, the Muslim Brotherhood by far the most organized force there: its scouts shouting: *"We want them veiled! Veiled! Veiled!"* So sad and Yubi—headstrong as she is—had wanted to see for herself, dismissing his "pedantics" about the natural course of any revolution in history.

It has a way of educating us about the shenanigans of fate. It's inevitable. The demagogues will prevail, whichever flavor they come in. It's a mandatory lost century. It happened in France, China, Russia, you name it. Egypt isn't the exception, he has preached to her. Doesn't your baby speak to you as *it* does to me?

And when Ernest finally arrives to drive them to Dr Ihab's hospital, Yubi clings to Ernest's chest, nearly rips his shirt in agony.

"You'll be okay, Yubi." Ernest is so sweet to her. "I know a shortcut. We'll make it okay."

Hector sits in the front seat glumly.

Baby doesn't feed. They go to see goddamned Afanasy in Masr el-Gedida, the upscale neighborhood far east. The great clinician has set up an illegal clinic in his fancy-dancy big empty flat. He was a pediatrician back home, he claims, not revealing where "home" actually is. A resident pediatrician, Afanasy backtracks. A "promising" resident of pediatrics. An applicant for a residency in pediatrics. But he is a good doctor in pediatrics nonetheless. Hector stares at *it*, the baby, and succumbs to *its* will. Baby is quiet in Afanasy's hands. At three months, Wayne weights twelve pounds and has a developed rooting and stepping reflexes. Wayne does not roll over or grasp objects nearby. "Bad sign." Afanasy shakes his big head. "Bad nutrition for the baby. I give you good program for milk in the boobo. Baby throat is inflamed can't suck. I inject in the baby excellent antibiotic. Come to me every day and I inject. Discount for my friends."

And when they are home, Hector thinks about the connection between Wayne's illness and the massacre of two dozen Copts on this same day. Coincidence? No way. Wayne, you are the light of this world.

Baby teethes, gets sick often—massacres and riots continue.

But Wayne is no longer *it*.

Screw the divine portents. Revolution, you go to the devil where you belong.

My son will never suffer again

He will no longer carry your sins.

———— ❧ ————

And suddenly, almost deliberately, *he* was gone.

18

PLAY

W hat're you doing here?" Hector frowned at the unlikely figure seated behind the desk.

"Sit down, Mr Kane." Fred Zhang said. "Please."

Behind Fred's head was a window. Far south, in the Central Business District, Hector made out a handset-shaped tower buffeted by roily whirlwinds. Yet it stood fast, this giant handset: The whirlwinds, spiced by the ash of a great man, only made the rooftop flags flutter faster. And there was a huge, gilded sign on top:

AIIB

Asian Infrastructure Investment Bank, China's new investment leviathan, which wouldn't open for another year.

Pulau had crafted for its Chinese fetus the zaniest cradle in the history of finance. No wonder there, Hector decided. The Pulauis were very good at choosing their mates. They wouldn't have survived the Oil Crisis, the Asian Financial Crisis, or the more recent Global Financial Crisis without this essential survival skill.

"Mr Kane…?"

Hector surrendered to the chair.

The MED director was dressed in a smart dark blue suit. He was tied, pocket-squared, and perfumed—a rarity among Pulauis. Fred was the eldest and the most seasoned of the MED diplomats. Although Hector never admitted it even to himself, he slightly trusted him.

"How can we help you?" A bureaucratic smile, the director's knotty digits making a pigeon chest on the blotter as he tipped forward, elbows on the chair's armrests.

Hector shook his head. "*Uh-unh*. I didn't ask for you, and I've no business with you here. I wanna see *him*."

"That is true, sir," Paul elaborated, still standing. "He has asked for a meeting with Ambassador Lee."

Fred balled his right fist and covered his lips with it, listening to his man's candor with raised eyebrows. Then his eyes flitted toward the door. Paul got the message and left immediately.

At almost the exact moment, Siva came through a side door with a silver tray bearing a bottle of Hennessey and two overturned flute glasses. Once all was set on the desk, Siva repaired to wherever he came from, and Fred rose.

"Let's relax and be good friends first." Fred began pouring the cognac into the flutes. "Life is too short to hold grudges, someone very smart once said that."

"Who? Your dodgy boss?" Hector took his flute.

Fred walked to a solid bookcase obliterating the wall behind Hector. "Do you read, Mr Kane?" His left holding the drink, Fred's right hand pawed the backbones of many volumes in the bookshelves. Till it parked on a certain white leather-bound book. "This isn't a rhetorical question. Sometimes people in ivory towers forget that they must read like those down below."

"Says the man on top of the mountain," Hector scoffed.

"Exactly. That's why we never stop reading. Because we can't lose touch with the common man. It's very tempting in our trade to mistake oblivion for ignorance."

"Are you saying *I* am ignorant?"

"Reading isn't for the weakhearted. It takes courage. Sometimes your whole reality can shatter."

"I have people waiting for me in the other room. Tell me something I don't know already."

"I will, I'll show you," Fred said energetically.

Hector replenished his flute. "What is it? Snepp? Agee? Philby? You think you're very mysterious, Freddie, don't you?"

"Not at all. We're being as transparent with you as you aren't with yourself, Mr Kane."

"Oh, how gorgeous!"

Fred returned to the desk with the white book. He placed it, so reverently, between Hector's elbow and the silver tray. Hector looked at the thing. The title was in gilded Chinese. And that made him giggle. "And I thought I was drunk."

Fred turned over two pages and landed his neat fingertip on an English word that stood out against the jaundice of the blank page:

PHARAOHSTAN

Obviously this was a Chinese copy of Mr Kero's historic foray into the literary-verse, his orphan play, his winning lottery ticket by virtue of which he not only had lost his family, his medical career, and his religion, but had become a tramadol junkie too.

"Is this a bad joke or something?" Hector said.

"On the contrary. This is a matter of utmost seriousness. Especially for you. You, of all people. You have suffered a lot because of this play."

"Have I?"

"It cost you a marriage—one you never had to be in, in the first place."

"Get this jabberwocky out of my face!" Hector snarled.

"But it didn't stop there. Did it, Mr Kane?"

Hector pushed the book with his elbow. The tray, with its cargo, tumbled down to the floor.

The Hennessey bottle smashed on the floor, the silver tray clanged.

And in an instant, Siva materialized at the side door.

"Problem?" the good servant inquired sharply, one hand on the doorjamb, the other on the handle in case he was to lock Hector and the director away. (A wave of guttural banter—Cantonese?—came bursting from the room behind him.)

Fred waved him away, then looked down at the mess at his feet. "It pains us to see what you have become, Mr Kane. Maybe alcohol wasn't the right treat for you. We are to blame. Your soul is in great distress."

"What are you, the Dalai Lama? Take me to see your boss. One word from His Excellency will heal my soul."

Fred avoided the glass with a wide sidestep and pulled Hector up by his shoulders. He walked him away from the shattered glass, saying, "But before we do that, would you like to know a secret?"

"What secret?" Hector shrugged him off and stared at him.

"It starts with a Muslim imam you once killed."

"Goodness, aren't you raving!"

"By proxy. Remember a Mukhabarat officer named Mourad *Bey?*"

Hector was silent.

Fred was now leaning his back on the wall. Above his head were two framed photos of Fei Guo and his son and successor, the incumbent prime minister of Pulau, Richard Fei.

"Mourad *Bey,*" Fred said, "from the Egyptian Secret Service, al-Mukhabarat. Mourad *Bey,* Mr Kane, who is blessing us with his visit today—thanks to you."

Hector wanted to cry, to shut this man up, but his voice was gone.

"Mourad *Bey.*" Fred pocketed his fists and walked slowly to the cornered CIA agent. "Mourad *Bey,* a man you smuggled across our border, *brought under our very roof.* Mourad *Bey.* Or shall we call him *Ahmed al-Shatby?*"

———※———

The director's face was now two inches from Hector's. He breathed sweet cognac and victory.

Hector felt defeated and groggy. "Why are you telling me this?"

"Because you don't know the full truth, yet."

"What makes you think so? After all you said, I must be the shiftiest spy on the planet."

Fred smiled sardonically. "If that's what you think, then tell me one thing. Where do you think our *bey* is right now?"

"In the room where I left him. Under your 'very roof.'"

Fred's smile broadened. He shook his head. "No, sir, he isn't. But before I show you how oblivious you are, I have one question, Mr Kane."

"'Agent,' if you don't mind."

"We'll come to that later." Fred paced about the room, holding his chin with his fingertips and looking at his shoes. "Why did you let him use you? You knew he was up to no good. We can't believe a man with your experience could fall for a junior Mukhabarat officer so easily."

Hector shrugged. "Is that it? Your big question?"

"It's one piece of the puzzle."

"Well, he'd changed his name—or it was his real name, I don't know—and he came asking for admission to AIMES. By that time, many State Security officers did everything they could to avoid the purge. The Revolution had made them vulnerable. Some of them were even hunted down for sport by the Revolutionaries. And now with the Muslim Brotherhood in power, he either had to convert or to flee the country. Well, Mourad—or Ahmed—later actually married into a Brotherhood family. But before that, he asked me to help him get an education. He'd left the police for good, he said, and was looking for a fresh start. So I... believed him. At least at first I did."

"And then what happened?"

"I noticed he wasn't paying attention in class, wasn't doing his assignments, and was dodgy and lied a lot. This wasn't someone looking for a fresh start. This was—"

"A cover," Fred provided.

Hector nodded emphatically.

"Did you know he'd moved to Mukhabarat from State Security?"

"Not really. But I suspected it. He's been very keen on

buddying up with Westerners on campus—especially army and Company guys."

"And why didn't you report that to the Company?"

Hector shrugged with his whole body. "You can't just accuse someone of being a spy. You need evidence for that."

Fred shook his head and grinned, still pacing the room. "You're lying. But I'll bridge the gap for you. Because you weren't even an active agent at the time."

Hector daggered the MED director with a suspicious look. "How do you know about all that?"

"I told you. We read. We read a lot."

Hector decided to accept this ultimate defeat. The Pulauis knew far more than he'd expected. Now he should avail himself of this wide knowledge.

Hector turned and picked the white volume from the floor. The book was wet with cognac. He shook it before the Pulaui director and demanded, "I gave you my piece of the puzzle. Now it's your turn. So tell me, Freddie, why is this trash in your library?"

"Who do you think wrote this, Mr Kane?"

"You're the bookworm."

Fred joined his hands and touched them to his jaw. "The story behind this play is very strange, Mr Kane. More of a fairytale. Here's our version of it. Once upon a time, there was a policeman. An SSP officer, someone we both know. Only he had an eccentricity, a little vice: He wrote fiction. Someday, he thought, he would sit right next to Balzac, Mahfouz, or maybe Márquez. But he wasn't as good. In fact, he wasn't good at all writing long-form fiction. All that came out of his pen were silly symbolic plays, and a few short stories of the magical realism persuasion. Nothing Orwellian, but still dangerous to publish in a police state like Egypt. So he gave up on his literary dream.

Until one day…" And here Fred released a pneumatic chuckle. "This is a very creative policeman, let me assure you. Until one day, a strange idea popped into his head: What if—he thought— what if I gave my writings to my prisoners? The Egyptian State Security cells are never empty, as you're well aware. Insulting national symbols, violating public decency, blasphemy, you name it. So our desperate author gave his first manuscript to a journalist accused of defending Israel. It was an erotic play, and it didn't work. The next, a Kafkaesque retelling of Egypt's nineteen fifty-two coup d'état, didn't fly either. Thus the third, Mr Kane. A prophecy of Mubarak's downfall. A medieval play where the king dies and his body rots without leaving his throne. This one he gave to a Coptic doctor brought in on charges of creating a silly Facebook page." Fred halted, hands in pockets, and looked at his pale guest. "Do you know how the story ends, Mr Kane?"

By now Hector thought he'd seen it all—unfolding, synapsing, making belated sense in his brain—so he nodded gloomily.

But the Pulaui managed to surprise him once again. "No, sir, you don't. The story is still happening."

Fred walked back to the bookshelves. He wormed his right hand inside the very hole made by *Pharaohstan*'s absence. A soft click was heard, then the bookcase swung open like a thoracic cage in an open-heart surgery.

Hector went to check the entrails of this chest.

Niched inside was a monolith-like server glittering in greens and oranges. Left of it, a triptych of security screens stood on a chest-high black table. Each screen was divided into rectangles corresponding to the different cameras—visible or hidden— dominating the MFA inside out—washrooms included.

And it was in one of the washrooms that Hector's eyes happened to land first. He eyed a scene he'd long suspected. A waistline washroom camera—probably camouflaged as a tap sensor—panned four toilet stalls: Three were empty. But in the fourth Fifi's Gypsy brown curls bobbed up and down above the door. Underneath, a pair of black Converse tiptoed with every thrust.

Whether Fred had noticed this or not, Hector wasn't sure. The MED director had stepped back to allow his CIA guest a liberal view of their voyeuristic accomplishments.

At length, Fred came and tapped his pinkie on a rectangle at the top of the middle screen. "Here, sir. Look here."

"What's that mean?"

"Judge for yourself." Fred double-tapped the rectangle to maximize it into a full-screen audio feed.

On the same security desk where Hector had cosigned the Swiss knife incident report, Ambassador Tommy Lee is now seated. Lee, young-old, is grizzly but fit, with very few wrinkles. He is in casual dress: a patterned turquoise button-up hanging, untucked, over ink-blue jeans. On his right wrist is a Bollywood leather-and-beads bracelet. To his right earlobe clings a golden earring resembling—in striking exactitude—the topography of Pulau, the teardrop island.

Across from Lee the crowns of two African men—though only one of them, the one born outside Africa, identifies as such—face up to a low ceiling camera.

Baxter and Mourad *Bey*.

Baxter and Ahmed.

"You're delusional," says Lee in his crisp, traceless accent, upbeat and cocky. "Modern Egypt isn't so old. Even China is by and large a child of the present. Do you wish to tell me Ramses, Saladin, Nasser, and Mubarak are leaders of the same country? *Huh!* Shame on you, Mourad *Bey*. I was expecting more from you."

"I'll repeat what I said in a language you can understand." Mourad leans forward for emphasis, his elbows resting on his knees. He enunciates in far better English than he's ever let on. "The Muslim Brotherhood do not share our history or culture. The year is nearly over, and our leaders have exhausted their stock of patience. The Muslim Brotherhood *will* go."

"Let me share a fact of life with you, pal," Baxter says. "Democracy doesn't just—*poof*—go. It stays. It might sting in the beginning, but it grows and grows and it becomes something big and beautiful. We in Washington will support you only as such, a democracy. And as a representative of the Central Intelligence Agency, I can assure you, the Brotherhood *are* staying no matter what your army folks think."

"Why not tell your superiors to focus on their own internal problems, Baxter?" the Egyptian returns. "This is so pointless."

Baxter pleads with the Pulaui mediator, tittering, "Do us some translation Mr Lee. Please!"

"Who guarantees a safe transfer of power?" Lee inquired of the Egyptian.

"Whoa, whoa," Baxter interjects. "Who said anything about a transfer?"

"Our tanks on the streets," the Mukhabarat officer answers.

"How about the Brothers, won't they fight back?" Lee asks.

"Fight who? It was the people who brought them to power. The people can anytime take it back."

"So what're the tanks for?" Lee asks.

The Egyptian leans back and scratches his beard. "Let's call it 'insurance.'"

Baxter jumps back in. "You're scared of your own people, admit it."

"If I may ask," Lee says to Mourad, "what's your personal opinion about all this? Are you seriously for a new military regime in Egypt? Don't you know where that will lead?"

"Do you?" the Egyptian scoffs.

"I do," Lee says gravely. "Not a good place."

"We don't come from a good place, Mr Lee," the Egyptian says. "Egypt is a forty-degree-Celsius navel of hell. It's rich, but an incredibly poor country. We have been ravaged by every conqueror on earth. Do you think we want more? Please. Let me finish. The SCAF—those military assholes—*are* us. And we are them. Our flour is in our dough, as our people say. But the Muslim Brotherhood? No, no, no. They don't belong."

The mediator turns to the CIA officer. "Rebuttal, Agent Simmons?"

Baxter stands up and looks down on his Egyptian classmate. "Enjoy your trip, bro. Your SCAF won't be there for long."

And Baxter is about to exit the scene, when Ahmed calls: "Is that what Hector thinks, too? As per your request, I have not approached him. But I think he's a better negotiator than all of you."

Baxter flashes his trademark grin. "Well, there's a reason why he's not here. I'll see you upstairs, bro."

Hector flopped on his chair. "You want to buy me. That's what you guys always do. Buy, buy, buy. Buy anything. Land. Franchises. People."

Fred rocked a little in his swivel chair. "Look around you, Mr Kane. As you can see, we're not big on buying. We're a do-it-yourself kinda people."

"So what's your deal?"

Fred simpered, the ridges in his face deepening. "You came asking for answers. That video was your tester."

"I'm not leaving without the full product."

"The product you think you want isn't going to appeal to you. It's not even valid, at this point."

"I decide what's valid for me and what's not." Hector looked sharply at him. "Who do you really work for? The Chinese?"

"Aren't you a typical Westerner," Fred said sarcastically. "Imagine me asking you if you work for the Canadians."

"That's not the same thing."

"Why not? They're two different countries. Aren't they? Does Canada sneak spies south of the border? Would it? Does it need to? Why yes and why no? Cogitate about this, and when you see the answer, you'll understand our situation."

Hector was agitated and, in effect, bedumbed.

"Asia is a very complex continent, Mr Kane. Identity doesn't always mean nationality or loyalty here."

"I'm Irish-Armenian-Lebanese-Canadian-American. Don't you think I *know* that?"

"But you're luckier than us." Fred fell into a morose pause. "You get to choose who's dominant in the Western hemisphere to plead fealty to. In Pulau, we have a problem. Most of us are of Chinese descent. But not *all* of us identify with China. In fact, most Pulauis have somewhat a negative view of the country known today as 'the People's Republic of China.' But we are

Chinese after all, and there's nothing we can do about it."

"And where does that leave you?"

"Division, if we're lucky enough. But you need well-rounded factions to divide. And we don't have that."

"So what do you want from me?"

"Your Agency has given up on you. Even if they promote you to chief deputy, they'll still keep you in the dark. You're like an old bike in the basement. Your best shot is to be with other bikers."

"But I'm not for sale, thank you."

Fred shook his forefinger. "A spy is a spy is a spy. Once you know so much, it's impossible to accept being left out. I know so much about you, professor, perhaps more than you know about yourself. For instance, you *had* a respected day job, but it wasn't enough. Our offer is simple. We do services for big powers. We help them meet the people they want. We organize liaisons, so to speak. We bet on people. And right now, *Agent Kane*," Fred enunciated, "we are betting on you."

───── ❧ ─────

"Oh, man, I forgot my knife," Baxter reported on the bus.

"But that's what you went down for," Yubi said, surprised, "to get it."

"The security office was closed," Baxter said.

Hector remained silent. He had reclaimed the knife himself but had been ignoring Baxter ever since they'd left the MFA.

A conundrum split his mind: Why would Langley go to the trouble of concealing so much information from him—when he would be promoted soon?

The only logical explanation was that Agent Kane was not

an "old bike." He was in danger. Leaking. Compromised. And Langley, in its infinite wisdom, had opted for a quarantine until they eradicated the problem.

Which meant—they must know about Yubi.

19

SCARE

For lunch, they chose a place called *Lau Pa Sat*. It was a big hawker center tucked away in a crease in time, between Chinatown and the Central Business District, the glorious past and the rewarding present.

The place was teeming with people and suffused with food odors and a haze miasma. But in a way, it was real, a reprieve from the government buildings they'd bustled in the whole day. Their fellow lunchers weren't super-friendly, over-the-top, smarmy as most officials were. Nor were they bitter like Mrs Chu, or unreasonably aggressive like Mr Li—the driver—and whatever-his-name, the concierge at the res. In this very human place, people were spontaneous. Which was all Hector needed.

Hector noticed a long queue before one of the stalls. He piloted his group there and asked one of the men what this stall sold. The man shrugged and said, "I don't know. It's busy so I wait here." Another man, who had his entire family lined up in front of him, said he didn't know either: He'd been ordering food at another stall when he'd seen this long queue.

"We'll join the bandwagon, then," Hector declared.

Paul nudged at his scapula.

"What?"

"I'll go reserve the seats," Paul said.

"You're our guide, for Christ's sake. Stay with us. No one can read a word of this Mozambican." Hector referred to the glowing overhead menu, all of which was in Chinese.

"They speak Portuguese in Mozambique, sir," the Christian spy corrected him politely.

"Aren't you a straightforward fellow."

But after they'd gotten their orders, Hector felt he owed Paul an apology. It was impossible to find a vacant table.

People had used all sorts of stuff—menus, empty bottles, chopsticks, masks, shoes even—to reserve the entirety of the ironing-board-like wooden benches spread under the cast-iron dome. So Hector and his group had to wait out a septet of suited salarymen, seated at the distant end of the court, before they got to taste their choices of the exotic food.

"In Pulau," Paul explained, hunched over his pork ribs soup—which made Zainab wrinkle her nose with disgust—"we have a culture known as *kiasu*. We're not as proud of it now as we once were. But anyway, sorry for the hassle."

Fifi, radiant, her hair collected in a loose ponytail, her hip glued to Kero's, said, "Yeah, I think I know what you're talking about. You compete over every little thing. Daddy likes it. He says Arabs need just this *kiasu* to prosper."

"We're not Arabs," Kero objected, fishing for the beef pieces in his Shanghai noodles with a pair of defiant chopsticks.

This remark gave Zainab an excuse to dislodge her eyes from Saint Paul's baleful pork. "Maybe *you* aren't. But we all *alhamdulillah* are."

"Does 'all' include Baxter and Yubi?" Kero returned

combatively.

There, her overzealous hubby stepped in. "Egypt is an Arab country. If you don't like Arabs, leave!"

"What do you think I'm doing here?" Kero muttered, shaking his head.

Hector busied himself admiring the beauty of the overhead gazebo. A great Chinese lantern dangled from the center. Around it, five long-armed steel fans spun to the aesthetic standard of slow motion.

It was hypnotic.

He heard Saint Paul steer the argument away.

"Your father is mistaken, Miss Noman," Paul said. "*Kiasu* isn't about competing over trifles. It literally means 'fear of losing out.' It runs the gamut from food stalls to test scores to marriages. It's been a driving force for excellence in Pulau for decades. It makes sense. Pulau, after all, has no assets but its citizens. We aren't like you. Nile and Pyramids and old temples. We are only *us*."

"You have King George Port," Fifi proposed.

"You mean *the Bay?* We seldom call it 'Port.' Yes, that's our lucky charm, passed down from the British." (A distant tower clock chimed once.) "There would be no Pulau without the Bay. And yet, we are not the Bay. It doesn't even turn in enough revenues anymore."

"Why not?" Yubi asked.

"Asia is teeming with big ports. Two in Malaysia, and not a bad one in Thailand. There's also Saigon. And Manila, too. We're lucky if we get five million containers a year now. That's not much, but we need that to keep the Bay open. Our main revenues now come from services industries. Mainly banks and tourism."

Hector scanned his table. Zainab was struggling not to hate

246 . *The Haze*

her black chicken soup, whereas her husband took conservative bites of his vegan noodles. Kero was still trying to tame his chopsticks. Fifi had chosen Pulau's trademark, the Hainanese chicken rice. But she expressed her distaste for the ginger-garlic-chili spicing by fishing for the poached chicken chops inside.

Paul noticed this and said, "That's called *grave-digging*. It brings bad luck."

"What?" Fifi almost laughed. "That's ridiculous."

"Paul, tell me," Hector interceded, "what's the problem with *kiasu*? It seems like a very positive idea."

"You see, professor, *kiasu* was based on meritocracy. It's an ideology, perhaps a good one. Not without blemishes, but it's done us more good than harm. It was necessary when our people were poor and struggling. But now we're well-off. We need no *kiasu* anymore. Can you imagine? Some of our schools require IQ tests for parents before admitting their kids! That's not how things should be at all."

Baxter said, "Guess your flunkers can teach at our MIT," and snickered merrily.

Yubi said, "But that's crazy."

And Saint Paul concurred. "We know it is crazy, ma'am. Or, at least, we once knew." And the apostle raised his eyes to the haze and declaimed: "May your soul rest in heaven, Fei Guo. Craziness all started after you were gone."

And he crossed himself and slurped his pork.

———— ⁂ ————

Zainab asked Fifi if there were any black chicken shreds stuck in her teeth.

Yubi, having deserted her shrimp soup, leaned against her

husband. Her warmth, mixed with the Boss fragrance Hector had bought her at *la place Vendôme* during the Paris trip, the shrewish hiss of her voice on his eardrum—not to forget the tramadol in his blood—aroused him.

He contracted his traps to distance himself, however a silly inch, from her *presence.*

"Baby, you okay?"

"I'm good."

"You don't look good."

"I think I'm fine."

"What's the matter? You're so—"

"What?"

"Distracted," she said.

He swiveled and stared at her. She bit her lower lip—it dimly glossed, a soft hue of pink—and blinked multiple times. This was her method of telling him she was both empathetic and embarrassed. She reached her arm behind his back.

But thank goodness his phone buzzed right then.

———❧———

By which time, all of them—except Fifi—had finished or given up on their dishes.

"Sorry, babe, I need to take this." Hector hurried off to answer the call.

He'd half-expected Jeff, or the dean. But this call was local. He obscured himself behind a garishly tarped scaffolding near the exit and touched the green accept icon.

"Hello?"

"How's the food?" It was the Cardinal's voice.

Hector fought the shakiness in his voice. "Sir."

"We're moving in right now. You know the drill."

A masked young girl, who looked too proud of her red-tied hair, frolicked past him, followed by a couple of jolly middle-aged parents. A coffee aroma rose in the air from the nearby stall, heavy, heady.

"What I remember is that I shouldn't react," Hector said. "That's my part."

"That's the plan. Your appointment as deputy chief has been approved, by the way. Congratulations, Hector. The paperwork is gonna take a week or two. But you can tell your wife now, if you want to."

"But, sir—*triple-eye*. I'm supposed to—"

"Don't worry about that now. Let your colleagues do their job. You've pretty much done yours."

Hector peeked at the table. Paul was discoursing closely with Yubi. Baxter was quieter than usual: shooting regular glances in *his* direction. Fifi was laughing with Kero. Ahmed and his wife were clearing up the dishes.

"Hector, are you still there?"

"Yessir," Hector said. "I am here."

When he returned to the table, Hector found his wife in an almost drunken state. Yubi was ebullient, her cheeks and neck the color of ripe apricot. She cackled. "Hey, baby, what did you tell Ambassador Lee about me? Hah? Did you say you had 'a hot Asian piece back in the room waiting?' *Hah. Hah. Hah.* Hector, honey, what's happened to you! You're silly, but more charming. *Hah. Hah. Hah. Hah. Hah.* I love this island and *you*. Come sit beside me, baby. This guy"—she pointed both her manicured forefingers at a grinning Paul—"is trying to steal your hot piece away from you. He's a doll, though. Come here, baby. What's wrong?"

"We're behind schedule," Hector said. "We need to go. Now."

"But I haven't finished my rice yet," Fifi complained.

"You're gravedigging, not eating," Kero said.

"It's too spicy."

Hector clapped his hands. "Come on, guys. What's our next destination? Chinatown? We can get there on foot, I think. Let's get out of here."

"Why the rush, boss?" Baxter gave him a sharp look.

Hector ignored him. "Come on. Where are Zainab and Ahmed?"

"They're throwing out the empties," Yubi said. "Anyway, Chinatown isn't our next destination. It's the National University."

"Can someone go find Ahmed and Zainab to—"

A siren, mingled with a distant, protesting shriek, froze him. Hector tossed his eyes toward the entrance. The crowds didn't allow him to see the emergency. But Fifi climbed onto the bench, followed by Kero, then Yubi, who revealed: "It's like a CDC bust or something."

Hector glared at Saint Paul—the Shrugger.

Zainab and her husband came back running. "Vomit! Vomit!" Zainab exhorted them. "I vomited in the garbage. Vomit now. Everybody vomit!"

Two phantoms in white positive-pressure suits approached. Hector recognized the sleepy-looking visa clerk from the Embassy and Fabio, itchy mustache wiped off but smugger than ever.

Visa Clerk collected the leftovers from Fifi's dish, while Fabio headed to the next table.

"Don't panic," Visa Clerk reassured the students. "My name is Dr Joseph Street, from the World Health Organization. We're here to make sure everyone is safe. Please, if you have purchased any food items from the first four stalls in the market, proceed to our booth outside and get vaccinated against H7N9, commonly known as 'bird flu.' Please, everyone, do not get scared. Early immunization should lower your chances of infection up to forty percent. Please, walk out slowly. And, again, do not panic."

Fifi's face was the color of ash, Kero's a shade of blue. Yubi squeezed Hector's arm in fright.

"Out, please," Visa Clerk said. "Do not touch anything on your way." He turned to Fabio. "Dr Santiago."

Fabio was trying to reassure a quartet of backpacked Swedish tourists at the next table, all of whom looked like copies of the same person in various stages of shock.

"Dr Santiago!" Visa Clerk called louder.

Fabio turned.

"Please take these good people outta here. I'll collect and seal everything."

———— ⚜ ————

Panic had verily overtaken the market. Everyone was filing out in jittery queues. Most stalls were either gaping or wax-sealed. The owners of the first four stalls were shouting at the white-suited helmeted aliens as the latter dumped the precious birds into man-sized CO_2 boxes. Hector couldn't but secretly admire the Company's plan. It was simple, but legit.

And in a few minutes, the daughter of the most vehement antivaxxer in Egypt would be inoculated with the perfect pathogen, a *cadeau* from Central Intelligence.

Fifi was sobbing. "I'll die, I just know it."

Mini hugged Fifi's shoulders. "Don't say that, sweetie. I promise you, we're all gonna be okay."

"You should have vomited," Zainab reproached them, walking behind with her silent hubby.

"Nobody is going to die," Hector said. "Kero, you're the physician. Has anybody died of bird flu at all?"

Hector was counting on Kero's flimsy knowledge of his deserted profession. Yet Kero didn't seem to have heard him: He followed behind Fabio, his head slouched and swinging on his chest like a slaughtered bird.

The jumble of shouts, the babel of tongues, the shuffling of feet, the noise of storefronts coming down—all this created the atmosphere of a concentration camp, the stinky haze outside like the fumes of Auschwitz.

"Our booth is right there." Fabio pointed at a parked ambulance with a green-gloved pinkie, beside which stood a blue awning carrying the Red Cross logo.

Fifi was still weeping. "Thank you, you're a godsend," she said.

The retiring Cairo deputy nodded gloomily. He retraced his steps, brushing his successor's shoulder on the way.

Saint Paul rubbed his hands, as if he were on the verge of a repast. "I'll get you through in a jiffy. I know someone."

Hector tapped on Fifi's shoulder. "Your aunt called," he whispered. "I think your daddy's sick."

20

HOT PURSUIT

O nce upon a time, there was a University. The University was betrothed to a King. The King died. The University broke her betrothal.

That was the biography of the National University of Pulau in a nutshell. Formerly, Fei Guo International University. Or just FGIU. Acronyms are typically more resistant to conversion.

This brief gloss over the university's history, a sullen intro to their next visit, was Paul's only concession to his tour-guiding duties before he called it a day. He'd made his way to his front seat on the bus, plopped there roughly, crossed his arms, and for a long while had refused to engage in any conversation.

Now Hector said, "Egypt has a similar story."

"Yes, doctor," Zainab seconded him, rubbing the vaccination sting on the posterior of her left arm. "We have a better story. We removed King Fouad because he was a British agent. And we removed Mubarak for the same reason. Thank God our current president is a good Muslim man."

Same symphony. Yet Hector was playing a different chord.

"Cairo University was once King Fouad University. King is dead, long live the republic."

Hector was in a good mood. His ruse, blame-free but tricky, had worked. One call from the panic-stricken daughter to her anti-vax daddy—"Dad, are you okay? Good. Cause I wanted to say goodbye. I'm about to die here, Dad. They say I need this vaccine for the bird flu because of some rice I ate..."—and the radical, anti-medicine man roared. He would call Richard Fei right away. He threatened the MFA apostle: No meddling with his daughter's immune system whatsoever, or he would see that it became a diplomatic crisis, if not a global scandal. He wanted his daughter on a plane to Cairo in forty-eight hours, tops.

Mission accomplished. Good job, Deputy Chief Kane.

FGIU was situated on the northeastern ridge of the island, overlooking the rolling South China Sea. Hector looked at the haze-ridden shore out his window and envisioned the nation of Brunei, far off on the other side, engulfed by the great Indonesian state of Sarawak. Same way Lebanon is held in Assad's maw: Hard not to get bruised when the Lion takes an interest in you.

And only a walk north of the university was America's naval base, occupying the tip of this teardrop island. And the piers there pointed—in serendipitous accuracy—toward Vietnam, wary of what lay beyond: namely, China.

The South China Sea was but a contest for who got the biggest ship.

So childish.

And so salacious.

So *kiasu*.

So realist.

Si vis pacem para bellum!

FGIU had no wall and was just a cluster of bubble-like buildings connected by bridges or tunnels. It looked like a mushroom farm undergone radiation.

"They have protest inside," said Li, the bus driver. "I wait here."

They got out at the gate and walked inside.

"What the heck is this all about?" Fifi said, relatively put-together now since she hadn't died yet.

"I'll ask," Yubi said.

She approached one of the girls carrying placards and asked her. The girl came with Yubi, and this was her tale:

So this protest had to do with the last World Touring Car Championship. A Pulaui racer—an Indian guy, who'd been on the German auto racing team *Wiechers-Sport* for two years—had stepped on the Chinese flag seemingly by mistake after the Race of Austria (the Salzburging circuit). He'd released both a public statement and apology, stressing his fault had been the result of post-race vertigo: The flag had fallen off a fan's hand and he hadn't noticed it.

"But the cameras tell a different story," the girl said. "He walked over the flag with both feet!" The girl stomped her own feet on the ground for emphasis. "He is a liar. We demand he lose his citizenship."

Paul, mask on, hands joined behind his derriere, stood ten feet away under a fig tree.

Trees were plenty. Vines covered the concrete bubbles.

Yubi asked the girl whether she was Chinese. The girl looked at her with contempt and said, "Doesn't it show?" And she walked away.

The protesters were a sea of livid Chinese faces, peppered by a few Malay sympathizers. The placards were scripted in Chinese, except for one:

REMEMBER THE CURRY WARS?!

———— ❧ ————

The story of the Curry Wars was related, twenty minutes later, by the university's provost himself.

This was a man by the name of Phillip Northrop: sixtyish, bald, scruffy, decked out in a Panama suit the color of coffee grounds. He was a quick friend and loud, the kind of man who features in a comedy of manners as "larger than life." His life, anyway. Hector didn't like him. And he didn't like the fact that he turned out to be an old acquaintance either.

This late fact came to Hector after he'd been left alone with the provost in his office.

It was a small, claustrophobic office on the basement floor with a high open window from which the haze poured in. And to make the atmosphere more toxic, Provost Northrop decided to light a cigar.

"They have issues with one another," he said. "Part of it is historical rivalry. Part is *kiasu,* as they call it. Part is race. But you care for my theory, Hector?" He'd used a first-name basis with Hector ever since he'd shaken his hand at the lobby, where Hector had broken away from his group. "That chap, Fei Guo, he *destroyed* them. But first, the Curry Wars, yes. What a fancy name for sectarian strife. But the government contained it. One

Chinese family, sometime before Christmas, griped about their Indian neighbors' 'cooking customs.' The smell of curry coming from their kitchen window. And what followed was two weeks of riots. Five people were killed. It could've been Pulau's first civil war, for all I know." He circled his cigar in the air. "And now this race squabble we have on campus. At your institute, you must have seen a significant analogy—students protesting against each other all the time."

"Nothing of the sort, provost," Hector said. "Most of our students are either rich Arabs or Western."

"What a shame." Northrop smoked dreamily, his eyes on his high window, reclining in his squeaky chair. "There's no politics without conflict."

"Oh, we have that. But…" Hector stopped. "Provost, you said Fei Guo *destroyed* them?"

The provost nodded. "Haven't you noticed the hypocrisy yet? I can't have overestimated you, Hector."

"What hypocrisy? You mean him holding power for over fifty years? That's typical in a non-Western country. Look at Turkey. Or Israel. Or the Arab Gulf states. Or Malaysia. As long as he did his job—"

The provost swung forward and enunciated, "*Fei Guo.* Why should one man brandish his clan name before other mortals? He set himself on a pedestal, forcing his countrymen to upgrade their names, tongues, and professions to square with a fancy fantasy he had. 'The New Deal,' as he called it. *Humph.*"

"Yes, we've been lectured about it," Hector said gloomily, recalling the disconsolate Mrs Chu.

But the provost continued his lecture.

The New Deal, Phillip Northrop explained, had commenced on Pulau's National Day Rally of '73. For the first time since independence, Fei Guo abstained from speaking Mandarin or patois in his speech, declaring in his textbook Oxfordian English, "History has sailed away, my brethren. Tomorrow is here to stay!" And it didn't take long before the purge started. The British edifices of yesterday were torn down, and kinky skyscrapers grew in their place. Western investors were lured with cheap labor and low interest rates: They were copied off, ditched, but tenaciously kept on as friends. Fei Guo disliked the local patois—an amalgam of Mandarin, Malay, and Hokkien spoken by almost all islanders—and called it "lowlife and abhorrent!" Fei Guo, this champion of independence, chose English, the language of his former masters, to be "the language of tomorrow." The Americans had whispered their prophecies into his ear, and Fei Guo was a believer. And his belief in Western supremacy did not stop there. He forced his whole nation to switch first and last names, as per the European custom. All but himself. Only *Fei Guo* was clan first, first name second.

The provost dropped his ashes in a china tray, then out of the blue said, "Hector, how is life in Egypt? Good?"

This change of tone threw Hector off. He pondered a reply, but then the provost's secretary—a middle-aged Chinese lady in a rather tight pantsuit—came in to place a plastic tray carrying a can of Spright and a glass of ice on the coffee table at Hector's knees.

She left, and Provost Northrop, head kinked to his right shoulder for some reason, said, "You don't recognize me, do you, Hector? It's been years, but still—"

"Provost, have we meet before?"

Phillip Northrop blew out a thick cloud of smoke. "Brussels. August. Twenty-O-eight. The European Consortium on Non-Proliferation and Disarmament. I was with double-I SS, you with

SIPRI. I was no provost then."

It was a different time zone. The night chases in the Grote Markt. The Moroccan brothers who cooked tabun in a hot-dog cart parked outside La Monnaie De Munt opera house. And Ozgur's bullets, skidding inches off the statue of the Peeing Boy.

"After the conference, I ran into you late at night," the provost continued. "It was a pub. What's it called?"

"*Delirium!*" Hector provided quickly, his memory ablaze.

The ancient stone-paved streets. The blithe, dissolute, smelly air of the EU's capital. And the two Swedish chicks—Lina and her friend, whatever-her-name-was—and he and Ozgur guzzling *Chimay* beer and spinning a silly scheme to pick the girls up: Ozgur was a Goldman Sachs dude and Hector a Silicon Valley startupper who sent safaris to war zones guided by robots. So stupid it almost worked. Enter this annoying conference vermin and he boomed—

"*Our SIPRI chap, missed me yet? Ha ha ha!*" The provost winded down his chortle in a quiet cough. "Even back then, you found it hard to remember me. I often get that. My wife says it's a gift: I have quite a forgettable face. Perhaps I should use it to some glorious end." The provost circled the cigar again. "A private investigator, let's say. Or MI-six." He paused, bit his cigar, and his eyes moved away from his guest. "You had company that night," he said, tapping his cigar on the ashtray.

"Yes. Unfortunately, my friend is no longer alive."

"Oh."

A weird silence followed. Only the sparrows' twitters and echoes from the protest outside were audible.

Hector took one cordial sip of the Spright, then stood up. "Well, it's been nice to catch up with an old friend. Too bad I have a group to attend to."

Silence.

Hector walked to the door, then he looked back. He barely remembered this man. Yet now he wished he had known him better—better enough to explain why Northrop looked so crooked, head chronically tilted on his shoulder, and why he'd stopped smoking his damned cigar.

Hector was one foot outside, when the crooked figure said, "What have you gotten me into?"

Hector backed up and closed the door. "What do you mean?"

"What do *I* mean? *What do I mean!* Ask your dead friend!"

Hector pulled the provost up by his striped tie. "Speak up," he sizzled. "Or I swear to God I'll kill you."

"I don't… They said… they were CIA."

Hector's right hand tight on the tie, he vised his arm around the provost's neck. He took Baxter's Swiss knife from his pocket and opened it, then walked the serrated blade on the provost's neck.

"I only booked them… for the room." Northrop's eyes popped out, staring at the blade under his jaw. "Please!"

"Which room?"

His captive smelled of stale smoke and showerlessness. Hector let him go. The provost coughed and spat dark phlegm on the crisscrossed tiles. Throughout, he did not abandon his cigar.

A moment passed before the provost, regaining face, wheezed, wiping his lips with his jacket sleeve. "We should hurry up. Their booking ends in ten minutes."

———※———

Hector followed the provost up the stairs to the dais-like lobby where a dozen tables or so carried cardboard signs for different student groups. *Learn Mandarin Now. Chinese Cuisine Aficionados. Green Economy...* Et cetera.

A student stopped the provost to ask him about something, but Hector hooked his arm through the provost's elbow and pulled him away.

The provost led Hector to a street crowded with shrubbery, little palms, and cherry trees. The air was thick with the haze and difficult to breathe. Yet neither man bothered with his mask.

The provost put his hands in his pockets and balanced himself on the edge of the curb. Across from them was a giant bubble. Hector's eyes were bloodshot from the haze—add to that, his rage—but he made out a funny-looking academic cap on top of this gray bubble. He saw tens of students go in and out through a couple of sliding doors. Atop the "IN" door large silvery letters read:

DENG XIAOPING LIBRARY

So much for global American hegemony.

Hector asked, "Are they inside?"

The provost nodded sullenly. "Second floor. Room two-O-two. I'm so sorry..."

But Hector dashed across to the library.

The entrance was blocked by a flap barrier. Hector had no time for this, so he jumped right over. The girl at the information desk called after him, but he ignored her and cantered on. The ground floor of the library was larger than he'd expected. Hundreds of oak bookshelves stood tall everywhere like Tolkien's Ents, menacing but alluring. The carpeting itself was the color of healthy grass. The decor was so breathtaking, disorienting, that Hector lost track of his steps. He felt that he was lost in a literal forest of books.

"Hey, you, sir! Come back. You must sign in," enjoined an angry male voice a few feet behind.

Hector paced faster. His eyes spotted a sign for the staircase hanging from the ceiling, pointing left. No sign for the elevators. He rushed through the first left aisle.

"Sir, stop!"

He cut through one aisle to the next, bumping into fearful students, literally jumping over a squat student who was too absorbed in his book to even notice. And finally, the staircase loomed: mosaic slabs suspended in the air, supported by ultra-thin wire slings, the plastic frame mostly invisible. Hector leaped up the slabs and saw two heavy security personnel jogging under his feet.

"Wait, mister, stop!" demanded a female guard on the flight beneath.

The second floor had fewer bookshelves and more study spaces. It was floored in vermilion carpeting and hosted spaced squads of hazel carrels. Right on Hector's left was an alcove for the washrooms. On his right was a line of cherry-wood doors with silvery knobs. Steel lozenges on the wall told the room number. Hector saw that the first room was numbered 230, the next 228, the third 226. He was going backwards.

Radio static burst somewhere behind him, and a male voice growled, "Officers Sigma-Five and -Six, report on the subject."

"Sir, come back," the female guard pleaded with him. "We

have police."

"Stop where you are!" ordered the male guard.

Hector had to dodge them. He darted back through the hall, the two guards chasing after him. Amid the carrels a few large tables were set in a common reading space. Shaded lights hung from the ceiling. Pots with ferns or flowers grew in every corner. Hector asked the first librarian he ran into where Room 202 was. She pointed a hirsute arm toward a printers alcove. Then she saw the guards. She stared at Hector in fright.

Hector raced to the alcove. A table stood in his way. He made a vault over it, but this landed him on a twisted right ankle, his temple banging into a concrete column. Piled on the rough vermilion carpet, sprained and bleeding, Hector belatedly realized that libraries were not made for hot pursuits.

His disappearance prompted the male guard to ask everyone on the floor to leave because "a dangerous individual" was on the loose. Hector shook his head, wiped his wound with his jacket sleeve, then stood up. The room was right there.

Room 202 lay at the corner of the printers alcove. Hector attempted the doorknob, but it wouldn't turn. The glass panel in the center of the door was plastered with cardboard from the inside. He rapped his fists on the wood, but no one responded. He moved to the next door, but the lozenge read 203. He retraced his steps to the alcove, and there he saw the banner:

Get your N-95 mask fit for free
It WILL save your life!!!

Deep in the alcove was a woman in a two-piece black dress, standing behind a hostess stand. Hector approached her and saw that the door to her left, in continuity with the wall, read 202 too. Obviously the room was too big or too special to boast just one entrance.

The woman smiled at him, quite mechanically. She was in her mid-forties to -fifties and her lined eyes skipped the wound on his right temple expertly. "You have a booking?"

"My students are inside. The American Institute in Cairo? I just came in late."

She joined her black-manicured hands in an apologetic gesture. "Unfortunately, I cannot let you in. Once the test starts, it can't be interrupted, since it's a closed environment. They're using a strong bitter material to test if the masks are sealed. So hard luck for you. *Ha ha ha.* I have spots for Monday, though."

"Listen to me," Hector hissed through his teeth, flashing his Swiss knife in an instant. "Step aside or you're gonna regret it. I'm the craziest man in the world right now."

The security shouts echoing from the hall emphasized his point. Only now the woman in black squinted at his bleeding forehead. She stepped away from the stand and raised sweaty palms. "I work for the library," she said. "I have a strong son. Black belt taekwondo. And I bite. Stay away."

Hector folded the knife and put it back into his pocket, then went for the doorknob. Like its sister, this one was also locked.

"Open the door," he demanded. But he didn't hear a reply. He turned his head and only glimpsed the taekwondo mother's wedged heels rounding the corner.

He bent on the glass panel, sending the hostess stand whamming to the floor with his back. The glass here was not opaque. He made out seven figures helmeted inside, toeing an invisible line. Before them stood a girl whom Hector recognized right away: She was the girl from the Embassy, the Louisiana girl. Louisiana Girl pantomimed with a spray canister and a mask: sticking out her tongue, tilting her head right and left, reading off a paper that a muscular man stepped forward to hand her—the agricultural attaché!—then donning then doffing a white mask.

Hector knocked on the door. But nobody heard him. He pounded his fists. Now one helmet turned. Fred Zhang! Saint Paul had obviously abandoned this heathen feast.

"*Stop!*" Hector shrieked outside. "*No, no, no, no!*"

The girl tested the helmets one by one. She sprayed something into their mouth-holes. But when she came to the seventh helmet—Fifi—she acted as if she'd run out of the spray. Oops. We're going through them too fast, aren't we?

The agricultural attaché handed her a new canister.

Now it's your turn, sweetie pie. Sorry for the delay. This test *will* save your life. Don't you worry. You're in the world's safest hands.

Hector took the wooden stand and hit the glass panel. After four strokes, the glass yielded.

"Stop right there!" a voice cried behind him.

And a pair of strong hands cuffed him. "Do not move. You're under arrest."

They held him in a ground-floor room, brought him a bottle of mineral water, and allowed his wife to nurse his wound.

Yubi was mute most of the time. She dabbled a piece of saline-wet gauze on his temple, then asked for Betadine. A female guard—a Malay woman who'd been keeping a watchful eye on them both—sent out for the university's nurse. But Hector said no, he was fine, just a Band-Aid please and please he must speak to Mr Fred Zhang because Mr Fred Zhang was onto something beyond anybody's ken, a global conspiracy, a deal that would change the face of the planet. Do you know which planet this is? It's Mars for all he knew, 'cause he couldn't recognize anything anymore.

"Betadine, please!" Yubi shouted to the guard. "My husband has a concussion. He's not responsible for whatever comes out of his silly mouth!"

Fred did not show up, but Paul did, about twenty minutes later. Yubi had by then anointed her husband with a red smudge of Betadine: The color seeped through the thick dressing plastered on the right side of his forehead.

Paul showed the policemen his ID, discussed the situation with them in patois, and gave them his cell phone to speak directly to Fred. Yubi then went outside to exercise her womanese with the library personnel. Paul entered the room and closed the door.

"We'll get you out," Paul said. "But you will never disrespect our laws again. We are not America or the Middle East. Strict laws mean our survival in Asia. We live in a literal jungle. You will abide, or you will suffer the consequences. Are we clear on the terms for your release?"

Hector snorted.

"Agent Kane, feel free to insult me if that's going to release your anger."

And Hector did.

Saint Paul smiled, relieved. "I'm not the man you should be interested in blaming. I was actually trying to help."

"Help? You? You ran away like a chicken."

"I was called away, yes. Unfortunate. But it didn't have to be that way."

"You're speaking nonsense, Paul. Spare me, will you?"

Paul walked to the window. He looked out at the haze-haunted campus. "It's going to be beautiful tonight. There's a gap in the haze. Not much, but it'll give you a reprieve from this Hades. Don't think much about the truth, Hector. The truth will reveal itself. Enjoy the moment. Take your wife on a romantic date. Sing, dance, and love. Make choices. Live. And when the time is right, you'll be ready to face the truth."

Hector chuckled in pain.

Paul turned. He bowed and said, "It's been a pleasure to guide you for one day, Agent Kane. May God guide you through the rest."

And he left the room.

21

LORD OF THE DANCE

S he sent the students away.
"Now it's just the two of us?" he said.
"Yeah, whatever."

———— ❧ ————

Tooth Temple. Built in 1965. Renovated shortly before Fei Guo's death. It had cost the Pulaui government over 150 million dollars. Yet it was worth it. Here the lower right canine of the Buddha was buried. Tang dynasty architecture. Brick masonry replacing lumber. Doors badged with graphics of General Yuchi, the fierce soldier holding his long ax. Five stories high. Glaring red.

She told him about her daddy.

"He really converted to Christianity when he met my mom. But not really. He was Buddhist to the end. He loved my mom, and me, and he wouldn't let us live the life he'd had. He was very bitter about his past. All first-generation immigrants are like that, have you noticed that? They escape. That's what they are.

Escapists. Professionals in avoiding pain. So Daddy never liked me reading about China or the Cultural Revolution or any of that. Did I tell you he had a PhD? Yeah, right? Can you imagine? He was a well-educated man. In Canada he was just a landlord. He was lucky, you know." She wrapped her arms around his neck, pushing him against the yard's wall. "I used to work with a guy at Tim Horton's who was a general in the Pakistani army. Can you imagine that? Yeah. He was a general, giving orders to people, and then he was just a baker. And a bad baker. That's why I liked you, baby. You kinda reminded me of this guy. He was so tough and awkward. Yeah, you were. I know men. You thought you ought to have me because you were, like, the perfect spy or something. But girls don't care about that. They want a man, that's it. Not a psycho. But you're very likable when you're crazy, you know? It's crazy."

In the prayer hall dozens of monks in saffron robes chanted for the Buddha with a devout congregation. A leading monk paced back and forth before a dozen crouching monks or so with their backs to the altar. And this altar was a congress of the *Buddha Maitreya*—the future Buddha—flanked by two *Bodhisattvas:* the strivers for *nibbana.*

Two women took photos of the congregation. Everybody— even Hector—recited the panegyrics off the prayer booklets.

"Buddha is the awakened one," Yubi said, massaging Hector's back. "*Samsara* is reincarnation. And we must end it. We can't live forever. It's scary, right? Time-wasting and so scary. It's like the Buddha said after his birth, 'I'm the best of the world. This is my last birth and I will never be born again.' See? It's all *dukkha.* We suffer. And if the Buddha achieved *nibbana,* you and me can do it too."

Hector caught up with her in the foyer. He pushed her

against a glass-locked god and sucked her scarred ear. "I'll reach *nibbana* with you right here and now."

She coughed, she was sweating, she was horny but devious. "But I wanna see the temple."

"Look at me."

She did, and she gave him a long, warm, hungry kiss. Her lips were sweat-salty, her tongue bitter with the mask-fit spray. She breathed fire from her nostrils. Her jet-black eyes reflected the votive candles burning for the Buddhas. It was their first kiss in fourteen months.

Hector took her hand and tugged her to the foyer. "Tell me about your God."

"Which one?"

"These statues. I wanna know you better."

Okay. So this one is the Buddha *Acala*, the black-faced, angry god with fangs and the sword and baton. And in the other hand he holds the noose of judgment. *Acala* burned away both sins and barriers. And this one is *Manjushri*, the oldest *Bodhisattva*. He holds a flaming sword in one hand, a lotus in the other.

"It's all wisdom," she said. "It's like when things become really clear. When the truth blossoms."

"I love you," Hector said.

"Are you sure you're okay? Maybe we should go see a doctor. It looks like a concussion."

"Did I tell you how I got my first girlfriend, in high school?"

She shook her head, giggling.

"I banged my head at a football match. She was the cheerleader who took me to see the medic."

She kissed him again. They went out of the temple.

———— ✦ ————

The sun was high, the haze thinner.

"It never goes down," Yubi said. "Even when it's down, the sun is like hiding. Because of the smoke, it feels like it's always here."

They bought ice cream. Walnut-macadamia and straight chocolate in biscuit cones, thank you.

"Did we eat?" Yubi asked

"Uh-hmm," Hector voiced. "Breakfast."

"I'm starving."

"Little India is around the corner. They're always eating there."

The Hindu temple was a pyramid of gods with big wooing eyes. No sign of the deity Hector was most familiar with: the dancing Shiva, haloed by his eternal ring of fire, bugged by Konstantin Bronzit's fly. No, this temple belonged to a mightier deity: the sexy, lethal Kali—Shiva's wife.

The goddess glowered at Hector and Yubi—this foreign, interracial couple—with protruding bloodshot eyes, her tongue serpentine, her fangs long and sharp.

"She's so scary," Yubi said.

"Not scarier than your *Acala.*"

"Maybe because he's a guy."

He held her tight. "Do I scare you?"

She laughed coyly. "You're so cute when you're edgy like that."

In the outside hall a half-naked man was dancing with a crown of flowers and leaves, a jasmine garland jiggling from his neck. The hall was madly crowded. The chants, the drums, the cheers were earsplitting.

They raced out of the temple and soon lost themselves in

laughter.

"You're bad," Yubi said, slugging his shoulder. "They'll hate us for it."

"You're so bad and crazy," he said.

She sniffed his lips then said, "What is happening to us?"

"I don't know. I don't care."

And they kissed again.

Their restaurant stood kitty-corner to the temple, its buzz visible through the glass. It was nearly full and the music was as tasty as the food: sad *shehnai* weaving into lively *sitar* jigs.

"Nasi biryani," the waitress provided the name of the spicy rice dish. (Yubi jotted this down into her phone notes.) "Murtabak," was the garlicky stuffed pancake. All was greasy, sizzling, delicious, redolent of a thousand definitions of spice.

"I thought you don't like Indian food," Yubi said.

"I don't."

She didn't argue. "I like Indian people," she said as if in redress. "They're so full of life, of bravado. Hey—what do you think?"

Hector shrugged. This close-bodied, extended-family ambiance was not appealing to him for some reason. "Don't you have an Indian girlfriend or something?"

"Yes, Padmal. At Loyalist College. But she cheated on her boyfriend with mine. But then, she came to work at Sick Kids. So we patched things up. She sent me a teapot for our wedding. Remember? It was so beautiful."

"I can never understand how women can get along after stealing each other's men," Hector said.

"Take it easy, okay?" She'd sensed the surliness in his voice. She opened her purse, dropped her phone, then pulled out a pack of wet wipes. "I'm so hungry," she said.

———— ❧ ————

Fish Spa Aquarium
Leap back in time
Get back the skin of your 20s without botox or lotion
Meet our Doctor Fish for $15 only!!!

Yubi prevailed, and in a jiffy they were dangling their feet from an emerald-green velvet sofa into the empty glass aquarium. Shadows of elephants, giraffes, deer, and donkeys spun around them from the rotating lampshade.

"You hold her close." The aquarium owner, capped by a Super Mario hat, instructed him. "They freak out."

"Not my girl," said Hector.

The man guffawed. "They all say that."

"What's that about anyway?" Yubi asked worriedly.

"Relax, sweetie. It's an adventure."

At Yubi's side a Malay boy stood behind what looked like a rusty railroad-crossing switch. With a loud, grating sound, the aquarium began to bubble. Yubi shrieked and wiggled her feet, digging her nails into Hector's shirt. Hector laughed. He tickled the soles of her feet with his toes just as hundreds of tiny fish swarmed the aquarium and began eating away the dead skin on their feet.

———— ❧ ————

"You like dogs?" he asked.

"I guess."

"My grandfather had a dog. And I really hated it. He liked his dog more than me. We didn't get along anyway. Guss, that was the dog's name. A black labradoodle. As in a Labrador sleeping with a poodle."

"Ugly match."

He agreed. "That was in Cayuga, ever heard of it?"

"Uh-unh."

"My Toron'o gal. 'Course you haven't. Who has? It's a podunk town across the Grand River. For me, it was just 'the River Town.' Seven years I biked over that river, looking at the railway bridge on the other side, and dreaming of the day I got out."

"And you did." She pecked his chin.

"I went back to sell that house when I was a bummer in New York. My grandfather had passed away. I didn't even know, we weren't in touch. All I knew was that I had a little farm to sell to some Chinese guy who called me out of the blue. He said he would pay me two hundred K for that dumpster, and I said, 'Gimme a couple o' days.' So this hippie Brooklyn dude, so full of himself, well-fed on big city crap, in his slim-fit fancy pants and fedora, goes back to the bush to sell the family farm. And what does he see? First he sees wind turbines and solar panels on the way. (Over there *in Cayuga, Ontario!*) On Highway Three, I almost crashed my Enterprise Micra into a Lamborghini. The bridge I used to bike on every day and dream of my escape had been rebuilt. Lots of new shops and pretty chicks. (Where were they when *I* was around!) I didn't recognize my hometown, I didn't recognize my farm. My grandfather had painted the house in a weird metallic shade of gray, and there were a couple of tractors rusting away in the barn. So I park my Micra, and step out. And guess who comes out to greet me? Right! That bloody dog! I thought he'd died, but there he was, coming at me, barking and growling and wagging his tail. And then he moaned and licked my hand. A woman came out of the house and said she was my grandfather's girlfriend or something. And I was sorta embarrassed. She made me ginger tea and told me stories about my grandfather. Silly small-town stories, but they made me feel as if I'd never known the man. It was all... so nice, I guess. So I couldn't sell that place. It would've been like selling my history."

She was listening to his heartbeats. "My whole history is here," she said, eyes fixed on the bazaars in the distance. "I feel I'm stuck in endless *samsara* that begins and ends with this island. You know, the years we've been together kind of don't count here." She was silent a long while. "Will you take me to see your grandfather's farm?"

"Sure, when we get back."

"Will we?"

———— ❧ ————

The haze was so sparse it was invisible. All things were starkly visible a hundred feet off. Chinatown got busier and busier. And the alleyways and the marketplace buzzed, bustled, and exuded tropical heat.

They walked into a bazaar.

"So, you wasted your time getting fixed for a new mask, when the haze is slipping away," he said.

She'd taken off her bolero and was walking in her scoop-neck, tie-dyed shirt. Hector leaned over her nape to kiss it, but she laughingly pushed him away.

"How much?" Hector asked the bazaar attendant.

"Which mug?" The attendant was a racially ambiguous girl with wide hazelnut eyes and smooth skin, who couldn't be over sixteen.

"Not the mugs. This *thing*. This frog."

"Oh, this one." The girl removed a bronze statuette of a fat toad crouching on a pile of coins. Its eyes were red, and it looked as if it'd vomited its bed of coins: There was a coin dangling from its fat lips. "Jin Chan. We call it 'the lucky frog.' He brings luck, and love, and karma. Do you want it? This heavy statue is… *hmm*… fifty dollars."

Yubi shook her head. "How about this elephant god?" she asked.

"Lord Ganesha." The girl's voice wimpled. "Lord of success and wisdom."

"They don't go hand in hand," Hector muttered.

"It is a good statue. You take it. I give it to you for fifty-five dollars."

"But that's even more expensive than the first one," Yubi said.

"You take two for a hundred. Three for hundred and thirty. Final discount. We close soon."

It was then Hector found his Shiva. "I'll take *that* one," he said.

The girl picked the dancing god's statuette and proffered it to her client in awe, head bowed. "Nataraja, our Lord of the Dance. Our creator and preserver. Also our destroyer. God of birth and rebirth. He will set you free, as the truth will."

———— ❖ ————

Her lips tasted of sparkling wine, her breaths were warmer than the tropical wind. Their cruise had taken off at Peel Quay, civilization shimmering on either shore of the artificial river. City lights replaced the haze in invading the sky.

An Italian waiter, who seemed too proud of his paunch, laid down the hors d'oeuvre: fried seaweed drenched in coconut milk, topped with cumin.

"*Umm…* I think I'll stick to the pasta," Yubi said, giving up on the heavy plywood menu.

"But which type of pasta, *signorina?* We have maybe forty types of pasta." The waiter replenished her glass with Martini sparkling wine, his left palm bracing the paunch under his black vest.

"She's spent too many years in Cairo, Egypt." Hector winked to the waiter, a mild headache clenching his right temple. "She's lost her fine taste."

"I worked in Dubai for nine years," said the waiter. "Rich people. Very large appetites."

"Not us." Yubi moved her forefinger back and forth, pointing to her husband and herself. "Our pockets aren't that deep."

"Oh, that is silly, *signorina.* I'll make sure you don't pay me a penny. I want you to enjoy the food. Enjoy the romance. And the nice weather. I love you both. I just want you to be happy."

Hector placed the orders. Two fettuccine Alfredos: one with shrimp, for Yubi, and the other with chicken. That should be it, thank you. We'll talk dessert later.

"He's so good, eh?" Hector said.

"He's charming," Yubi confessed.

A jazz band was playing on the open deck. The ship was now slipping out of the river's estuary, the South China Sea dark and intimidating ahead. The ship turned southward to pace alongside the curving coast of the island. Hector took his wife to dance.

"Wow, what is it?" Yubi yelled, triple-stepping forward, then retreating, mirroring him. And they were mirroring dozens of other dancers on the deck.

"You're killing me," he responded, grabbing her wrist, touching the balls of his feet then twisting with her, switching spots. "*Night in Tunisia*. Miles Davis. Ray Brown. Ella Fitzgerald. Where did you grow up? Spadina?"

She burst out laughing, walking in place, shoulders swaying, elbows flexed, fingers slapping to the rhythm. She shouted something.

"I know," he cried, his headache growing.

"I feel I'm in New York." She giggled, and they touched hands and jerked opposite legs. They touched hands again, and they jerked legs.

The saxophone guy got down to show off. A few dancers backed up and clapped to the performance, bouncing on balls and tiptoeing. Hector and Yubi were still swinging away.

"What do you know about New York?" he taunted. "You're from the T-Dot, New York's bad copy." His headache got worse and he closed his eyes.

Mercifully, the band switched to sad Sinatra then. And Yubi, nestled in his embrace, put up with him stepping on her toes once in a while.

"You're tired," she said.

"*Uh-unh.*"

"Your head?"

"It's fine."

"I have some Tylenol in my bag."

"I'm good," he said, thinking of the tramadol in his pocket. He would pop two as soon as possible.

Sinatra was calling out to *Stormy Weather* to *keep rainin' all the time.*

They slow-danced for the rain, when Yubi's eyes flitted askance. "Holy, look who's here!"

She had her arms around his neck, and she was swaying against his hip. Her cheek was against his. His eyes were closed. "What?"

"Look! Baby, look!"

He looked. "This Sinatra impersonator? Good Lord, he's our concierge. *Ha ha ha ha.*"

"His voice is so calming." She rested her head on his shoulder, and they swayed to the concierge's charming baritone. Hector's headache was getting crueler. He scowled and ground his teeth.

Before long she nudged him again. "Hey, look. Look!"

"What now?"

Everyone was crowding to the taffrail, magnified. The ship was cruising by the island's southernmost landmark, a heavyweight contender for the new seven world wonders.

Across from the Indonesian island of Batam, a lighthouse in the image of the mermaid goddess rose to over 400 feet. Our Lady the Mermaid—as the lighthouse was known—smiled a Buddhist, serene smile, her teeth platinum, her wavy hair sunbeams of silver, her scales shining gold, her cleavage deep between two colossal breasts of white marble.

And from Our Lady's eyes, two shafts of light landed on the strait, setting the water aflame.

———— ❧ ————

A ponytailed blonde, with a nose so straight, so delicate, cheeks like blossomed begonias, and a pair of sinister, transfixing chestnut eyes—she was decked out in a crimson double-breasted jacket, a frilled white collar exploding into a ruff around her beautiful neck—grinned at Hector. "Welcome to the George Bay Sands," she said. "How can I help you today?"

European. Probably not Dutch. Mostly Danish. He knew some words but decided not to ruffle her feathers. The transaction must be smooth and low-toned.

She was standing behind a heavy black granite front desk. Behind her was a typical portrait of George IV in his fancy tight breeches and Garter robe, His Highness's face too juvenile for the disgrace to come.

Hector said, "*Mademoiselle, parlez vous français?*"

She did. *Un peu.* She could call for the Senegalese bellhop, who spoke excellent French, if Hector was willing to wait for just a few minutes.

"No, thank you. That is not necessary. Your French is good enough," he said.

His disguised head—a Tommy Wiseau wig headbanded by a pair of Thug Life pixel sunglasses—momentarily turned and winked at his wife. Save for a straw hat with a blue ribbon, Yubi was not disguised. Acting so blasé about it—Just another crazy rich Asian checking into one of the most expensive hotels on the planet—she busied herself acting drunk: dancing… giggling… and binging on the gateau laid down for guests in the lobby. She'd left her shopping bags and purse on her chair. Hector had her passport. Not without a token of coyness, his wife—prey to too much sparkling wine, too elaborate a romance, fine food, and music—had acquiesced to his risqué, pricey fantasy fully.

Hector leaned over the cool granite and spoke in an undertone to the receptionist. "Mademoiselle, my *belle* companion there lost herself to *le vin.* I met her on a cruise only an *heure* ago. She was *tellement charmante* and delicious. I don't know. She said she is booked here." He slid Yubi's blue passport, the Royal Arms half-effaced by use. "Can you, perhaps, ascertain?"

The girl looked inside the passport and saw Yubi's last name. She squinted at the Asian girl called Kane—now tickling the plants in the pots, guests stopping on their way to smile at or take shots of her kissing the flowers—and typed on her keyboard. "Does she have her keycard?" the receptionist asked.

"*Je sais pas.*" His tone buckled. His heart trotted to a race. Here he was, in the British namesake of the king conqueror, the hotel where his wife had—*allegedly?*—slept with the other man last night... this student of his... this friend of his... this *boy* who seduced her with his crisp foolishness. Had Hector really believed that the moment of truth—*he will set you free, as the truth will*—would not come?

"Does she have a booking, then?" he asked. "I thought she was a little bit"—he circled his fingers beside his bruised, wig-covered temple—"*folle,* if you know what I mean."

"She can keep the passport, Mr...?"

"Randy," he answered without thought. "Guillaume Randy. I'm from Québec."

Neither his name, nor Yubi's, added up. Yet the receptionist was helpful all the same. "Our bellhop will take you up to her suite."

She lingered there, rouged lips parting, one eyebrow rising. She'd been in the hotel business long enough, *mon ami,* and had seen it all before. She could smell the sizzling desire, feel the flame of the moment.

"I'll issue her a new keycard," she said. "Would you be so kind as to let her come over to sign up for it?"

———— ⚬ ————

"Wow." Yubi wrenched his arm. "Kill me now. I wanna die with this picture in my head."

The bellhop chortled. He was carrying a day's worth of shopping bags, his crimson cap tilted, his feet fidgeting on the rising pellucid floor. "Some of our guests take the elevator up and down, up and down, nonstop. We can do that, if you want, madame."

The madame's prize for the night—this sexy Frenchman, whom she squeezed impatiently in the elevator—said they had better things to do. "*Vrai, bébé?*"

"*Ouiiii!*" Yubi ate him alive with her eyes.

Chortles from the Senegalese bellhop again.

Why's the atmosphere so blithe, so sensual? thought Hector. And the answer struck him as very pedestrian. Money. It bought everything. Laughs. Comfort. Other men's wives.

The George Bay Sands had a very innovative, monstrous design. Rising to almost a thousand feet, it looked like a great octopus. Five tentacles of floors were never short of high-paying guests. Hector did not know how much his wife's lover had paid for the suite exactly, but he estimated the price to be between $200k-250k a night. You're expensive, Yubi, he thought, biting a kiss of her gateau-tasting lower lip. You're a delicacy. I'm so proud of my taste.

A glimmering spectacle of Pulau's hard-earned civilization

unrolled below them. As the glass elevator went up, and up, and up—slow and seemingly nonstop—the city glimmered under their feet. Little India. Chinatown. Orchard Road (where they had shopped after the cruise). Mermaid City never slept. Hector also saw the domes of the Royal Botanic Gardens, the destination they would seek tomorrow (if there would be a tomorrow). And up north, Mount Victoria lay murky under a canopy of verdure, like a homeless giant covered by a green blanket. Nature, with all its health and glory, didn't measure up to a man-made monstrosity such as the George Bay Sands.

The elevator ascended... and ascended.

At long last, the door slid open. The bellhop stepped on a black carpet. Hector and Yubi followed. A couple of maids in black smock uniforms and white aprons bowed right and left, as these two elite guests walked down the aisle. It was a short corridor, and it smelled of sandalwood with a spike of orange. Oil paintings and gold lanterns, shaped like human hands carrying torches, hung on the walls. And there was only one door at the end: dark oak, painted over with a gilded image of a sultan smoking shisha, the smoke whirling around and around and making the figure of a fanged Chinese dragon.

"Oh, my God." Yubi froze. She nudged her husband's shoulder. "Hey, did you check the price? It looks too much! How're we gonna pay for all that?"

Sprinkling generous grins on the two maids, the lucky Frenchman held his rich horny Asian closer to him. "I got a raise," he whispered to her.

"This chief deputy thing you told me about? Even that—"

"*Shshsh.*" He kissed her.

She looked at him and, reluctantly, smiled.

You're good, Hector thought. Worth every petro-penny!

$250k a night was the most conservative estimate for this paradise. The hall was furnished with a golden grand piano. There was a golden dragon statue with ruby eyes. And there was an original Turner on the wall, a painting that Hector knew of only through hearsay during his New York years: *The Congreve Miracle*, a harrowing depiction of two frigates, British versus Napoleonic, firing at each other at close range. The waves were frothy, the clouds smoky, the feel ominous.

A single plush arabesque carpet centered the hall. The flooring otherwise was seamless, a frozen pond of honey. A warm breeze came in from the French window.

Yubi dropped her jaw and let out a choked curse.

Hector gave the bellhop six hundred dollars—which he figured was below the tip average for this hotel—and hugged his wife's back.

"Hector, this is insane."

He turned her around and kissed her passionately, almost roughly.

She felt his aggression and broke loose. "Hey, what's wrong with you?" She contained him with her eyes. Then she yanked his stupid wig off and looked at him again. "That's better."

This time, she was the aggressor.

They opened a bottle of *Veuve Clicquot* and sipped quietly, locking eyes but not talking. Hector wanted this rich ambiance, this romantic trap, to weigh down on her, to suffocate her. But so far she looked more solid than the diamond candelabra overhead.

It was in the octopus's mantle, its vacant forehead, that this suite nested. Beneath the terrace was a lower deck, reached by a bifurcating staircase, where a T-shaped pool unfurled over the edge. They undressed and swam awhile. The water was warm, and Hector was quickly aroused. She laughed and swam away.

So they came back in and raided the fridge for snacks. *Royal Belgian* caviar was the choicest delicacy, yet Yubi declined. She sipped a bit more of the champagne.

"They're sleeping together," she said.

"Who?"

"Fifi and Kero. They argue a lot, but they love each other."

"Is that why you were late yesterday?"

She nodded.

"What happened?"

"They were having a fight. He wanted to make it up to her. So I told him to go and take her out."

"And why doesn't he want me to know?"

"It's not that, baby. He just can't tell you directly. He thinks very highly of you."

"Yeah, yeah. He thinks I can read a whole novel in just one day."

She giggled. "What novel? Oh—I remember now. It's that English memoir he's been working on. He doesn't want anyone to see it. He says he'll try to get it published in New York."

"New York?" Hector simpered incredulously. Then he changed the tone of the conversation. "So what are the lovers gonna do now?"

Yubi was silent. She landed her champagne flute on the marble table, then ran to the bedroom.

Hector ran after her.

He tried to kiss her there, but she desisted. "Take a shower first, baby."

In fifteen minutes, he was out, lightheaded with tramadol and lust, redolent of a *Clive Christian* aftershave, dressed in honey pajamas he found inside.

Yubi looked at him and giggled.

He pounced towards her, but she deftly dodged him. She went into the washroom and closed the door. "I won't take long. Don't fall asleep!" she said.

She wore the lilac-blue lingerie he'd picked for her at Victoria's Secret, and over that a skimpy bloodred robe, one of the hotel's endless gifts. She let the robe hang open.

Hector leaned back on the bed and whistled. "I never had *that* on my first honeymoon."

Yubi clapped her hands and the lights dimmed to an ember glow. (The bellhop had given them just this serviceable tip: Six hundred dollars bought only so much.) "Don't be sad, pretty boy. After tonight, you won't remember your old honeymoon."

She cat-walked to him in a straight line: too long a line. Fireworks and other city lights penetrating the floor-to-ceiling window painted her impeccable profile. She dropped with a heave in his lap. She kissed him very slowly, nose to nose, teeth to teeth. Her breaths were watermelon, her hair spicy clove, her neck a garden of tobacco leaves and vanilla.

22

BABY

Could she have *faked* it?

Hector was lost. He studied the woman cushioned on his right arm. Her breaths were deep, the pulse on her neck was regular on his biceps, a cherubic smile flickered on her lips. Once in a while, her stomach gurgled: He felt it against his kidney.

They were one flesh.

He moved his arm, and she snored. He readjusted the pillow to make her snores go away.

He stood naked by the window. Outside, Pulau was rowdy. Post-50th-Jubilee hangover. He looked back inside. On the nightstand beside the bed, the dancing god winked at him—this harbinger of revelations to come.

This destroyer of old life.

Hector sank in the yellow velvet sofa in the hall. His headache wouldn't revisit him. He knocked his knuckles on his bruised temple. Nothing. Not even annoyance. A soft current of wellbeing washed over him. He was accursedly alert and thoughtful.

He went through to the kitchen and fixed himself a blue-cheese sandwich with rye toast. He took two bites, then laid it down and reexamined the contents of the fridge. It was chock-full of pleasures, and everything was labeled and dated. He headed back to the bedroom, careful not to make any noise. He opened the great purpleheart wardrobe. An umbrella, fur jackets (seriously?), silk robes of different colors and sizes, a brown leather cigar case, a gentleman's accessory bag, a tiered Sephora makeup toolbox, all sealed and labeled with the following tongue-in-cheek remark in Shakespearean English:

The whispers art true, mine lief cousin. I am a free gift from the George Bay Sands. Feeleth free to taketh me with thee wherever thee wend!

The suite had two spacious washrooms. One was adjoined to the bedroom, which he and Yubi had showered in, and the other stood behind the golden dragon statue in the hall. Hector hadn't found anything significant in the former, so he made for the latter.

In the hall, he smirked at the beast. "What can you tell me, my angry friend?"

He entered the washroom. The floor was slip-resistant, so spotlessly white that Hector was momentarily snow blind. Blinking and squinting, he made out a sink with a mirror cabinet, a toilet, a bidet, a shower with a thick blanket, then a tub that reclined under a portrait—some generic acrylic thing—of a naked damsel in a thick Germanic forest.

He inspected the cabinet first. Other than the usual shaving and toothbrushing gear, nothing stood out. All were untouched, stickered, so well arranged they didn't look to have been touched in eons. The sink was dry and it smelled of a detergent with a citrus note. The toilet and bidet were also clear. The tub, though, had been recently drained: He knew that when he inserted his index finger down its hole and it came out wet. Now whole genres of scenarios reeled in Hector's head. Most of them told him he was reading way too much into a wet drain.

So he examined the shower and the curtain. Dry both. And the curtain was double-layered, made of some synthetic fiber that didn't feel like plastic.

He was about to give up, pat himself on the back for the effort, when his fingertip sensed something on the curtain. Some aberration there. A discontinuity. He stepped inside the shower and drew the curtain, then he gave the curtain a diligent reexamination. What his finger had snagged on was a half-inch perforation in the inside layer. The white polyester batting was popping out. But Hector's eyes took a special interest in the edge of this perforation: It was serrated and dark brown.

He was looking at a cigarette burn hole.

Like an Indian tracker, Hector dropped to the shower's base to examine it. Dry—typical—yet the drain matched the tub's: His fingertip came out sheeny.

This shower complex was a unique one. The showerhead was molded in the shape of a fanged dragon. The base was the dragon's wings. In the wall was a two-by-three sliding window that overlooked the pool in the lower deck. Hector flipped the latch and opened the window. The ledge was clear, not even a mote of dust. Yet his eyes caught something down there—a rod of dirt on the hedge.

So he stormed down to see.

Hector leveled the half-smoked joint to his eyes. He sniffed the stuff. Bona-fide Afghani hashish. He'd spent many an hour smoking this very stuff with someone he thought he knew.

Someone he thought was his friend.

Hector wanted to feel angry, but what he felt instead was commiseration. Perhaps also wistfulness. To distract himself, he went back up to the bedroom—he avoided looking at his cheating wife—and soundlessly as he could removed the cigar case from the wardrobe. The case came with a lighter, a golden boy kicking a soccer ball. He took the lighter down to the poolside, and gently put the remainder of the joint to use.

He reclined in the chaise lounge and looked up at the clear skies. He saw it all now:

Room service, sir. Can we come in?

W-w-w-what? No! I'm having a shower.

The little prince opens the shower window and tosses his contraband with a flick of his finger. He gargles some mouthwash, brushes his teeth, then takes a deep breath and opens the door—to meet his captors.

Hector blew out the dope into the haze-free sky. A helicopter zoomed by, its rotor too loud. He realized he was a thousand feet above the rest of humanity: on top of the world. Stars were reachable now, the truth—*O Lord of the Dance!*—at arm's length.

After a while he found himself weeping. A moment later, he was chuckling. He sprang up and spread his arms and howled, "I'm Hectorata, god of the dupes! I'm light of the world!" He flung the lighter over the hedge. "I was born once, but I'll die so many!"

The helicopter's sound was in his chest, in his head. He wanted to take refuge.

He dropped—facedown—into the pool.

The pool wasn't precisely T-shaped, but more of an arrow, its lateral expansion curvy, anchor-like. The edge was made of a special alloy of acrylic plastic. King George's gills—for that was what the expansion corresponded to in the great octopus— enjoyed a bird's eye view of Mermaid City, from coast to coast, strait to strait.

Hector crawled along the edge, gliding under the surface every now and again, or clutching the wall, to look down at civilization. Teardrop island. Its northern notch pointed at Vietnam. Its left convexity lay parallel to the Malaysian state of Pahang across the tense strait. Its fat bottom faced the island of Batam across another strait. And its right double curvature harbored two South China Sea recesses: George Bay (& Port) and the Disraeli river.

Small thou art, but mighty.

Made of light and secrets.

A nodal point for contending world impulses.

So unlike defeated, history-ridden Cairo.

Gliding twenty feet under, staring at the Playboy logo glowing in the deep, Hector thought about his dead son.

His wife's affair must have started shortly after his death. Yubi had never been a whole person since. Even her late conversion to Buddhism—all these meditations—didn't so much help her.

Wayne had died on the same day the Coptic Orthodox Pope Shenouda III had passed away: March 17, 2012. He was eight months old, the pope eighty-eight. Coincidence? A sign? A cosmic pattern? Hector couldn't care less. For him, whatever the reason, his baby hadn't had a fair shot at life. And however cruel it was, life was absolutely worth living.

At first, Wayne had watery diarrhea. They took him to Afanasy, who prescribed an oral solution. It was a "light illness," Afanasy said, so he would abstain from adding the usual antibiotic injections.

Overnight, the baby got a little bit better. But in the morning he began crying again. Yubi checked his diaper and saw blood therein. So they took him to a *real* doctor, a university professor in Doqqi. Kero knew him in person, so they got to skip the booking and go right in. He was a genial fifty-ish man. He palpated Wayne's bloated belly and took an X-ray. Then he sadly communicated the diagnosis. "Intussusception," he said, which was "a telescoping of the bowel." Part of the intestine, *Ostaz* Hector, moved faster than the rest, went inside the next segment and got jammed. We'll try an air enema. If it doesn't work, surgery is needed.

Kero's availability was both a good and a horrible happenstance. Since September, he'd been living downstairs to them in the Zamalek hostel. This was the year he got accepted into AIMES's prestigious Bin Hakam Fellowship for Arab Leadership on the strength of his highly popularized profile in the Egyptian Revolution—and thanks to Hector's approval. Kero was a former student of Yubi's from her brief stint as English tutor at St Mark's Cathedral. Despite being atheist, Kero had gone to the cathedral to benefit from the cheap courses. He needed a high TOEFL score to stand any chance of admission to AIMES.

Now this church business was brought up by Kero, just after baby Wayne had been declared dead. The enema reduction had failed, and the baby didn't live long enough to be prepared for surgery.

Yubi was shrieking about wanting to hold her baby, when Kero said, "He will go to heaven. Come on, Yubi, don't cry. I feel so bad for you. I like you as a friend very much. Isn't he baptized?"

"He was always sick. We never had the time," Yubi wailed.

"I'll pray for him, then," said Kero the atheist. "Today is a blessed day. Even the Pope is dead."

Yubi collapsed on the clinic's floor. Hector carried her to one of the beds, and a nurse took her blood pressure and was about to insert an intravenous line into her wrist, when Yubi came to.

She sat up with eerie energy. She'd had an epiphany. She would take her dead son to the cathedral, to the Pope's funeral. "I want my baby to be with Jesus and the angels in heaven, Hector," she said. "We did this to him. He should have been baptized!"

"Honey, that's so wrong," Hector tried to reason. "I'm sure he's in a better place now. Don't listen to crazy people." Hector looked at the sticky Kero.

"*I want my baby!*" she shrieked. "*Get me my baby!*"

"I'll go get the baby," Kero volunteered.

Hector barged out to get the doctor. But when he came back, Yubi, Kero, and Wayne's body were all missing.

———※———

Yubi had mentioned what had taken place there only once, following her return with Wayne's stiffened corpse, after three a.m.

"It was horrible, Hector. A nightmare. Millions. Millions of millions of desperate people. And they all jostled and hit one another, and me. I saw someone die there, I walked over him. Oh, it's so terrible I feel so guilty of everything. And, hey, this pope, he was so yellow. The soldiers were up there protecting his body in the casket. And he's so yellow and old. Ernest came there too, and he took me to the front row and I raised the baby over the dead man's body." She sobbed heavily. "So atrocious, I can't get it out of my head. They were both dead, Wayne and the pope. And Wayne is kinda grayish, and this guy's yellow. I hate myself, I can't do this anymore. I wanted to drop my baby in a garbage box. But Ernest carried it all the way. So horrible, Hector. Oh my God. I can't have children anymore."

That was when she made him sleep on the couch.

They had weird fights. His socks were too stinky, he was spending too much, he was away, he wasn't working out enough, or he spent too much time at the gym. What are we doing in Cairo, when is this Revolution ever going to end. She hates Muslims, she hates Christians, she wants to move to Greece(?).

"Why aren't you spying?" she asked him one day, utterly serious. "At least you would make me more excited about you. You're a lazy troglodyte now."

On another day: "Baby, you're so pale and skinny. Let me cook for you, baby."

On a third: "Hector... are we really gonna die?"

She invited Ernest to their apartment a few times without him being notified. Husband comes in, wife is dressed in a side-slit skirt, her bosom peeking through a dusty pink surplice blouse. Ernest is lighting wife's chocolate-flavored cigarette.

"Hector," she says loudly, "Ernest sweetie was talking about his thesis. You'll approve it, baby, right? It's about China or something. Right, Ernest? He was asking me about my family history. Oh, you're so nice, Ernest. Hector, baby, where have you been? I texted you about groceries. The fridge is pretty much empty. Go buy some mortadella and cheese and come back. No, Ernest will stay here with me. Your students won't slave away for you. *Ha ha.* Go! Go!"

23

SPIES AND LOVERS

D ry up," Ozgur said, dropping a green towel on the poolside.

Hector climbed out of the pool and picked up the towel. "Somehow I was expecting you."

"Put some clothes on." Ozgur turned and sat in the chaise lounge, one suede on the slate-gray tiles. "And don't wake her. You got a fine piece in there. You must be working really hard to please her." He circled his finger to indicate the superb penthouse suite. "Don't take too much time, buddy. We're kinda running out of it."

Yubi hated covers. Always a messy sleeper, she would kick the sheet, blanket, and bedspread to the floor. It only took a man in her bed to stifle this pent-up revulsion of bedly restraints. Only in a man's arms was Yubi complacent. Some incident in her childhood, she'd told him, her father saving her from her mother's punishment or some such Electra theme.

That was why she liked older men.

Wasn't that what she told him?

Hector pulled the sheet and coverlet from the floor and spread them gently over his wife. He tucked the edges under her elbow and knees.

Yubi opened her eyes. "Where're you going?"

"Get some air, sweetie." He kissed her forehead. "I won't be long."

"Have you been smoking?"

"Sorry, babe. I need to get some air."

She closed her eyes, and Hector skirted the bed to the nightstand. Beside the Shiva statuette was his wallet, his charging iPhone, and the suite's keycard. He dropped them all into his jeans' pockets and checked his watch. One a.m. Let's play, Ozzie, he thought.

Out in the hall he checked his phone. A few administrative emails, but only one missed call. Kero of all people. And one text, also from him:

Hi Doc I'm looking for you to give you my novel! I found the door open so I left it there inside. It is on this small glass table in front of your couch. This novel is partly autobiographical based on our trip to Paris. It is a silly romance maybe you will not like it but please Doctor READ it QUICKLY. I need it back. I love you Doctor and wish you everything good. See you soon.

Hector shook his head and ignored the text. Then he glanced at the lower deck. Ozgur was motionless in the chaise lounge in his light sandy suit and suedes, a frozen picture from the past.

Hector then thought of something. He stepped away from

the balcony and heard six beeps before the voice answered:

"Yep."

"You're ignoring me," Hector said.

Jeff hawked up phlegm and coughed. "Nope. Been kinda busy with the Egyptian drama that never ends. What're you up to? Spying away, huh?"

"What have you got for me?"

"Royal flush. You're spot-on with this guy. This one is like bin Laden, al-Zarkawi, and Mosa al-Damawy mashed into one son of a dog. He's the most dangerous man on earth. You've nailed it, buddy."

"And you say you hate drama?"

"It grows on you. Politics is nothing but drama, Hickey."

Ozgur now flickered. He was growing impatient.

"So he's in the clear?" Hector asked hastily. "And don't call me 'Hickey.'"

"Why, Hickey? She still talks about you. She loves you, man." Sound of a chomp: some fruit, or a carrot. "*Grinch. Grinch.* Your Afanasy isn't even Russian. He's Ukrainian. I'm looking at his passport right now. Blue. Emblem looks like a goat in a witch sermon. *Grinch. Grinch.* I made some calls. My sister's fiancé—"

Ozgur was already up.

"Get to the point, Jeff."

"Okay. He went to some sinkhole on the Vorskla called Poltava Medical U. Redid three years. Graduated by a miracle in eighty-four. After that, he got a B-one visa to visit his brother in San Fran. Broke it. USMLE board exams: failed twice. I'm telling ya, this guy is lucky to have a job at all—"

Ozgur was walking.

Hector dashed to the kitchen. "Yeah, yeah. Carry on."

"Pizza delivery, cleaner at a mall, the whole illegal immigrant enchilada. Paid some chick to marry him. He wanted a green card. Rejected. Got deported in eighty-seven. Marital status: divorced. I'm reading the State Department file on him. You wanted me to give this guy a scholarship? Screw you."

"So he came to Cairo to be a doc?" Hector said. "What a stupid idea. How?" His rye blue cheese sandwich was there.

"Ask your dean. She gave him the job: met him at a conference in Kiev, and he boarded the same flight over with her."

"Why would she do that?"

Footsteps in the hall. The suedes stopped.

"*Grinch. Grinch.* Why do you think? American university in the Middle East. Pay is too low for a real doctor from the States. He looks white enough and he's desperate."

Hector sank his teeth into the cold rye bread. "No Russian connection, eh? *Grind. Grind.* Who knows, they could've recruited him along the way."

"Would you?" Jeff said sarcastically.

Fair enough. Hector thanked him and ended the call.

The cheese was soft and buttery, a mold bomb in his mouth. And when Ozgur came in, Hector proffered, "Want a bite?"

Ozgur shook his head and turned back. Hector followed him.

———— ⚜ ————

They walked somberly back to the lower deck. In the ferny hedge, there was a discontinuity: the wire net carefully clipped, sharp edges bent, allowing a hole they squeezed through.

Now they were on a terrace of sorts. Behind them a two-story complex—the octopus's siphon—stood before a narrow view of the Bay and the Royal Botanic Gardens. Centering the terrace was a big circular tub glowing in green. Flower pots dotted its circumference, and a woman was lolling there. Green bikini, blonde, French, a prodigy in environmental science. A cigarette was burning in her fingers, sending a smudge up to heaven.

"I booked the flights," she said to Ozgur, almost defiantly.

Ozgur walked on silently.

Hector said, "Nice flowers," and followed suit.

When they reached the complex's side door, the same girl from the Embassy—the mask-fit criminal—emerged through the French window. She was wearing a yellow bikini and carrying a martini glass with an olive pick.

"Hi," she said jauntily, devouring the olive. She giggled and hurried, unsteadily, off to the tub.

"Langley will go bankrupt," Hector said to Ozgur. "Do you have any idea how much this hotel charges a night?"

"The Pulauis are covering it all," Ozgur said glumly. "Besides, ask yourself. Who's paying for *your* stay?"

"Prince Mohamed," Hector answered simply.

"I didn't know you were lovers."

"It's his farewell present. I'm leaving the Institute soon, you know."

Now the same agricultural attaché—the *second* mask-fit criminal—eased out onto the terrace from the lower floor of the complex. He folded his arms and breathed in the haze-free air. "Shame it's such a good night. How long are we staying for, sir?" he asked Ozgur.

"As long as it takes you to pack up," Ozgur answered.

He walked out of the door, and Hector followed.

The octopus's siphon drained into a different tentacle. This side faced east. As the elevator descended, Hector was mesmerized by a sweeping view of the Bay. Its Jubilee festivities. Its stock of toy ships. And, blotting out the rest, the murky beyond: the South China Sea.

The view was so breathtaking that Hector didn't notice the elevator had stopped, the door opened, and two passengers had walked in.

"I see zis and I think Paris after dark," a tenor voice said behind him.

Hector turned and was briefly stunned by a phosphorous blow of blue. The man standing before him was wearing a laughably garish shirt. He was a paunchy fellow with the broad, low-slung build of a veteran weightlifter. His head was big and bald and acne-scarred, punctuated by a pair of small, dark eyes. Eyes that were puzzlingly, if not mystically, cold. Eerie detachment shone from them, and his smile didn't take away from that.

He'd gotten sturdier and meaner with age, but the eyes remained the same. Hector knew who he was. Or at least who he *had been*.

"I do not blame you," the *starshy leytenant* Hector and Ozgur had monitored for two weeks in Paris, eight years ago, said. He crept closer under Hector's nose. "I struck with glory vhen I come here. I here four days. Zis island is miracle in time and destiny. I vish I have voman here." And the *leytenant* let out a sonorous laugh: It too didn't assuage the rotten vibe coming off him. (For who laughs with open eyes!)

Ozgur stuck out his hand to the *leytenant,* the Bay's panorama quickly slipping out of view, imploding into tawdry glimmers, street lights and car lights. "Kerry Grant," Ozgur said, shaking the man's hand. "Have we, by any chance, met before? You look a little familiar," he added with a phony smile.

Hector was so taken by the *leytenant*'s presence that he hadn't noticed the other man until now. That one stood back by the dial pad. He was a brown-haired, six-foot fellow about Hector's age, dressed in a blue aloha shirt, black gabardine shorts, and matching leather sandals. A pair of pilot sunglasses covered his eyes, making him look passive-aggressive.

Ozgur dismissed him completely, narrowing his gaze on their old booby-trap defector.

"I do not think ve met, no," the *leytenant*—whatever his rank was now—responded, his hand resting longer than usual in Ozgur's hand. "Cary Grant like in cinema? *Ha ha ha.* You like *Charade* I vonder. Got many names like in movie picture. *Ha ha ha.* You like me then, love beautiful vomen. Audrey Hepburn. She crushed my heart when I vas teenager." The man whose heart Audrey Hepburn had crushed slapped Ozgur's shoulder in camaraderie. "Glad to make acquaintance, Agent Grant."

The elevator's door opened. The Russians stepped out.

"*Pakah!*" Ozgur called after them.

But neither *pakah*ed back.

———— ❦ ————

Hector had expected one of the thousand hawker centers strewing the island, but this restaurant was Thai. It was only a three-minute walk from the hotel, and it had the air of a Cairo café. A dozen tables or so occupied the sidewalk. Same illicit, ad-hoc feel.

They opted for the more distant of two available tables, and soon the waiter materialized beside them: a thirty-ish man with a broad Stalinistic mustache and glistening brown skin, his gut stretching his yellow polyester polo, armpits sodden with sweat.

Ozgur ordered pad noodles and a butter chicken sandwich, and Hector only coffee. Two minutes later, the waiter came back with the orders. Pad noodles was a mix of fried noodles, bean sprouts, tofu, chopped green onion, beaten egg, soy sauce, and chili powder on top. And the chicken sandwich had a lot of big onion tranches bulging out of it. Hector's coffee was a typical Southeast Asian *kopi*, heavy with milk and sugar.

Ozgur's teeth ground the food with relish. The noodles squirmed in his lip. And slowly, a sore smile manifested.

"So," Ozgur said.

"So," Hector replied.

"Quite the company we had in the elevator. Any insight?"

"You're the one who's seen God." Hector sipped his *kopi*.

"Even your humor is stale."

"That's authority for you. I was officially promoted today. I would've made it last year if the Company hadn't fired me. But anyway."

"Knock it off, will you?" Ozgur quickly scarfed down his noodles, sweat droplets breaking out on his forehead. It was getting warmer and a veritable stench heralded the haze's comeback. But the atmosphere was lively. Customers plenty. And Pulau's endless trees respiring, twigs rustling, fruit and flowers blossoming.

"Why the signal?" Hector asked.

"What are you talking about?"

"The perfume. Your *secret* night visit to my neighbor and

replacement. What was that about?'"

Ozgur turned to his butter-chicken sandwich, then he laid it down. "How do you know he's your replacement?"

"Let's say I have my sources."

Ozgur was silent awhile, debating whether to eat his sandwich at all. He looked up at Hector. "Believe it or not, I wanted to warn you."

"Against who?"

"Yourself. You have no idea what you've gotten yourself into."

Hector took a painful swig of his *kopi* and studied his old friend.

Ozgur pushed the sandwich away, giving up on it completely, and began, "Tell me—"

"I've nothing to tell you."

"Do you have something *not* to tell me, then?"

"I don't know what you're talking about."

"Ask me," Ozgur said. "I tell you my story, you tell me yours."

"Okay," Hector said. "For starters, I need to know where you went after you passed away."

"Order another *kopi*," Ozgur said. "This is going to take a while."

"Everything starts and ends with a woman," Ozgur said. "You come to life from a woman's womb. You fight the world to get a woman. When you die, you also wanna make her yours. Your widow, your daughter, your bereaved mother. It's always about you and *her*. Nothing more. When you're a young stud, you fail to see that. But once you hit forty, everything becomes terribly clear. Life falls into a pattern. You see what you didn't care to see. You see *her*. And mine was a girl I met eight years ago in Paris. You've seen her yourself. How not to fall in love!"

"Who're talking about?"

"Sally. The environmentalist. My Frenchie. The mother of my child."

"I don't buy any of this."

Ozgur pulled out his wallet and let Hector see a picture of a toddler, or old-enough infant, in an ornate pink romper. She had Ozgur's wolfish eyes and his strong forehead.

A soft curtain fell before Hector's eyes then lifted. He handed the wallet back to Ozgur.

"Her name is Courtney," Ozgur said.

"Like the guy I mentioned yesterday?" Hector said dubiously. "Don't you think this is too coincidental?"

Ozgur raised his salt-and-pepper eyebrows. "Life has a mystical pattern, a code if you will. But my Courtney is eleven months old, and we live in Paris."

"I was there in March," Hector said dryly. "I would've dropped by if I knew the address."

Ozgur went on. "Ever heard of a guy called Mosa al-Damashqy?"

Bloody Moses? Sure. A Syrian "martyr" who'd blown himself up in Damascus last year.

"He didn't just blow 'himself' up," Ozgur said. "He blew up Assad's whole National Security HQ. The explosion killed Assad's brother-in-law, two defense ministers, and a man called Suleiman, the godfather of Egyptian intelligence."

"Thought he died of heart failure, in Cleveland."

"Hah, how convenient! A year after the Arab Spring the man

who knew *everything* about the region dies of a heart attack. But anyway, he was an Assad supporter. Not a good guy. Useful sometimes—remember the Algerian guy from Marseilles?—so good riddance."

"I have one of his pupils riding with me on this trip," Hector blurted out.

"Good word. 'Pupil.' Is that how you talk in Canada?"

"I'm American, Ozgur."

"And Canadian. And Irish. And Armenian. We never forget. I remind myself I'm Greek *every single day.* But you know what I do when I feel lost? I check my pay stubs. Wherever they come from, that's my home." Ozgur gave Hector a penetrating look with his slate-gray eyes.

Hector was halfway through his second mug of *kopi*. He sipped silently, then asked, "The Egyptians: What's their part in your story?"

"They have no part. They just happen to pass by. Suleiman is gone, so no more trouble. Lisa's Crazy Horse will make sure they're cooperative."

"Then why the fuss over this Mosa al-Damawy episode?"

"Because you're looking at him."

Hector felt a tingling in his jaw. The *kopi* spilled over his pinstriped shirt.

"Bloody Moses," said Ozgur, "the emir of the resistance! He cries to heaven and—lo and behold—it rains M-fourteens and RPG-sevens. He strikes a rock—*Allah akbar!*—we have sarin. No wonder Assad was frustrated. How could he beat a CIA prophet?"

Hector stared at the man sitting across from him, this old friend of his.

This twice-dead spook.

This symbol of the Syrian resistance!

And he was about to utter something—he didn't know what—but Ozgur was faster.

"But that's not where the story begins," Ozgur said. "As I said, it starts with a woman. She was a silly teenage girl at the time. A girl Bloody Moses—before he *was* Bloody Moses—meets on a blown-up operation in Paris in twenty-O-five. Know which operation I'm referring to? Bin-go. It was your first run in the rain. Your baptism. Remember those funny clothes I brought you? Damn right. It was her! The Jewess from *les puces de Clignancourt.* You know me, I'm not the romantic type. But these things just happen. And for that reason, I ran away and avoided her for six whole years. Till I was burning in Syria. And where would I go? Yep, straight to Paris! Spy meets girl, they hook up, spy skedaddles. Perfect spy story. But not when the prophet is on a diet of sea salt and cumin, sleeping on explosions in Assad's camp. Not when he's preaching celibacy to horny jihadists. Not in those cold February nights—the Phoenician sky a waltz of winks, whispers in nightdress-red. Not when you drown in milky dimples and wake up wet and disgusted with yourself, and you are pushing fifty. Spy calls girl, and girl is pregnant. The spy stages his second death and becomes husband and father. That's my story, Hector, and I can't wait to hear yours."

Yet Hector's story was no match for Ozgur's.

Ozgur's Odyssey was finished, definite, indisputable.

Hector's was still *hazy.* He had to clear it out before he could share it with anyone.

So he downed his second *kopi* and deflected. "That doesn't

explain the window."

"What window?"

"The guardhouse."

"That wasn't me."

"Then who was it?"

"I'm the one asking questions now."

"And I've got no answers for you."

Ozgur slammed his fists on the table. A customer turned and frowned at them. "Here I am," Ozgur rasped, "talking to you in private before anybody can lay a hand on you. And what d'you give me? Claptrap. Let's talk about your library *adventure*."

"Guilty." Hector raised his hands with a smirk.

Ozgur glared at him. "You're finished, buddy! Legally, professionally, and—as far as I can see—mentally. So unless you're suicidal, you should be grateful we're having this conversation."

"Arrest me now if you can," Hector said.

Ozgur rotated his neck to see if anyone was watching them. "Do you know what you're about to be accused of? It's treason, idiot!" he hissed. "Please, Hector, let me help you. Turn yourself in. It's not too late. We can figure out a way out of this."

Hector stood up. He examined the *kopi* stain on his shirt, then said, "Next time, call before you show up."

And he walked back to the hotel.

24

MIDDLE-MIDDLE MAN

S trangely, Hector slept really well that night. He held Yubi in his arms and dreamed of a labradoodle racing in a garden populated by whispering maple trees.

Yubi hated his *Enter Sandman* ringtone. He rose to shower-dive in the pool. She said she would follow in just a few—falling instantly back to sleep.

While deep in the water, Hector thought he'd seen a dark phantom looking down at him from the poolside. He kicked himself up and gasped the polluted air. His nose, lungs, and eyes twinged. There was no one. The pool was covered by coal motes, burnt reeds, and Fei Guo's ashes. The horizon was obscured by the haze.

Hector climbed out and walked to the hedge. "Hullo," he called out. He didn't see a soul. No Sally, no girl in yellow bikini, no agricultural attaché. And no Mosa al-Damawy. He only saw dead flowers, an ash-ridden tub, an overturned chaise lounge, a shuttered French door. It was like a scene from a post-apocalyptic movie. And the fence had been mended perfectly.

He made for the opposite railing and looked down. A thick cloud erased the streetscape. This swanky suite on top of the world was a cocoon. A nest for clandestine affairs. No wonder Prince Romeo—who'd dreamed his pants off about doing *la cour* with his professor and friend's wife—had chosen this celestial nook for his cuckolding dare, getting especially high for the occasion.

Despite that, Hector couldn't deny that he still loved Yubi.

Even with her hideous crime, he couldn't help but forgive her.

But their marriage was over.

He was dressed in a cocoa Hackett blazer, deep blue jeans, and a sky-blue-on-white striped shirt, all of which Yubi had picked and paid for yesterday using her HSBC Mastercard. She was sick of his navy Zegna, she'd told him. She'd also suggested a future beard. She would resketch him, color him however she liked.

And he had yessed, yessed, yessed.

She was so late getting dressed. At nine-forty she emerged from the bedroom still in her red silk robe, with one shoulder peeping deliciously out. She'd showered and brushed her teeth. Her smile would magnet a man ten miles off.

Hector scowled, looked at his watch. "Did you call the students?"

Yes, baby. She texted Kero, 'cause he didn't pick up. And she called Fifi, Zainab, and Baxter. Everyone should be here by ten.

Still the coquettish voice, the fetching smile. "We still have half an hour," she said with a giggle. "Take off your blazer, baby. It's so hot."

—— ❧ ——

Inviting the students to the hotel was her idea. But Hector made her call the day's guide as well. His name was John. Yubi instructed John to come straight to the hotel, instead of boarding the bus with Mr Li, eavesdropping and annoying the students.

Around ten-fifteen they went down to the hotel's restaurant. John was sitting there, helping himself to a mountain of salmon sashimi iced by cantaloupe and pineapple slices and with a bit of wasabi paste on the side.

He stood up and shook hands with both of them. "I'm so glad to meet you again," he said.

"Sit down, please," Hector said.

Yubi went on to sit with the students at the next table.

Hector wasn't too impressed. No cultural connoisseur was needed to tell him that filling one's plate before the guests' arrival wasn't very diplomatic. And yet, thanks to the sex euphoria, he was only cognizant of his disapproval at the diplomat's behavior. All issues withdrew into the distance. They were objectively valid, yes, but irrelevant—all except what was to be touched, licked, sniffed, heard, and seen: Those were *gorged* with presence. The cool marble tabletop under Hector's hand. The fresh smells of food. The petite cutlery clanks and clatter. The sienna crisscrossed tiles. The old-lace camisole Yubi was wearing. Everything exploded with the sensory.

A short, athletic man, John was clad in a cream short-sleeve and brown slacks. And he smiled religiously. "Do you smoke?" John asked.

"Not really. Excuse me." Hector left the table and targeted the big platters in the center of the buffet. He served himself a plateful of sushi rolls and turkey, then came and sat back with the diplomat. He was ravenous and suddenly enraged. He didn't know why.

"Sir," John ventured after a while, "I would like to offer you a cigarette if you smoked, sir."

Hector's eyes flitted over the neighboring table. Keroloss had conveniently seated himself beside Fifi, slanting toward her like the Tower of Pisa. Yubi and Baxter were in conversation, and Baxter's eyes met Hector's and the rookie spook flashed him a meaningful smile: It made Hector rage all the more.

Hector looked at the Pulaui. "Sorry, Johnny, I don't smoke really."

"My name is John. Please call me John, sir."

"All righty, John."

"Can we step outside for a smoke, sir?"

"Why, I've just told you I don't smoke, John."

"I'm obliged to offer you a cigarette as soon as possible, sir."

Zainab suddenly jumped off her seat and scurried over to their table. She leaned a hand on the diplomat's left shoulder and said, "Can you help me with a mystery?"

John's chest and shoulders wavered with laughter. He cocked his head to gaze at this gorgeous Muslim-Brotherhood scout. Zainab was dressed in an emerald-green dress, her headscarf light cyan. A *houriya* out of Paradise!

"Of course!" John celebrated.

"How you people are so thin? I came here and I gained two kilos already. But I don't see a single fat person in Pulau." Bearing on the man's shoulder, she turned her free hand right and left, left and right, as if working an invisible doorknob, and asked, "How?"

John guffawed copiously. "We work out," he said, shoulder-pressing the air. "We go to the gym. We walk all day. We're always on the move. *Ha ha ha!*"

Ahmed bared his teeth and started off a round of applause.

Hector stood up, throwing his towel down on his barely touched sushi. "Let's have a smoke, John."

"Where're you going?" Yubi asked.

"I'll be back."

"Yes. We will have coffee then come back," John paraphrased. Then he followed Hector out of the hotel.

⚬

"Coffee or cigarettes?" Hector said. "You're dithering."

"Coffee is good enough. There's a *TCC* nearby. It's really nice there. I'll show you."

Hector fished his mask out of his pocket and donned it. He took off his blazer, undid two buttons on his shirt, and followed the diplomat away.

The haze had come back with malevolence. It was muggier, stinkier, and *outbreak*-ish in feel. Five million people were stuck together on this spit of dust, all of whom were masked, wary of one another, highly competitive, individualistic, yet nationally prideful.

We are all Fei Guo! the mask-donners screamed silently. Citizens of the New World Order. *God walked among us one day, but we have burned Him into ash.* They were a colony of busy motes—a germination of Fei Guo's legacy. An outbreak of civilization. And everything mourned. Not even the pervasive greenery could take away from that.

Hector followed his guide down a four-lane road flanked by apartment blocks and retail stores. For five minutes or so, they strode together in silence. Then John veered onto a side street, and Hector followed him. The buildings there were low and luxurious, clearly new. BMWs, Porsches, and Lamborghinis were parked behind conspicuously open gates. Palm trees, ferns, and singed shrubbery dolled up the sidewalks.

"I grew up here," John said. "It wasn't an upscale neighborhood then. But the city is changing. It is always changing. It's like a new city every day. Buildings rise and fall. Even people are changing."

At the end of the street there was a fenced coffee shop. Big steel fans staved the smog off a bunch of deserted outdoor tables. Big parasols flagged the name *TCC* in bold green letters.

John pulled the door open for two Chinese ladies to come out first. They laughed and chirped something in patois to him. John bowed and chirped back. Then he held the door for Hector. "After you, sir."

"What a gentleman!" Hector scoffed. "If you were an inch taller, I would date you."

"Who knows. In a few minutes, you may change your mind."

They chose a distant table with gaping wooden planks. Overhead were anchor-shaped lanterns, which fit well into the general décor of the coffee shop: a pirate ship. The cashiers and baristas wore eyepatches and tricorn felt hats with a Jolly Roger imprint on all of them. Rum bottles were lined up along the baseboards. A cartoon of Captain Hook hung on the wall. This hilarious setup made Hector smile while sipping his Earl Grey tea.

John cut to the chase: "I'm the middle-middle man."

Like an hourglass, the world flipped over and started counting anew. Hector uttered, "Ow."

"Forgive me. I didn't mean to startle you. Our president is

very interested in your friendship. One day he will be glad to shake your hand himself."

Our president. The words reverberated in Hector's head. Pulau didn't have a president, only a prime minister. "You're Chinese?" he asked.

And John nodded. "Ministry of State Security, sir. Middle East Division."

"Since when is there a 'Middle East Division' in the MSS?"

"Since the Arab Spring." John stirred two sugars in his cocoa. "It came out of the blue."

"It sure did."

"You understand that we feel very sorry about the girl. We tried our best to save her."

"Girl? What girl?"

"Your target. Fifi. The Big No's daughter."

Slowly, the world began to flip the other way.

"We tried to spare her and her father this tragedy," John said. "We switched the vaccines in the ambulance. But we made the mistake of not reaching out to you first. After that, it was out of our hands. Bloody Pulauis!"

"That's strange coming from a Pulaui."

White mug on lips, John corrected him, "I'm basically Chinese. I was born in Shanghai to Chinese parents who immigrated to Pulau when the New Deal was still hot. It isn't anymore. And I wholeheartedly identify as a Chinese. It's no secret. Even the MFA leadership is aware of it. The truth is seldom that simple, but mine is."

"That doesn't sound simple enough."

"In the West, you spend too much time plotting against one another. We're human too. But we don't adopt a Machiavellian backstabbing ideology to prosper. We're prospering already, because we believe in who we are. Your problem is that you don't."

"Are you trying to be radical, Johnny? 'Cause I used to kill radicals."

John took a sip of his cocoa and landed his mug gently on the table. "Please relax, sir. You have requested this meeting, so make use of it. I'm all ears."

A child vociferously cried behind Hector. Hector turned and saw an Indian lady carrying a trayful of cold drinks, struggling to keep her toddler quiet. Hector took a long while to turn his head back to the Chinese. "Well, it's not *you* I'm interested in meeting. I would like to see *him*."

"'Him,'" John echoed with raised eyebrows.

"Yes, *him*. Ernest. Are you dumb or what?"

John's eyes wandered to the same Indian mother. He whispered something in mandarin over his collar. Promptly, two suited Chinese men came into the coffee shop and asked the mother politely to escort them out. The tubbier of the two pushed the stroller out himself.

"Sorry about that," John said. "I should've let you know. This meeting is being recorded."

Hector felt a bucketful of ice pour down his spine. He leaned back and sighed. "I still have to see him. Is he alive—still?"

"Of course he is. Alive and kicking."

"What do you want him for?"

A stupid question, but it needed to be asked.

John grinned. "We are practical people, Agent Kane. We care only about money and power. The real question is, why do *you* feel you must see him?"

"Let's say I don't trust you. Friendship is a two-way deal. If I'm gonna be your friend, then I must see how you treat your other friends."

"We have big plans for the little prince, yes, but friendship isn't one of them."

"Don't kid yourself, Johnny. You're shooting for a friendship with the *big* prince. *That* is worth billions. Isn't that true?"

John thought for a while, then nodded. "Maybe. In some indirect way. But as for yourself, Agent Kane, *that*'s a friendship we really want."

Hector opened his arms theatrically. "I'm all yours, Johnny. Just take me."

"Please don't call me that."

"Call you what?"

"Johnny."

"Your MFA buddies have been calling me 'Mr Kane' For days. I never objected."

John's eyes shone suddenly. "I tell you what, call me Johnny," he said brightly. "I have changed my mind. It didn't occur to me at first, but now it sounds okay. What do you say, Agent Kane? Aren't we all strange creatures? How do we know what we like and what we don't? How can we better predict ourselves? We're very complex creatures."

"Sure, very complicated."

"*Uh-unh.*" Johnny waggled his finger no. "Not complicated. *Complex.* Big difference."

"Yeah? How's that explain my wife working for you?"

Johnny chuckled heartily. "Please don't be ridiculous. Of course she doesn't. A girl like Yubi, born and raised in North America, she doesn't speak the language and is married to a white man. She's never even been curious to visit China, not even once. She's a typical *banana*—yellow on the outside, white inside."

"Then why me? I'm feta cheese if Yubi is a banana."

"But you have a soul, a presence we can communicate with."

Hector looked at him. "Say that again?"

Johnny laughed quietly. "You're a complicated man, Agent Kane, I'll give you that."

Hector parodied him with a wagging forefinger. "*Uh-unh.* Not complicated. *Complex.*"

"Right, I forgot."

"What's the difference, anyway?"

Johnny was electrified. "That's exactly why we need you! To figure *that* out!"

Hector sipped his Earl Grey.

"You see, Agent Kane," Johnny explained. "A car is a complicated machine. You know its parts, you factor in the laws of dynamics, you get how it works. Totally predictable. A human being, on the other hand, is a *complex* system, like a garden. Both are creative and unpredictable. Have I lost you yet?"

"Johnny, what's your background, exactly?"

"City planning. I received my MCP from Berkeley six years ago."

"And what's a city-planner doing in 'foreign service,' if may ask?"

"Well, I started out at the Urban Redevelopment Authority, the URA. My interest was streetscape. Trees. And we already had a vision in that regard."

"Oh, I know about that. *Come visit the City in the Garden.* This dreamy motto. It was all over the travel guides. My wife is fascinated with it all."

"*City in the Garden* is the new motto. Back in the day it was just *Garden City*. In fact, sir, this ties in very closely with the Arab Spring. Would you like to hear a story?"

"I'm a grown man, Johnny. I'm a bit old for bedtime stories."

"It's not a bedtime story, sir. It's a story about a foolish man who creates a monster he can't control."

"That's *Frankenstein*." Hector coughed, looking at his wristwatch. "We should get back to the hotel. We can talk along the way."

They left the coffee shop, and Johnny related his strange story:

"I might fool you, but I'm not an ambitious man. When I first started at the URA, I was only looking to maintain the status quo. Maybe shake things up a little bit. But that was it. Come twenty-O-nine, the prime minister asked us for longer jogging tracks. So we did it. Pulau increased its park connectors from seventy to two hundred kilometers in less than two years. But that didn't satisfy the prime minister yet. He wanted more, and bigger parks. So we did that as well. Our National Parks Agency now boasts more than three hundred parks on this small island, all thanks to our work at the URA. But like an addiction, our prime minister's zeal grew with every green patch we sowed, with every flower and shrub we imported from Asia or Latin America. He got totally *whacked out*, if I may say so. Next he wanted more 'biodiversity.' He had always dreamed, he said, of giant rain trees to ward the sun off our streets, of pygmy flame trees on each and every corner, of genetically engineered palms with fragrant canopies, of self-reproducing acacias alongside our sidewalks, et cetera, et cetera. This was dangerous. I wrote him a long memo expressing my concerns. But he brushed it off. Come twenty-ten, the scientists in our Royal Botanic Gardens started reporting weird occurrences with their plants. Their plants, in brief, were no longer behaving properly. A green demon seemed to have taken possession of all green stuff in Pulau. Flowers died for no reason and newer, mutated versions replaced them in the pots. The National Parks arborists I'd helped a few months earlier also reported the same thing with their trees: The trees I'd planted myself either grew up to be giant monsters and had to be trimmed or taken down to keep the traffic flowing—or they withered and died, being replaced by genuses we had never seen. Our bioengineering did work, sir, but not to the results we expected. In a word, our garden grew on its own. It is independent, self-aware, and—yes—alive."

Then what happened?

"Well, then the minister mentor asked to meet with me."

Hector stopped and gawked at him. A biker nearly crashed into him at the crossing. "Minister mentor... as in *the* minister mentor?"

"Agent Kane, Pulau had only one minister mentor, and it won't have another."

Hector asked him to continue.

"He'd recently retired. But like all Pulaui elders, he still followed up on things. I went to see him in his Oxley Road house, the house he ordered to be demolished after his death. Ambassador Lee was also there. They looked so stressed. Fei Guo was in his wheelchair, holding *my* memo! The same memo I'd written to the prime minister four months earlier! Fei Guo said to me, 'Show me what these fools did not want to see, son. No summaries.' I was so overwhelmed, I stuttered, it was such a great honor! But I managed to make my point."

The hotel loomed, a nightmarish octopus towering over the Bay of its namesake. Pedestrians and trees were in continuity to the gate. Hector had not noticed how tree and person interlaced so finely in Pulau... not before now.

Johnny resumed his story, crossing the street with Hector. "You see, like all complex systems, our garden developed its own identity. We no longer understand it. It's alien culture to us. You come from a different culture, for example, but we have a common denominator—biology, media, literature, money. We understand one another. But that doesn't apply to our new force on the streets. Does the garden understand us? Debatable. But we can safely say that it is of a different mind from us. The sad conclusion is that Pulau is under green occupation, Agent Kane."

Hector was totally mixed up. A thin thread of logic underlined this tale. He was hooked, he was a slave for the narrative, he *wanted* to beat the monster garden.

What else do you use as bait? he wondered. Women, intel, money—and now fairytales?

Chapeau to the MSS. You guys have definitely outdone us.

"That doesn't put you in foreign service still," Hector said.

"When we failed to understand our creation, we had to find a different model to study, sir. Say, a complex system with established bridges for communication."

"Like human relations?"

"Like political science."

"Which avenue of political science? It's a huge discipline."

"How about the Arab Spring? Does it ring a bell?"

Hector thought of the millions shrieking on the streets and the chants and the fireworks and the unexpected outcomes. "Very risky," he concluded.

"Because it's uncertain?"

"Because it's not well-understood. Nobody has a clue what made Arabs revolt in the first place. And no one can expect what will happen next. You can't build your study of a garden on human behavior, Johnny. We, for the most part, don't make sense."

"Your father," the Chinese man said, dawdling before the stairs leading up to the hotel's plaza, "wrote a book called *The Dunes of Ignorance*—"

"I know where this is going."

"In it he preached that Arabs would never revolt."

"So you decided to hire his son?"

"Exactly, Agent Kane. That's why *you* are the one. You're the closest to Rocky Kane we can get. Only you can help us understand where the great Rocky Kane went wrong."

25

NEW HEIGHTS

We have, on average, a million different species of plants on the island," Johnny said in a raspy voice on the bus, his squeezed neck a diagram of sinews. "But you haven't noticed that, have you? It's because you're blind."

"I can only count to fifty," Fifi said blithely, sitting over her flexed leg. "Some people are just not Chinese, you know."

This had everyone on the bus—excluding Johnny and the driver—in stitches. Fifi was wearing a somewhat frilly sleeveless violet top and faded jean shorts. Beside her, tittering ever so loudly, sat Kero in his eternal Bart Simpson T-shirt. The shirt looked washed, though, and Kero had on a new pair of jeans, matching the color of his girlfriend's shorts. Ahmed and Zainab, in their usual middle seats, laughed open-mouthed, their eyes narrow crescents. But Ahmed's laughs were not audible. Either the gaiety had knocked the air out of his lungs or he was so preoccupied with his failure to negotiate yesterday that he couldn't fake it. He was dressed in his typical sunflower-yellow shirt and black pants. Seated beside the glamorous Zainab, he looked like a rotten picture of her grandpa. Zainab was laughing ebulliently and clearly. Hector noticed that all the women on the bus were content. Only the boys were restless.

"Interesting remark, Miss Noman," Johnny responded finally. "Do you wish to say that we, Asians, have higher IQs than others? I can't agree more. That's one of our many gifts. But what's yours? And what are you, by the way: Arab, Egyptian, Gypsy, Austrian, or just a rebel?"

"Whoa, whoa, whoa." Baxter rose to the victim's defense. "Hey, brother, what's your problem? Careful, we ain't takin' none of your racist crap here. 'Sides, you said *blind?*"

"When people invite you, you do not insult their country," the driver rejoined.

"And you are indeed blind," added Johnny.

Yubi stepped in. "I'm Chinese and I'm feeling really ashamed of both of you right now."

"You are not Chinese," the driver said, his hands tight on his wheel. "You do not speak our language."

Hector raised his hands to defuse the situation. "Stop this nonsense right now!" He was more amazed at his temper than the others were. "Johnny, why do you think we're 'blind'?"

"No offense. There is a point I was trying to make. You're *plant-blind*. Most human beings now are. We tread on ferns we don't see, sit under trees only for shadow, give each other flowers we can't name. What makes a rose a rose? A tulip? A lily? A gerbera, or an orchid? Anybody?"

"I tell them," volunteered the driver. "Ignorant people they are. Orchid is yellow and she dances."

———— ✻ ————

Li made a wide left turn, driving over a small concrete bridge that crossed the Disraeli river. Having departed from the east coast where the Sands was, the bus was taking them close to a hundred miles southwest for their first stop, the United Nations Development Programme (UNDP).

Hearing Yubi question the driver about his sanity—in response to his gloss about the orchid—Hector looked over the bridge and couldn't see Peel Quay in the thick smog. He thought about his romantic night with Yubi, and about Mosa al-Damawy, and couldn't but marvel at how remote those memories felt. The haze didn't only cover distance, it eroded time also.

Hector carefully pulled his phone from his pocket and stationed it between his knees. His walk-and-talk with Johnny had been, overall, a success. Not only had Johnny agreed to let him see Ernest, but he'd sent word out to his comrades to set up a meeting with their "Russian friends." It was time for Hector to send this piece of intel to the Agency. Yubi was innocent—at least of being a spy—and he would love to see the people who'd tortured him over the past couple of days suffer.

He first inspected the phone's screen. No missed calls or texts. Only the usual email notifications, most of which were from fellow academics or former students keeping in touch with him. (Never Ernest: The bastard had cut all contact with him since he'd left Cairo.) As per the Company's protocol, Hector had not stored any Company contacts on his phone. Not anywhere. But he memorized a few. His first choice would have been Ozgur, but this ghost of a friend hadn't given him his phone number and, realizing it now, Hector hadn't really asked for it. Hector did remember Fabio's number, though. It was the same Vodafone Egypt number, working on roaming service in Pulau.

Hector began writing a text for Fabio:

Howdy. Is Miranda okay? Tell her I'm getting you guys two
fine bottles back with me. Baijiu and Absolut. Each is over $

He stopped. He knew not, yet, the time nor the location of
his rendezvous with the other sides. So what would the CIA
make of such an incomplete message?

Hector was already under suspicion, and he might as well be
under surveillance. (Baxter's voice, barking at the driver,
confirmed this latter thought.) Hector decided that there was no
point in asking for the Company's attention right now, for he
had it already.

He decided to keep the message for later. So he pressed the
home button and redirected his attention to the ongoing
altercation on the bus.

Kero was chortling rather jumpily, squeezing Fifi's bare
shoulders, while Zainab glowered at them from the seat behind.
Hector was a little concerned about this now-public affair. He
had no gripes about Christians dating Muslims or whichever way
it went. But he was worried about their safety. Once they
returned to Cairo, they would be uncoupled. Inevitable. The
Islamists were confident and powerful, and they wouldn't mind
stoning the infidel and his lover in public to set an example.

But then something interesting captured Hector's attention.

Ahmed/Mourad *Bey* chimed in, in perfectly articulate
English, "The orchid Mr Li commented on, it's the Ballerina as
you people call it, is it not, John?"

The shock was greatest on the *Bey*'s wife. Zainab crept slowly
away from her husband and, blinking with her long lashes, gazed
at him incredulously.

"Excellent." Johnny lauded the Mukhabarat officer. "You have acquainted yourself with a very fine piece of our iconography, Mr al-Shatby."

"Well, it was in the *Eyewitness* travel book," Ahmed said. "Nothing spectacular, really. It was a red orchid that you then genetically bleached. First it was orange, and you called it 'Lady Sunshine,' because you were hopeful about this Franklin D Roosevelt New Deal knockoff of yours. Your bankers put it in their breast pockets as they laundered money from Hong Kong and New Delhi. Your students chewed on it, thinking it gave them brainpower. A rumor went around in the nineteen-nineties that Mr Fei Guo himself added it to his teapots. And it was a fad for years."

"It is yellow now," said Li, a regrettable flavor to his honk. "Not good for tea no more."

On their left, Middle Road intersected with Prinsep Street, which meant they were close to the residence and to the southwest coast of the island.

The bus juddered on, and Johnny continued where Ahmed had left off.

"So we hunted our Ladies down," said Johnny. "It was called exactly that, 'the Ladies' Hunt.' And we dumped them, or used them as fertilizers for the new garden we sowed."

"Why?" Yubi asked.

"Because Fei Guo didn't want a new gum epidemic," Johnny said. "Early after independence, ma'am, our port workers were so overworked. They worked twenty- and sometimes twenty-four-hour shifts. And they needed a relief, a recreation. Booze was prohibited, and smoke was out of the question. So gum it was. And gum it was for years. Till it infested every home, every shop, every government institution on the island. Tons of cheap sugary fruit gum, produced in the mainland, flooded our stores.

It came in a zillion different flavors in blue ship containers we called 'Dream Fairies.'"

Li uttered a rare laugh, low-pitched and wistful. He shook his grizzled crown. "Best days in life!"

"The gum was often mixed with tobacco, or aspirin, or even opium," Johnny carried on. "For years, the gum allowed our workers to bear the brunt of menial labor—manually paving the road for our bright future—but then it created too much pollution. The streets were covered with it. You found it in your hair, in your food. It was quite an epidemic. So we abolished it, barred every sort of gum from crossing our border forever."

"But why yellow?" Yubi asked. "Your flower is yellow. I think Mr Li said that. But Ahmed just said it's red."

"More bleach," Ahmed answered. "Whitewash the thing a bit more. Add a poisonous chemical or two to deter people. Give it a new name."

"The official name for our national flower now is 'Golden Shower,'" Johnny said. "But we hardly stick to formalities."

"*Ballerina!*" proclaimed the driver, drawling the last vowel.

Fifi heard that and cackled, ending in a strident cough.

"You okay, sweetie?" Yubi asked.

Still coughing, Fifi nodded. "I'm good."

Hector interlocked eyes with Johnny.

———— ⚜ ————

Hector exited the bus last.

"Doctor, did you get my text?"

"Not now, Kero."

"When will you—"

"Not now, Kero."

The sham artist walked away with a bowed rastacap.

Good Lord, thought Hector. Given all I'm going through, I can't wait to read this silly romance about Paris!

He joined his group.

Under a thin layer of haze, a beauty greeted him. After all, this was the Pulaui southwest. And like in all the west this year, the haze was merciful. The kilns of Sumatra were silent to honor Fei Guo's departure.

The driveway was paved with exposed aggregate of a mosaic complexion. It drew you into it the longer you gazed—like an optical quicksand. For this reason, everyone stepped away from the aggregate and stood beside a triad of strong palms centering the yard. This whole complex was called *King's Terrace,* and it was a two-tower affair connected by a one-story bridge.

"This way." Johnny pointed to the roofed entrance. "We'll cross the sky-bridge on the seventeenth floor."

But when they got up there, Kero got cold feet. The sky-bridge's walls were glass, floor to ceiling. The floor was a thin, streaked black ceramic. It looked—it felt—like tightrope walking between the two towers.

"I hate this," Kero said. "I'm bad with heights, man."

"How're you gonna survive the Monsters Park, then?" Yubi laughed. "You won't last a second on the rides!"

"I don't do rides," Kero said, still unable to move.

Fifi put her hands under her armpits and flapped her elbows and cock-a-doodle-doed. "Chicken! Chicken!" she teased him.

At this point Kero braved it up and with heavy feet—and a lot of encouragement—finished the walk.

Hector had no problems with height, and he gazed down through the glass wall. Only now he understood what had been so fetching about the mosaic driveway. It was, in fact, not mosaic at all. The aggregate made a distinct pattern. A face. Liver-spotted crown. Cloudy eyes. Tight, stretched lips.

The same face that had made him dizzy during his time-travel, yesterday.

Seventeen stories below, Fei Guo smiled widely at him. *I am earth and air,* the dead founder said. *Run no more.*

The office was called *The Global Centre for Public Service Excellence*—which had little to say about its parent organization, UNDP.

It was a single apartment with windows facing south, through which a sweeping view of the Batam Strait mesmerized them. The haze was stronger down south, but patchy. The water was serene and shimmering. Hector wished he was a fish—specifically, a vigorous carp—shooting beneath the surface... eating and procreating peacefully until the time came when he would be baited and slain on the spot.

Being mindful of one's journey in life, and struggling to find meaning in it, was man's greatest affliction.

There was a computer lab and a conference room. But Hector and his group were received in the hall. An athletic Chinese girl in a slanted black skirt and a white blouse ushered them to an oval glass table surrounded by black leatherette chairs. The air was redolent with jasmine. The pots in every corner nursed green plants with big leaves. In a few minutes, a lanky Swede, mid-forties, came to welcome them. He was dressed in a white shirt and clay-brown slacks. His face was bony and his nose was sharp and his hair was very thin. His eyes were chestnut, and muted. Crossing his legs, he revealed two different socks. He welcomed them again, said he'd been to Cairo once, and yawned.

Then the Chinese girl offered them peppermint rings out of an acrylic jar. This seemed to set the Swede in motion. He leaned his elbows on the glass table and spieled away.

He talked about the UNDP and his affiliated office—in great detail, in a deep baritone, maintaining eye contact with his guests and jotting down notes to address them later, no trace of his earlier sleepiness whatsoever.

Hector found this metamorphosis—from bored bureaucrat to "sustainable development" expert—entertaining. The Swede reminded him of himself. Hector had nearly forgotten about his Europe days. How he sold baloney to EU politicians, rubbed knees with impressible artists, slept with post-doc fellows who couldn't afford their rent. The whole international relations enchilada.

Ahmed asked about the office's funding.

The Swede made a cage with his slender digits. "We rely substantially on donations from stakeholders. We do receive token funding from the UN. But this goes into paying our electricity bills." The Swede cocked his head and smiled at his Chinese secretary, or assistant, or bed-buddy, or whoever she was. "Anyway, let's stick to our topic, shall we? Since the mid-sixties, the UNDP has helped over one hundred-seventy nations move up the GDP scale. Our offices build resilience, foster development that is sustainable—"

Fifi chuckled. Then she bowed her head and raised her hand in apology.

The bureaucrat carried on. "Again, sustainable development is our goal. Our Pulau office, for example, has assisted ASEAN countries in fulfilling the UNDP's sustainable development goals. We improved their public sector capabilities, including education, health care, poverty—"

"Do you pay for this?" Kero asked.

"I beg your pardon?"

"Those sustainable development goals, does your office pay for them?"

"Well…" The Swede's eyes flicked to his assistant, this time with a plea.

"Banks take care of that," answered the assistant.

"Local or international?" Kero persisted.

"I would say both," the Swede said. "But for big projects, infrastructure stuff, usually MDBs. Multilateral development banks. For instance, right now we're drafting a plan for renovating the flood management system in the Philippines. The World Bank Group will cover a big part of the expenses. The rest, well—"

"Well what?" This time it was Baxter who interrupted him.

Hector was very amused. His students had absorbed his classes handsomely. They inherited his loathing for sustainable development agencies to a comical degree.

"It's up to Asian countries to figure that out," the Swede returned. "We are on the cusp of a new era of regional financing in Asia. More and more Asia-based MDBs are coming into the picture. Chinese in particular. Not only is China becoming *the* dominant financier of Asia, but it has reshaped our whole understanding of economics—"

"Ooh," Zainab moaned. "So sad. Go on, sir, please."

"Back when I was in school," the bureaucrat said, trying to regain control, "the marriage between MDBs and sustainable development was clear-cut. Developing countries sought aids, and we—Westerners—provided for them through our traditional systems. You're aware, of course, that the first MDBs were born out of the Second World War to help rebuild Europe. Then the Cold War made it necessary for these banks to continue. Come the two-thousand-eight World Financial Crisis, both creditors and borrowers became iffy. Especially in Asia. They lost trust in us completely—"

"Unbelievable," said Ahmed.

The Swede nodded, feigning unawareness of the badgering. "Absolutely. The Chinese in particular took up the task of redrafting the monetary system. And they began with Asia. They kind of feel... I don't know how to put it—"

"Entitled?" offered Baxter.

"No, that would be inaccurate. It's a sense of duty that drives them. A duty to correct, to improve, to return to Chinese norms. In other words, they feel they have to, or the world will suffer. In their collective mentality, they are made to lead. And that is the bind. China so far is one of the world's largest borrowers. It is a developing economy. And yet, it is steadily becoming a heavyweight creditor. Especially in Asia. For the first time in history, ladies and gentlemen, a developing country, deep in debt, is calling the shots—"

"Sorry." Zainab stood up. "We must leave. It's almost time for the Zohr prayer."

———— ༔ ————

Sultan Ahmed Mosque was built circa 1825, with a special grant from the East India Company. Five thousand pounds Sir Fullerton had commissioned to help Sultan Ahmed Shah—the last Malay to rule Pulau—immortalize his name.

Legend had it the Dutch architect who'd designed this wonder was executed by the sultan shortly after, so as not to replicate it.

A century later, though, the mosque was falling apart. And here was where Fei Guo came into the picture.

"In the late eighties," Johnny related on the bus, "to show his goodwill to the Malays, Fei Guo budgeted a million dollars to renovate their great mosque. Sultan Ahmed Mosque now boasts golden lamps and door knockers. Original Persian rugs. Its grand dome has glass-bottle windowlets similar to those in Hagia Sophia. There is a courtyard with peach and gelam trees that I have planted myself. And there is a well there, which can heal anything."

"Anything?" Fifi said dubiously.

"Anything and everything," confirmed the guide.

Zainab was so excited. She would gorge herself on that well's water. This would clear the infection from yesterday. Allah would make it go away.

Kero rolled his eyes.

Li dropped them far from the mosque. He said the streets were too bumpy and narrow for him, so they had to leg it.

Hector piloted the pack with Yubi's hand in his. Ahmed and his wife followed. Then Fifi and her infidel boyfriend. Lastly Baxter and Johnny trailed behind—which made Hector somewhat uneasy.

The neighborhood was called *Arab Street* though no Arabs had ever lived here, as Johnny explained. It was a ghetto for the aboriginal Malays. Its historical name was *Kampong Gelam*, which literally meant "the village" in patois. Thinly bearded men in drab two-piece outfits bustled around like ants. Some of them had pants chopped off above the ankles, conforming to the Muhammadan Sunnah: Beware of frills, my children, those dirt-smeared hems. Earth is unholy. Ostentation has a sister in hell.

"Is this Pulau or Kandahar?" Fifi puffed.

"We're multicultural," said Johnny with a smile.

"Kandahar is more modern," said Baxter. "I went to some fashion shows there. Pancakes."

"Keep your voices down, please," Hector said.

With their masks, they threaded their way through the beards, niqabs, and chadors. The neighborhood boasted some very lush trees, which made the hazy alleyways yet more impenetrable.

Zainab and her husband headed to the mosque, while the rest lingered in the only open restaurant in the vicinity. The place was without a sign, dirty and empty. And soon the Zohr prayer, aired from a platoon of strident loudspeakers atop the mosque's minaret and parapet, reached them inside. Very few noises came from the deserted streets.

"Gelam is the leafy tree you see at every corner here," Johnny said. "It's a hardy queen, tough, and it can take anything. Fire. Drought. Cold. Haze. Anything." He sat back and relaxed. "The Malays have got it all."

A teenage boy clad in a dusky tunic and white pants brought Johnny's choice of the local delicacies. Aside from what looked like *basbosa*, what stood out most were a dish with cubed yams swimming in coconut milk, and some moss green cone covered by a shell of hexagonal flakes.

"*Ew*," Fifi said. "What *is* that?"

"Alien corn." Kero chortled.

"And it has a name," said Johny. "*Delicious monster.* Don't let that faze you. It doesn't bite." And he laughed his fill at his own joke.

Fifi stabbed it with her fork and said it tasted like banana with pineapple.

"No, thank you," Baxter said, opting for the yams in the

coconut milk.

Yubi giggled and crawled closer to Hector, plastering herself to his perspiring side. She hugged his back, rested her head on his collarbone, and tickled his ankles with her big toe. Hector breathed the lavender in her hair. Her scalp, which he rubbed with his jaw, was sweaty and soft.

"Oh," Fifi moaned, "that's so romantic."

"Eat your monster, Fifi," Yubi said.

"I don't do monsters, honey. I do nice guys just like your guy," Fifi replied in a mock slatternly tone.

Yubi laughed, her happiness ringing inside her husband's lungs.

"Thought you already *had* a guy," Baxter said slyly.

Kero chewed his monster mutely.

"This ain't none of your business, yo," Fifi said jovially.

"Why do they call themselves Arabs?" Hector asked Johnny, to change the mood.

"Mid-eighties," Johnny said. "*Al-Takfir wal-Hijra.* Brainwashed losers."

"This *takfir* thing," Yubi said, "it's like calling someone a *kafir*, right? Like an infidel."

"Yes," confirmed Kero. "*Takfir* means infidelity."

Fifi looked at him and hiccupped with laughter. She dropped her fork.

"What?" Kero said.

Yubi said, "Let's talk about something else. That's so gloomy."

But Baxter wouldn't hear of it. "This movement is dead, bro," he said to Johnny.

"What's ISIS, then? A boy band?" Johnny riposted.

"So what's your point?" Hector interceded. "So far we know

that *al-Takfir wal-Hijra* is dead. Not that it's lost its audience. But it's been replaced by more sinister groups."

Johnny shrugged.

"Come on," Baxter said. "Show your cards, man. You ain't the first one here to blame others for your problems. What is it this time? They made your Malays wear the hijab and grow their beards? Bring it on, my man. Bring it on."

Yubi frowned. So did Fifi, revisiting her sweet monster.

Johnny smiled. "We live in a globalized world, now, don't we? And who invented it? Wait, wait. I'm not saying America brought it on. I'm only suggesting that when a head is chopped somewhere on the planet, a baby cries on the other side."

"That's not what I teach." Hector decided to take Baxter's side, mainly to stymie suspicion, noticing his wife's body detaching itself from his. "We live in a world dominated by power. And power seeks more power. Culture is power, yes, but only if it sells. So it needs to be buyable."

"It doesn't have to be good, no?" Johnny said.

"And who decides what's good?" Baxter said. "Beijing?"

Johnny released a string of low-voltage chuckles. He wolfed down his *basbosa*-like dessert, then said, "What sells is power, yes? Imagine a world where they brainwash your kids, force them to buy things they neither need nor really want. We don't need 'Beijing' to say that's not good."

"America isn't responsible for your problems," Baxter said. "Please own up to it and move on. Stop blaming us, man."

"Is that the case, Mr Simmons?" Johnny gave the CIA rookie an amused look. "America has made the Gulf Arabs filthy rich. And what's an Arab do but conquer and preach? Let's say Arabs have quite an influence over our poor, simple Malay. An influence so great, in fact, that the name of this neighborhood has changed from *the village* to *Arab Street* thanks to a bunch of radical *al-Takfir wal-Hijra* preachers sent out from the Arab Gulf. How do you find your bubur cha cha, Mr Simmons? Good, or do want me to ask 'Beijing'?"

"My *what?*" Baxter said, gazing at his strangely named yams in coconut milk.

The Chinese gave Hector a conspiratorial grin.

Li said he would park at the nearby Ion Orchard shopping center and insisted on being called before they headed back.

"I sleep," he warned. "Driver is very tired. You do not give rest. Go now, leave. Be there long time." And he pulled his door shut in their faces and pulled away.

"He is *charming!*" Fifi chanted.

The Royal Botanic Gardens were a cluster of three domes stuck together on the bay shore like mushrooms. The place was close to the George Bay Sands, but between the hotel and gardens was the king's Bay: its water melted lead, dozens of ships grazing in its smoky yard.

The atmosphere was harrowing: muggy and stinky with hundreds of people waiting in line and coughing in their masks. The haze-filtered sunlight laid a matte blanket over the ticket office, the wooden ramps, the verdure bursting out of the three domes in vines and ferns. Color paled. Faces—all faces—were anemic.

Unlike his two predecessors, Johnny wasn't one for tickets. At the gate, he flashed his ID to the guards and let everybody in without a word.

Hector looked up inside and saw no dome. A holographic

sky fluttered with carefree birds and slow, cottony clouds against a limpid blue background. The air was warm and pregnant with a boutique of fragrances. Noises intermingled with the symphony orchestras of bird sounds.

They walked down a lane of bright green grass that broke shortly into trails too many to count. Johnny led them up one of the trails, and soon they were in a rolling park. Yoga and tai chi were huge here. The crowdedness gave meditation a sanguineous uplift. Blood vessels relaxed. Lungs took in deep refills of the blissful air. The grass shied under their feet.

They left behind memories of their former steps.

"Royal isn't monarchic," Johnny exulted. "Our Gardens are *exquisite* gardens, *excellent* gardens, *superior* gardens. You won't smell it, but the air is purified by ultraviolet filters. Every germ is counted. Flies are numbered. Species rise and fall on their own. This is a true genetic pool. Careful what you tread on."

Behind a cluster of sea guttas—bifurcated, small-leafed trees native to the rocky soil of Pulau, as Johnny provided—was a serene pond spotted by what, at first glance, seemed like lily pads. Hector almost saw a crowned frog crouched there. But then he eyed two chirpy teenage girls racing on the pads. He realized the pads were actually stepping stones.

They crossed the pond and came upon a thicket of huge, lush, wide-spreading trees gaping to allow a passageway. Retro kerosene lamps dangled overhead from the tree branches, and white-on-pink flowers fell upon them as they walked down. It felt wondrously claustrophobic. The bark was wizened dark brown, the leaves as big as elephant ears, curled like a wizard's scrolls.

"One of my early accomplishments," Johnny bragged. "*The Hot Rain Tree*. Basic genetic play. You fiddle with the tree's sex organs, make it unable to satisfy its lust, so it flowers nonstop.

Trees are no different than us. They eat, drink, and they *love* mating."

"You kept them from enjoying sex?" Fifi said, walking behind Hector. "That's torture!"

Baxter snickered at the rear.

"How long is this tunnel?" Zainab asked in front, behind Johnny.

"We're already there." Johnny cleared a lock of dead twigs at the end. "Brace yourselves, ladies and gentlemen. You're about to get lost."

They found themselves in a bloody maze. The hedges were made of pruned red robin shaped like horseheads, giant mice, or boy-and-girl silhouettes. A pale statue of Our Lady the Mermaid stood in the center atop a tiered, algae-covered fountain. A gleeful, golden elf welcomed every correct turn, an ugly leprechaun every dead end. Fifi found this exhilarating. She chased after Kero in and out of the bloody passages.

And before long it was inevitable. They were kissing.

Baxter whistled. "Holy shmoly. Get a room!"

Zainab faced this transgression with tearful eyes, yapping to her husband ireful hisses. And the instant the lovers uncoupled—Fifi dropped to the grass, coughing—Zainab was quick to shame the hussy. "Fatima, come right here, *ya safla!*" she yelled in Arabic. "If I were your mother, I would lick you in public with a bamboo!"

Fifi's reaction was even more provocative. She didn't even look at the angry Muslim-Brotherhood lioness. She cocked her head and broke down in a coughing guffaw.

"Save some laughs for the theme park," Zainab said. "Or do you want to go to a strip club instead? Given the way you're dressed, you'll fit right in."

"You've got your husband to strip down for," Fifi said with a dismissive flick of her hand, still coughing. "Why are you harassing me, you terrorist?"

Hector nudged Yubi's elbow, and Yubi stepped in immediately. She helped Fifi up on her feet, and together they moved ahead of the pack.

Kero was frozen at the fence, red-handed, wide-eyed, lips quivering like a hare under siege—before he dashed to join his girlfriend and Yubi.

Zainab was now sobbing profusely, shaking in her husband's arms. "She called us terrorists, Ahmed. That's what you get when you lower yourself to the level of apostates and infidels. *Sniffle. Sniffle.* They hate us, want us dead. This she-devil will slit my throat. I swear to God, she will. I'm so scared I want to call the police. *Sniffle. Sniffle.*"

Hector dawdled behind them, allowing Baxter to bypass him too, then he gripped Johnny's arm and raised a forefinger to silence him.

After they were a safe distance behind, Hector demanded, "I'm fed up with you and your trees. You're a time-waster of the first class. When and where *is* the rendezvous?"

Johnny answered in mock thick Chinese English, "But don't you want to make sure your wife and your students are having good time first? *Tut-tut.* Not good what you do. No. No. We are one happy trip. We cannot leave in a storm like this. Not good policy."

Kero fainted on the skyway—which was Johnny's plan all along.

They'd trekked in lands of exotic venues. The Whispering

Flowers Garden. The Living Stone Farm. The Stinking Corpse Lily Colony.

So by the time they'd hit the heart of the Botanic Gardens, the Supertree Grove, they were terribly "knackered," as Baxter put it.

At the center of the Supertree Grove seven great sycamores rose to record heights. They were sheathed in glimmering steel buttresses, with a transparent skyway weaving through their boughs.

Shrieks rose from over two hundred feet high.

Kero had cold feet at first, naturally. But Fifi challenged him this time as she'd done at King's Terrace—instigated by subtle remarks from Johnny.

Finding himself between disgrace and a hard place—accepting the "Cuckoo" pet name Fifi brandished to tease him, versus facing up to his phobia—Lover Boy went for the hard place. He took the one-person lift to the skyway to beat his acrophobia.

They cheered for him. They witnessed his historical first step. But then… Cuckoo's innate fear got hold of him.

All Cuckoo's hopes for glory, for making his girlfriend proud, for living up to his name—whether Revolutionary, authorial, or papal—were shattered.

He was rendered a dirty smudge against the fake sky—a curling, cry-baby one.

"Kero!" Fifi screamed, then raced to the lift.

Followed by—of all people—Ahmed.

The remainder of the group were instructed to stay put.

"We can't risk crowding the skyway," Johnny rationalized. "Wait for us till we get the paramedics. Professor, shall we?"

26

INVISIBILITY, HECTOR

J ohnny's pace was relaxed, his tongue agog with whatever snippets of botanic trivia his soon-ending guidesmanship called for.

"Check the sea almonds on your left, Agent Kane. Every one is larger than any sea almond on the planet. Not my design, no. I give credit to myself where credit is only due. These are my brother's. Typically, a sea almond sheds its leaves twice a year. But we've made ours evergreen. Downside is, you never get to see the aging shade, the change from red to yellow to orange as the leaves grow older and fall. These trees are forever young! The crown is different too, as you can see. Have you ever seen a tree layered up like this? We call this a *pagoda*. A sea almond has a pagoda-like crown. It's natural. But not in this heightened form. You know something? Architecture in the West has always puzzled me. It lacks—how to say this?—the *hierarchy*. We often say in the MSS that Emperor Ming achieved *nibbana* not by his good deeds or conquests only. No, no. But by dreaming up this abstract form, the pagoda. Do you know who invented the chair? The wardrobe? The table? You should read your Plato. (Watch out for the joggers.) One wise man once said, 'All western philosophy consists of footnotes to Plato.' And our man Ming beat Plato down in the dust. You first. Our stop is at the end of the line. We'll sit right there."

———— ⚜ ————

It was some kind of streetcar. But it was built in the form of a red dragon.

Soon the doors slid shut, and the dragon sped through an underground tunnel.

Hector gazed out the window over Johnny's right shoulder. Johnny looked out too, and the glass reflected his proud smile. The tunnel was lined in phosphorescent green.

"Dragon's gold," said Johnny. "Freakish, don't you think?"

Hector had been counting on Johnny's vanity, and Johnny had swallowed the bait. Hector deftly picked his phone out of his back pocket and double-tapped the home button to retrieve the stored message for Fabio.

His eyes never left the window. "It's beautiful," he said.

"It's moss. A special kind of luminous moss. We call it 'dragon's gold.' Believe it or not, it's not here by our design."

Feigning shock, Hector now shifted his face around to get a fuller picture of this luminous infestation—through the other windows. He only needed a glimpse of his phone's screen. And now he had it. He tapped *send* and slowly slipped the phone back into his back pocket.

"So is there *anything* by design here, Johnny?"

"Yes. I'm afraid there is," Johnny said with macabre dejection.

For the next eight stops, as passengers thinned out till there was no one else left, the two spooks sat side by side in mourning silence. Then the train slowed down, its screech piercing. The green moss discontinued, and darkness overcast the tunnel. The overhead fans whooshed, lights twitched, and there was a smell of dust.

Then the dragon slithered to a stop. Doors tinkled then opened.

"We've arrived," Johnny said. "I hope we aren't too late."

They climbed down onto a macadam platform. Hector saw a huddle of squat golden trees at the end of the platform. A hot breeze blew from there, tickling the golden leaflets. It made Hector hot. He undid another button on his shirt. He distinguished a trail among the trees with a wooden sign on top of it. The letters were too dim to read from such a distance.

He felt a hard object pressed against his mid-spine.

"Turn around," Johnny said.

Hector turned with what he believed was a combative smile.

Johnny was holding a Glock 17 semiautomatic. Behind him, the dragon was making a U-turn in a cul-de-sac.

Hector whistled. "You've got deep pockets for someone your size."

"It was under the seat," Johnny provided flatly. "Empty your pockets, please. Slowly."

Hector did. Leather wallet, check. Keys and hotel card, check. Dirty napkins, check. Useless mask, check. Peppermint rings, thrown away to the dragon on its way up.

"Your watch and your phone, please. Put them on the floor."

Hector did. And the MSS spy picked the phone up and looked at it a bit. "Did you send for help? The devil can't reach you here."

"I thought you were the devil."

"Then I should have warned you. We don't have network coverage underground." Johnny powered the phone off, then asked Hector to strip down and pile his clothes on the floor, too.

Johnny took his own belt and genuflected to examine Hector's clothes. Diligently, he moved the buckle over every item on the floor. Finally, he stood up. "Lucky you."

"You've got it." Hector grinned.

"Not a beep. The Agency has given up on you."

"Which means?"

"That you're single again. Dress up."

Hector began doing so. He felt humiliated and a bit confused. He'd half-expected the Company to have sewn a tracker in his jacket or his jeans or even in his shoes. Had the MSS really outdone the West's most powerful intelligence agency?

"May I ask what the gun's for?"

"The Russians have trust issues," Johnny said.

"And you're the zens of love and confidence?"

"Don't think too hard about our motives. That's totally irrelevant."

Hector tucked his shirt into his jeans. "You know? That episode about my father—where he went wrong and so on— doesn't make any sense."

Johnny was silent.

"I've been thinking about it," Hector continued, slipping his feet into his loafers. "Academia is a surrogate reality. Too structured to be of any good. The real world doesn't work that way. That was my father's problem. He was too much of an academician. Too structured. A simpleton."

"You aren't your father," Johnny said.

"But I inherited his brain. His tendency to believe in the

status quo. His structured brain. His naïvety."

Johnny finally put his gun away, stowing it behind the front of his belt.

Hector put his wristwatch on, then slipped his phone—still turned off—into his back pocket. "All I wanted was to live peacefully with my wife. And now I'm being dragged into this inferno for a quest that keeps eluding me."

"Not for long," Johnny said.

"Why am I really here, Johnny?"

"Because you wanted to see your friend."

"I never said he was my friend."

"Agent Kane, we're running out of time. If you want to stay behind, be my guest. But otherwise, we must hurry."

There was no walking back, Hector realized. And he knew the Chinese man knew it, too.

Hector followed his captor down the platform to the huddle of golden trees. Only now could he read the sign over the trail. It read:

GREEN CATACOMB

Banana, rubber, red cedar, fig, custard apple, and many nameless trees hemmed them in—as if wanting to take a bite of them.

Johnny battled the tangles head-on. Hector followed.

"We used synthetic granular fertilizers at first," Johnny said. "But they didn't take. Mother Earth has a way of saying no. Imagine five million bastards stuck on this piece of rock, this 'spit of dust,' as the Malaysians call it. And we're aging. Twenty-five thousand deaths a year. Where to bury all those, Hector!"

Hector took hearing his first name from the MSS spy as a good sign.

"Organic is the way to go," Johnny carried on. "That's the future. We're destined to live and to die in our garden. Not a shabby existence, don't you think? If you're a Gaia-worshiper, that's fine. But… (There you go, they regrow the moment you cut them. Watch your step.) What was I saying? Yes. We don't believe in the garden, Hector. We decorate our homes with it, fine. We use the trees to streetscape, fine. We promise tourists a green paradise, a tropical Vegas, well, at least we're getting paid for it. But this…"

A midrib of a banana tree lashed against them, the blade grazing Johnny's neck. He let out a curse and shrugged his left shoulder to stop the bleeding. But they soldiered on.

"So what you see here is a green cemetery. And it runs deep and far. We offer the garden our dead to keep her satiated, to keep her away from the living. The Russians think that's crazy, but we don't see eye to eye on a lot of things."

"What's the deal between you and the Russians?" Hector asked, fighting his way through a thicket of regrowing fuchsia-colored ferns.

"At this point we're sidekicks. Associates at best. We don't call the shots, yet, but we count the bullets."

Hector perceived movement high up in the canopy. The chirping of so many birds drew closer, and closer. He dropped, and a swarm of the birds, quacking insanely, missed his head only by inches, spearheaded by a four-rotor drone.

Hector rose gingerly and took in the new environment. The trail had ended, and he was now in some kind of spacious, sett-tiled court. At the center was a tiered dark stone oasis of neatly assorted flower pots. Tables, chairs, a couple of barbecues, a

Hawaiian bar, and even a bike were dispersed here and there.

And beyond, ship hulls, anchors, propellers—dozens of them—hovered in midair!

Hector scowled at this surreal spectacle. Gradually, he realized it was not air the ships were suspended in, but water. Specifically, the Bay's water, as seen through a pellucid glass wall.

"Hector, my chap!" someone hailed him from his left side.

Hector turned and gawked at his interlocutor.

The voice registered. But the face did not. Not at first. And when it slowly did, the voice slipped away like a mirage.

Reality wobbled around him.

It was the same grizzly, young-old face. Even the teardrop earring was there. Here was the celebrity who'd dodged him for days!

Yet something about seeing him face to face made Hector wish he could bury himself in this garden of death.

Ambassador Tommy Lee drew closer, spreading his arms, ready for an embrace. "Finally!" he cheered.

And then the truth shone in Hector's head, with the force of an exploding star. The face was the correct match. But not the body. Those black slacks. The white tunic, the silly Chinese logo on the left breast. Those—did not belong to Lee!

Not *Lee*.

But *Li*. The bus driver.

The mere existence of this composite figure made Hector sick. He felt the sett quake underneath him. He took a step, two steps, three steps backwards, as the bicameral Chinese-Pulaui dignitary walked closer and closer, arms outstretched and far-reaching.

"Like our healthy graveyard?" Lee grabbed his shoulders. "Fei Guo is our air. And we will be the trees to breathe him. Hector, my boy, do not be so shocked. The biggest shock is yet to come."

Hector could now see that even the bus company's logo wasn't, in fact, in Chinese at all. These crisscrossing sticks in traffic-red were in English. An "M" neighbored by two italicized mirror images of "Z."

M S S

The Ministry of State Security.

The Chinese had given the CIA the biggest slap in the face in the history of espionage.

The drone drove the birds down. And Hector winced. Then he heard a snorty, raspy laugh, and the swarm swooped back up.

"You've got yourself a dangerous toy, Mr Lebedev," Lee said.

Hector peered in the direction Lee was facing and saw Siva— in his eternal charcoal suit—walking toward some kind of frondy sugar-apple tree. Hector hadn't noticed the man under the tree until then. He was the same Russian he'd run into in the elevator yesterday. The booby-trap "defector" of Paris.

Eight years ago "Lebedev" had been "*Starshy Leytenant* Popov," Hector remembered.

Strange how spies changed names—Popov to Lebedev, Ozgur Alexopolous to Mosa al-Damawy to Kerry Grant, Li to Lee—while Hector, all his life, had been stuck with just one infamous name.

Lebedev was dressed in a pair of dark blue jeans and a black blazer with a matching tight-fitting V-neck. He looked like a bouncer. Hector looked beside the tree and saw a three-step dais leading up to the glass wall. Johnny was standing there, and beside him was a wrought-iron table. To the right of the table stood a figure in a pinstriped suit. He turned his back on Hector, looking up at the ship bottoms floating in the Bay.

"Where is Ernest?" Hector asked Lee.

"Hector, let's put the past behind us. We're here to make history. And we really need your help."

"Where *is* Ernest?" Hector repeated.

Lee shepherded Hector away with a firm, paternal grip. "In our trade, son, a spy can't afford to be edgy. It's a disagreeable, seductive trait, for sure. But triumph and seduction don't necessarily go together. (Move on, my boy. It's senseless to fight now.) I'll let you in on a secret. Most successful spies in history were never heard of. Not due to obscurity, but by design. They were neither glamorous nor sexy. What I have come to realize in my dotage, my friend—and you're the son of my dear old friend (remind me to talk about this one day)—is that a spy's greatest weapon isn't brains or weapons or testosterone. But *invisibility*, Hector," said the bus driver. "It trumps fame, glory, and even love."

They bypassed Lebedev and Siva and climbed the stone steps hip to hip, leg to leg, eye to eye.

On the dais, Lee let go of him. Hector was overwhelmed by the sea. The ashen light seeping through the glass wall gave the Bay a cosmetic ambiance. Flamboyant sea fauna swaggered before him—pastel yellow sweetlips, orange butterflyfish, magenta grunts, green perches, brown eels—and ships of different shapes and shades roofed the horizon.

There was one ship in particular that received the lion's share of this skyview: Its vermilion rudder overlooked the dais at eight o'clock, its berth barely visible two hundred feet up, to the south.

Now Hector turned and saw him: the man in the pinstriped suit.

The man's neck was red, as if by inflammation, his hair

brown, his eyes green, like his, but hostile. *Authority* radiated from him. He was Lebedev's taciturn companion in the elevator.

Invisibility, Hector.

Between Hector and the mysterious man the wrought-iron table hosted a minibar on a silver tray. Lee filled three flutes with Grand Marnier and called for both sides to join him for a toast.

"To death!" Lee said, clanking his flute against theirs.

"To peace!" said Johnny.

"To revisionism!" said Lee again. "To anarchy!"

Both Hector and the man in the pinstriped suit were silent.

Johnny went down to take over control of the drone from Lebedev, and the latter came up to take his flute from Lee. Lee said merrily, "Our trees are obliged, *Kapitan* Lebedev. Hope you'll always remember today. Even I have not had the honor to scatter Fei Guo's ashes yet. But, hey, we're in happy communion now."

Hector sipped the liquor. His molars were itching to grind, but he controlled himself. "We haven't been introduced," he said to the man in the pinstriped suit.

"Of course," volunteered Lee.

But Hector stopped him. "I want *him* to speak for himself. I'm done talking to bus drivers."

Lee gulped his insult with the dredges of his Grand Marnier, fixing himself another. Lebedev also asked for a refill.

"The fact that you don't know who I am," began Pinstriped Suit, his English clear and fluent, "speaks volumes about your *situation* at the Agency. For the record, it's *Polkovnik* Volkov you're guilty of colluding with."

Hector trudged after the *polkovnik* as he paced away from the table.

"Look at the sea, Hector," Volkov said. "Even in this horrid weather, it's alive and cool. Fish are better than us humans. Some of them get fat, some get eaten, but life always goes on. They don't stop living because some of them are too weak to endure. There is no *Mastermind Fish* that controls the deeps. What kind of world would it be—when you have only one superpower? One fish. Fish need to scavenge, to fight and die, to parade, to languor, to strive for whatever makes life meaningful for each subspecies. Put your hands on the glass and feel the undercurrent, Hector. It's music! A godly rhythm. Can you hear what it says? It says, *Power! Power!*—as loudly as it can."

"Maybe not so loud." Hector removed his palms from the glass and picked up his flute from the sett floor. "We swim and scuba-dive. We send ships. We wage wars. We make money. And money, my dear *polkovnik,* is power. Not rhetoric."

The *polkovnik* smiled, revealing a row of small, pearly-white teeth. "You're better than we thought. Alas, we should have met years earlier, before things spiraled out of control. Listen to me, Hector. See this drone my aide was toying with? It's got your people's camera mounted on it. We've disabled the audio, but they still have you on video. Do you understand me?"

Hector swiveled and looked hard at this ash-scattering devil spying on him.

Volkov gently tapped Hector on the shoulder.

Hector turned.

"Before you ask any questions, you must listen to our side of the story. You people strike, run, get hurt, then hold grudges against us, without bothering to listen. Would you be so kind as to listen, Hector?"

Hector did not answer.

"Only yesterday," Volkov said, pacing around on the dais, "the Syrian Army responded to a new attack on Aleppo's Central Prison. The same happened in Egypt during the Revolution—or what you call revolution—to tragic results. Cut to Kabul, yesterday. A suicide bomber attacked a convoy of NATO troops, blowing up a dozen soldiers or so. Poor kids, they go to war hoping for a scar and a medal, they don't make enough corpse to bury. Iraq, same bloody day. Yesterday. Eleven bombs shook Sadr City, killing God-knows-how-many innocent people. The same people who suffered genocides under Saddam are praying for his Second Coming. Do you see a pattern, Hector?"

Volkov stopped a foot from Hector's face.

Hector said, "We're just trying to help."

"Did anybody *ask* for your help?"

"Did anybody ask for *yours?*"

The Russian smiled and moved back. "You remind me of one dictator I know. When he was asked why there was no opposition in his country, he said, 'It's not my job to raise competitors to run against me.'"

"You're confused. This is not a competition. We don't *rule* the international system. Nobody does. We're only trying to make it safe for everyone."

"And make a profit along the way, no?" Volkov turned with a sly smile.

"Success breeds success. It's infectious. And democracy *is* success. It's a profitable business, if you want to look at it that way."

The Russian looked at the vermilion rudder in the sea-sky. It was stirring with life now, its blade adjusting for the ship's next destination, waving goodbye. The anchor rose slowly from the deep, dark and rusty, mesmerizing.

"Where is he?" Hector asked, suddenly worried.

"The Middle East is by far the most volatile region in our world," Volkov said slowly, as if in a trance. "Political violence is one thing. We can deal with it, it's part of life. But volatility is another. It's like cancer. It's not part of the rhythm. We are, in fact, doing you a great favor."

The propeller spun slowly. The ship distanced itself from the berth. Then the rudder changed direction and the propeller sped away.

Volkov pointed at the departing ship and said, "Say goodbye to your student and friend, Hector."

Hector stared at the vessel, at first confused, then incredulous.

And at length, his eyes grew hot with tears. "What will happen to him?"

"He will be okay. His father *will* submit to our demands. All parents eventually do. You think you live for yourself. But the moment your kid trips on the grass, you lose your sanity."

"Then why did you bring me here?"

The *polkovnik* did not answer that. He nodded at his aide, who put his drink on the table instantly and headed to the sugar-apple tree. "For all it's worth, you've made a great sacrifice for world peace."

"Excuse me?" Hector said.

Volkov walked to the steps, Hector following him like a sticky peddler. "Hey! We're not done yet!"

"I'm afraid we are, Mr Kane. Say hullo to our friends in the Company."

Two pairs of hands held Hector in check, as he saw the Russians disappear in the trail. He kicked and screamed. But he could not move.

"What did we say about edginess? Ha?" Lee said blithely from his left side.

And Siva said, crazily becalming on his right side, "It is over, son. Accept your destiny."

⁓ ❧ ⁓

There they were, waiting for him after the dragon had vomited him up.

Three angry, patriotic men.

"You shouldn't have done that, boss," Baxter said, his lips taut into a hyphen.

And Visa Clerk eyed him with contempt.

And Agricultural Attaché motioned Hector away with a theatrical bow. "My Liege. I haven't gone for my jog yet. So make my day and try to run."

Baxter and Agricultural Attaché flanked him. Visa Clerk secured the rear. They walked him off of the platform, passed by a group of Japanese high-schoolers who sang loudly and cackled with every refrain, then walked out through a gate hedged by spider lilies and vanilla shrubs, through legions of curious tourists. Everyone seemed to have just learned about the Green Catacomb. It was high time to witness the Pulaui afterlife, to be pawed by lusty twigs, to tread on ravenous roots, to worship and be worshiped by the underground forest of death.

The spooks picked a different route out of the Gardens. They sauntered down a valley of swaying poplars and mellifluous canaries: The birds sang a plaintive eulogy for Hector, and he chuckled in reprisal. His captors said he'd gone bonkers. They paused on a bridge over a pond teeming with fat piranhas. Visa Clerk said he'd killed someone in a pool just like this one, up in Manila, in the bloodiest operation he'd ever seen. Agricultural Attaché crossed his forearms on the railing and smiled, getting to know Visa Clerk better. "You should've stayed there,"

Agricultural Attaché said. "You get two girls for a tequila, plus a hot massage. A wife on the bargain if you'll pay for the hysterectomy and the postage. *Ha ha ha hah!*"

They strolled through a chilly garden where blueberry-blue topiary trees were sculpted like dolphins or sharks. Baxter left them there. He said he must rejoin his group at the Supertree Grove. Hector wondered what Baxter would tell Yubi and the students. But he dared not ask.

Visa Clerk and Agricultural Attaché escorted him silently out of the Gardens, into the haze. Hector reached for his mask reflexively. But then he looked at it and tossed it down to the ground.

From now on he would put up with the stench, fill his lungs with the dead man's ash.

He would face life without armor. No mask. No trama. Not even hope.

He got into the car

PART THREE

27

TRAITOR

T he US Navy was not generous with its interrogation rentals. This one was a ten-by-ten room with dingy ivory walls. Other than a single lightbulb in a wrought-iron cage, a pan-tilt-zoom camera stuck to the far-left corner like a robotic insect, a gray metal table, and four lyre-backed chairs, the room was unfurnished. Hector was stripped of his cell phone, wristwatch, keys, and wallet; was given coffee and a slice of pepperoni pizza to nibble on; was allowed one bathroom break per hour; then was left alone fretting.

He'd been sitting there for over two hours, when the electric metal door swung open and Ozgur, Fabio, then Visa Clerk walked in respectively, all dressed in black suits.

Visa Clerk targeted the farthest chair by the wall and kind of reclined on it, crossing his legs. Ozgur and Fabio sat at the broad side of the table across from Hector, avoiding eye contact with him as they lowered themselves on their chairs.

"How are you doing, Hector?" Fabio began breathily, crossing his wrists on a dogeared red folder he'd positioned squarely before him on the table.

"Fabulous! Cut the jelly, Fab. I know how ugly it looks."

Fabio arched his eyebrows and rocked his head awhile. He opened the red folder and spoke at a higher, formal notch. He started with the time and date and purpose of the interrogation, then read Hector his Miranda rights—which Hector laughingly dismissed: He was innocent, he said, and wanted to get this done with as smoothly as possible.

Next, Fabio stated his name and designation, then introduced Ozgur as "Agent Kerry Grant"—which made Hector chuckle—followed by the mysterious visa clerk, who turned out to be "Agent Matthew Rossini from the Defense Intelligence Agency."

"The DIA?" Hector whistled. "I never thought I was that important."

"Don't be modest," Ozgur said dryly.

"What did you say your name was again?" Hector said.

Ozgur drummed his fingers on the tabletop and shook his head silently.

Now Rossini leaned forward and said, "You may begin, Mr Kane. Tell us what happened."

Hector obeyed, and in excruciating detail he relayed the events of the past two days: from the prince's call and the suspicion of his wife, to the MFA deal and the middle-middle man, to the bicameral creature — Lee/Li — and his guest the *polkovnik,* up to his apprehension out of the dragon tube a few hours ago. The DIA man kept nodding with each major turn of events; Ozgur didn't seem to be following the narrative as much as Hector would have hoped; Fabio jotted down tons of notes on a couple of folded A4 papers—in cursive, minute handwriting which looked close to Anglophonic Arabic or Farsi to English.

"And… why didn't you report any of this to the Agency?"

Fabio asked finally.

"In fact, I did." Hector remembered his failed text. "At least I tried to. Check my phone."

Ozgur volunteered to fetch Hector's phone. Two minutes passed, then he returned with a zipped evidence bag holding the iPhone. Fabio powered the phone on, then reviewed the messages. Ozgur followed, before passing it to Rossini.

"That was," Rossini said, eyes on the phone, "really smart of you."

"What's that supposed to mean?" Hector said.

Fabio doodled on his folded paper, crossing out most of his extensive recent notes. "Is that the end of your story, Hector?"

Hector folded his arms. "We're smart people, aren't we? Show me what you got or let me go. Simple."

Fabio glanced over at Ozgur, who nodded to him gravely.

Thereupon, Fabio reopened his red folder. The topmost paper inside was a punched timeline. Hector's eyes scanned it, upside down, and he concluded it had to do with the start and end of Operation C.O.R.O.N.A. The first date was sometime in March 2013 and the last, at the bottom, was today's date. Fabio now removed this paper and laid it aside. Underneath was a colored photo of a bloody, bludgeoned face. Fabio dealt this photo across the table, and Hector frowned at it for a while. The face looked familiar. It was sharp, olivy, and lightly bearded. The hem of a Yasser Arafat's checkered *keffieyh* was visible under the broken jaw.

Ozgur rose and walked around the table to lean over Hector's shoulder. "His name was Mukhtar al-Halabi," he said, tapping the photo rather aggressively. "He was only a kid, barely twenty."

"And he used to work for us," added Fabio. "He reported to the Crazy Horse."

"Where?" Hector asked.

"Syria," answered Ozgur. "He was Mosa al-Damawy's finest *pupil.*"

Hector swiveled and frowned at the ghost of Mosa al-Damawy. Then he looked back at the photo and asked, "Who did this?"

"Any theories, Professor Kane?" Rossini said.

"I've already told you my story."

"Assad," Ozgur said. "Assad's men."

"Actually it wasn't al-Assad," Fabio corrected. "Not strictly. It was one of us."

Hector's eyes widened. He looked at Fabio, then at Rossini, then back at Ozgur. "*Us?*"

Ozgur returned to his chair with a frustrated air. Fabio pulled the photo back, then handed Hector another. This photo was one of the Yakhont photos he'd seen during his trailer briefing with the Cardinal two weeks ago. It showed a TELAR vehicle painted with the red, white, and black colors of the Syrian flag.

"*Us* in the know." Fabio tapped his pinkie on the edge of the photo. "Mukhtar was the one who took this."

Hector raised his head. "Did you figure out who he, or she, is?"

Fabio only smirked. Ozgur rubbed his jaw and let out a desperate sigh.

"Tell me something," Rossini said. "At what point did you become aware that the Cairo station had informers in Syria?"

"Is that really a question?"

"I'm afraid it is, yes."

"Formally, never. But that's common knowledge on the street."

The DIA man didn't seem to like this answer. "How about

the Yakhont intel?"

"I knew about it on April twenty-eighth. Sunday. During my briefing with the CIA director."

"And before that?"

"Never."

Ozgur snorted and rubbed his face.

Fabio extracted a document from deeper in his folder and passed it to Hector. This document was an incident report undersigned by Lisa McConkey on April 26, 2013. It detailed her encounter with Hector's suspicious activity in her office. In half a page, she'd succinctly documented his fake resignation, his snooping around her cabinets, his unsatisfactory answer when caught in the act. Everything.

Hector wadded the paper up and flung it behind his back. No one moved to reclaim it. Hector then bowed his head and squeezed it. He couldn't believe the mess he'd gotten himself into.

"My advice is to open up right now," Rossini said.

"Jesus, man!" Hector said. "You've made quite a theory based on one rash mistake. I was desperate for information, I confess. But—"

"Is that a confession?" Ozgur interrupted him.

"A *what?*"

"This session is being recorded, Hector," Fabio said.

"But I didn't do *anything!*"

A moment of silence weighed on the table. Then Rossini said, "Exactly eleven days ago, Agent Kane, we received intel from our source in the GRU. Our source said the Russians had infiltrated one of the CIA's most important stations. Namely, Cairo."

Hector processed this piece of information quickly. So the Defense Intelligence Agency had infiltrated their Russian counterpart, the Main Intelligence Directorate (commonly known by its dated acronym, GRU). Splendid. Why do we still have war in Syria, then? We should be in Bog's head by now!

"'Buratino' is what the Russians call him," Rossini continued. "Are you familiar with the name?"

Hector shook his head.

"It's a character in a children's book," Fabio said. "Aleksey Tolstoy's plagiarism of Collodi's *Pinocchio*."

"With a big difference," Rossini pointed out, sticking out his forefinger. "Buratino never becomes a real boy. And his nose doesn't grow long if he lies."

"He's a pretty good liar," Ozgur growled rather condemningly.

"He acts himself on stage," Fabio said, "defends other toys. Proletariat feel-good stuff. At any rate, whatever weird code the Russians have for their spies, we didn't know who Buratino was, but we managed to narrow our list down."

And the Cairo deputy patted his red folder with glee.

Ozgur said sadly, "That was my mission, Hector. To prove it wasn't you."

Hector stared at him, feeling his whole body stiffen.

"And I was proven wrong beyond my wildest expectations," Ozgur added. "Really, really, you've managed to impress not just me, but all of us."

Hector cried, "That isn't me! I'm not your 'Buratino'! I've no connection to the Russians whatsoever!"

Yet the next seven photographs, which Fabio passed along with relish, made Hector regret making that claim.

They were taken from the four-rotor drone, and they spotted him toasting to what looked like a victory with the *polkovnik* and the bicameral Chinese/Pulaui spymaster.

After a long pause, Hector pushed the incriminatory photos away. He took a deep breath, then said with defiant clarity, "I am not Buratino, and I would like to speak to my lawyer."

Fabio declared loudly, "Session concluded at twenty-one fourteen, May seventeen, two thousand thirteen."

The folder was closed, and the three interrogators stood up.

"What if I'm telling the truth?" Hector said. "What *if* I've been set up?"

"Then you should have come to us first," Ozgur said.

"Heads up from a friend, Hector," Fabio said. "Whatever 'innocent' is, that's not you."

"And Yubi? What're you gonna tell her? She must be terribly worried right now."

Rossini exchanged looks with the others. "For caution's sake, we can put her in loose confinement for now."

"What? Why? She's not part of anything!"

"I believe you've lost track of your lies, professor," Rossini said, undoing his tie. "What you mentioned to this committee was that your wife took part in the abduction of an American citizen. Think well about your next lie. You'll have plenty of time to cook it up in solitary."

Hector jumped from his chair with a groan, throwing the table away in frustration. Ozgur leaped back and avoided the impact. But Fabio wasn't as lucky. He tripped on his lyre-backed chair, and the table landed on his left leg. He yelped with pain.

"Sorry, Fab!" Hector hastened. "I didn't…"

The door buzzed open, and two broad-jawed Navy sailors in digital-blue camos raced in and dragged Hector out of the room.

28

JUST A LITTLE ROCK 'N' ROLL

he US Navy was not generous with its prison rentals. His room was a lampless dungeon cell from hell. The haze got unrestricted access from a high window with three rusty bars. Hector boxed the padded walls, until the pain in his bones forced him to stop.

He sat down and sank bit by bit into himself.

He decided to taste the food, as a distraction. Beef barley ("I'm an Irishman, gimme barley, barley can't come out bad for an Irishman, gimme barely," his grandfather used to say). Coleslaw (reminded him of Cairo's KFC, Tahrir Square, which the protesters pillaged then transformed into a squatters' paradise). Diet Coke (God bless the olden days, when he'd been a boy in the Middle East, Coca Cola was the world's unrivaled elixir, and he could swear it had tasted better). Cashews (his mind went blank on this one, for this tropical plant always resisted his taste buds).

He started to weep.

He breathed the haze. Thank goodness they weren't generous enough to offer him a mask. He wanted this celestial poison, these spirits from the passing forest. He was high.

The sky dimmed ever and ever quicker. Few fat stars winked. And the boots on the ground. The repeat-after-me-sailor:

> *I'm a steam roller baby*
> *And I'm a rollin' down the line*
> *So ya better get outta my way now*
> *Before I roll all over you*
> *It's just a little—*
> *(Ho!)*
> *A little—*
> *(Ho!)*
> *It's just a little rock 'n' roll.*

The shrieks were in his head. The boots tramped all over him.

The haze was one with his DNA.

He was aching with every cell of his body.

Darkness enclosed him.

———— ⚓ ————

The US Navy was generous with its air conditioning, though.

Hector awoke with a sneeze. He lifted heavy eyelids and slowly examined his environment.

He was in a different room. Spacier. More personal. There was a double-hung window overlooking the base's hazy and noisy yard, and a folding plastic table pushed to the far wall, coupled by a hazelnut wooden chair. On the table were a cylinder water bottle and a modest pyramid of books. (Rudyard Kipling's *Kim*—an unusual find—topped the pyramid.)

Beside the table was a closet, and inside he saw a pair of jeans, a cocoa blazer, and a sky-blue-on-white striped shirt—which looked too familiar not to be his.

He was ensconced in bed, the edges of the bedding annoyingly tucked under the mattress: a fluffy pink duvet and a couple of white sheets. He was dressed in scrubs of some sort, moccasin in color. He wiggled his toes and didn't feel his socks. He turned on his right side and looked at the floor. His loafers and socks were there.

The door opened and Ozgur came in. He closed the door behind him, and chanted, "Hey, fighter, rise up, it'll soon be brighter."

Despite his smile, Ozgur looked disheveled and tired. His stubble was longer, his eyelids heavier. He was dressed in the same black suit from the interrogation, but the tie wasn't there and the shirt was rumpled. He was holding two paper cups.

"What time is it?" Hector croaked, propping himself up on his elbow.

"Ten-twenty."

"What day? Where am I?"

"You're in eternal bliss, Hickey." Ozgur handed him one of the cups. "Double-double. I haven't forgotten."

Hector pointed at the water bottle, and Ozgur brought it to him. Hector quenched his thirst, then tasted the steaming coffee. It was medium-roast Colombian, and the cream was smooth and fresh. "You spiked the food?" he asked.

"I wasn't expecting you to take the bait. But, hey, you're unpredictable, *complex* like a garden."

Hector stared at him. "Don't be so melodramatic. What happened?"

Ozgur drew out the wooden chair from the table and sat astraddle it. He folded his arms on its back. "How much do you remember?"

"Not much. Shadows. My life reeling before me. Sadness and happiness at the same time. What was that?"

"A hyoscine analog. Something to stimulate your memory."

"It's horrible."

"Don't feel pressured." Ozgur smiled. "A thank-you is more than enough."

"For what?"

"For saving your neck. You're as innocent as lettuce, as the Egyptians say. Stupid. But innocent."

Hector downed his coffee in a few nervous guzzles. Then he tossed the cup on the comforter and got out of bed. He took off his scrubs and began dressing himself. "Is Yubi okay?"

"She's been cleared, too," Ozgur said. "The DIA is pulling out of the res right now."

"She's at the res?"

"We checked her out of the Sands. What a story you told us last night, man! I've known you for years, but never assumed you were that romantic."

Hector sat down on the bed and began slipping his feet into the loafers. "How's Fabio, by the way? I need to apologize to him in person."

Ozgur was silent awhile. "That's what I came to talk to you about."

Hector looked at him. "Is the injury really that bad?"

Ozgur shook his head. "Hector, don't freak out, okay? Fabio is dead."

Hector's eyes contained the room in just a moment. It was a small one, comprising a small desk and two armless chairs. Agricultural Attaché was seated on one of the chairs, cross-legged. He smiled casually without getting up. Matthew Rossini stood in the center of the room. Like Ozgur, he looked sleepless but triumphant.

"Agent Kane." Rossini strode to give Hector a firm hand-squeeze. "My sincerest apologies for the way we handled your inquest yesterday. You understand, this was an issue of national security. I was just saying that to the director. Come on in. (Agent Grant, the door please.) The DIA is looking forward to your full cooperation."

Hector freed his hand from Rossini's, then walked to the man standing by the window.

"Sir," Hector said.

The Cardinal didn't turn. "Did you have a good night's sleep?"

"Yes, sir."

"Good. You have a long journey ahead of you. We booked you all for the three p.m., straight to Cairo. All first class. Air China. No layovers, and they have an open bar on board. You can drink yourself to oblivion for twelve hours straight. As for that student who passed away—he doesn't have a family, does he?"

"No, sir," Hector answered.

"We'll sort it out with the Egyptians, anyway. The most important thing now is *you*, Hector. How are you holding up? We're not sending you back if you're not ready."

Hector looked out the Cardinal's window, at the haunted piers. He couldn't help but compare this view with the sweeping Mediterranean. Out his window, an Arleigh Burke-class destroyer was anchored only fifty feet away, its tripod mast too bulky for practical use, its hull too grand for this spit of dust known as Pulau. At the next pier was an Ohio-class submarine, open to supplies, a dull gray monster with a distinctive hump. Battle paraphernalia. It used to evoke his appetite. Now only his grief.

"Hector," the Cardinal said.

But Hector did not hear him.

"I'll tell you what," the Cardinal said. "Why not take your wife on a *real* vacation? Vienna or Venice or anywhere with clean air. This island is cursed. It's no wonder we've been played like fiddles by the Russians. Who can think straight in this inferno!"

When Hector still didn't respond, the Cardinal looked at Ozgur.

Ozgur shrugged.

"Did Oz"—the Cardinal quickly corrected himself—"Kerry tell you about our alternative offer?"

Hector nodded slowly.

"So what d'you say? Deputy chief or dean? Of course, we would love to have you. But it's your choice after all. In theory, you can take over AIMES, if you want to. Both are excellent choices."

"In theory he would be working for us," interceded Rossini. "AIMES is our training yard. So Agent Kane would be reporting to the DIA—if he chose the academic route, of course."

Hector turned away from the window at long last. "I have other plans," he said.

"What plans?" the Cardinal said.

"I have a family farm in Cayuga. I'll go there with my wife and we'll start over."

After a long silence, the Cardinal said, "You need more time to think this over, son."

"Too late, sir. I have already made my mind. My flight off of this island will be to Toronto Pearson. I will never set foot in Cairo *ever* again."

29

SMOKE AND FIRE

Shortly after the Mercedes had taken off from the naval base, Agricultural Attaché, in the driver's seat, tossed Hector his stuff in the backseat—the iPhone, the black leather wallet, the keys, and the wristwatch, all contained in a large zipper bag—while Ozgur related the story of the CIA's overnight success.

"Imagine a plan so devious, so perfectly aware of human insecurities, its main strength—and defect—was the seduction of fear. Fear of everything. Of leading an entire life as a *kaffir* in the *Kenanah* of Allah. Of being the bane of your family. Of losing love." Ozgur raised his hoary eyebrows, the car speeding through the hazy streets. "Once upon a time, there was a Copt. Like all Copts, he was persecuted in his home country from day one. So when he grew up, he was determined to do *anything* to flee. Your Copt wasn't rich, or handsome, or religious—tragedy is easier for the religious—but he was good in school. And after *thanaweya amma* he became a doctor. Which was a profession he hated. So picture him. Miserable, neurotic, lost in dreams beyond his grasp. Then—*bada-boom!*—he's a literary sensation. Poor kid, he lost his head in the spotlights and the cameras. He thought he'd become someone he wasn't. Someone who actually could flee. But that's not how life works. So our Copt goes to the US Embassy and applies for a visa. Rejected. He sucks it up and tries again. Same result. Show me your passport, Mr Mikhail. How many visas have you garnered so far? None! Hand me your bank statement. *Umm.* Not a penny! So you told me you were a doctor? Do you have an apartment? A car? A wife? Oh, I don't understand the Egyptian economy. Please try again later. Bye."

Hector tried to power his iPhone on, but it had to be recharged. So he handed it to the driver, who hooked it up to the car's charger. The car was now easing into the tunnel under Mount Victoria, which led out to the Central Business District.

Ozgur scratched an itchy point on his shin and continued his tale:

"It was then that he flashed on the Russians' radar. On his fourth visa rejection, the kid made quite a scene at the Embassy. He yelled and demanded to meet with the ambassador himself. So the security guards—Egyptians, all of them—threw him out. The famed genius, Egypt's Chekhov, was humiliated beyond measure. The guards saw him weep outside, waddle in his country's dirt. And then, was Paris—thanks to you. You see, Hector, they got to him under your nose. It was in the City of Light that Kero met his mysterious spymaster: a man who promised him a panacea for all his suffering. Need a pass to freedom, Kero? Free sex with your girlfriend? Escape Islam for good? Come to *Umarica!* All you need to do is prove your loyalty, pass the Patriotism Aptitude Test. One little thing you'll do for us, and your asylum is granted.

"I verified the details myself. One perk of living in Paris is that you get to hang out with a lot of DGSE vets. My source confirms the recruitment started at *Shakespeare and Company*. Our writer met a man who promised him a first edition of *A Moveable Feast*. He had to lose Fifi at *Amorino*—the ice cream shop—to continue his transaction aboard a small boat in the Seine. The cameras of Notre-Dame recorded only snippets of their forty-minute rendezvous. But they were enough. You don't like what you see happening in the Arab region, Kero, do you? The violence. The rise of political Islam. The cannibals in Syria. God, Kero, how savage! How have we come to this? We Americans are naïve. We believe people. But not anymore. This sweeping madness must stop. And we need *you*, Kero.

"Soon, Ernest Perkins-bin Hakam was brought into the dialog. This half-blood Saudi royal is dangerous, Kero. Don't let him fool you. He's not who you think he is. He's pro-Islamist. Yes. We, the CIA—*now you know!*—have been monitoring him for years. He's a loony leftist, you know. A nihilist. A multicultural ideologue. He came to Cairo to do no good, and he's no good. We want to rid the world of him, use him as leverage to stop his father from supporting the Islamists in Egypt and Syria and everywhere. Would you be so kind as to help us? Again, this is an aptitude test to prove your loyalty. So here's what to do."

There was a red sign. The driver braked suddenly. Hector looked at the weekend gaiety outside. In this green dystopia, this suffocating haze, Pulauis still managed to enjoy themselves. Colored masks and winking eyes and sprightly old couples. Children flying balloons in the smog—which looked like dialog bubbles in comic books. Palms canting over the bustling roads. Ferns tickling the car's roof.

Traffic unjammed, and the Mercedes moved on. Ozgur said:

"Our spymaster offered a simple plan, generic but reliable. Kero would contact Ernest and somehow persuade him to leave DC. We didn't catch their final words. Both Kero and his recruiter were gone by the time the cameras zoomed back to the boat. But we hacked the kid's laptop at the res. And this is what we've put together. For weeks, Kero chatted with the lonely prince in DC, allowing him to vent his frustration with his father and the entitled millennials he met in America's passionless capital. All with Fifi's stupid help, for she was closer to Ernest than Kero. Then Kero took over. You should read the texts. This kid wasn't Ibsen, but his manipulation is worthy of respect. *Grass is always greener on the other side,* he wrote to Ernest. *Here in Egypt the people have gone all fanatic, either radical left, radical Islamist, or radical anti-Revolution. And we miss you, buddy. Even the professor is asking about you all the time. Why not come hang out with us? There is this trip that's coming up and you can see Dr Kane and Yubi and all of us. A reunion party! A surprise! How about that? Don't worry. I won't tell a soul. That's our little secret.*

"Everything went as planned. Ernest landed in Pulau on May fifteenth, at seventeen-fifteen. He checked in to his fancy hotel around eighteen hundred hours. He showered and waited for his buddy to pick him up. But only the Chinese came. They served him up to the Russians on a golden platter. He was taken, as the hotel's security cameras show, in under an hour after his arrival."

The car got stuck in the traffic again. Hector looked out his window and saw the white domes of the Royal Botanic Gardens afar like giant airbrushed bees. "But how does Yubi fit into this?" Hector asked.

"Well, that's a Russian classic. We got in touch with our old prince. The Russians wrote a script for him. I'd suspected that myself when you recounted that call that ticked you off. Think about it. Without this call, you wouldn't have gone after the Russians at all. They *knew* we were digging for their Buratino, so they framed you to mislead us."

"But I checked," Hector said. "Yubi's name *was* registered there at the hotel, as a guest."

"And I made further checks," Ozgur said. "The suite was booked to a 'Mr Ernest Perkins,' paid for by his daddy's *Dubai First Royale Mastercard*. Obviously, the prince cared for his son more than he ever let on. Only two hours after his son was taken, the prince called the hotel and added a 'Mrs Yubi Kane.' Next thing he did was call you. And you swallowed the bait like a stupid fish. Any husband would have done the same. Their plan was airtight. We probably wouldn't know anything if it weren't for a tiny glitch—something even the best minds of the GRU missed in their calculations."

The driver now let out a muffled chuckle. Hector hadn't, up to this point, bothered to ask the so-called "agricultural attaché" about his true identity. But something about this chuckle—its conference with the car's rapid climb onto the concrete bridge over the Disraeli, the head-shake that followed—prompted him to ask. "Who the hell are you, anyway?"

The driver said, "Derek, sir."

"And who is 'Derek, sir'?"

There was a pause, before Derek replied, "Agent Derek Moore, sir. Far East Division."

Hector crinkled his nose. "Daddy's boy?"

Daddy's boy slugged his wheel. "More like a taxi driver right now."

"And if he wants to keep his job," Ozgur said, looking at Daddy's boy, "he'd better hurry up."

The car lunged forward with a screech. The two men in the backseat cursed.

Hector then turned to Ozgur. "You haven't told me about their 'glitch.'"

"We believe that what tipped the balance of their scheme," Ozgur said, "was its main selling point. *Fear.* They simply didn't know about the kid's fear of heights."

"But the Chinese knew."

Ozgur's lips stretched into a wolfish grin. "Exactly, *mon ami.* Which is to say, our MSS sidekicks screwed the Russians over on that. Whether it was on purpose or by lack of proper communication, they'll have to make it up to the Russians somehow."

"How did it happen?"

"This was after we arrested you at the Gardens. Baxter went to tell your students and wife that you'd been invited to a 'private dinner' with Richard Fei. You would catch up with them later at the theme park. So off they went, those innocents. Kero, in particular, was so excited about it. He wanted to clear his name of his latest scandal on the skyway. He would go for it again, soar in the air, prove his mettle to his girl. But his girl had actually broken up with him—before she would break up with him, if it makes sense. She'd thought it out and decided she wasn't eloping to *Umarica* with him. No way, bro. She was going back to her loving puritanical father in Cairo. The New World was the future, not a place. She was going to pour it all out to him, ditch him up in the air—if only the bugger would muster his courage and get onto the bloody ride. It was a Greek monsters kinda ride, and Kero's seat was the cyclops. Fifi made fun of him and called out to Baxter to replace him. And Baxter jumped right in, kissing her on the cheeks. But even that wouldn't get Lover Boy on the ride. The ride was about to leave. But then… something interesting happened."

"*Very*," emphasized Derek.

"Baxter gets a phone call. And who do you think it is? Our Cairo deputy. Some bosh about Yubi trying to escape. Meanwhile, the ride is mysteriously waiting for Lover Boy. The tubby Chinese worker is looking at Kero with *shame* written all over his face. He wants Lover Boy to be the cyclops. Everyone wants Lover Boy to be the cyclops. So cyclops with reluctance he becomes. And before he has a chance to change his mind, the ride locks and takes off. It climbs the railway with a shuddering noise. Every creak is a tick toward the final hour. Finally, he'll defeat his phobia, be a man once and for all. And as the lever continues to creak, and our cyclops mounts to the hazy sky, he's sweating and his smile widens. Beside him Fifi is gasping and laughing in her Medusa seat, gripping her belt with terror. And then the ride drops. Fifty feet from up high at a twenty-degree angle. Shrieks burst out. But he, Kero, can't breathe, can't even cry. He doesn't feel his face. He gasps, and the ride sweeps him up with a left tilt and he is relieved now. He whoops. He screams in ecstasy. He tears off his mask and gulps the toxic haze. Fifi is avoiding his hand. He tries to reach out to her, but this thick belt is restraining him. The ride yaws and slews. They reach down to the bottom, upside down. Then they shoot up a hundred feet or so for another plummet. Kero shouts to her, 'What's wrong with you?' And there she drops the bomb. She wants to break up and won't go to America with him. The ride rises, and our cyclops is crying. It is then that his belt unlocks and he drops to his death. You should see the video. He didn't even realize he was falling until he hit the ground."

Hector's heart was torn between grief and rage. How could Kero be such a perfect swindler and a dim bulb? Was it love? Hector himself must, then, be guilty of the same crime.

As the car neared the dreary intersection of Middle and

Prinsep, Hector asked, "How about the girl? Is she alive?"

"She'll be all right, Hector. We're, in fact, indebted to her. Without her we wouldn't know a scrap. She's the one who clued us in on this whole Paris adventure. Kero had told her on the first day. He'd booked their flights to JFK without her consent, popped the question, and acted like a lunatic. When she pressed him, he cracked. He didn't tell her the whole story, though. Nothing about Ernest at all. Just that he'd met a 'very important man in Paris,' who'd asked him to spy on the Muslim Brotherhood. For his 'reporting prowess,' Kero was then rewarded with a job in DC to fight terrorism. *Huh*. Poor girl. So—what's the word?—clean, I guess. She had no idea what danger she narrowly escaped."

"How about the virus?"

"That's history. We gave her the antidote. Not because of our good hearts, to be sincere, but because her stress level messed up with her immune system. She was sneezing and coughing when the Cardinal and me interviewed her yesterday. She wouldn't have made it to Cairo."

Hector wanted to feel the triumph of good over evil, of life over death, but the victory felt tasteless. Earlier at the naval base, Ozgur had told him that Fabio's body had been found floating in the Disraeli river this morning. The Russians had slugged his body with six .380 ACP bullets. The Cairo deputy had been a fugitive through the night, with the full force of an American naval base scouring the island for him. So it made sense the Russians had weighed the odds and decided to eliminate their man while they still could. Yet something else troubled Hector.

Ozgur noticed his silence. "What're you thinking of?"

"You told me *Buratino* was a children's book?"

"*Uh-huh*. A version of *Pinocchio*."

"Why not Pinocchio? Why the knockoff, not the original?"

Ozgur frowned and thought about this for a moment. "People like to remake stories. The Russians baptized their man with a Russian name to make him theirs. We may never know for sure. It's like Churchill said, 'Russia is a riddle wrapped in a mystery inside an enigma.'"

"Put yourself in Kero's shoes. You meet a guy at a bookstore who claims to be a spy. What's the first thing that pops into your mind?"

"That he is? A spy?"

"Seriously? Just like that? Even *I*—with my family background—didn't buy a word of what you said in New York ten years ago. Not at first, and not without evidence. Remember?"

Ozgur took out his peppermints box and tossed two lozenges into his mouth. He ground them with haste. "Do you know why spies fail often? 'Cause they think too much. Go take a shower, man. Say hullo to the wife. We'll visit you in Cayuga sometime."

Hector got out of the car. He stood there awhile, in the haze, thinking. He waited for a closing line, an epiphany, something. But nothing came.

The Mercedes drove away.

And Hector walked toward the residence.

———— ❧ ————

The concierge's kiosk stood in the hazy gloom by the gate. It was dim and its damage not yet repaired. The acrid saxophone player had not even wiped the lipstick off his broken window—this mark of sadist criminality by the seven travelers from the

American Institute in Cairo who'd wreaked irremediable havoc on this eco-utopia.

The sun rendered the haze coral in color. The day was exceptionally hot, and moments after Hector had left the car he was perspiring heavily. He had no mask and the haze felt stinkier and heavier. He was coughing as he stepped under the boom gate, alarmed as he walked inside, frightened as he saw Baxter running with his distinctive limp toward him.

Baxter was barefoot and wearing his boxers only.

"What's going on?" Hector inquired.

"We better run, boss. This place is on fire."

"What? Where?"

"Our building. Our floor. I was lucky I caught the smell before I became a turkey. Hey, boss, where're you goin'?"

Hector saw the few summer students scurrying away in terror. On the bridge, he blocked the way of one boy with long hair and asked him to lend him his mask. The boy looked defensive, so Hector snatched the mask off his face and ran on. The boy screamed after him, but then his roommates caught up with him and pushed him on.

Hector crossed the bridge and knelt by the glowing pond and immersed his mask therein. Then he rushed to save Yubi... if she was still alive.

The stench was closer. And the smoke too. It had the color and quickly dissipating form of a murder of crows. Hector rushed through the dorm's entrance and up the stairs. The stairs were dense with smoke and he held his breath the longest he could. On the second-floor flight, he banged into a late survivor bumbling downstairs. Hector opened his mouth to ask him about the source of the fire, but an insuppressible cough prevented him.

He pushed himself up to the third floor with growing nausea. The fire was there in full bloom: vivid pumpkin, hot, hissing, and hungry. It'd caught the ceiling of the hallway, and the dead fumes were seeping from under Hector's own door.

Unit 301, as it happened, was the nucleus of this inferno.

Hector coughed incessantly. He felt dizzy. But he managed to kick his door, and the smoldering wood fell without resistance. A tongue of fire pounced on Hector now, like a lurking nemesis. Hector retreated to the hallway, coughing and covering his masked nostrils with his sleeve. His eyes were burning. He looked at the glass windows of the hallway and tried to smash one of them. Yet the glass was too strong.

He swung his head toward his apartment and screamed, *"Yubi! Are you inside?"*

He walked back to the flames. The woodwork was a ring of fire, the blaze vehement on the left side. He peered through and saw his carpet and sofa ablaze. The curtain covering the wide glass window behind the sofa was the cradle of a growing baby of hell, which crawled to the ceiling before his burning eyes.

Something was keeping the fumes at bay, though, slowing their accumulation. The hallways and stairs, Hector realized, were overwhelmed by smoke because they were closed spaces.

And finally he spotted it. Above the sink there was a small hopper window that he'd never bothered to close even when the haze raged. And this small window made his heart rejoice. Hope!

Before his excitement paralyzed him, he charged through the door then to the sink, *ouch*ing and cursing all the way. He opened the faucet and quickly immersed his head and mask in the warm water. Then he took off his shirt and wetted it too. He spun around and scanned his burning residence. Yubi was nowhere to be seen.

"Yubi! Yubi! Where are you?"

No reply.

He wrapped his wet shirt around his trunk and maneuvered his way back toward the doorway. In the bedroom, he saw only fire. The bed, the dressing table, the curtains, the wardrobe, all coalesced into one giant blaze. This was the hub of the fire, its hellish womb. If Yubi was there, she was no longer among the living.

Hector felt like bawling. He coughed and rasped, "*Yubi! Can you hear me?*"

At length his cough got more strident and his nausea revisited him. He lurched back to check the one area of the apartment he needed to see last before he saved his wife—or perished with her.

The bathroom was on the southeastern side of the apartment. It had a folding plastic door, which had melted from the heat, and inside it was full of toxic smoke.

"*Yubi, you there?*"

Only the gases greeted him.

He closed his eyes, held his breath, and waded inside, fumbling for the sink on his right, then for the four pegs on the wall to his left. Then for the shower at the far-left corner. There he found her. He opened his eyes and saw her, lying on the shower base. She was holding a book close to her bosom, curling like a frightened child on a stormy night.

He dropped to his knees and held her. "Yubi, I'm right here, babe. Right here."

She only moaned. She was alive but weak. Her face was sticky all over. He swung the faucet to the right side to let the cold water drench them. But *cold* was boiling hot. He quickly turned it off and heaved his wife away.

The hall was a veritable sitting room of hell now. The fire

had grown out of the bedroom to overtake the whole apartment. The ceiling looked like a skyscape from the apocalypse. There was literally no square foot free of fire on the floor. The doorway was obliterated by the blaze, one with the wall. It was not visible anymore.

Hector hoisted his wife tightly in his arms and thought of an escape route. But there was none. Even the big window behind the sofa was covered by the burning curtain. It would take a lot of power to smash it, anyway. By which time both of them would be dead. And even if he managed to crack it, what awaited them was a free fall from forty-five feet—not a nice death.

The demonic pumpkin, masquerading as flame, drew nearer to his feet. Hector stepped back coughing, fighting to stay conscious. Yubi was getting heavier. His chest wheezed. The hot plastic stung his back, and he yawped with pain.

He stumbled back into the bathroom and laid Yubi on the floor. Through the melting door he saw the Pumpkin Demon laughing at him, its eyes hollow, its smirking face kin of Fabio's. It had teeth made of white plastic, a maw dark with smoke. It drew nearer and nearer, and it licked his face with its toxic, serpentine tongue.

And then he was swimming in heavenly white clouds.

30

VILL BE IN TOUCH

The first face he saw was Daddy's boy's. The prominent zygomata and the smug smile raised the blood pressure in Hector's vessels.

Hector croaked, "What brought you back?"

"You're lucky you're old enough to forget your phone," Ozgur said.

Ozgur came and dropped Hector's iPhone on the bed beside his right hand. Hector noticed the intravenous line running a clear fluid into the back of his wrist. He tried to rise, but the pain in his left side overpowered him. He let out a curse and lay back in agony. Only then did he become aware a nasal cannula was hooked to his nose, breathing oxygen into his nostrils at a slow, almost imperceptible rate.

"You're alive," Derek pointed out.

"How's Yubi? Is she alive?"

"You really wanna know?" Ozgur looked foreboding.

"I can take it."

Ozgur chortled. "She's okay, buddy. She had surgery to drain the blood out of her head. It's like an 'epidural hematoma,' as the nurse said. They drilled a hole in her skull and sucked it all out. She'll function as much as you want her to."

Hector was silent awhile. He looked up at the bisque-colored ceiling, then asked, "What place is this?"

"A hospital?" Derek said, a little gigglish.

"Winston Churchill Hospital," Ozgur said.

Despite his pain, Hector chuckled. "Man, I love this country."

"And they love you, too," Ozgur said. "That's why they tried to kill your wife."

"What?" Hector's blithe was all drained. "What are you talking about?"

"Your concierge," Derek said, stepping away from the bed, "was found dead inside your bedroom."

"Take it easy," Ozgur joked. "I don't think Yubi had the hots for this guy—"

"Get to the point," Hector cut him off, a crushing pain in his ribs.

"Point is," Ozgur said, "your concierge was a bastard. The Chinese ordered him to kill your wife, on Russian orders of course. Obviously the Russkies have it in for you. You're a free man, and their best mole in decades is dead. But again they screwed up. Simply because you went there and saved her. She resisted her attacker, so he hit her. And she hit him back—killing him, actually. Then she ran to the bathroom to hide. That's when the fire started."

"At least, that's our interpretation," said Derek.

Hector felt needles piercing the sac of his heart. "Did she say anything?"

"She's not conscious yet," Derek said.

There was movement outside the room. A stretcher carrying

a chattering patient moved past the doorway.

Hector asked, "And what caused the fire?"

"Electric short circuit," Ozgur said with a puff. "That's the Pulaui report."

"No kidding."

"Yep," Ozgur said.

"A lot is gonna change, sir," said Derek. "We're rethinking our alliance with Pulau in the first place. This country has gone bonkers now that its founder is gone. We were aware there were some Chinese sympathizers among them, but nothing like the thorough infiltration we have seen. And it's happening all over Asia. China, in this day and age, isn't fazed by us. No country is. And this"—he paused, fumbling for word—"is scary."

Hector thought about his late tragedy. Before he'd come to this island, he'd been a firm believer in the global American hegemony. That is to say, he'd seriously believed that the United States was the mightiest nation on earth. Now, he wasn't so sure.

After a moment, he asked the Cardinal's son, "Is your father still in town?"

"Yessir."

"Then let him know I'll be accepting his offer. It seems Liza and me are stuck together for another round."

Ozgur leaned over the bed with a victorious grin. "Is it the fire?"

Hector raised his hands helplessly, indicating his current condition. "The world is a much meaner place than I thought. I was delusional about my happy retirement. Spies can't retire. Once you go underground, you can't walk in the sun anymore."

"But why not AIMES? You still can be dean, and work for the DIA on the side," Derek said.

With pain, Hector shook his head on the pillow. "I'm not going back to academia. It took me thirty years to learn that I'm not my father."

Ozgur agreed. "Good call, buddy. We can call the Cardinal right now."

A nurse came, carrying a load of supplies. She was dressed in a retro white dress with a matching apron and cap. She looked like Florence Nightingale risen. "Dressing change time," she said.

"Oh, I don't wanna see that," Ozgur said.

"My friend here is very *squeamish*," Hector said to the nurse with a smile.

"Black chicken or sushi?" Ozgur bade Derek choose.

"I'll go for sushi," said Derek. Then he turned and looked at the patient, then at the nurse. "Is he allowed to eat at all?"

"He's on DAT," said the nurse. "Diet as tolerated. But take it easy on salt and spice."

"What do you say, homie?" Derek asked Hector. "Is sushi okay?"

"'Homie'?" Hector objected with a rise of his head, instantly regretting it because of the pain.

Ozgur let out a chuckle, patting Derek's well-formed deltoid. "We'll see you soon, *homie*."

And they left Hector alone with the nurse.

Now the nurse went around the bed and began setting up her dressing equipment on the veneered overbed table. She was a smooth-faced mid-thirties woman with the body of a multiparous mother.

Hector told her, "I like your nail polish," and she laughed

with a guttural cough.

"You smoke?" Hector asked her.

She shook her capped head. "With the haze? We smoke twenty-four seven on this island."

By now she'd unfolded her aseptic drape on the table, dropped her gauze and forceps, and begun pouring out her saline into a white plastic tray.

"Do you," she asked him, "smoke?"

"I smoked my lungs out last night. Why am I feeling so much pain?"

"I'll get you something for the pain in just in a moment, dear."

"But I thought…" He turned his head on the pillow to peer at the IV bag now three-quarters empty. "Isn't that morphine?"

"You wish. Narcotics are emergency medicine in Pulau. They gave you some at Emerg yesterday. What you have now is Hartmann's solution, dear, to restore your fluids."

"Heart-Man? But I'm a man with many hearts," Hector said with a groan. "You can have one if you want."

"*Huh.* You're so sweet. But your wife won't be so happy about that, will she?"

"Did you see her? Is she okay?"

"She's in ICU, ground floor. You're in Acute, third floor. But the story of you going into the fire to save her is all over the hospital. You must love her very much."

The nurse put on her blue gloves and bent to remove the old bandages off Hector's left-side wounds. She removed the dressing on his left-hip would, and Hector yelped. "How bad is it?" he asked.

"This one isn't too bad. Second-degree with the fascia intact. I'll put a little bit of honey there. But I need to cleanse it first."

"How many burns are there?" Hector tried to squeeze his

head and gain a full view of his damaged side, but the pain, and the nurse's gloved left hand, pushed him back.

"Don't look," the nurse said. "You have a thirty-percent burn area, mostly on your left side and legs. We covered the ones where the skin is near or totally gone. My biggest worry isn't the one I'm doing right now, but the one on your left leg and foot. It's a third-degree and it might need a graft."

"Anything on my right?"

"A few ones, yes. But mostly first- and second-degree. I'll put some cream there in just a moment. You need rest and a good diet and antibiotics."

"And painkillers." Hector *ouch*ed as the nurse swiped the wet gauze along the exposed nerve endings on his wound.

The nurse did another—longer—dressing on the lateral side of his leg and covered his foot wound with some black sponge, which she soon sucked using a vacuum device and put a clamp on to keep the negative pressure. She moved to apply a silver cream to his relatively superficial right-side wounds. Hector could see now that his entire right leg was purple, vesicular, and swollen. But the skin was still there. He was wearing a rather skimpy pale blue hospital gown with spades in deep blue all over it. Underneath he was naked. Something about the nurse's gentleness made him unusually shy.

The nurse finished her job and dumped the dirty pieces of gauze into the garbage box, then her metal forceps into the yellow sharps container on the wall. "I can get you some briefs if you need some," she said, as if she'd read his thoughts.

Hector refused politely.

"Can you move up by yourself?" she asked.

Grinding his teeth, Hector raised his head, then dangled his legs on the right side of his bed to the floor. He balled his fists and pushed himself up on his tender feet. He groaned with pain, but he was able to hold a stance. He took two steps, then tripped on his oxygen tubing. In a fit of rage, he snapped his nasal cannula off. "Goddammit, I need some painkillers!"

"Don't use such language, please."

"I'm sorry."

"Glad you said so."

"What's your name again?"

"Gaia," said the nurse.

"Are you serious? That's your name? Anyway, Gaia, I'd like to be left alone now."

Gaia left, and Hector limped with his IV machine to the washroom, which stood in the alcove-like narrow end of the room.

He rinsed his face, then looked in the mirror. It took him a long while to adjust to the man who looked back at him. Most of Hector's beautiful dark hair had been lost to the fire, giving his scalp a mangy appearance. And his left eyebrow was scarred. His skin was Cabernet Sauvignon in color, and his lower lip was swollen and chapped. He had a patchy, two-day stubble with more white hair than he remembered.

He lathered the hand soap and cursed as he rinsed then dried off his face with a scratchy, rough towel. He dragged his IV machine out of the washroom.

Before he went back to bed, he lifted the venetian blinds on the window at the end of the alcove. The view wasn't good. Save for a few ventilation orifices, a bald roof greeted him. Obviously Winston Churchill was in some parts still under construction. Beyond the bald rooftop of the hospital, Hector could espy the outline of Mount Victoria. Everything else—the sky, the sea, the streets, the trees, the people—was invisible.

The haze had eaten away most of the visible world.

Hector drew the blinds down.

He sat on his bed and felt a searing pain from his leg through his torso. He cursed louder and fumbled behind him for the call bell. Winston Churchill's beds were equipped with a lavish control device wired to the wall, which did all sorts of functions, from managing the lights to programing the overbed TV to calling the nurse to ordering food. Hector pressed the nurse button multiple times, then he flung the device away and picked up his phone and powered it on.

———— ⚜ ————

Dean Noman had sent him an email, timestamped only an hour ago. Citing her brother's gratitude, she thanked him also for Fifi's safety then wished him a speedy recovery. Fifi had told her about the fire. The dean, then, moved on to bemoan Kero's miserable death. "Keroloss was a stellar student, a poor and very tortured soul. His mother and two sisters have been found, do you know that, Hector? Yes! Thanks to Ibrahim's efforts, a private investigator who used to work for the State Security has traced them to a nunnery in the city of Nag Hammadi. That's where the Gnostic scrolls were found, Hector." The nunnery had a strange name that the dean had not heard of before: *Anba Bedaba,* after a bishop and martyr during the reign of Diocletian. ("A rich but ignored history, Copts have!") And the SSP had forced the three women there, or else—the SSP had threatened them—Kero would die. "How savage! Kero would have met them right at the airport once he returned to Cairo. This was going to be a big surprise for him. But, alas, he passed away for real, and not by the SSP. His mother and sisters are heartbroken. They feel, somehow, guilty for his death…"

Hector decided to wait on composing the reply. He needed to explain himself in the best, most careful way possible. No other email was worthy of attention.

But before he left his emails app, a new email popped up in real-time. This one was from Lisa. The Agency was obviously too eager to have him back. The email was dry and formal. Lisa welcomed his return to Murphy & Associates as "chief operating officer" starting July first, and congratulated him on being "selected" for this position among "a large pool of candidates."

Hector checked his home screen and found a Facebook message from Zainab. He read her good wishes for him and Yubi and wrote a quick reply, expressing his thanks. He wondered about her husband's next move. With Kero's death, *Pharaohstan* would get international hype. Would *invisibility* still satisfy the Mukhabarat officer? And what would become of his personal life? A whisper about his true identity to Zainab's family would certainly end his happy marriage—maybe even jeopardize his very life.

Hector was thinking about this when he went back to his home screen and tapped the messages icon. He inspected the list of first-few-words, then scrolled up and down. He was confused. Kero's last message—about the new novel—was nowhere on his phone.

He remembered that Fabio had fiddled with his phone during the interrogation. He could have simply swiped "Delete" and the message was gone. That made sense. But still, a deeper question lingered in Hector's head.

Gaia came in. "Is everything all right, dear?"

"Can you get me some pain pills? I need something really strong. If you can't do opioids, at least give me a high dose of Advil or Tylenol."

Gaia walked to the oxygen dispenser on the wall and turned it off. "Your cousin is coming back to visit you at noon, by the way?"

"Why, what time is it now?"

"It's ten-fifteen."

There was a shrill cry outside, which added to Hector's confusion. "You said 'cousin'?"

"Yes. He asked how you were doing and I told him you wanted time alone. So he went down to check on your wife. He said he would come back later, at lunch, which is noon."

"Which cousin? You mean one of my two pals who went to buy food?"

"No, dear. He's a funny-looking guy. Short and bald with a hard face and small eyes. And he speaks in a funny accent, too."

Hector jumped off his bed. He yanked his IV line off and lurched to stare at Gaia, who was about to scream.

"Relax," he said. "I'm not gonna hurt you. Did you tell him where my wife is?"

Gaia nodded. "I'm so sorry. I'm so..."

Hector dashed to the door.

A clerk from the nursing station yelled, "Hey! Sir!"

Hector raced to the floor's automatic sliding doors. His gown hung by a thread from his neck, his right hand dribbled blood on the floor, and his legs ached with every step. He was back into the fire, emotionally, physically, and mentally. His brain moved faster than his damaged body could.

The Acute Floor's door gave way to a circular elevator lobby where an elderly Chinese couple was waiting. Hector had no time for this. He went down the spiral staircase the fastest he could without stumbling. Every touch of his bare soles on the steps sent an electric shock to his brain. He winced and felt tears well up in his eyes. But he kept going.

On the ground floor, he found himself in a vast, crowded, disorienting lobby. There were many stores on one side and a coffee shop—*TCC*—midway between the staircase and the front door. There was a security desk there, indicated by a hanging sign. Hector lurched toward it and approached a tubby security guard in a blue security vest. He asked the guard about the ICU and the guard, scowling dubiously, pointed at a long corridor behind him.

Hector bolted through the corridor, feeling his heart about to explode. It was a long and empty corridor and he couldn't feel his legs. His brain had apparently given up on him seeking help. A generalized soreness of his body ensued. The left side of his skull, where the fire had left its most visible mark, pulsed with every movement. His vision began to suffer.

He crashed into the ICU's double door to open it, slipping on the floor with a shriek.

Hector pulled himself up and examined his surroundings.

He'd expected a dynamic place, but the ICU was almost deserted. Only one nurse was at the nursing station, under a daisy chain of overhead monitors. The place was U-shaped and stuffy, hosting only seven rooms. A beep echoed regularly.

"How can I help you?" the nurse—chubby, wearing horn-rimmed glasses and too much makeup—said with a bored air, chewing gum.

"I would like to see my wife. Yubi Kane. She came here yesterday. A burn injury."

"Do you have ID?"

"I'm her husband!" Hector quickly toned down his voice. "I'm in Room Three Twenty-Two on the Acute Floor. I've lost all my papers in the fire. And, for crying out loud, where is everybody?"

Horn-Rimmed Glasses looked up at him. "Room Four," she said flatly.

Hector lurched around the nursing station and traced the white-in-black stickers to the room numbered 4. The steel-boarded, honey-colored door was ajar. Hector pushed it gently and stepped inside. The room was twice the size of his on the Acute floor, dimly lit, and Yubi's bed stood far against the dull bisque wall.

She was covered jaw to toe with a couple of white sheets, from under which a mesh of wires fed into a vital-signs monitor on her left. Hector looked at the monitor. The blood pressure, pulse, temperature, and oxygen saturation readings were marked in green. Which was good. But she was still unconscious.

"Yubi," he crooned, gently touching her forehead. "You'll be okay. I'm here."

"So let me get this straight," said a voice behind him. "They tell you it's a 'corona' virus, and you'e sold. *Huh huh huh huh*. Oh boy, oh boy. And I thought *I* was the best liar out there!"

Hector spun and stared at his interlocutor.

The man was sitting on a padded chair behind the door. A half-burnt red notebook lay open on his lap.

The man closed the notebook and stood up. He walked toward Hector, stopped, then shoved the notebook against Hector's chest like a compact disc into a drive. "You should read it. It's trash *par excellence*. Third-world symbolic junk. Everything has two or three meanings. Jesus and Satan and Darwin are one and the same person. What a waste of time, man."

Hector was stupefied. At length, he accepted the ambassador's gift. "Why, Jeff? Of all people, you had everything."

The United States ambassador to Cairo joined his hands and touched the tips of his forefingers to his lips. "Precisely. You see, Hector. *That* was my problem. Remember when we first met? I told you I wanted to go to Russia's near-abroad. And what a lousy lie that was. Anyone who thinks the Cold War is over needs psychiatric help. I have *always* wanted to be in Cairo, where time doesn't even exist. It's an easy job, with a good deal of gory drama (fine by me) and you live like a sultan by the sheer color of your passport. Where else would I go? But you… you, Hector, you never doubted me. Even when I gave you your Russian doctor's name all mixed up, you didn't care to look it up. And not only you. No one ever questions *anything* I say. It's so boring. I just couldn't stand being the only player in the league."

"But," Hector stammered, "I called you. You were in Cairo. How—"

"Technology." Jeff flicked his hand disdainfully. "It messed everything up. It's become more and more difficult to get any good intelligence nowadays. I don't blame you. Even the State Department thinks I'm in Thailand right now. You'll be amazed how much I get away with."

Hector looked at the red notebook. "What's in this bloody book, anyway?"

"That's the funny part. Nothing. He wrote me off completely. As everyone does. He must've thought I wasn't *story material*. I met the bastard only once, when Fab couldn't close a deal with him. Egyptians are so paranoid, man, thanks to sixty years of living in a police state. He wanted to meet someone he trusted. Say, the United States ambassador. *Huh!* Stupid jerk. I'm glad he went to hell."

"Why are you really here, Jeff?"

"I wanted to see you."

"But I don't want to see you. I don't even know you anymore."

"You can call me 'Buratino.'"

"Was Fabio innocent, then?"

Buratino smiled, scratching his chin. "Not precisely. This is what I've come to tell you, Hickey. This whole charade, this whole *Corona* business, is just a way to replace one Pinocchio with another."

"*Pinocchio?*"

Buratino nodded and sighed. "The Company lied to you. They *knew* about me. I wasn't 'Buratino' then. Names would come later: The Russians have a soft spot for drama. Fabio was my doppelgänger, my 'Pinocchio.' At first, the CIA sent him to me as a bait, to feed the Russians false intel. But then—you know dear old Fab—he got *sneaky* about it. He told me everything and asked for more money. But overall, he did what I wanted him to do. He was a good business partner. Selfish, but isn't everyone?"

"Is that why you killed him?"

Buratino shook his head, a sympathetic simper congealing on his face. "No, buddy. That's another lie. Your Company did. Their deal with him was for him to bow down after this operation. Retire in his hometown in Cali and never be heard from again. They never imagined he was working on something bigger than their silly little scheme to make you hate them. People with small plans have small minds. So they became insecure about it. Imagine him in the Kremlin, airing their dirty linen. Another Philby! *Huh.* It would've been a show worth watching. But they canceled it before it premiered."

"You're a terrible liar," Hector said.

"Do you see my nose?" Buratino leaned forward and raised his chin. Then he chuckled. "You're more like him than I thought. Oh, my God," he said thoughtfully.

"I still don't believe a word of this."

"*Cairo's Obligatory Replacement Of Needless Apostate.* CORONA. That's your operation."

"*Apostate?* You're lying."

"I'll give you two scenarios and I want you to think which is more plausible. The CIA—with its Service, Integrity, and Excellence—is seeking to infect a young lady with a deadly 'corona' virus to blackmail her father. The other is that Langley has noticed its Pinocchio has been acting in a *vague* way. He's neither good bait, nor a confirmed traitor. He's—let's say—a *needless apostate.* So what'd they do? They seek a replacement. There is this one hothead who flopped in Europe, this agent. You know who I'm talking about? He once swore there were nuclear smugglers across the Baltic, and there weren't. He said the Big No was a crazy old man, and the Big No turned out to be our modern Gandhi. Now our agent is in Cairo wallowing in his sorrows. He's friends with Buratino already and he's pretty much useless. Ditch him. Make him bitter. Cook him slowly. Give him a mission that makes him question all his morals. So maybe—maybe—he'll end up a new and better Pinocchio. A full-fledged traitor we can use against the Russians. The American version of a Russian spy."

Hector's pain made it impossible for him to process this clearly. He looked at the man who was both his friend and his country's highest representative in bloody Cairo. Could this really be the truth?

He will set you free, as the truth will.

"If that's true, why are you telling me this?" Hector growled.

"To give you the chance to live up to your true potential. To be the man my first Pinocchio wasn't. You see, Hickey, Fabio's problem was that he was loyal to one and only one thing. Himself. But that's not how it should be. A beautiful island like Pulau," Jeff exulted, "can change a spy's view on anything. This haze they produce and live with every day. Their shifting loyalties. Their always-changing society. Their lack of firm religious beliefs. This, Hickey, is the future of the trade."

"What are you saying?"

Jeff turned and gave Hector a serene Buddhist look. "You can be more than what you are. Not a double, or a triple, or a quad-whatsoever, but a mosaic spy. A spy with no loyalties, not even to yourself. A *hazy* spy. Invisible to yourself as to others."

"You're crazy." Hector gawked at him and gasped.

"I am yes. But I always win. And I want you to join me, bud."

"It was a big mistake for you to come here, Jeff. They'll be coming for you."

Jeff looked around him and said, "Where is everybody, Hector? Where are the mighty Company men?"

Only the rhythmic beeps filled the silence.

Buratino walked toward his new Pinocchio and added, "How is it that you're magically alive after the fire, Fifi is safe in Cairo, and the bad guys are all dead?"

"You're a bad guy," Hector said.

"I'm a liar but I'm no bad guy. And my proof is her." Jeff nodded toward Yubi. "I could've killed her if I wanted to."

"But you tried to!"

"Another lie. They filled your head with poison."

Hector remembered the red book. He looked at it, then stared at Buratino, and snarled. "But you wouldn't be here, Jeff. Would you? You're here for *this!*" Hector threw the book to the floor.

It took only a fraction of a second, yet Hector spotted it, a glancing twitch on Buratino's nasal folds.

The whiz was sharp and quick. Then Jeff's body dropped like a dummy whose strings were torn.

Lebedev strutted into the room with a Glock 19 fitted with a silencer. He looked at the blood pooling from Jeff's skull over the red notebook, then said, "He took his chance. Bad liar ve need no more." He looked up at Hector, who was tense all over. "Do not vorry. Ve do not kill innocent people."

"Was it all lies?" Hector asked.

Lebedev's small dark eyes did not blink. He backed up toward the door.

"Hey!" Hector followed him. "Don't go before you answer me!"

The Russian turned and pointed the gun at him. "Ve vill be in touch."

"What? No! I don't wanna be in touch!"

"Hector... Hector..."

It took him a dazed moment to realize it was Yubi. He nearly tripped over Jeff's body, running back inside.

"Who was that?" she asked feebly. "What a nightmare."

"No, sweetie. I'm here with you. It's all over. The bad guys are gone, I'm here, you're here. We're both alive."

"You're raving."

"I know."

"And you look terrible."

"And you look damn beautiful."

"You're a bad liar," she said with a sad giggle.

"I'll be working on my lies from now on."

"Please don't lie to me again."

Hector looked at his wife. Her hair was singed; her sinewy, marmoreal neck was scarred on both sides; her face was bruised;

and the surgical wound on her forehead was covered with a thick, dirty bandage. She looked more beautiful than he ever remembered.

He kissed her. She tasted like Betadine, bitterness, and fire.

"I'm not lying," he said.

Burnaby Hawkes's stories have appeared in *Heater*, *The Raven Chronicles*, and other magazines. He read English and philosophy at the University of Toronto and holds a master's degree in international security. He has worked as a researcher for the North Atlantic Alliance and a contributor to multiple international organizations and think tanks. He lives in Canada.

CPSIA information can be obtained
at www.ICGtesting.com
Printed in the USA
LVHW021136300520
656237LV00010B/85